SHADOWS IN JEROME

MW01537933

SHADOWS IN JEROME

A Novel

Curtis D. Vick

Copyright © 2003 by Curtis D. Vick.

Library of Congress Number: 2003094570
ISBN :   Hardcover   1-4134-1958-5
                  Softcover   1-4134-1957-7

All rights reserved. No part of this book may be reproduced or transmitted in any
form or by any means, electronic or mechanical, including photocopying, recording,
or by any information storage and retrieval system, without permission in writing
from the copyright owner.

Shadows in Jerome is a work of fiction. The town of Jerome does exist, but no
character, event, or place created by the author of this novel is intended to be real.
Where real names, places, dates and historical facts are used they are a part of public
record and have been included only to create a sense of authenticity in the setting
of the story; there is no intent to tie actual people, places, or historical events to the
characters, events or places of this narrative. Any attempt by anyone to do so is as
imaginative as this story itself.

This book was printed in the United States of America.

To order additional copies of this book, contact:
Xlibris Corporation
1-888-795-4274
www.Xlibris.com
Orders@Xlibris.com
20135

This novel is for my lovely wife, Dorinda, who suffered long hours alone while I worked on it and gave me the time and support I needed to finish it. The book is also a tribute to that dear old town on the slopes of Mingus Mountain which I first found in my youth and could not forget. Finally, it is in recognition of that hauntingly beautiful face which spoke to me from the past of her tragic life as I looked through a book about the old place. Sammy, I hope you found your own forever.

ACKNOWLEDGEMENTS

Thanks must be rendered to those who helped with this book by serving as readers of the manuscript in its initial form. They are: Mr. Robbie Robinson who is the finest English teacher I ever worked with, his wife Kris whose comments were especially encouraging; my daughter, Pamela Martin, my niece, Lynn Bridges, and Marjorie Martin whose encouragement came at just the right time and who gave me insight into the marketing and naming of this book. I must also thank my good friend Roger Kolbo for his help and support. Special appreciation must go to my wife, Dorinda, for her hard work as my editor. Her knowledge of the language and of writing was crucial to the completion of the book. Finally, I could not have written this novel without the assistance of the Jerome Historical Society and its archivist, Mr. Ronne B. Roope. The cover photograph is from the Society's collection of pictures of Jerome and is printed with permission of the Jerome Historical Society.

ONE

In 1927 Jerome was alive. Highway 89A wound up the side of the mountain from the Verde Valley, went through Jerome, climbed over the mountain and on to Prescott. It was a two-lane passage of crushed, macadamized granite. Graded, and engineered as well as the mountain's own flanks and the current technology would allow, it was a hundred times better than the dirt road it had replaced. And the dirt road it had replaced had been very good compared with the wagon track before that, then the mule trail and the footpath it began as.

Heavy trucks, such as they were in 1927, could negotiate the crushed granite, but once in a while one went over the side. Then people had to come and see as much about the accident as they could. They gawked at the break in the wooden guard rail, or rock wall, which outlined the curve where the luckless driver had lost control and broken through. Sometimes, there was no guard rail or wall. In such cases they edged up to the side of the road and gaped at the slash in the earth's surface the vehicle had made going over. Always, they rubbernecked at the actual wreck itself, somewhere down the side of the cliff below the road on which it had lost traction and failed to make the turn.

Usually, by the time people came to look, the driver, and any passengers he might have had with him, was already in Jerome's new hospital, the finest facility of its type within hundreds of miles.

Jerome needed a good hospital. Men got hurt in the mines that tunneled into the side of Mingus Mountain where the town sat holding on with the help of pilings and retaining walls against gravity and the 30 degree slope known as Cleopatra Hill.

Men were sent to the hospital on a regular basis. When they got there, most paid a visit to the great operating theatre that occupied the stone building, which sat above the rest of the town on a southeast to northwest axis. The entire ceiling of the operating theatre was filled with lights. In years to come, artists would put paint on easels, and create interpretations of the old building in all the colors of the spectrum. But in 1927, the surgeons who worked there to salvage a semblance of life out of what remained of the men brought to them, labored not with brushes and palette knives but with exquisitely sharp scalpels and suture needles and strong cat-gut. The main colors they saw were bright scarlet and maroon. These were often mixed with the yellow of fat or the ivory of bone. Still, the doctors cared more for texture and shape than hue, being more like sculptors than daubers in oils or watercolors. The men they worked on didn't know the difference. Brought in with their senses diffused by pain and fear, they were soon sent into the black of unconsciousness by means of the gaggingly awful ether that put them to sleep and kept them in that state while the doctors cut and sewed and re-made their poor, injured bodies.

The hospital sat at the south end of town, looking down on a spine of land that jutted away in a northeasterly direction. This piece of topography was called the hogback. Highway 89A ran along the top of it, passing the high school on its left as it rose from Deception Gulch where it had doubled back on itself in loops and switchbacks in order to climb out of the lowlands.

The hogback was the portal to the town on its southeast side, affording 89A the footing it needed. Several streets branched from the highway toward the north as, coming up from the lowlands from the east, it topped the high point of the ridge. It was called Hampshire Avenue here. Some of the streets connected with

Deception Gulch to the southeast; others led north and down into a valley which bore a patchwork of names to go with the various places and peoples located there but which, in general, took the name of Bittercreek Gulch after the stream that had once flowed through it.

Along 89A, drivers felt tension as they climbed, for there were hundreds of feet of space there. A man-made rock wall lay against the hill to the right, and in one place, a little cave had been built into it where some lucky person could park his car and walk up by means of concrete steps to his house on the heights above the hogback. This high land held a street called East Avenue. The few houses on it provided their inhabitants the pleasure of looking down in all directions.

Route 89A curved around this area, passing rooming houses perched on the side hill to its left for three blocks before it became Hull Avenue and finally entered the business part of Jerome. It passed Hotel Jerome. On the left side of the street a variety of businesses took up space. Other establishments sat to the right, some with their back portions hanging out over a hundred feet of empty air. The street kept going; past the jailhouse, another hotel, a furniture store, a cigar shop, and a shooting gallery whose second story was the Royal Theatre with its front on the next street up. Then it went by Ray's gas station and made a left turn at Jerome Avenue, where the American Café occupied the corner; past that in front of the Fountain Theatre on its right to the Conrad Hotel on the corner where it met Main Street running to the southeast, downhill, one-way; then 89A turned right and proceeded two blocks past the T.G. Moulter Company building on the left, another hotel on the right, a brothel known locally as Janie's place, and a car dealership called Trustate Motors, where it made a sharp curve back to the left, passed the Holy St. Mary's Church sitting to its right on the hill above, then the Delacroix Apartment Complex, more houses and the Baptist Church, then more houses above and below, and finally, took a gradual turn to the right and up the mountainside, where it wound its way south, out of town and on to Prescott.

The route ran through the town in the shape of a jagged bolt of lightning, confusing in the already complicated and compact little place with its streets laid out like pieces of discarded twine on the side of the mountain.

It was a demanding drive for anything larger than a sedan. The men who drove the trucks despised the few miles it took to get through Jerome. None made the trip unless they had to. Most found a route around the mountain and then on to Prescott if headed south, or across the Verde and on up to Flagstaff if going north; though this route was just as treacherous as it went through Oak Creek Canyon.

Surprisingly, there weren't many fatal traffic accidents in Jerome itself. There was no way to get enough speed built up to make any kind of crash deadly on the ascent through town. And coming down, from Prescott, the road was so tortuous, and most of the drop-offs so dramatically evident in their danger and absolute hopelessness as they sunk out of sight into what appeared to be the very abyss of Hell itself, that drivers were always moving slowly when they came into town from that direction.

Nevertheless, it was on this very stretch of highway south of Jerome, between Jerome and Prescott, that most accidents did happen. It was a hard route for anyone to drive who was afraid of heights or unsure of himself. Truckers who had been there talked about it wherever they met. Adding to their accounts was the fact that the highway leading into Jerome from either direction wasn't paved until 1938. Fourteen years later the town ceased to be a living thing with its own heartbeat and life-force and became a ghost town and eventually a tourist attraction.

In the early days the town had suffered the dirt and mud, the wooden walkways of all Western towns. This gave way to heavy cut stone blocks for most of the streets themselves. And by 1927, the dirt roads and by-ways of Jerome were paved with some kind of water resistant surface. The sidewalks, with the exception of some made of wood, were either of sandstone blocks mortared together, or concrete.

Very little was level in Jerome. It was an up and down town. Common fact for a resident of one house was the ability to look down on the topmost part of a neighbor's house. Sidewalks went between elevations by means of a slight slope or a series of steps; some were often no more than long stairways passing from one street—down or up—to another.

No plot of ground was wasted. People erected buildings that jutted out over empty air. As long as there was space at the front for a sidewalk and a street to give an address, structures were built. The backsides of these brave creations were supported by pilings resting against the descending slope, or by concrete walls that often rose as much as four stories at the rear and showed only a single story beneath the roof at the front. Construction was constantly going on somewhere in town.

Fire had swept through Jerome four times; there were few wooden buildings left by 1927, except for private homes. Included in these were one or two true Victorian mansions and many lesser houses which copied them in style if not size. However, for commercial purposes, the most popular materials were brick and concrete. The bricks were used to form the more traditionally imposing structures; the primary hotels, of which there were several, stores and offices, schools and churches—though there were some church buildings made of wood. The Holy St. Mary's Church was of brick with a wing made of wood.

But it was concrete, poured into plank forms in stages until walls reached desired heights, then finished with stucco, that was employed for the most part in Jerome. It made for strong walls, and with buildings often standing wall to wall, only the front had to be finished for aesthetic purposes.

Commerce was everything, and it was everywhere. Jerome was a twenty-four-hour-town. The mines ran multiple shifts seven days a week. Nothing stopped. The life of the town slowed only for individuals when they went to bed, where they were forced to find sleep amid the clamor of the endless activity on the streets. It was the price they paid for the town's economy. As long as the mines operated, it was a place where everybody worked if they wanted to, where there were never enough people for the jobs available, and where hunger and poverty were things one had to put honest labor into achieving. Amazingly, a few did.

People dreamed and despaired, lived and died, loved and hated, schemed and committed crimes in Jerome just as people did everywhere else. But people also fought, gambled, whored, murdered, made and lost fortunes in Jerome in such a degree of concentration that it was unusual. In its less than two square miles of land on the northeast slope of Mingus Mountain, the little town contained nearly all categories of things that could be found collectively across the entire United States. It even had international connections, carrying the name of the distaff side of Winston Churchill's family; his mother was Jenny Jerome. And, as if to underscore its European ties, men came to Jerome from all the countries across the Atlantic to work in its mines. Asia was represented there by the Chinese. Mexico sent her sons and daughters as well.

Despite Jerome's unique qualities, the thing that drove the town was an ordinary thing, something always found where men congregate. That thing was greed. On the most basic level it was labor in exchange for money. But it gained in complexity as the level of need rose. On its highest level, it was the lust for power as well as wealth.

There was gold taken from Mingus Mountain, silver too. For a common individual the amount extracted daily would have been a tremendous fortune. But as important as it was, and not to be overlooked in any measure, it was not precious metal of the gold and silver kind which the two principal companies, The United Verde Mine and the United Verde Extension Mine, depended on for their huge profits: it was copper. In a world which had learned to depend on electricity, copper was more valuable than gold or silver—if it could be found in large enough quantities. In Jerome, an enormous amount of copper was taken out of the mines every day.

Getting that copper required men and machines. The machines were often massive things of iron and steel. They consisted of huge wheels which revolved on heavy axles by means of belts and chains moved in turn by engines powered by gasoline, steam, or electricity. There were ore trucks and digging machines and trains. Some of the trains were smaller than their larger cousins which transported the copper to other places in the United States. They had to be small in order to travel the tunnels and the ledges of the open pit, but they were powerful dwarves just the same.

As an adjunct to this front line of giants and mini-giants, there were countless other systems of pipes and lines and collections of vehicles and shops and machines and tools of all kinds. And the whole thing had to be run by men. It was necessary, then, that each man know his job well.

Serving this mass of men was the town. It provided them with living quarters, stores and shops for whatever they needed; there were restaurants, bars, and houses of pleasure. Jerome had two schools in addition to the high school. There were churches for every denomination in the town, for not all of the people who lived in Jerome visited the bars or the whorehouses. And even some who did went to church, where they made what amends they could to assuage their guilt. The Protestants and Catholics led in popularity and membership in the religious category.

Jerome had dentists, doctors, and lawyers. There were fancy clothing shops for the ladies whose husbands had the more important jobs in the mines and made the highest salaries. And there were plenty of other outlets for goods in the town; everything from tools to toys, food to fuel, items to fit every wallet or pocketbook. The town lacked for nothing, except morality; sadly, though there were good and righteous people in Jerome, that blank space in the mural of human character was as conspicuous there as it was anywhere else.

And it was because of this fact that job capability was perhaps the easiest thing for the men who lived and worked there to have. A far more difficult thing for them to do was live together and survive. At work this was easier, but in town, off duty, this sometimes became the hardest of all tasks the men who mined Mingus Mountain had to perform.

TWO

By 1995, when he came winding his way over the mountain from Prescott with the top down on the canary yellow Volkswagen convertible, Jerome had officially been declared a ghost town since 1953. It was summer, and the sky was blue and vast overhead. The wonderful weather and the asphalt that now layered the roadbed masked the road's evil. Still, he had been aware of the awful heights the little car whizzed by so effortlessly, its engine whistling happily, as if it were alive. But when he saw the houses behind their front yards, protected by fences and closed gates, and except for the ravages of weather and neglect, looking as if they had just been moved out of the day before, seemingly waiting for the next family to come and take possession of them, he became transfixed.

Turning to the young woman beside him in the front seat of the car, he said, "Think of it. Families lived here, babies were born here, made here, people had their dreams here. Now it's all gone."

She shook her head as if to draw notice to her long black hair streaming in the wind, looked at him with piercing blue eyes, and asked through full lips that defined a too-large mouth, "Why did the people leave, anyway?"

"The copper," he said, "it just ran out I guess. The people all left, at least most of them, about 50 years ago. Just look at it."

She did. To their right, where she thought houses should have been, there was only empty space. Rooflines edged the roadside where walls normally would have been. With her head turned in that direction, she could see all the way to a mountain range.

"All you can see are roofs," she said, "and a lot of space."

"Oh, I don't know," he mumbled absently, craning his neck to look at the buildings sitting on the heights above and to their left. He was drifting now, going back in time in that way he had that nobody seemed to understand.

God, to think of it! Here on this mountainside people had lived and done all of the things they did everywhere else. That was part of it, but there had been an earlier time, too. He liked to think of the primitive, empty ground, the land with nothing but wild things on it, and then imagine the people coming and the houses being built and the activity beginning and the town growing: all out here in this lonesome place. It had happened that way. And over time, where only animals and Indians and the occasional mountain trapper had trod, kids had eventually trudged down paths to school and men went into barber shops and women called grocery stores and had their groceries delivered to them. In this once wild place people had sat on porches in summer, drinking lemonade and listening to baseball games on the radio. They had done it all here where the wind had blown cold and hard for centuries, where the wolves and the grizzly bears had roamed and been hailed as kings in their own right; where the Indian had walked and ridden and hunted and set up camp. Here it had been wilderness and then it had become a town with paved streets and telephones and churches and cars and trucks and people. Dammit! He just wanted to get out and roll in the soil of the place, touch the worn and weathered concrete of the sidewalks and try to contain it all in the effluvium of his imagination.

He was not always a present-tense person; not even a simple past-tense person; he was more of a past-perfect-tense person than anything else. He liked to carve out a piece of time within the past and explore it. Sometimes, he started in a certain place where a certain thing had been done before and was still being done. Then came the part he loved: in this place a certain thing had been done during a period of time when other things were being done. The time he always focused on was special in some way, it was always a piece of time within another piece of time, and all of it was in the past; the past within the past, the past-perfect-tense.

"Hello, Mike. You've got that expression on your face again." She turned away from him and shook her head. Then, looking down to her right, where the road they were on bent sharply back on itself as it descended to the next level, she said, "I hope you don't get us killed. Pay attention to where we're going for God's sake! I could understand if you were looking at some woman walking along, but not at a bunch of old sagging houses sliding off the side of a hill somewhere. God, look at how far down it would be if a person lost control of their vehicle!"

Beside her, he worked the controls of the little car, hardly hearing her, lost in the reverie he always felt for things of the past, especially when they were so well preserved as the old town of Jerome was.

*   *   *

His full name was Michael Albert Peale. He was known as Mike Peale. He had dropped the more formal Michael and gotten rid of the Albert completely. People had turned it into a joke. He was 32, with dark hair he feared someday he would lose. Not tall, but not short either, he stood 5' 10" and weighed a too-heavy 180, which he had begun to tell himself must be shaved down to 170. But he probably wouldn't because he liked to eat too much. He wasn't athletic, but he wasn't a klutz either. He had a soft voice, a Southern voice, toned and trained on the drawly dialect of Georgia, where he had been born. Later, it had been honed to an even finer point in the environs of Oklahoma City, where, because he had taken a class in photography while at O.S.U. in nearby Norman, he had been able to get a job as a photographer in a Sears store after graduation. He never intended to keep the position for very long, but it worked out that he did, and it was two years before he moved from the Sears store and the absolute hell, from his point of view, of working with mothers and their children in the creation of family portraits, to being unemployed. He found that he liked being out of work even less than working in the portraiture business. He had majored in accounting in school, so he got a job doing that. The quiet, solitary labor of it made him wonder what had taken him so long to get a real job. But the dead dreariness of numbers and the artlessness of business were forces which he soon came to see as destructive to his personality, and he realized why he had remained at Sears as long as he had.

He learned something about himself, then. What he really liked was art and history. He had become confused about these two veins of interest while in college, he reasoned, and that explained the photography and accounting. He would keep the photography. He liked it. In fact, he was in love with it. But the accounting, an act he must have thought was vaguely historical since it involved keeping records of other people's financial transactions, would have to go. He would have to channel the taste for history into something he could love as well as taking pictures.

The result of all this cogitating was that he'd decided to become a free-lance photographer and make calendars or greeting cards, posters maybe. Or, at least take the pictures that went on the calendars and greeting cards and posters that companies which made all that stuff made. He would travel the country and find the most interesting things he could to photograph. It would require a few items.

He set to work immediately on the task of getting his outfit together. He found the little yellow bug advertised in the Daily Oklahoman. He needed a good car in order to do all the driving he had in mind, so he went to see it. The old Chevvy Camaro he had driven out to Oklahoma from Blackshear, Georgia, was not suitable. As soon as he turned the corner on Park St., which was the address given in the advertisement, and saw the bright, little Volkswagen sitting in the driveway with its top down and the "for sale" sign on its windshield, he knew it was for him.

The remainder of his equipment hadn't been hard to assemble. He had learned a lot about cameras and taking pictures while working at Sears. All he needed was a 35mm. with some good attachments and a tripod. As for luggage and personal things, he had always been a levis kind of guy. Maybe a sports jacket with a nice sweater over a shirt and a pair of jeans with some good casual loafers.

Before he sent Oklahoma City fading away at seventy miles per hour in the little bug's rear-view mirror, he secured a place to send his negatives, and arranged an agreement with an agent there to sell his work. He had drawn on the connections he'd made while at Sears. The experience taught him that you needed the help of other people to do the things you wanted to do. He'd been frugal with his money, so he wasn't broke when he turned the little yellow car onto the first on-ramp he came to and ran through the gears, bringing her up to freeway speed and, finally, heading west.

That had been two years ago. And during those two years while he had been traveling and taking pictures, he'd found that art would not pay all of the bills. There had been countless other jobs; some as lowly as washing dishes, others as professional as helping out at tax time in creaky little businesses in small, run-down towns.

Along the way he had met lots of people. She had been one of them. Her name was Julia Raemy. At least that's what she told him it was. He'd met her in west Texas, where he had taken a series of pictures he called "nature's vacancy." They had been together six months now. She thought every photograph he took was good. It was all she ever said, that they were good. She was tall and pretty, and easy to be with most of the time.

He was aware that she found what she called his "dreaminess" irritating. And when she thought he was in one of his "states," also her term, she could be fairly irritating herself. Otherwise, she demanded little, except for one thing: she was a sponge when it came to making love. He sometimes found himself playing "catch-up" with her. But he realized it was a problem most men would see only as a blessing—and he knew that should include himself. So he learned to give even when he had little to offer.

She was intelligent beyond the average. She had graduated from high school and had claimed to have taken two years of junior college, but the conversations he'd had with her told him she was not learned. Still, like the bright little car he had come to love, she went right along day after day in a happy state of being. And that pleased him.

They'd spent the last two months in Phoenix. He had come to Arizona for its ghost towns. A prime target for his camera was the ghost town of Tombstone. But he learned upon going there that it was not what he'd thought it was. Someone told him, then, of the little town of Ruby, a true ghost town set in the high desert of southern Arizona, where commercialism had not gone, they'd said.

They traveled there and he found his informers had not exaggerated. He gloried in the spirit of the past that seemed to be in the air itself of Ruby. The few old buildings and abandoned machines, rust eating them like a fungus, made good pictures, but they lacked something, they were like every other such photograph he'd seen. They were too typical, too similar to what people thought a ghost town should be. In fact, while in Ruby, he and Julia met a family living in a rusted motorhome who turned out to be more interesting, photogenically, than the old town itself. They were characters out of a John Steinbeck novel.

*   *   *

It was while he was poking around in the Phoenix Library that he came upon information about Jerome; located on the side of Mingus Mountain, overlooking the Verde Valley. It was just twenty-five miles north of Prescott, which had been the territorial capitol of Arizona.

Jerome was a mining town that had lost its mines and become a ghost town. It had begun its identity in 1883, its mines remained in production until 1951, when they officially closed and the town lost its primary reason for existence. The people began to leave in 1952 and it became a real ghost town. But a movement in the 60's to rehabilitate it and turn it into a tourist attraction was responsible for keeping the heart of it beating. Now it lived again as people came in droves to walk its up and down streets and gawk at its old buildings and buy the art of the artists and hippy-hangers-on and others who lived there, making a strange, non-traditional, permanent population.

In a way, the place seemed just as unreal and phony as tombstone. But something about the pictures he saw in the books the library had on the old town reached out to him, and he decided to go there.

It wasn't long after that that he and Julia emptied their motel room of their few things and put them in the little car. Soon, it was whistling along all the way up the freeway to Cordes Junction, where they turned to the west and headed toward Prescott. She had wanted to stay in this very interesting old town. But he gave her only a few hours there before turning the yellow car northeast and headed resolutely out onto the plains of central Arizona and ever upward toward the mountains. They left the flats behind and he played the game of momentum with the gears and the little engine in the rear; always keeping it running at high speed, using the gears to attack the ascending spirals and occasional flat lengths of road to move steadily toward the top. Once there, it was still a game of gears to slow their descent as gravity pulled on them now from a different direction. They wound downward then, past the awful drops to the right of the road, slipping easily through the high meadows surrounded by big ponderosa pines, and rolling along the few level spaces where aspen patches could be seen in the foreground, framing the far, blue mountains and sun dappled valley below.

Finally, the little bug purred effortlessly downhill, negotiated a turn and was suddenly on the stretch of Main Street running north just before it curled down to another level to go south through the business district of Jerome. Ahead and to their left rose the brick structure that he was to learn later was the Holy St. Mary's Catholic Church. A street slanted off from Main Street near the old church, just past a tall building of stucco in the process of being restored, and headed upward to several grand old multi-storied houses clinging to the hill there.

Mike had to fight the impulse to turn onto that street. There was too much to see! He wanted to park the car and walk everywhere at once. It was what he was thinking as they rolled past the church. The retaining wall that held back an expanse of green lawn seemed to move like a brown ribbon along with them until they came to the hairpin turn to the right.

After the turn, the street was lined with business structures on the left, their fronts obliterating the view of the San Francisco Peaks seventy miles to the northeast and twelve thousand feet into the clouds above the town of Flagstaff. The buildings also wiped out the sight of the stark drop-off of at least a hundred feet that began only a yard or two beyond the sidewalk edging the street.

On the other side of the street, to the right of the little Volkswagen, was a place where a large building had once stood, but where now a smaller structure housing bathrooms for the tourists sat on a slight rise above a series of parking spaces. Next to this was a sign over it proclaiming it to be the Jerome volunteer fire department. Straight ahead, the street took a dive and ran downhill past other lots, some vacant, some with the bones of a building still protruding from them.

There were restaurants and stores, and everywhere there was art. Most of it was very good. Some of it was not. But the tourists crowding the sidewalks and ambling carelessly out into the street, unmindful of the traffic, hardly seemed to care or know the difference.

Mike steered the little car into a parking space and shut off its engine. Turning to Julia, he said, "We gotta' get out and walk."

She took his hand and he pulled her along. He seemed to find everything interesting. But he was no ordinary pilgrim. He scrutinized the place, examining the different layers of paint on the buildings, marveling at the very gutters, and seemed to be in a world of his own.

They walked for an hour before she looked at him and said, "I can't do it anymore, Mike. We have to find a place to sit and rest."

He gazed at her uncomprehendingly, but only for a moment. He had seen that expression on her face before, heard that same tone in her voice. In his favor was the fact that he did not realize how long they had been walking and looking. The place was like a dream come true for him. He felt no fatigue, no hunger, no thirst. They had walked through countless old buildings renovated into art studios and antique stores and shops of every kind. He had touched old doors and windows and had once even gotten down and run his hands over the surface of the concrete sidewalk.

It had surprised and unsettled her, but he seemed oblivious to the stares of the people who'd stopped and then walked around him while he was down on his hands and knees. Her plea for him to call a halt to the endless tour of the town, although motivated by hunger and a desire to rest, was also the result of embarrassment. She was not moved by the same passion as he was, and without her own personal type of awe and wonder to shield her, the all-too-obvious looks thrown first his way and then at her, as if to say, "Are you really with this guy?" had begun to take their toll.

"Alright," he said, "we'll get something to eat. You can relax for a while. Isn't this place amazing, though?"

She made no reply as he led her toward what appeared to be a restaurant. Then he stopped, caught again by something which he found wonderful in some way unknown to her. He stood with his mouth open, staring upward.

She looked where he was looking. It was the marquee of an old theatre. The few dead stubs of neon lights still attached to it echoed the meaning of the older and more substantial lettering painted on the brick wall behind it; The Fountain. They had passed it from a distance three times already. But, now, something about it had touched him and he stood gazing up at it.

"God," he said, "think of it, Julia, they all played here. They played here before I could watch them back home in that dinky little theatre I used to go to on Saturdays as a kid."

"What do you mean?" she asked.

"Lord!" he exclaimed again, not hearing her question, "kids out here had already seen some of the same things on the screen that I saw later; seen it and grown up and gone away from here before I was born. Think of it!"

"The only thing," she began, with just a tiny bit of disgust in her tone, "I want to think about is a place to sit where I can have something cool to drink."

He turned toward her then and, shaking his head and smiling, took her hand and led her once more toward the building with the sign out front marking it as a restaurant: The American Café.

THREE

At its juncture with Hull, where 89A came into town, Main made a sharp point of, not only sidewalk and curb, but the very building standing there, so that people coming up saw a three-story structure that seemed to deflect the traffic's flow like the bows of some great Titanic cutting through the ocean's surface; one-way going up to the right, one way coming down from the left.

It was in this very part of town, on the third floor of the building with the unusual shape, that a room with bath and kitchenette existed which was advertised for rent. Immediately upon seeing this advertisement, written on a dirty square of cardboard inserted in the window of the second floor, which was street level on the Main Street side of the building, Mike inquired about and subsequently rented the rooms for $400.00 per month.

Later, shortly after the sun had dropped behind the shoulder of the mountain, he stood in the main room of the little apartment at its "bow" section, looking out of the large, single window. He could almost see the traffic coming up as it had in the old days when the term "ghost" meant something lurking in the night, and not this grand old town in the time of its decay, a time when it had become a thing like some Egyptian mummy, able to lure and attract only because of its connections with death and the strange notion that somehow life was still lying within it, dormant in some way, waiting for a spark of something to bring it surging from the nether world and into this one.

He grinned to himself as he thought of how his mind was playing tricks on him. It was, of course, the memories generated by seeing the old theatre which had made him select such a macabre metaphor. Again he found something humorous about it: Lon Chaney and The Mummy Returns. His college friends had made fun of him for seeking out and watching the old classics. Television shows that featured them had been his favorite programs. For even then, his senses had turned toward times past. Modern thrillers, while almost technically perfect, lacked the drama, the musty, rotting-cloth-smell needed to move him as those old movies had.

Still, he mused, his imagery hadn't been too far-fetched. This place had been vibrant once. Not so quiet and empty as now. People lived here, true. Money changed hands here. There was a bit of life here. But, he thought, it is merely a sigh, a momentary blush on a cold cheek, hardly anything at all when compared with what it once was.

*   *   *

He did not know just how accurate his speculative thoughts were. In 1893 a narrow guage railroad had run through very hazardous terrain to the top of Mingus Mountain within a mile of where Jerome sat. Later, in 1912, a spur of the Santa Fe railroad was built to Clarkdale, at the foot of the mountain. By 1919 an extended branch connected it with Jerome.

But by 1927, the rails carried only ore and mining equipment. And the little narrow guage had been abandoned. There was the road to Perkinsville, thence to Paulden and Chino Valley, where the connection of the narrow guage to the main Santa Fe line had been made at a place called Jerome Junction. The lifeblood for the little mountain town of Jerome was derived from two places: Flagstaff to the northeast and Prescott to the southwest. North of Flagstaff was wilderness, east of it lay an equal vastness. South of Prescott lay southern Arizona; Phoenix and Tucson were the primary cities. All of these places were far from Jerome, with the exception of the Prescott and Camp Verde areas. And they all depended on the transcontinental rail system. But in 1927 roads connected them all. And the automobile, the killer of railroads, was about to appropriate the community on Mingus Mountain.

It was the hard macadam surface of the new road, dubbed 89A that made it possible. It spiraled in smooth two-lane convenience up and over the mountainous route in both directions, bringing everything to Jerome that the town needed for life. And by 1920, the year it was finally completed, the edge of dominance in heavy freight was worn off the rails by motorized transport.

The trucks that traveled the new route hauled food and goods to the little town on the mountainside. They brought the medicines and the equipment used in the hospital. They brought the hardware and the furniture and the clothing, they brought the out of town newspapers and the magazines, the mail, and the movie reels that were needed at the theatres; the Fountain did not enjoy total dominance of the town.

Men coming to find jobs in the mines and the stores and shops hitched rides on trucks, sometimes they rode with the girls who came to work in the brothels; though every wayward female who came to the town on the mountainside was not a tramp. Some came to work in the restaurants and the stores. A few were professionals: nurses, secretaries, or teachers. New citizens also came to Jerome in their own cars and trucks. And it was the road that allowed those to whom life no longer mattered to be taken away. The dead rolled along in hearses, some were buried in Jerome, some in Clarkdale or another place in the Verde Valley. Others went on to the train depot in Clarkdale where they were shipped to far-away places to be buried near their own kin.

Few people who willingly left Jerome with intentions of never coming back were seldom noticed. It wasn't a place for leaving. It was too vibrant. The copper and the road saw to that. Copper was Jerome's soul, and route 89A was the artery that fed its heart. And even though the angle at which it had to send itself upward through the body of the little town was such that traffic along its single, main line was made to go slow, the center of town pulsed steadily day and night, week after week, month after month, and year after year until 1953, when the last load of copper ore had been taken out of the mines and the people left and the town became a skeleton of itself; only hollow houses and empty streets remained.

*   *   *

As he stood before the window, at the apex of the triangle made by the streets of the little town, Mike's feelings about the town almost became physical, like fields of energy they emanated from him and moved ahead of him while he traveled, not as mortals do, along lines of distance measured by time spent, but across time itself, down the avenues of his own imagination.

Inside the little room, behind the glass which showed him as much of his own reflection as it did the quaint scene of the dark street and the old structures it served, he was not aware of a sudden, sharp force of wind whipping past the corner of the old hotel across the street and toward the walls of his own room; whipping past and halting momentarily to form a vortex above the vacant pavement that reflected the light from the window, where he stood peering through the out-dated blinds into the gloom like the captain of some vessel sailing into unknown waters. Behind him, Julia left the small bathroom and came through the kitchen to stand at his elbow.

"Whatta' y'see out there?"

At her touch and the sound of her voice he felt a rippling of the skin on his back and he shuddered as if cold, even though the little flat was a bit warm from the heat of the August evening.

"What's the matter?" she asked.

"Don't scare me like that," he said, raising the bottom half of the window with some effort and turning toward her.

She laughed at him, then reached up and touched his face. "Silly," she said as he pulled her to him and their lips met.

Through the now open window, the sounds of the night rushed in with the cooler outside air. On the streets below, people were still walking, but only a few headlights inched their way up the steep road to the town. Even fewer cars went from the little town toward the valley. Most of the tourists had left before the sun went down, having vowed to do so on their way up as they looked in awe at the places where the land dropped away from the level pavement for hundreds of feet as if a giant knife had carved it.

In the little apartment they lay together on the bed, listening to the people still moving in the town, still entering the few shops that were open, and the restaurants still serving customers. The main attraction for most of the people on the streets was the bar near the center of town. A country band was playing there. Music from it, along with laughter and talking, spilled into the warm night through the bar's open doors. But the sounds all seemed muted to Mike and Julia, softened by an even greater auditory presence. It was the hush of the mountain above the scar on its side that was the town.

The mountain stood above and beyond the town in great dark folds of stone and soil and timber—though only scrub oak and salt cedar grew where the great Ponderosa had once stood which the miners had taken to support their tunnel ceilings. That part of the forest which at one time had reached green and vibrant toward the blue sky, now made up a huge wooden skeleton of beams and framing, lying silent in the shafts and tunnels hundreds of feet below the town, in the solid rock of the mountain itself.

Mike and Julia made love as a breeze pushed aside the plain white curtains in the open window, gently rattling the Venetian blinds. Then they lay quietly in the increasing stillness until sleep came to them.

*   *   *

There were two full blocks of buildings on either side of Main Street where it became a one-way going down through the town. But past First Ave., where an old hotel sat gutted and naked, its grand entry-way a reminder of the glory it once knew, for most of its length the east side of the street held only vacant lots and the foundations of buildings long-since gone. Only the last hundred feet supported buildings on that side; one of these was the odd shaped building where their apartment occupied the third floor.

They had parked the Volkswagen in front of one of the abandoned sites. After he'd rented the rooms, Mike returned and put the little car's top up and locked the doors and jokingly told it to enjoy the rest.

Across the street, some of the original buildings still remained. Once they had been dentists' offices, lawyers' offices; some had been clothing shops, one had housed a drugstore. There had also been a surveyor's office on the street. Now, the same buildings were tourist traps where art, jewelry, souvenirs, and t-shirts were sold. The upstairs quarters were used as apartments for the people who owned the shops below them. Some rooms were rented out to the drifters who came through town, stopped and worked long enough to make a stash and moved on.

There were two or three restaurants along that side of the street. One was a long and narrow affair set into a part of the ground floor of a three story structure that had once been an apartment building; lettering chiseled into the rock facing running in a continuous band just below its high roof proclaimed the date of its construction and gave its name; Sturdevant Apartment Bldg. The restaurant it housed was called Rooster's. A wooden carving of a green and yellow fowl hung over its pink door with the name burned into a smaller plaque fastened to the carving with rusty wire. It was where they had their first breakfast in Jerome.

They awoke at six o'clock. Normally not averse to rising early, especially when he had something to look forward to, such as the continued exploration of this old town, Mike was surprised to find himself still sleepy-eyed and grumbling as Julia rolled against him and said affectionately, "Hey, you said we had to get up early, remember?"

"Yeah, I do," he said, his eyes still closed, "but I didn't sleep much last night. Had a lot of crazy dreams."

"You're just excited about this old place. Come on, get up. Even I want to see what the day has in store for us here."

He didn't answer. But a half hour later, as they stepped inside Rooster's, and he smelled the rich aroma of bacon frying and coffee brewing, he brightened. They slid into one of the booths along the wall. A waitress came with coffee in thick brown mugs.

"How'd you know I wanted some of this?" Mike said, looking up at her with a warm smile.

"You look like a coffee person to me," she answered, her face showing a deadpan expression. She didn't feel like the usual banter this morning. She believed people should be in their own homes on Sunday. But she knew quite well that the tourists would soon flood the place. And by noon, those coming up from the valley and over the mountain from Prescott would add to the crowd already there and no peace would exist until the middle of the week.

"What'll you have? Need some time to look at the menu?" She shot the questions at them like bullets. A cigarette lay burning in the ashtray behind the counter. She wanted to get back to it before it turned into an ashy caricature of itself.

"I need eggs, bacon, hash-browns and pancakes—and more coffee," said Mike.

Julia looked at him with disapproval. But she didn't say anything, only ordered her own breakfast instead. "I'll have toast and orange juice," she said, "and a cup of coffee."

He paid no attention to her order. Unlike her, he was willing to live and let live where some things were concerned. Diet was one of them. By the time the waitress brought the coffee, he was already busy looking around at the interior of the old place. "I'm gonna' get some real good pictures here," he said, happily, finally awake.

She lifted her coffee cup and drank without replying to his statement. She was noncommittal about his work. He always got good pictures. The important thing was finding something to interest her while he took them. She had no intention of hanging out in the rented rooms while he went about researching and photographing this old town. And sitting and watching him read silently for hours might mean togetherness, but it would also be a bore. If he ran true to form, they would spend another frenetic day roaming the place. Then he would be settled enough to focus on something about it, and that would free her up to look around herself.

But it didn't take an entire day for him to run into the snag that would hold him for awhile. As she had correctly predicted, he wanted to resume the exploration started the day before. And so began another marathon of walking, looking, examining and head shaking. She followed along, but with a purpose, now.

Two hours later, they had just finished a mid-morning cup of coffee in the American Café, on the corner of route 89A and Jerome Avenue, the same eatery they had stopped at the previous afternoon. After they paid their bill and left, he began talking a mile a minute to her as they walked along the south side of the street. The Fountain theatre stood directly across from them. But it no longer excited him in the way it had at first. He only glanced longingly at it once, then continued talking.

The thing he was so interested in had to do with the café itself. There was a history behind the old place. Part of its story was printed on its menu. Amazingly enough, probably due to his excitement about the old town, that and the theatre across the street, he had not noticed the narrative on the menu the day before. Now, he almost shouted as he talked about something or someone called the wobblies.

"The I.W.W., Julia. The International Workers of the World!"

She looked at him blankly, uncomprehending.

"They were here," he said. "Well, of course they would be," he commented on his own statement, as if her vacant stare was exactly what he expected and it didn't matter too much that she knew nothing about what he had been saying. "This was a very capitalistic place," he continued, "it's just that, well, you study about something and all of a sudden find yourself standing right where some of it all happened. It's fascinating, Julia."

She looked at him, her blue eyes filled with introspection, and said, "What if I got a job in one of these little shops here. It wouldn't hurt, would it? Maybe a waitress. That gal in the place where we ate this morning didn't look too happy."

He couldn't speak for a moment. He had told her something of importance and was amazed that it had gone completely past her. Then, with a heavy sigh, he said, "You want to be a waitress?"

"No," she said, "shaking her head and running a hand down one side of her long, black hair, forcing it to lie behind her shoulder, "I'd rather sell art in one of these so-called art galleries. I could dress weird, my hair's already right . . ."

They both laughed then. "However," she continued more seriously, "to be realistic, I think slinging hash is more of a possibility. It would keep me productive while you get on with your work. I wouldn't mind for a while. Who knows," she was smiling again, "I might learn some stuff you could use."

"Damn!" he said, stopping suddenly and taking hold of her so that she was partially turned toward him.

"What?" she exclaimed, the humor quickly leaving her voice, while her brow furrowed and her face tightened with concern. "It was just a thought, Mike. I won't do it if it bothers you that much."

"No," he said, turning her toward a flight of steps leading downward between the sidewalk and the wall of the building to their left, "I think your being a waitress is a good idea. I was just reacting to this."

"This? What do you mean?"

Letting go of her then, and with a flourish of both arms as if he were presenting some grand setting to her, he said through a broad smile, "This, my love."

It was not the stairs themselves that interested him, but a sign, a painting of a human hand with its forefinger pointing down the stairs. Below the hand with its finger were the words, "Jerome Public Library. Weekend visitors welcome."

"Oh, hey! She said, reading the sign then turning quickly back to him with her own broad grin. Yeah, this would do it, she thought happily. He'd be here all day. Now, she could explore for herself.

It wasn't the original site of the Jerome Public Library. That had been in the building known as the Clubhouse, which had started life as the town's hospital. Later, when the new hospital had been built, the Clubhouse became the site of an organization for mine employees. When the mine shut down in the 50's, its collection of books and other materials was taken to one of the mining company's warehouses. The collection remained there for awhile until it was finally given to the Jerome Preservation Society, which housed it in the basement of what had once been a saloon. It was the basement they were about to visit, the one with the sign pointing down the flight of stairs dropping out of a section of the sidewalk in that old-fashioned way that was common in cities built early in the century.

It was a close and damp place. An older woman with a grim face sat behind a small desk with a sign on it that read: "Donashuns needed. Must be a resident to check out books. Please feel free to browse. Jerome Preservation Soc."

Mike entered the makeshift library with reverence on his face and respect in each quiet, slow movement, the only kind of movement he permitted himself to make in such places. He was soon engrossed.

Moving along the cramped aisles between bookshelves, Julia could almost see his facial expressions as muted exclamations came to her from where she had left him sitting in one creaking little corner, books strewn around him on the old wooden floor. Smiling, she went to him and told him she planned to walk around the old town and see what the possibilities were for a job. He mumbled acknowledgement, never lifting his head from the book spread open in his lap. Then she left him with a few words about meeting him back at the rented rooms that afternoon.

*   *   *

That night, Mike lay on their bed with the books he had brought from the library spread out next to him. Julia was in the bathroom. She had told him earlier that she had done something significant after leaving him in the library. He knew she wanted to talk more about it with him, but that conversation would have to wait until the lights were out and he could no longer read from the old books.

He'd been able to convince the volunteer librarian that he was indeed a resident. By chance, she knew the owner of the apartment. When he was able to describe that person to her and supply her with a name, she issued him a library card and allowed him to check out the books he wanted.

The copies were assuredly old. Purchases for the library had no longer taken place after 1951. The librarian had told him that. He had selected a book on Arizona history, another book about Jerome itself, a text on mining, and a copy of Spoon River Anthology by Edgar Lee Masters. He had included it in the books he borrowed, not for the content of the text itself, but for the notes which were written in the slim volume. Someone had written on the fly leaf and everywhere else there had been a blank space to write. In one corner of the inside cover, the upper left, was writing and a date: "To M., from Me. 1926. Allow me to share your grief."

It was this thin book of verses he was examining as Julia walked into the bedroom from the bathroom. He had just lifted it from among the other books. She turned to the window before getting into bed beside him, checking to see that the shades were drawn and that their privacy was assured.

He read the inscription aloud as she finally settled in and snuggled close. Outside, the wind, which had begun to blow soon after nightfall, suddenly hit the old building with a powerful burst. The curtains fluttered, and the glass in the window rattled.

"Ooh," she said, "we could get a storm. I like making love in the rain. You know that, don't you?"

He chuckled. But he didn't put the book down. Instead, he told her about it, explaining that it was not the poetry it contained, but the handwritten notes which interested him. "I wonder who M. was," he mused.

"You know," Julia said, propping herself up on an elbow beside him in the bed, "the preservation society probably got that book from one of these old houses here. Otherwise, how would it come to be in the library collection?"

He looked at her vacantly. Of course he had already surmised that. "Well, that's why I checked the book out, Julia. I'd sort of like to see where the idea might lead."

From somewhere higher on the mountainside, a crack of lightning split the quiet of the evening, and another pane-rattling gust hit the building. Then the rain began to fall. It was the start of what was locally called "the monsoons," usually arriving near the end of June, the rainfall was late by more than a month.

"Come here," she said, reaching up with one hand to turn off the light emanating through the shade of the antique lamp standing on its brass pole that curved toward them like some old-fashioned maid, bending as if to ask if they needed anything.

"You know," he said, as she kissed him, "all this walking up and down these streets has made me kinda' worn out."

She laughed and kissed him again. "You stayed in that musty old basement looking at books all afternoon. Don't talk like that to me. I'm the one who walked all over the place today. You'd think I'd be too tired for this," and she lifted her leg and ran it upward along his.

With a sigh of resignation, he dropped the book over the bedside and pulled her closer to him. At that moment, the thunder rolled once again from the heights. For an instant, an image of the old houses perched on the slopes high above the town flashed into his mind, there had been one area in particular which had attracted his attention the day before as they had come into town.

But his thoughts were soon filled with the passion she caused him to feel, and he made love to her while the rain fell heavily outside and the thunder grumbled its way down the mountain and on toward the valley.

Along the streets, the pavement glistened where lighted windows threw a glow onto its wet surface, the wind gusted; moving, seemingly, ever downward through the old town, from the highest streets of all where at one time the wealthiest residents of Jerome had lived in large multi-storied houses, built in the grand style of the previous century, the style known as Victorian.

FOUR

She moved from the main bedroom on the top floor out to the landing, then down the grand staircase and onto the ground level of the house, past the great front door, onto the porch and into the rain. She descended the levels and layers of the town encased in the storm itself, until she reached the place where 89A and Main came together. She paused there, and the wind whirled around her, as if, like some impatient steed she rode, eager to hurry on. The rain fell to the street in heavy waves. The window was dark in the apartment. But she sensed what was going on in the little boat shaped room anyway.

The apartment was well-known to her. It had played a role in her life once, long ago. Like many things in Jerome, it was a place of unhappy memory to her. But the couple there now had no knowledge of the two-room flat as anything more than what it appeared to be. To them it was just a quaint piece of history to live in for a while.

She moved on. The curious attraction she had felt earlier when she had seen him standing in the lighted window of the oddly shaped building, appearing to move as from a force apart from the real world, adrift almost in time itself, was not there tonight—though something did tug at her senses.

Past the edge of the street and downward, she moved along as she had done for all the years since the last, the one holding the event which kept her there.

Around her now the thunder and the lightning played their parts in the drama of the rainstorm. Ahead, like everything else in the town, her destination lay on the slope of a hillside. Illuminated by the lightning, some of the stones flashed wetly as the thunder rent the air. The bent and rusted old fence glistened. But she had no need of the light to guide her. It was a place she knew well.

*   *   *

Their lovemaking over, Julia lay quiet and satisfied. Outside, the rain still fell steadily, though softly now. The wind had become a breeze, and the scents it bathed them in were fresh as only new-fallen rain could make them. Now, she would tell him of her own little victory that day.

"I got a job at Rooster's."

He wasn't surprised. And she could tell he wasn't. "Well, that's good, Babe," and he meant it. He knew she needed something to do while he made the pictures.

She smiled to herself at his seeming indifference, knowing he would be this way until he did his thing. She turned away from him, then, and sank into the sleep that came to her easily, now.

But beside her, he was wide awake. Finally, he eased out of the bed and crept into the tiny kitchen. He took with him the copy of the book with the notes in it. He sat down in one of the two rickety chairs at the small table and turned to the page with the inscription on it, "To M., from Me. 1926. Allow me to share your grief."

Again the thought ran through his head, I wonder who M. was? Perhaps even more important, who was Me? And what might the grief be about? He turned to a page within the book and began to read.

Spoon River Anthology was a book of verse. He did not think of himself as a poet. He had never written poems. But he often found himself selecting books of poetry to glance at, sometimes to read at length. It was why he had taken the book from the shelf in the first place. He had never considered his strange manner of looking into the past, as he called it, and seeing beyond that part of life often held up to be observed, and just as often the only thing seen of it by most people, as being a poetic thing to do, an act of poetry. But others had seen it as such. And others had seen him as being a poet, too. Some had scoffed in derision at such a useless thing. Some had been made to stop and think further than that about it. And a few had smiled knowingly.

He had heard of this book. The poet, Edgar Lee Masters, was said to have been that kind of writer with only one great work to offer. Spoon River Anthology was the story of people in a typical American town during the early part of the century. The poems were presented as epitaphs taken from gravestones, and as the reader progressed through the selections, a picture of the town and its people gradually emerged.

He found himself reading about a young woman, used and thrown away by one of the town's most prominent citizens. Her pain and suffering as she tried to live with herself in the light of love given and honor taken, all in sin and forbidden association, cried out to him as he sat and read in the dim little kitchen with the rain falling on the roof overhead.

He soon deduced which of the two hands by which the book had been marked and written in was M. and which was Me. Further, he believed M. was feminine and Me. was masculine. He thought it was M. who had written the most. And of course it was M. who had marked the various poems. Some entire lines were underlined. In other instances, individual words had been shaded, circled or underlined. Only the page bearing the inscription had received the written attention of the hand he thought was Me.

The rain had stopped long before he became aware of the velvet weight of silence that lay around him in the little kitchen lit by the single bulb. Looking up from the book, he sat back in the chair and stared straight at the dark square that was the window on the west wall of the room, the wall nearest Main Street. Past the dingy curtains, the glass lay dark and impenetrable. Because of the night and the light in the little room, only from its other side could it be seen through.

He closed the book and placed it on the table, then lifted both hands and rubbed his face. He was finally tired and ready for sleep. He shoved the frail chair backward and stood, then reached down to retrieve the book. It lay open before him. Absently he closed it again, turned off the light in the kitchen and felt his way into the bedroom. He placed the book on the floor with the other books he had checked out of the library earlier that day, then he crawled quietly into bed. Julia's warmth drew him and he moved to her, put his arm across her, and was asleep in less than a minute.

*   *   *

Coming back up the side of the mountain on which the town lay, she had stopped and looked at the single lighted window. Again she felt an odd sensation. Not un-like the one she had become aware of the first time she'd encountered the man. She intruded her senses then, and suddenly, the old sadness draped over her in all its hurt. A moment's intense anger at the man almost overcame her, but she held herself. Carefully, she felt of him, then, and surprise drove away all other emotions. After that, she withdrew hurriedly and continued upward to the house that sat on the second highest street of the town. She did not see the light go out behind her, but she knew when it did. Far across the valley below, the thunder rumbled faintly. Morning was not long to come.

FIVE

Sitting at the counter with his usual large breakfast before him, feeling good at seeing Julia happily working there, Mike got to meet Rooster. The small man, about fifty years old, emerged at Julia's call from the tiny kitchen that was walled off from the remainder of the restaurant, and extended a hand with a spatula in it toward him.

Julia took the kitchen utensil from the little man, who turned with a nod of thanks to her before announcing himself to Mike with a broad grin and a proffered hand now empty of the spatula.

"I'm called Roosta,' he said with a single shake, "from New Yoak. I heah y'take pictchas."

Looking at the man, who had wisps of reddish-gray hair peeking from beneath the white chef's hat he wore, Mike thought how much he resembled a clown. If he just had a big red ball over his nose he'd be one, he thought. Aloud, he answered with a nod as Rooster grinned up at him, "Yes, I take pictures."

The owner of the restaurant continued as if he had gotten a broader reception than the single, simple sentence. "Y' gal's a talka. Just like mine," and he pointed to the ceiling and winked, "upstauhs. Good f'the customahs. Not so good f'you 'n me. Say, I gotta' go. Mondays, you'd think they could stay home, but, no. Mondays are too close t'Sundays. They'll keep comin' till mid-week. Nice meetin' ya." He winked and went back to his grill.

Mike looked around. There were a few places empty. But for a Monday in a ghost town, business did look good.

Julia grinned as she leaned over the counter and asked him what he intended to do for the day.

"What about that other woman," Mike asked before answering her question, "I don't like it that you had to take her job."

"She offered it to me," said Julia. "She's alright. Has a family down in Cottonwood. She hated having to work on weekends. I told her we'd be leaving in a couple of weeks anyway. She needed a vacation." Then, nodding toward the kitchen, "The little guy's a sweetie, he'll take her back."

Mike leaned away from the counter and looked at the high ceiling. It was made of tin with a pattern pressed into it. "God, I love this old place!" he exclaimed. "Do you see that ceiling? I mean, it's like going back in time to be here. Think of it."

An hour later, he was on that part of 89A, the section known as Clark Street, that fronted what he assumed had been an old-style apartment building. There were people walking about. But the crowd was nothing like it had been during the previous two days.

He turned his attention back to the old place rising above him. It was built on a level above the street. A retaining wall ran along the front of the property. A set of stairs led up from the sidewalk and into the building. Chiseled into a single heavy lintel stone over the double doors were the words, The Delacroix House. The doors had been chained and barred. He was able to look inside. There was little more to view except a long hallway

Back on the level of the street, at another part of the front wall, he peered through a dirty pane of glass in a window that had been partially covered with plywood and saw a small kitchen with cabinets and a sink. There was junk piled in a corner. He decided to explore at the back of the building.

Walking around the structure, he found a long drive that served the entire building. It was cluttered with trash and overgrown saplings that seemed to flourish everywhere in the old town where there was a bit of bare earth.

At the driveway's far end, he saw something that seemed to be made of metal among the saplings. He walked toward that end of the building. As he traversed the drive, he could see into the back windows of the old place. He realized he had been right about its purpose, then. It had been an apartment building. He could see that fewer precautions had been taken to discourage prying eyes on this side of the Delacroix House. Most of its windows were uncovered. It appeared to have had three kinds, or sizes, of accommodation: two room kitchenettes, three room flats, and larger, four room apartments. The building consisted of three stories and a basement. He could see hallways running from front to back. There was a similar set of double doors at the rear of the building, though they were of a plainer style than those at the front. And he believed a hallway also ran at right angles to the one he could see. He estimated that the place probably had fifteen to twenty apartments in it. He could imagine a furnace in the basement with a system of pipes for steam heat.

Looking through windows and walking slowly along, he finally arrived at what he had seen at the end of the driveway. It was a set of rusted railings that ran upward along what had served as one of the many up and down sidewalks in the old town. Past the stairway, the driveway stopped where the body of the mountain halted it.

The concrete stairway led to the next street above. Craning his neck, he could see part of a wooden porch on a big house there. Beyond this sagging structure, and one more street higher, another house sat large and partially hidden in the growth of trees and saplings on a built-up yard. He could just make out the large cut blocks of stone that made the retaining wall which held it. Something else seemed to occupy the yard along with the house and the saplings. He couldn't tell what it was, but it appeared to be unusual.

Disdaining the stairway, which was filled with various kinds of trash, he returned to the street, followed it upward toward the back of the house he was interested in.

The streets were like stairs themselves as they rose against the mountainside. Several old houses on the street below his present position formed a barrier between himself and the apartment building and the remainder of the town. Their fronts led onto the street where he now stood. The house he was interested in was behind him, on the next level. He stood just below what was its backyard. The retaining wall of heavy cut stone blocks rose to a height of eight feet before giving way to an overgrowth of weeds and saplings.

Finally locating places to put his hands and feet, he climbed the wall and stepped onto the surface of the yard. It was here, on the high crown of the still ascending surface of the lot, beneath a huge oak, that the thing sat which he had seen from below.

He made his way up the slope of the yard and walked with his legs swishing against the growth toward what he could see now was an old car. It was covered in trash and nearly hidden by the saplings. It was a rag-top sedan, he thought, but the top was missing and the body was badly dented. He supposed that it could have been in a wreck at one time. He looked at an emblem on the side of what had once been a barrel-like hood and read, Cadillac.

The tires, what little remained of them, were on wheels with wooden spokes that had collapsed in decay. From inside the metal body came the smell of old upholstery and wood framing rotting in the weather. The old body was marred by rust, now, but in places that had provided protection from sun and rain, some of its color could still be seen. Paint on a piece of metal which had been bent and curled in on itself led him to think the car might once have been dark green. Inside the cavity of the engine compartment, the motor was layered in rust. On the earth beneath it, there was no trace of oil or grease. Years of rain had washed it clean.

Tall weeds bearing tiny blue flowers grew around the abandoned machine. He lost himself in thought for several minutes as he walked around the old wreck, examining it and imagining what it must have looked like when it was showroom new.

He peered around at the yard and the house. It was a grand yellow thing, its paint was peeled and faded almost to a white in places. There were signs on its walls that said no trespassing. A weathered structure he felt had once been the garage for the old car stood at the far side of the big house. It was posted as well with signs telling visitors to stay away. But the signs appeared faded and ragged. Perhaps they no longer meant what they had once been intended to mean.

The place was one which he had to return to. He knew that, but he would forego more exploration today. He would leave, but he would come back. Before he left, though, he wanted a picture of the old car sitting in the shadows. The sun was just high enough now to afford the light needed to bring out the rust in the metal and the color in the wildflowers.

He took the picture, then walked back through the weeds to the end of the yard and slid down to the street. It was his first shot of the day. Actually, he thought, the first shot of the entire project. A throw-away though, probably. There was one thing about it, it wasn't a typical western-ghost-town scene. An old car beneath a tree; could have been taken in any slummy part of town anywhere back East.

His thoughts were suddenly interrupted. From somewhere above and to his left a strange sound was made. He stopped and looked around for a moment, then he whistled in surprise to himself as he saw the church sitting on the level below. Forgetting the strange noise, he hurried downward, toward the old edifice.

*   *   *

It was two hours later that, in a sort of mental fog, and feeling thirsty, he stepped into the wide doorway of Mcallister Beer Co. & Emporium on Main Street, at the corner where 89A paused to look back to the left before running up the hill and over the mountain to Prescott.

It was a high-ceilinged room, with two entrances, one on Jerome Avenue and the other on Main; both on route 89A, though. It was dark inside, but he could see by the light from the opened doors that the walls were a dingy white.

Commercial beer signs decorated the walls. The bar ran from north to south, like the street outside. A mirror covered the wall behind the bar. A big clock with the famous horses and beer wagon covered the north wall.

In a corner across from the bar, on a little platform raised a foot or so from the floor, a hard-looking woman in levis, boots, and a man's cowboy shirt sang into the black cone of a microphone on a chrome mic-stand. A younger female, he would have said a girl, accompanied the woman on a fiddle. The music they made seemed to lose itself in the nearly empty place. There were two or three couples at tables, and a man and a woman were dancing in the small area that was the dance floor. An old man in a black hat sat at the far end of the bar.

It all seemed out of place time-wise for Mike. He felt it was too early in the day; not just for drinking, but for the singing and the dancing. He slid onto a red leather stool anyway and met the bartender's silent query with, "Give me a beer, please."

Mike placed his camera at his elbow on the bar and turned to look out of the open door into the street. More people were walking there, now. The strains of the two-woman band felt like light rain in the heavy air of the bar. He was beginning to return to normal. Up there, on the hill inside the old church, he'd done his thing again; gone back, at least he felt he had gone back. That old church was special in some way.

When the beer arrived, he held the bottle to his lips and allowed a good long drink to fill his mouth and slide down his throat. From his left, the old man spoke.

"Looks like you enjoyed that."

Mike turned his head toward him. He liked most people. And he knew from experience that the way to get to know a place was to talk to the people who lived there.

"I sure did," he said. And he shifted on the stool and faced the old man. His invitation to talk further was accepted instantly.

"You don't look like most people that come here," said the old man, an expression on his face that showed he thought he was being sly. "You a newspaperman or a tellyvishun anchor?"

"I'm neither," said Mike with a smile.

"What?" asked the old man, his hand cupped behind one ear as he leaned toward Mike.

"I'm a free-lance photographer," said Mike, raising the level of his voice.

The old man jerked backward as if he had been hit with an object. He studied Mike for a moment. Then he said, "By-God, I know whut a free-lance photographer is. Used to be one. Name's Cyrus Dooley."

He slumped sideways against the bar after he said this, took out a cigarette from a pack in his shirt pocket and lit it. With the first drag he succumbed to heavy coughing. When this subsided, he continued to smoke and observe Mike, as if waiting for a sign of recognition of the name.

In turn, Mike studied him. Cyrus Dooley was well past sixty-five he would guess; a gold tooth and a dark place where there was no tooth, the usual leather-skinned testament to years of smoking, there was white hair beneath the black cowboy hat that matched a dirty western shirt. He wore even dirtier levis held onto his skinny hips by a broad belt with what seemed to Mike to be silver-trimmed turquoise studs on sections of it. A pair of scuffed cowboy boots finished the outfit.

Mike rose from his stool and moved to one closer to the old man. Holding out his hand he said, "I'm Mike Peale. Glad to meet you." And he sat down on the stool. The old man took his hand, gave it a shake and then dropped his own hand back into his lap. "Hey, Ralph," he said, as he turned and hailed the bartender, "give us both another."

Mike looked down at his watch. He was surprised to see that it was nearly eleven o'clock. Even so, it was a strange time to be drinking beer, he thought. But with the heat beginning to make itself known outside, and the holiday feeling of the town, especially with the tourists coming out, now, into the morning sun, it seemed the natural thing to do, and it felt right. Must be why I ordered one in the first place, he thought with a smile.

Seeing this, the old man chuckled. Then he had another coughing spell which he ended with a side-snap toward the wall and a muted curse before he turned back toward Mike.

Sliding the two bottles across the bar toward the men, the bartender said, in reference to the old man's use of cigarettes, "When you goin' to give 'em up, Cy?"

"By-God, I'll damn sure let you know, Ralph," came the quick reply as the old man looked up grimly at the bartender.

But when he turned again toward Mike, the smile was back among the wrinkles on his face. "Don't bother 'bout me'n Ralph. He's right, though, the damned things'll kill me I guess. So, you're a taker of pictures?"

Both men drank from their respective bottles before the dialogue resumed. Mike's mind was a bit clearer now than it had been when he'd first entered the bar. But the sensations he had carried down the hill with him still tingled. Maybe the old man could tell him a few things about the church sitting high behind them, catching the full blast of the mid-morning sun now in stone and mortar silence, holding central position in the dead and dried-up body of the town that had, after its life left it, lain on the hillside in the rain and the sun for nearly twenty years before the artists and hippies and just plain vermin had found its bleached skeleton and crawled into the shadow of its bones to root for lives of their own.

SIX

Her place was on a small daybed against the south wall of the great bedroom that occupied the north end of the third story of the grand old house. A rococo-styled mantelpiece divided the room at the north wall. French doors flanked the fireplace, each leading to a narrow balcony, the tail end of a much larger balcony that fronted the bedroom on its east side. The smaller balcony wrapped around to the west wall, but there were no doors there, only a great double window. At the juncture of the east and north walls a tower rose above the third floor into a point, like the spire of a gothic cathedral standing lonely vigilance somewhere in Europe.

It was here, in this room, so well known to her, that she existed. The old house, now in decay, creaked when the wind caught it. The wind also took the liberty of coming through the broken panes of glass; the wind, and the rain as well. Rot in wood and fabric, and other things, made up the perfumes of the old place, now. The floor coverings, the furnishings and the draperies all gave off the odor of mould. It was nothing like it had been. Few things were, including her.

But some things were unchanged. Her longing for those far-gone times with their own people and textures and scents and loves, ah, that longing never ceased. She allowed memory to come to her, and she enhanced it far beyond its usual parameters. Still, it wasn't the same.

It was her first night at the grand house that she sometimes revisited in this way. It was one of her favorite memories. But often, after re-living it, the bitterness and the hatred rushed over her, and the old house shook from a force other than the wind against its flanks!

It had been right at dusk, and the light from the fading sun fanned across the west in beautiful, amber strokes; parts of which could be seen even if the mountain's dark bulk did intervene. She had entered the great bedroom from the hall after spending a few minutes in one of the four baths and powdering rooms. It had been the curiosity of a young woman unaccustomed to such opulence of wall hangings and furnishings. The size of the place alone was enough to impress her forever, she had thought.

The double doors to the large room had been open. And through the spacious window on the room's far side, past the doubly-flanked fireplace, could be seen light from the sun, which in grand and glorious splendor was quickly falling. The light flowed down from the top of the mountain, but also from around the north flank where the open pit of the mine had lowered the massive earthen bulk and allowed the western sun to touch the town in its final minutes at the end of the day. The red-orange light made shadows that seemed to glide softly along the walls.

She had not been able to resist the beauty of the scene. She walked slowly into the room and stood gazing through the crystal panes at the failing glory.

Softly, like a shadow himself, he had entered the room behind her. Oh, she knew nothing of his presence at that moment, but the passage of years, and the anguish over a loved-one's death, and the secrets left behind, and the special powers sometimes given to those who know them allowed her now, in memory, to recall even his thoughts in that destined time and space.

He had wondered if she could sense what he was thinking; she stood so still and lovely in the evening hush. Then she turned, and he felt himself blushing, thinking without logic, yet with just a bit of guilt and a touch of the darkness of shame, that she could sense his lust. B.L. probably had his eye on her already. That thought, and the fact of her youth accounted for his feelings of guilt. Maybe the shame as well. But B.L. wouldn't give a damn how remorseful he might be, he knew that.

He looked as closely as he could while maintaining the gracious smile of the host, to locate the traces of her ancestry. Her ancestry, what a hell of a way to put it. She was dark. Her hair, like a beautiful, ebony wave, flowed across her forehead to frame her high, though not too high, cheekbones. It seemed to withdraw from her ample, yet delicate, jawline. A well-made, straight nose ended at the perfect place above a voluptuous mouth. Dark, innocent eyes set off by equally large and dark lashes looked back at him. The soft mouth smiled. She was indeed beautiful. A touch of fear, like a coiling snake, flicked at him. He knew he would not be able to resist her.

And then she spoke, and in the lovely timbre of her voice he felt himself swaying on his feet. From other rooms on floors below, and from the balcony nearby, he heard voices. There was laughter and the tinkle of glasses. From the main verandah on the ground floor, music wafted upward on the air of the summer night. Scent from roses, placed in large bunches throughout the house seemed to whisper to him. Suddenly, he found himself thinking of lips pressed against upturned faces, and hands caressing bodies. Dammit, he urged himself, don't forget B.L., him and your plans!

But despite his fears, his own, pleading caution, he felt his passion grow. She still stood at the far edge of the room. Beyond her, at last, the sun had set, and the curtain of the night had been drawn.

Good God! How long had he been standing there like an idiot? He walked across the hardwood onto the big woven rug that lay with its passionate purple unseen in the dim light, and approached her. The hand he held out to her was trembling. He could hear his heart beating. Never, never had a woman affected him so.

With a surge that rattled the old walls of the place, she shook out of the reverie! A rumble began in the corner where she maintained herself. It began, then rushed into a crash and a crack of sound akin to an explosion; her voice, now; her way of expression, now.

The dust motes swirled around her in the shafts of sunlight coming through the doors leading to the east balcony. It was too early yet for the light to come through the old French doors flanking the fireplace, one off its hinges at the top, so that it hung and swayed in the wind like a thing trying to escape. Most of the glass had been knocked out of these doors, as well as the window along the west wall. The elements roamed freely inside the old house.

It didn't matter to her. Few things mattered to her. But the few that did wrapped her in obsession. And she moved and dwelled in this cloak, along with the hate and sad, sad longing of love and one-time associations with those who had loved her too.

But love was a memory thing, now. For nearly all that had been loved by her was gone. Only that which she had sought to love but which now she loathed and despised with all of the fury allotted her, remained as the anvil upon which she beat out her hatred with every passage of the sun.

When the sun set, when it spread itself across the sky in amber strokes, and the day like a sacrifice was led by time into the past, then she rose. Sometimes she visited the streets of the town. She made sure she met no one. But there had been mistakes. Some knew she was there. She felt gratitude that they left her alone in the old mansion. Oh, a few children had come trembling in fear to the front of the old porch. But nothing had resulted from that. The house was on county record as being hers. It had been since 1927 when the deed had been quit-claim signed over to her. The sudden memory of why she had been given the house caused her to emit a mewling cat-scream that burst from the corner like the wrenching of a dry board against the few remaining rusty nails holding it to the side of the old structure when the wind clawed at it.

It was easy to stay hidden. And she had for over sixty years. Most people were unaware; a shadow within a shadow was only that to them. A dark and hurried figure passing quickly on a rainy night; a darker place within the darkness; and the few sounds made in the old mansion attributed to wind, or stray animals.

When all the people had left in 1953, it had been a good time for her. She moved freely, then. Ironically, that is when her presence became known on a wider front, and stories were born. It was said that lights could be seen in the old town on the hill by people in the valley towns of Clarkdale and Cottonwood. But by that time, most of the buildings in Jerome were unoccupied. And Company Row, that string of the very best of the old Victorian structures lining Hill Street, was no exception. Her house, standing halfway along Hill Street, overlooking the old Delacroix apartments, was less a candidate for searching and exploring than the others. It could not be sold. That had been taken care of legally. Moreover, it was protected from scavenging, though some had come to do just that. But she had sent them scurrying away in terror.

She had remained safe, then, over the years; safe from discovery, and in danger of nothing else. In the corner, she rumbled in her own rare version of humor at the thought of one of them doing her harm. Then the sadness returned, like the dark in a room when a curtain, held back momentarily to let in light from a setting sun, is dropped once more into place. Oh, but he had harmed her, those many years ago, he had. She had never been safe from him!

Below, in the yard, someone was walking around in the trash and the bushes near the old car. She didn't need to rise to see. But there was something about the sounds the person made, a quiet, thoughtful approach that could be detected by the rhythm of movement he created that drew her up from her place. And she rose in the morning air of the rotting old room and moved slowly toward the balcony.

Even if he had looked upward at the old house then, he couldn't have seen her, a shadow against the gray wood flecked with pieces of fading yellow paint. She knew that he was interested in the car. At the thought of the old machine rage rippled through her. But she held herself, and no sound escaped. She was aware that he took a picture of the wreck, and a flicker of something oddly familiar to her flashed through her senses. Suddenly, she realized the intruder was the man who had been with the woman in the little flat. Curiosity settled her anger, then, and she reached toward him. He was walking away now, walking in the direction of the old church.

She faded from view, back into the room. There was something interesting about this man! She had felt it the other evening, as well. Could it be? Then, in the old room there erupted a sound like a thousand volts of electricity short-circuiting, a rasping, gasping sound, her way of utterance now. Quickly she left the room. Passed along the hall and followed the great staircase downward. She left the old house and went into the street, crossed it and eventually entered the church where she settled in a dark place.

Outside, on the street, the sound had halted him. He looked up and around but could not tell its location. Then, a shaft of sunlight hit the old church's belltower and seemed to drizzle down its walls and flow onto the street like water. Almost as if pulled by a magnet, though he recognized it as the force that took control of him whenever he entered one of what Julia called his "dazes", he made his way downward and walked woodenly toward the old building. He climbed the steps and entered. The sight he saw caused him to suck in his breath deeply.

Before him lay the nave, the principal area where the congregation sat. The heavy wooden pews, dark in color, marched in rows toward the apse, the frontal area where the main altar and pulpit rose above them. A wide aisle marked the center of the old church. It was carpeted in a worn and faded fabric that had once been a deep blue. The walls were painted in glaring white. High, arched windows let in the light along the north wall through beautiful stained-glass scenes. It was impressive.

On a little stand, in hand-lettering, a sign informed all visitors to the church that it had been restored by the Jerome Preservation Society and donations were welcome. A box for the purpose was provided. Noting that the request for money had no incorrect spelling in it this time, he put a dollar bill into the box, then turned to look around some more.

To his right was a closed door, and beyond it a narrow stairway led somewhere above. He went to it, climbing slowly, yet with eagerness.

Two flights up he arrived at a landing. To his left were the inner workings of an organ, all brass pipes and mechanical levers. A curtain separated that part of the instrument from its grand keyboard, its seat and pedals arranged so that whoever played the instrument sat with his back to the congregation below. In front of this was the platform on which the choir stood and sang. He noted that the choir faced the nave. It made a kind of visual connection with the altar and the priest and his assistants there that he supposed provided the people with a sense of harmony and structure.

Retracing his steps down the little staircase, he opened the door and entered the room he had previously noticed. This was where the confessional was situated; two small booths, like closets back to back, hugged the wall nearest the street. He noted that along the south wall there rose a wide window, of normal glass. He walked softly over to this window and looked out. Below him, as if he were looking down on a model in a museum, lay the main business section of the town of Jerome. From here, one could see many of the places people frequented: clothiers, restaurants, stores, bars ; it was the heart of the town. Along with the stories told in sotto voice or even in tones of anguish and remorse in the confessional booth, visual augmentation, one might say, verification, could be had in daily observance from this one strategic spot. The coming and going of people could be noted, considered, and judged.

A stab of self-chastisement took him at this mental blasphemy. What priests saw and heard of a confidential nature remained of a confidential nature. And yet, he thought, perhaps not always. More accurately, perhaps not with every priest. He looked around at the walls of the room. Like the rest of the church they were stark white. Also, like the rest of the church, the doors and baseboards, woodwork and flooring, were of a dark brown. It was a place of light and dark, good and evil. Again came the stab of self-scolding.

He listened to the creak of the wood floor beneath his feet as he crossed it. Slowly, as if someone might see him, though the place was empty except for himself, he pulled back the thin curtain to the confessional and sat down inside the dark little cube.

Instantly, he felt himself falling into the depths of his imagination. He could hear the people's clothing rustle as they sat in the pews below. He heard the murmuring voices of children and their mothers' whispers of admonishment. He even thought he could hear the priest speaking from the pulpit, just to the side of the great altar. More importantly, he sensed a presence in the booth opposite him, the one in which the priest usually sat to hear those confessing pour out their sins. "Father, forgive me for I have sinned . . ."

As the perfectly logical phrase, under the circumstances, ran through his mind, the feeling that the other side of the confessional was occupied intensified, and he thought he could almost describe what the priest looked like who might have indeed sat there in earlier times, when the old town lusted and fornicated, lied and stole, schemed and gossiped and sinned as only such a place in all the fecundity of life pressed close in the tight confines of its up and down streets, and tiny scraps of smoke-plagued lawn, and houses sitting much too close together could do.

He lost the vision of the cubicle and began to see in his mind's eye the town in an earlier aspect. In the style of his musings of the previous few moments, it seemed that his mind continued to consider the old town in its past. And, he heard a voice. It was unlike his own, and it seemed to echo within his mind as if it were wired in, somehow, to his very nerve endings. It was a saddened voice, with a sepulchral tone about it that caused him to feel as if he were floating in a void of mists through which scenes appeared in conjunction with the words the voice spoke. It continued . . . *what she had to do, what she could not escape doing. When riches may be garnered in some place by the employment of labor and machines, riches that go beyond imagination for some, and make for a very good living for others, and provide life where life would not have been for many, a foulness is brewed. To such a place all that bespeaks of evil must surely come. Men of greater intelligence will use that intelligence to move other men for their greed. And those men moved will in turn exert their peculiar means to apply pressure to others, and so on. But evil, foul, stinking evil will be among it all.*

Lies will be told that will fester in the telling, the knowing, the believing. They will twist and turn in bunches, like worms crawling within the putrid bodies of the dead dropped into their narrow graves in porous pine boxes. And like such ever-hungry vermin, they will eat at the fabric around them until one day they gnaw through in all their wormy, ivory hued horror, their cutting, biting, filthy little mandibles moving greedily.

Lust will live well in such a place. Women on the street in innocent mien, on household duties, will be leered at, others will be asked to give and they will give and give again until truth, almost a lone entity of good in this place, will out; then anger, hate, jealousy and revenge will stride forth and murder will abound like a demon itself. Little children will be deprived of fathers, wives of husbands by its uncaring hand. Such despair will be set off by all the wants and desires that men have learned to hide in the light of day, pretending they know them not. But they know them: false pride, ego, greed, envy, carnal desire. In such a setting, even the cleanliness of true fact becomes an instrument of all that is bad.

Accident in this place is a blessing, for while it will bring pain and suffering, and even death, it will be all of a kind not touched by the filthy fingers of evil; except where greed has created the inevitability of accident, and sloth has set the stage for it.

And above it all, power will be supreme among the prizes. And pain and suffering will flow in invisible streams, except when sometimes caught in the faces of the suffering or in the gloating of those causing it, until the entire town is flooded more with the unseen suffering than it is the visibility of God's good, pleasing and healthful sunshine, or his high and peaceful stars in the velvet night sky.

Still, the people will come, they will come to the sources of whatever riches their station in life has prepared for them. All in some way will look to the leaders of the pulpits of the town; they will come to their lawmen, their judges, they will seek their preachers, their pastors, their priests. And always the purpose, to garner more, to be forgiven once again; always the question, surely now is not the end, not the end!

And when death takes them, they shall leave all they strove for, all they lusted and schemed and did unspeakable acts for. Death begins with the box. There is little space in the grave for all the things for which men strive!

And, so, when ye come, if ye have suffered at the hands of evil, if ye have little to leave except the breath you breathed at the last, then do ye begin all once again; except, except, Oh, surely not . . .

Suddenly, he felt as if he were in a vortex of light and dark, turning around and around to a heavy, hollow moaning that slowly diminished and finally ended with the disappearance of the dark and the light flashes and the sensation of spinning. He became fully aware of the stifling narrowness of the confessional, the old, musty smell of it.

Clawing clumsily at the curtain, he felt he had lost track of time. He stood, for a moment or two swaying slightly on his feet. His thoughts had been chaotic while in the little closet. He reached back into his mind to touch them again, but he could only remember their tone and style, not anything definite. Had he really tranced-out in there, he wondered?

He hurried from the room and onto the floor of the nave. The old church was as empty and quiet as it had been when he'd entered. Standing at the head of the aisle, he felt a chill at his back. He had thought to explore as much of the church as he could. But suddenly, he felt an urge to leave. I'll come back again, he promised himself.

He left the vicinity of the church then and looked up two streets above it at the old house he intended to explore as well. Then gravity and something else, he couldn't have explained what, drew him downward, and he eventually found himself standing before the doors of the Mcallister Beer Co. & Emporium in the building which had once been the Conrad hotel.

SEVEN

"Well, did you get a lot of pictures today?" Julia asked from the bathroom as she settled into the worn and stained bathtub.

He almost didn't hear her. He lay on the bed with both pillows beneath his head, reading again from the Spoon River book.

"Mike?"

"Yeah, uh, yes?" he answered, forcing himself to put the book down and go into the bathroom to talk with her. He sat on the commode, which nestled its cold and rust-stained cavity close to the tub. With her hair wrapped in a towel, she lay beneath billowy suds in water as hot as she could get it and still enjoy it. He looked at her and smiled while saying, "Tell me about your first day on the job at Rooster's. Are you tired?"

She looked up at the pea-green and brown cross-hatched wall paper that rose on the walls of the tiny room to the dirty, white ceiling. Then she rolled her head toward him and giggled.

"What?" he asked, looking around and then down at his feet.

"I just hope you aren't doing anything except sitting on that thing. God! It's bad enough in this place. How long do you suppose it's been since they gave it a good cleaning?"

He examined the little room closer. It was true, the place was musty and dirty. "I guess I could stay home tomorrow and get after it," he said reluctantly. He didn't like unclean living conditions either. But they had been in some bad places since they'd become a couple. This place wasn't beyond redemption. A good cleaning would change it a lot toward the better.

"Nope. Tomorrow's Tuesday. Rooster said probably I could take off during the afternoon. We'll both clean it then. Deal?"

He grinned down at her. Aside from her good looks, it was her best quality, she wasn't hard to get along with. "Deal," he said.

"Today went fine," she said, answering his original question, "but I expected you to come in for lunch. Then when you didn't, I thought maybe for a snack in the afternoon. Where were you all day?"

"I met this guy, an old man," he began. And it was as if she had broken a dam somewhere within him. She could tell that he was excited, but was trying to restrain himself so he could tell her as much as possible and still keep it all straight. She looked quietly at him while he spoke.

"He has a darkroom. Lives here. Anyway, I went into that old church we passed coming into town the other day. And, and we talked. I'd already taken a picture, we had a few beers at the saloon and I came home and began reading in the books again and . . ."

"How many pictures did you say?"

"One, I took one."

"One all day?"

"I guess I got side-tracked."

She held both arms up as if in supplication and said, her eyebrows raised and her tone sarcastic, "One picture, Mike?"

He looked at the nipples of her breasts rising above the suds in the tub and said, "Yes, one. I spent the time talking with this guy."

She realized then where his eyes were focused. "Didja' get drunk? She grinned, letting her arms fall back into the water, "'Cause if you didn't, you should've taken more pictures." They laughed together.

"No, Honey, I mean, this old man, name's Cyrus Dooley, been around a long time, has a darkroom. I was talking to him after . . ."

She noted the pause. "After what?" she asked.

He sighed. "After I sort of had a vision in the old church."

She smiled wryly and looked down at the hot suds just below her chin. She shook her head. "Well, I'm not surprised." Then she busied herself with her bath, finally asking him to help her with her back. "But don't get my hair wet," she warned him, bending forward while he scrubbed her with the washcloth.

He had hesitated to tell her of his "going back" as he called his peculiar trances, which she called his dazes, not because he was fearful of what she might say. It was just that he couldn't blame her for her skepticism. And she almost always expressed it in a bantering or sarcastic manner. It was this display of her attitude he sought to avoid.

"What did you see in your vision?"

It was a logical question, but one he hadn't asked himself yet, not since he had been in the old church. It took him a moment to respond to her. He relaxed his grip on her shoulder and allowed her to sit up straight. She noticed the serious look on his face. Then she became more reserved herself.

"A sense of evil," he said quietly, looking away as if not believing the words himself.

"Evil?" she exclaimed, bending over once more as a signal for him to give her back a few last swipes with the washcloth.

"Um, hm," he said, leaning toward her and washing her back, "yeah, I'd have to say that was it."

Without saying more, she sat straight in the tub, gripped the side of it and then stood, reaching out for the towel hanging on the wall directly across from where he sat.

He handed it to her, then leaned over and, sticking a hand into the water, pulled the plug in the bottom of the tub. The water began to drain. He rose to his feet and moved to the door so she could have room to get out of the tub and stand while drying.

As she began to run the towel over her body, he stepped forward and took it. "Let me do it," he said. He gave her a good drying-off, massaging her arms and legs and neck as he did so.

She shut her eyes and succumbed to the wonderful sensations his strong yet gentle hands encased in the towel caused her to feel. "I could almost fall asleep right here," she sighed.

"Tired?" he asked.

"Yes, I guess so. And that's what you asked me, wasn't it?"

"It was," he said, pushing her gently out of the small room so he could lift her into his arms and carry her to the bed. Placing her there, so that she lay naked on the sheet with the cover already turned back, he felt desire.

She looked up at him knowingly. "You will be surprised," she said while smiling wryly, "I know you will, but not tonight. That's what I was trying to tell you. The day was fine, but I'm tired as hell."

He looked at her and grinned. Then, shaking his head at the irony, he left to take care of his own preparations for the evening. By the time he returned, teeth brushed, himself bathed and in clean underwear, she was asleep. He eased into bed beside her, reached to the floor and picked up the copy of Spoon River Anthology. He read it completely through before finally turning off the lamp and going to sleep himself at exactly midnight.

*   *   *

Outside the flat, in the dark of the first minutes of the morning, she rose above the street. There was little light, man-made or from the sky. In the stillness, she began to weave as if the wind were blowing. Only a hollow rush of air could be heard, no more than a breeze in the treetops might make in the first stirrings of dawn. Below her, the blackened, oil-stained pavement of asphalt lay over the heavy cobblestones which had been placed there long ago in the old town. She had walked on those stones in her youth. She yearned to walk on them again. This day, in the beginnings of itself, he would walk on them. He would see them as they had been. And though he would not see all that he would eventually come to know as he knew his right and left hands, he would see some of it this very day, before the sun rose.

Later, hours or minutes, or even seconds—it didn't matter, since time that moved ahead in its spectrum was meaningless to her, she drifted down the side of the mountain, past old places now gone which she had known well; blank and empty pieces of land which she had once seen crowded with buildings and other uses mankind put land spaces to; past all that once had been alive and flourishing to the place where they who had lived in Jerome on the flank of Cleopatra Hill had taken those who had passed on to life's other side. There, in the lonely and forsaken piece of land which served the oldest use of all, was a very particular bit of earth which held value beyond value for her. She came to it at least once every day.

In the non-light of the earliest hours of the day she moved undetected. She had learned to use concealment in the first days after she had been seen in the light. She stirred only in the morning, or during the hazy heat of the afternoon, or at dusk. Any who saw her saw only hints of her presence; heat shimmering from an August sun, a dust-devil in the distance, a sheet of rain before dark clouds, a gray shadow on a winter day.

She moved along in the dark. Each time she went to the place, she felt great sadness, greater now that she was aware of things she had not known before; she was aware of them, and she viewed all the parts of her former existence from a different reference point.

It was her cross to bear that she must do this; come here and reflect. For her, it was a keen blade that was double-edged; sad because of the pain it held, and happy too because of the joy it caused her to re-live. But like a needle stuck on a phonograph disc, the same scenes were played and re-played. She had little control of that. However, she had learned over the years to break them up, to lengthen some parts of them and speed up other parts. Still, the pain was pain and the joy was joy that had already been. She came, though, in the dark, every day.

Many of the memories were of him. And as it came to her, she settled to it with a dry gurgling that was her way of sighing, now.

*   *   *

It had been dusk, again. Not that he thought of the parallel. And again it had been chance. This time, it was not B.L. he needed to worry about. He had very little to worry about anyway, least of all a man who had once been his boss. Things couldn't have worked out better.

He was walking along the great upstairs hall, just past the main stairway. Ahead, where the extra bedrooms led off to the left, he saw that a door leading out to a small side balcony was open. The fumes from the valley smelter were drifting into the house, the same deadly fumes which, before the smelter had been moved to the new town of Clarkdale, had killed most of the vegetation in Jerome. Since coming to this house, he had tried to brighten the grounds around the place with flowers and shrubs, as well as a tree or two. Even if the smelter smoke was now much less than before, there was still no advantage to allowing any of it inside. The door had to be closed.

Proceeding farther down the hallway, he saw that another door was open. Was she at home, yet? If so, she had been very quiet. The thought that she might be sleeping made him aware of his footsteps on the wood floor. It might be a good idea to walk softly.

And then, through the open door, he saw her. Maybe she thought she was the only one at home. It wasn't normal for him to be here at this time of day, either, as he often had dinner out. Usually, he wouldn't be expected here for another two hours. And Madeleine was gone as well; gone to Prescott with a group of ladies. "Going to do some real shopping," she had said, wouldn't be back until the following day.

He turned his head and prepared to walk past as quietly and unobtrusively as he could; he'd fully expected to do that. Why hadn't he taken Franklin up on his offer to discuss the new accounting procedures over a good steak at the Fashion Saloon that evening? A good steak and a couple of drinks and, since he knew Madeleine would not be home, perhaps something a bit better than mere steak a little later?

His steps faltered. Quick as lightning now his mind seemed to work. It not only seemed to concentrate in this new, undesirable direction, but was apparently able to make side comment on it as well. There was no noise from downstairs. The maid was in her quarters, without a doubt. His head wanted to turn toward the open door. Maybe just a look in to see if anything was wrong. He could not move farther along the hallway. He could always say he didn't know she was there, that he had just meant to pop in and close the door. After all, why were her feet shaking? The whole bed was shaking. Why? What if something was wrong with her and he had knowledge of it and did nothing about it? He would be accountable. His damned legs would not move!

But when he allowed his head to turn so that his eyes could take in more of the scene he had only caught a glimpse of earlier, he found that he could move, haltingly, though with a strange sensation of numbness in the legs, but move they would, even so, toward and through the open doorway.

And there she was. God! How old was she? Her ebony cloud of hair, like her sister's, streamed in dark shades across the pillows of the large poster bed. Long, perfectly shaped legs lay, still in their cotton stockings, slightly parted. With her dress pulled up, she was caressing herself.

Damn! He had never seen such a sight. He thought only men took care of themselves that way. Not young girls. Not sweet, innocent girls. He heard himself gasp, realized he was striding now into the room. He suddenly felt the bed beneath him as he sat on its edge. Her face, it was all he could see, was turned toward him. With her mouth open as if in mortal terror, she stared at him with those green eyes. He heard himself say to her, "What are you doing?" and all the while, his hand was touching, as he had seen her doing, her body there, there between those perfectly shaped outstretched legs.

On the hillside, in the dark, an explosive squeal of fury sliced into the surrounding terrain. At the sudden sound, a coyote, on its way back from the hunt, doubled its wiry body into a ball and leaped in terror past a far corner of the old graveyard. Fleeing something it felt with senses other than its keen hearing, it hurtled recklessly down the hillside toward Bitter Creek Gulch.

Behind the terrified animal, in the center of the old burying ground, the air where she stood at a sunken grave crackled with the energy of her hatred. This part of the memories would stop here. She would see to it. Later, it might come, but it would be quick then, a flicker to be experienced in a flash, but to be experienced nonetheless and so meet the requirement. There was another part to remember, a sweeter one.

*   *   *

Mike turned from his left side onto his back. The gray light of pre-dawn filtered through the windows of the little apartment. A clam-shell travel clock ticked away on the flat surface of the cabinet-style headboard of the bed. He believed the style had come out of the late twenties or early thirties and was called art-deco; all rounded corners, wood veneer in dark oak, leather and brass handles on little drawers which slid out to reveal small, green felted interiors with a few grains of dust and perhaps a hair pin or two inside.

The clock showed 3:45. Damn, he thought, too early. What was he doing waking up that early. Then he remembered the dream, and suddenly he was wide awake. It had been the most vivid dream he had ever had. And there was something about it, something familiar to him, some kind of difference to it that he had experienced with other dreams; like the time he'd dreamed about his cousin in the back seat of a car in a big city during what he'd surmised in the dream was the night. A few days later a letter notified him that she had been killed in an accident while driving her husband to work early in the morning. They had lived in Miami, Florida.

He'd had other dreams like that, too. With the odd sensation attached. It was a feeling he had while dreaming and then later while remembering the dream. A kind of identity tag that indicated the dream was special, different from all the other dreams he had ever had or would ever have. The dream he'd just had was like that. It had the tag on it.

"So, what do you mean, a tag?" Julia sat before the old fashioned dresser with the dark mirror, a piece of furniture which was not at all like anything else in the little apartment, and finished the job of brushing her hair and pinning it back on the sides, so that it would be out of the way when she worked. He still lay in the bed. Since he had awakened an hour and a half earlier, he had hardly moved from the position he had assumed after realizing it had been a dream which had gotten him up so early. He lay with both hands behind his head; staring at the ceiling. A moment before, she'd opened the bottom part of the window that fronted the bedroom, and a crisp breeze flowed through the yellowed Venetian blinds, occasionally hitting them with a gust strong enough to move the entire collection of blinds so that they clattered. Only she and the blinds seemed to reflect energy. Everything else in the room, except his chest rising and falling as he breathed, was dead still. It made a silence like a curtain of white, a blanking-out. Except in his head. In there he was seeing the dream in flashes of dark and light, and he was hearing the sounds of the dream. Then her voice broke through again.

"Mike, you alright?"

He turned his head in her direction. She was looking at him in the reflection of the mirror. There was concern on her face. This wouldn't do. With a surge, he rose from the bed and moved his arms down to turn his body. He sat with both feet on the floor. After a moment or two, he stood and went into the bathroom. He relieved himself and thought as he stared down into the rusted throat of the toilet that he had promised to clean it. Then he remembered that she had said they would both be home to clean it. That was not good. If he left her to do it alone it would look bad. When he came back into the bedroom she asked him again if he was alright.

"I'm O.K., honey," he said, pulling on his pants.

"Well, you looked so engrossed in your thoughts a minute ago that it worried me. Tell me about this dream. What is all this about a tag?"

"I've told you about that before. But you don't listen to that kind of stuff."

"You mean one of those funny dreams you have about the future, that supernatural bit you Southerners all seem to have buried in you somewhere?"

He laughed. "Yeah, that's what I mean."

"So, what about this dream, something going to happen to us in this little old mystery of a town?"

"That's a good way of putting it," he said, surprise elevating the tone of his voice.

She turned from the mirror and looked at him. She smiled. "It happens every now and then," she said, referring to the metaphor she had made.

He grinned at her, noting to himself that it was also a cliché, then shrugged his shoulders. "Hey," he began, dropping into an exaggerated Southern accent, "It was just a dream. As long as I'm with you, I ain't askeerd of nothin', sugah."

She turned back to the mirror and her hair. "So, what was this nothing sort of dream about, anyway? Come on, let me in on it."

"Nothing bad happened," he declared. "It was just a dream about this place and the people here and me walking along the street looking into all the stores and seeing the people. That's all."

While telling her this, he had walked over to the large window at the apex of the room and looked down on the street. He remained there a few seconds in silence. She watched him.

"Mike, what's wrong," she asked.

He turned back toward the interior of the room. "Nothing," he said. Then he walked over to the single window on the Main Street side of the room. If they had been in a ship it would have been the starboard side. He felt strange. For a moment he wondered if they were indeed in such a craft, and that perhaps when he looked out he would see heaving seas rolling along past them. But when he looked at the street again he saw the same asphalt he had always seen there. And even though it was early, a few tourists were already out. He sighed, somehow relieved.

"In the dream," he began, "it all looked different."

"What do you mean, different?"

"The streets were made of stones. Big, cut stones. The biggest damned cobblestones I've ever seen."

She let her hands fall to her lap and leaned against the rickety back of the old chair she sat in. "Mike, didn't you look at pictures of this place in the library the other day? Come on. Get your clothes on. I'll serve you a good breakfast at Rooster's."

"Like what?" he said, moving away from the window to grab his shirt off the back of the only other chair in the room, an avocado-green, overstuffed arm chair.

"Like a bran muffin, some fruit and maybe a poached egg."

"No thanks, my dear. I want bacon and eggs and a side order of buttermilk pancakes. All washed down with lots of strong coffee." He sat on the edge of the bed to put on his shoes.

She grinned at him and shook her head in mock disbelief. "Now, why didn't I know that," she teased.

Five minutes later, as they both exited the door of the stairway that led to the third floor of the building where the apartment was, the gravity of thought with which the dream had left him returned as he walked across Main Street and headed uphill toward Rooster's restaurant. Suddenly, he stopped.

"Come on, Mike," Julia said, looking back at him. "You can't stand there in the street. One of these people on vacation will run over you."

But he couldn't hear her. Nor was he seeing what she thought he was gazing at. It was as if he was experiencing the dream all over again, in broad daylight, and while fully awake. But it was only for an instant. As soon as it came, the sensation of re-dreaming left him. And as he looked up at Julia, who had another concerned expression on her face, he forced a smile and followed her along the sidewalk to Rooster's. But in his mind's eye, despite trying not to, he began to replay what he had seen in the dream.

Before him the town had been revealed as it had been in years past. He would guess sometime during the late twenties or early thirties; this because of the cars parked on both sides of the street, all facing downhill. It wasn't the way they were parked that was important, though. It was the cars themselves.

To his right was a furniture store. Most of the buildings were either brick or concrete block, the heavy scalloped type. A few were made of stucco over concrete. Many of the storefronts held large glass windows trimmed in wood. One or two businesses furnished a canvas awning for customers to walk beneath as they moved along the sidewalk.

Past the furniture store was a grocery store with a sign proclaiming "Fancy groceries, we deliver". Beyond that he could see a store with a large sign hanging over the sidewalk. It read, "Popular Store". Other storefronts and buildings lined the street all the way up the hill. He noted a drugstore, something that looked like an office, and a theatre front. At that point the angle of the street made further recognition on the east side difficult. But it was easy to see the west side of the street where a line of poles stood with wires swaying between them at about the second story level. There was a sign in front of a building identifying it as the Electric Light and Telephone Company. That side of the street also had a grocery store, a second-hand store, the Boyd Hotel, something which seemed to be a dentist's office, and a building named the Sturdevant Apartments.

A variety of colors had been used on the buildings. Paper and other types of trash littered the sidewalks. A yellowish cloud rose in the distance as the street leveled out. A large building sat to the left there, it bore lettering across the front: T.G. Moulter Co. A portion of the sky could be seen above the rooflines of it and the buildings nearby.

Most of the people on the street were wearing coats. He could feel a chill. It was probably a winter afternoon. There were a few men and women together, some younger boys walked alone, or in pairs. Everyone fit the scene except for one woman and her companion. She looked in Mike's direction, while the man with her, dressed in a fancy white suit, stood holding the door of a beautiful plum-colored roadster open for her.

The woman wore a light beige coat of heavy twill topped by a dark fur collar. On her head was a hat shaped to fit close. It seemed to be constructed of broad bands. Heavy curls fringed the bottom of the hat and covered the back of her neck. Dark brown, almost black, eyes peered toward him. The glow of intelligence lighted their depths. A strangely sad smile lay on her beautiful, full lips.

When she got in the car, the man with her closed the door and went around to the driver's side. In the dream, Mike had stood and watched the car as it backed out from the curb, then rolled slowly past his position on the street. Inside the car, in the single seat, beneath the tan canvas top, neither the driver nor the woman looked his way. He watched as the elegant machine moved away from him. Afterwards, he had just ambled along, taking it all in with senses that seemed unusually sharp.

It was a dream he would never forget, one he would be able to recall with exceptional clarity. Only when Julia's voice came to him across what seemed a gray void did he find himself and realize his surroundings. He was sitting at the counter at Rooster's. Julia stood behind the counter, leaning toward him, asking him what he wanted for breakfast. For a second, he thought how ludicrous it was that there was now a breakfast bar set up in the main entryway of the Sturdevant Apartments. Then he regained complete realization of the time and the place.

"Mike, listen to me, Mike?"

He shook his head and looked directly at her. "I'm alright. For god's sake give me some coffee."

"It's been in front of you for the last five minutes," she said.

EIGHT

This time, instead of heading for the library, Mike's destination was the offices and archives of the Jerome Preservation Society. Cyrus had told him about it the day before.

He had walked the empty stretch of street across from Rooster's for an hour after breakfast. A few tourists' cars had pulled in and parked near the little yellow bug with its top up and its windows closed, its doors locked. He recognized this area as being the spot in his dream where the street had been lined with buildings. He wondered what had happened to that side of the street as he stood at the VW's rounded nose and looked into the Verde Valley spread below. The beauty of it tempted him to take a few pictures with the camera that was always with him. He didn't usually photograph landscapes. He felt such pictures were too ordinary, that everybody did them. But this scene was perhaps different, he mused.

The valley held several small towns and outlying communities. Principal among them was old Camp Verde, originally a military fort which had been created to protect the homesteaders and miners from the local Yavapai Apaches; then there was Cottonwood, and next, Clarkdale; itself a model town built by the owner of the United Verde Mine of Jerome, Senator William A. Clark. Clarkdale had housed some of his mine employees; it was also the site of the main railhead in the area and was where Clark had located his smelter, which had once stood near the mine on the hills above Jerome. Finally, halfway along its length and to the valley's north, was Sedona, a town known for its art galleries and natural scenery. It lay along the banks of Oak Creek, among towering columns, cliffs, and escarpments of deep-red sandstone.

The remainder of the valley was a wild expanse that contained grass and scrub oak. Like a great red and green gash it ran for miles from the northwest to the southeast, fed by the waters of the Verde River and Oak Creek as well as two or three other streams with less than year-round flow. Along these waterways huge cottonwoods stood sixty to seventy feet high. Water had always meant life in Arizona. Here, it was abundant. In one of the canyons leading into the valley there were springs where the ancient Anasazi had built cliff dwellings; one, known as Montezuma's Castle, was famous the world over. The upper slopes of the far side of the valley grew cedars and thickets of oak brush and manzanita; then, at even higher altitudes the pines appeared.

Across from where he stood, nearly seventy miles in the distance, the land lifted thousands of feet in a ridge of granite and sandstone known as the Mogollon Rim. Beyond, the land ran even higher in blue and gray majesty toward the San Francisco Peaks, which even in the heat of summer carried a mantle of snow.

Standing there, taking in the beauty and great scope of the valley, he drifted back to earlier times in his imagination. Others had stood in this place and gazed at the scene he was now viewing, others who had been citizens of Jerome in its early history, right where he stood, where the little German car was parked. Here had been buildings, he could see a few old pieces of foundation. He had seen those buildings in the dream. If he could find out when the buildings had disappeared from this section of the town, he could partially date the time of his dream.

Behind him, the street that once had facilitated the movement of wagons and buggies drawn by horses and mules now catered to tourists in automobiles. They crept along down the old hill, gawking to the left and the right, in their Dodge V-10 club cabs with campers on the back containing micro-wave ovens and VCR's, or in their S.U.V.'s, and all makes and models of minivans.

It seemed a desecration of hallowed ground to him. After awhile, he turned and walked up the hill to the remaining business section of the old town. He arrived at the corner of Main and Jerome Avenue, where the Preservation Society's mine museum was housed in what had once been the Fashion Saloon. He crossed to the other side of Main and hurried up the hill through the little park there to the next level; the offices and archives building was in what had once been a church.

He entered the door and walked past another sign asking for "donashuns." Another volunteer, not the same one he had met in the library, sat behind the desk. She gave him a welcome smile. He wanted pictures, as many as he could get, and histories; the only requirement was that the subject must be Jerome as it had been in the twenties and thirties.

"I'm sorry for the mess," she apologized, "We haven't been in this building long enough to get things straightened out." She pointed to three large tables with stacks of books and papers on them. He saw that there were several piles of photographs. "You are welcome to look all you want," she said.

He almost ran to photographs. He had gone through a lot of material during his visit to the library. He meant to go through these pictures "with a fine tooth comb" as an old Southern saying he often used put it. He saw that there were some books he probably should check. He settled on the floor with his back against the end of a shelf. Soon, he lost all track of time. The old building was quiet.

Methodically, reverently, he turned through the pages of the albums the society members had arranged the pictures in. Sometimes a picture was a copy of a newspaper photo. At other times, it was a photograph taken by a professional photographer working for a commission, or for historical purposes. He looked at them all, wishing he had a magnifying glass. It was a thing he would have to purchase, but he could not leave yet. And then, as he turned a page and the scene from his dream appeared on it, he froze.

Looking closely at the picture, he found the furniture store. Then, he moved up the street in the old photograph. There was the grocery store, then the drug store, then a clothing store and another building with the marquee of a theatre out front. Was it? Yes, he could clearly see the word, Royal. Next came the store with the sign bearing the name, Popular. He looked for a date somewhere on the page containing the picture. He looked also in the text preceding and following it. But he could not find anything helpful.

It was only when the volunteer herself informed him that she would be closing for lunch that he stopped his activity and put the material he had collected back on the tables. After asking her, just to be sure, when she would return, he descended the stairway to street level in the bright light of the August afternoon.

He had an appointment to meet Cyrus at one o'clock in the Mcallister Beer Co. & Emporium, which he had learned the locals called Mac's. Looking at his watch, he saw that the appointment was nearly an hour away; time to find a magnifying glass.

At one o'clock he sat alone in the dark and beer tainted atmosphere of Mac's, looking at the lighted square of the open door, waiting for Cyrus Dooley.

The bartender was a young man of chunky build, hair to his shoulders, a heavy mustache, wearing levis and a white shirt open at the front with sleeves rolled to the elbow; not the same one, Mike decided, who had waited on him the first time he had been there. The bartender made comment as he leaned over and placed a second bottle on the table in front of Mike.

"That ol' man ain't never been anywhere that I know of on time," he sniggered. Then he straightened and said, "That'll be two dollars."

With a forefinger, Mike flicked the money toward him from change that lay on the table. He had asked about the old man when he'd first sat down, so it was his fault that the bartender had reason to become familiar. However, he didn't mind, He wanted to get to know as many local people as he could. In the corner behind him, the two-girl band was warming up. He turned in his chair so he could see them.

"You ladies play in here every afternoon?" he asked.

The older woman answered, "We don't come in on Wednesdays or Thursdays. But, yeah, usually in the summer we play every day, except them days." Then she motioned to the younger woman who was busy tuning one of the guitars, "This here's Evie an' I'm called Rube. That's short for Ruby. It's why we're called the Ruby Duo."

"There's an old ghost town in southern Arizona called Ruby," he noted, "it have anything to do with your name?"

She laughed and shook her head, "Naw, I've heard of it of course, havin' a name like I do an' all, but, I'm from Tennessee. Evie here, though, she's a native from a little wide spot in the road down below Presskitt. She might could tell you something about Ruby." She smiled broadly, "Ruby the ghost town, that is."

He looked at the girl called Evie. She had finished tuning the instrument and was softly strumming it in a chord pattern. He noticed a shy smile spreading on her face as the focus of the conversation shifted to her.

"Where are you from, Evie," he asked, "a ghost town, too?"

"It almost is," she laughed, "it's so little, nothin' happenin' there."

"Where is it?"

"It's a little ol' place called Yarnell, 'bout forty miles south of Presskitt."

He chuckled. "You sound like you're from Tennessee, too, by your accent," he said.

"You got a kind of drawl to your own talkin'," broke in the other woman. Where you from?"

Just then, the doorway darkened with the silhouette of Cyrus Dooley.

"There's your friend comin' in now," said the younger of the two performers, nodding her head toward the front of the saloon and smiling as if glad to be saved from answering any more questions.

With an almost reluctant movement, for he had been enjoying the talk with the two women, Mike twisted in his chair to look.

Dooley walked in slowly, his skinny old body moving with that less than smooth motion of the elderly. "By-God, Danny," the old man addressed the bartender, "you on today? What the hell's wrong with Ralph, it ain't his day off is it?"

"He went to Phoenix."

The old man stopped, jerked his head back and reached up with one hand to re-set the black hat on his head while uttering a single derogatory word, "Sheeut!"

"No," sniggered the bartender, "he went shopping. Took his wife."

A couple of patrons at the bar chuckled along with the bartender as the old man ignored the joke and moved toward the table where he saw Mike sitting. As he walked the short distance, he looked around in the corners of the large room, hoping some of the people there were from Phoenix,

"By-God," he began, loud enough for most to hear, "there ain't one Goddamned thing down in that hell-hole called Phoenix that'd make me want to take my wife to see—if I had one."

As Cyrus Dooley pulled a chair out and sat in it, looking around to see if anyone there would take issue with his last remarks, Mike said to him, "You don't like Phoenix, huh?"

"Hotter'n fire half the year, full of damned people all the time. Do you know," said Cyrus, peering hard at Mike as if they were negotiating the fate of the world, "the damned place is now bigger'n Los Angeles in land size?"

The bartender arrived at their table and plunked down a bottle of beer. "I figured you'd want this," he said.

Cyrus looked up at him," You figured right, Danny."

"That'll be two dollars."

"Damn, Danny! Can't you wait till I drink four or five first? You gittin' to be like some of them people we was just talkin' about. Money, money, money. Hurry, hurry, hurry."

"Here," said Mike, pulling out his wallet and handing the bartender a five dollar bill.

Cyrus nodded his head and smiled in acknowledgement of the gesture, then turned and watched the back of the young bartender walk away. When he turned to face Mike again he said, "He's from Phoenix, you know."

"Yeah?"

"Yeah, an' you couldn't get him to go back."

"Why's that?" asked Mike, taking a drink from his bottle of beer.

The old man looked at him blankly, then turned toward the two-woman band and addressed its younger member. "Evie, do that song you wrote about your hometown."

The girl blushed and looked at her partner.

"You know Ralph banned that song, Cyrus," said the woman called Rube.

"I know, but, hell! He ain't here." Then, turning and surveying the saloon in exaggerated slow motion, Cyrus said, "and there don't appear to be any tourists in here now anyway. Come on. Danny won't say anything."

The two women looked at each other. The older one raised an eyebrow and clamped her lips together in a straight line across her face. But she shifted the guitar hanging from her shoulders by a strap, tilted her head, and hit the chords. Evie began to sing.

"Yarnell, Yarnell, you know I love you well. But Phoe . . . nix is . . . a place right out of Hell . . . Yarnell . . ."

Cyrus smiled across the table at Mike during the performance. Mike, too, was amused by the song.

"It ain't much for melody but the lyrics sure tell it like it is," grinned Cyrus Dooley, lighting a cigarette.

In a more serious tone, Mike said, "The way I hear it, this place itself was a bit like Hell in its heyday."

Cyrus sighed, took a pull from his cigarette and said at the end of a long exhalation as he leaned back in his chair and looked across the table at the younger man, "You got that right, son. The damned Devil himself walked the streets of this place. He shore did." He punctuated this last pronouncement with a coughing spasm which ended in the side-snap at an unseen something to his right. Then he looked, watery-eyed and red-faced, at Mike and said, "Why don't we get out of this damned saloon an' I'll show you some things that might interest you about this old town.

NINE

It had washed over Jerome like a flood. Some of the debris it brought stayed, to finally rot of its own accord. Some had to be gotten rid of by the people there. But it could not have ignored the little town on the side of the mountain any more than it ignored the other hell-holes men created in their search for riches from the earth—or from each other's pockets.

Tombstone had its legend of Wyatt Earp and his brothers, and Doc Holliday, his friend. There were the Clantons, their adversaries. Dodge City knew Wild Bill Hickock. Earp had been there, too. Henry McCarty, known as Billy The Kid, came out of a range war in New Mexico. There was Texas John Slaughter, Batt Masterson, and the man who finally killed Billy The Kid, Pat Garrett. There were many others. All were relatively well-known, and all came in two basic categories: the lawman and the outlaw he was pitted against.

Jerome had its share of both types. There had been death, if not drama, in the contest between good and evil in the little mining town on the mountainside. It knew of no O.K. Corral, but a gun battle had taken place on the steps of its largest hotel between a killer who was inside the lobby firing through its glass doors at a sheriff who, though wounded several times by the ambusher, fired back with both his guns, one a new-fangled automatic type, and killed his would-be murderer. The lawman lived.

Another lawman foiled a bank robbery by standing flat-footed in the middle of the street and firing his forty-five at the windshield of the get-away car. He hit the driver between the eyes and sent the car into the wall of a nearby building. At another time, a property owner, on the advice of this same sheriff, waited in the dark for a suspected burglar and blew the top of his head off with a shotgun when he broke in. Nothing more came of the incident; it was routine.

In the area known as Bittercreek Gulch, where the immigrants lived, death and mayhem lay only as far below the surface of reality as a man's temper allowed it to. There, one afternoon, a man shot and killed his own wife and her lover as a crowd urged him on. In the brothels, violence came and went with the men who visited there. One luckless woman had her throat slashed by an unhappy customer. It took ninety one stitches to close the gaping slit. And on certain streets in the town, during the evenings especially, a man walked with his mind alert and his hands ready at all times.

But it was the mines which killed men in Jerome. Against death as a result of all types of crime, the mines were ahead two to one. Lack of adequate safety equipment and safety procedures was the reason. And if greed for profit and its resulting power was not illegal or immoral, it was just as bad as ignorance and jealousy, hatred and cruelty, in so far as it concerned the final result counted in men's lives.

*   *   *

For her, the dark side of the town put a fine point on a life of hardship and grief. She had come to Jerome with little except her determination; and her needs. They weren't many, and they were simple, but they were absolute. She must have work, for herself and her younger sister, a child of thirteen. She must have shelter for the same reasons, and she must have anonymity.

It would have been easy, and more profitable, to return to her old profession. But the younger sister made that impossible, and she was glad of this. Her own mother before her had been born in a brothel; the unlikely result of business done between an unknown harlot and a wayward soul who had come from China during the building of the transcontinental railroad. The odd combination had been repeated when she was born in a bawdy house along the Texas-Mexico border. Only this time the father was Mexican. It was this four way blend of the Asiatic, the Hispanic, the Indian, and the Anglo which made her beauty mysterious and unusual. And it was this unique beauty along with her mother's greed and lack of morality which had fated her for the brothels at a very young age. She attended the profession until she was forced to flee with her sister, whom she had never allowed to entertain the notion of working as a prostitute.

They came to Jerome. Behind them, they left death in the form of the younger girl's grandmother and the man her older sister had killed on a night of rage and insanity in the slums of a greasy little oil town called Greenfield.

She and her sister had ridden from the Verde Valley up the side of the mountain to Jerome in the summer of 1924. By that time the building of the United Verde's new smelter had been completed in the new town of Clarkdale, in the valley. The thick, gray smoke that had overwhelmed everything in the town from the old smelter was no longer in evidence, smoke from the valley took its place and rose against the flanks of the mountain. A new high school, a modern structure, had just been finished the year before, and she and her sister looked at it through the window of the bus as they passed it to their left, where it sat at the end of the hogback with many of its windows facing the expanse far below. She felt a sense of something good waiting for them ahead.

She quickly found a place for herself and the girl in the Hotel Jerome, not knowing how fortunate she was to have done so, for rooms in the town were at a premium. Some hotels and boarding houses slept men in shifts, so that a single bed served at least three men per day. In Jerome, after a downturn in 1921, the economy had revived. Not even the outbreak of a smallpox epidemic could mar what seemed to be an economic upsurge ahead. The mines were operating at full capacity and people everywhere were caught up in the frenzy of speculation in stocks.

Unaware of it all, she was grateful even if she did not realize their good fortune. The mess she had fled from in Texas was likely to be written off by the authorities there as just another killing in the red-light district, one which did not merit future inquiry, because the police felt the people involved had no merit of their own. Just the same, although she had ventured out on the first day to a grocery store and bought food in the form of fruits and canned meats, she and the thirteen year old huddled in the heat of the hotel room, going out only to visit the communal bathroom down the hall. Their only relief from the stress of boredom and insecurity was to look out the single window in their lonely little room. The view was of the building which sat at the end of the descending, one-way section of Main Street where it ran into the street coming up from the valley. Like others before her, she had thought immediately of a great ship's prow plunging through waves at sea.

But the yellow, dust-filled haze from the United Verde Mine, in its open pit stage by this time, and the smoke from the smelters in the valley, for there were two mines in Jerome, along with the hard, dirty surfaces of the streets, the walls of buildings, concrete sidewalks and painted clapboards rising up the hillside toward a gray sky, created a scene that was hardly a seascape. Yet, in another sense, she knew the town was indeed analogous to the ocean itself; alive with all manner of life in every variety of danger. It was the source of whatever she would find to sustain them there, and she knew she would have to enter it very soon.

*　　*　　*

Women in what had been her profession lived lives mostly without many advantages. But there were a few which were ironic in that they often provided opportunity which the women themselves would not ever be likely to put to good use outside of the brothel where they entertained all manner of men. One of them was being recipient to knowledge; as many different varieties of it as the men who came to see them were willing to let go of in the process; another lay in a more personal area, it involved knowing how to dress for every occasion. There was at least one more; much time spent in the confinement of a room or a house with little to do except read. In addition to this strange course of study, if the woman herself was of a quick mind, was the overall acquisition of knowledge of human nature. An intelligent and experienced prostitute was an actress who could play the role of a lady or any variety of femininity required—and look the part as well.

Madeleine was all of this and more. Her beauty was something she sometimes cursed and sometimes breathed thanks to God for. In Jerome it was an attribute she was to be grateful for.

It would have been much easier to seek a job as a waitress or a laundress or even a maid in the innumerable boarding houses of the town. But she needed to be out of sight as much as possible, and she had not fled a profession which often put her close to the dirty seams of life simply to take up washing men's underwear and making their beds and scrubbing the floors they walked across and spit on.

She had read in the paper she picked up the day she visited the grocery store that one of the mines needed file clerks. Further inquiry of a hotel maid she had begun a conversation with early on the second day at the hotel yielded the information that women were sometimes hired for such jobs, since they required an uncommon knowledge of reading and figures—but how many people had that?

She cultivated this source of information, gaining important facts about the town everyday for nearly a week. She learned where things were in the community. She learned how to hire transportation. Finally, she was ready. She decided to apply for one of the clerical positions at the United Verde Extension Mine. The maid, her friend by now, assured her that she could have a horse-drawn rig waiting in front of the hotel for her at almost any hour she wished. All she had to do was let her know and she would make the arrangements. But in no case was she to walk anywhere in the depravity that was this town of Jerome! No, not a lady as she so obviously was.

*   *   *

Of the two major mines in Jerome, the United Verde Extension was the newcomer. It had been preceded by the United Verde which tunneled into the top of Mingus Mountain until it became more profitable to use the open pit method instead. The United Verde had dismantled its smelter and moved it to Clarkdale, where a new smelter was eventually built in 1915. Named for the mine's owner, Clarkdale had been built especially for the mine's employees. It took some commerce away from Jerome. It also took most of its vicious smoke. What it left behind was an open-pit operation where the smelter and mine offices and buildings had been. This great hole in what had been part of Mingus Mountain lay to the northwest of Jerome. But in the deep valley to the east of the compact town, in what was known as Bitter Creek gulch, an adjunct to Deception gulch farther south, a new lode of copper ore had been discovered. It was developed by the Douglas family. The Douglases were not novices to mining. They named their new operations in Bitter Creek Gulch the United Verde Extension mine, but its less than formal name was The Little Daisy. Like the United Verde had once been before it, it was a stope mine with miles of tunnels beneath its tin and masonry buildings housing tools and equipment, storage as well as offices, all built on a few acres of flat land just down-slope from the town. The Douglas mansion sat only one or two hundred yards away. It only seemed ironic that the main offices lay in the valley in the town of Clemenceau, a town like Clarkdale, created for the housing of mine employees and the location of the mines primary business facilities. The mines themselves had been found and developed long before the new towns of Clarkdale and Clemenceau had even become ideas in the minds of Clark or Douglas. Vestiges in the form of "mansion row" and the buildings and clerical sections of the Little Daisy, not to mention the Little Daisy Hotel built up-slope from the mine to house workers, were testament to this fact.

It was the clerical office still on site at the Little Daisy which was Madeleine's destination on that day when she finally slipped into the rich, predacious sea that was Jerome.

*   *   *

The skinny, pimple-faced clerk who took her application simpered as he told her she would be reached if there was an opening, even though privately he intended to misplace her application the minute she left the office. She thanked him and turned to leave.

As she walked toward the door, she considered the thought that the clerk had not liked something about her and was not telling her the truth regarding the possible message to her if a job became a possibility. She had taken pains with herself that morning, telling her sister as she got herself ready that she must help her decide if she looked presentable for applying for a job.

"You look like some old lady," her sister had said wryly, observing the way she had put her hair up and noting the clothes she had selected. "Wear something with a little snap to it. Don't you want to knock 'em dead?"

"That's just what I do not want to do, sweetie," Madeleine said.

And she had made sure she did not look like someone who could "knock 'em dead" might look. Still, her beauty was there despite the old-fashioned hair style, the drab little hat, the plain eyes and lips, and the less than flattering dress beneath the even doudier shawl she had thrown over her shoulders.

If ever there was a brown and simple little bird, it was she; but only to one casually looking at her and failing to see beyond the disguise. To one experienced, her bearing, her manner of walking and moving would tell her secret readily. And if more evidence was needed, the lovely music of her voice and the dark lustre of her eyes would suffice.

Before her the single, large door serving entrance to the office she had applied in swung open and a tall man swept into the room, followed by two young men with anxious looks on their faces. The tall man's face, too, held a grim expression. But it softened quickly as he brushed past her. Then, just as she was reaching for the handle of the heavy door, she heard a deep voice call out to her. It could only be her, because she was the only female in the room.

"Madam," it said, "can I be of any help to you?"

She looked over her shoulder and, with her fingers clutching the door handle, paused long enough to say that she had just applied for a position with the clerk. Then she thanked the man, for it had indeed been the tall man who had spoken, the other two she now saw were hardly more than boys. They stood dutifully aside and waited on the man whom she sensed was their superior in ways other than the obvious.

The big man smiled at her. "And?" he asked.

It surprised her at first. "And, uh, and what, sir?"

"Did you get the position?"

*   *   *

The term, evil, would not be accurate if applied to Bartholomew Linnaeus Buenig. But neither would the word, good. Not if good meant sufficient distance from the a-moral plagues against character that men in general are heir to. He had them all. But B.L., as he was called, also had a sense of fairness that ran against the grain of mendacity ordinarily applied for the purposes of self-aggrandizement in the form of money and power; things which are usually the foundation for all that bad men do which, like volcanoes bubbling beneath the surface of the earth, eventually erupt, causing destruction, if not serious harm, of all who stand within their environs. There are many ways to name the phenomenon as applied to volcanoes. But in men, it is the wrong they do, which lives even after they have gone, it is greed and lust for power, it is simply bad seed blooming. And it is helped along by lies; either uttered or acted out, or simply supported by omission.

There were some things B.L. would lie about. If he thought what a person did not know would not hurt that person, or if he believed a person should have known whatever it was he did not know, then B.L. would take advantage of the situation. He saw life as a poker game. If you sat at the table to play, then he was free to take your money—if he could, and no holds barred. The difference with B.L. was that you had to sit at the table. He plied his skills nowhere else but in the game. And in this great game, he saw many smaller games. All had their own rules. And B.L. played by the rules. In that way he was an anomaly. Some would have said he was a man of honor because of it. Others called him a fool.

But in one way B.L. Buenig was like many men. He was a victim of lust. In Jerome he had sampled the best that the various houses of pleasure had to offer. He had passed most of the menu by, lifting his nose at the common fare that he knew quite well any of the lowest paid mine hands might have for the asking and a couple of dollars. But there were several women set aside by their respective madams for the "higher-ups" of the two mines, the aristocrats of the town because of the positions they held.

Even though The United Verde Extension also smelted its ore in the valley, and despite the fact that much of its management was conducted in offices there in Clemenceau, its division offices for men to work in the mine were maintained on site in Jerome, where most of these workers lived. Buenig lived there too. And while many of The United Verde's executives still occupied the large Victorian houses which sat conspicuously above Jerome, all together along two streets, Magnolia and Hill, he chose to be unlike them. His aloofness was not lost on this group. Still, most of them either feared or respected him, for not only did he carry his own measure of power as one of the Little Daisy's top managers, but he was naturally a forceful man.

Buenig lived alone in an apartment house, the Sturdevant; completed and opened for occupancy only one year before Douglas had built his town in the valley, in 1917. Chief of the Jerome section of The United Verde Extension's payroll and employment division, Buenig rated. And because he did, the sporting ladies of

Jerome delivered. Still, even in this most basic of relationships between men and women, he was not ordinary. He liked women, not just for the sexual pleasures they could provide, but he liked them because they were women, in the same way people liked anything simply because of what it was. And he knew quality when he saw it.

*   *   *

He turned his big head toward the clerk behind the desk at the far end of the room which served as the outer office to the real operation of the division. This was a bull-pen of clerks and file drawers. His own office lay in one corner with a window looking out on the buildings of the mining operation; the main tunnel opening; the attendant cluster of tin roofed buildings, the sheds and shops and roads and machines; close to the noise and the around-the-clock activity.

"Jensen?" his rich voice queried the clerk.

"Yes, sir, Mister Buenig."

"Give me this young lady's application. I'll interview her myself. I happen to know there are positions open in the division. We could use a member of the opposite sex around here." As he turned back toward Madeleine with a broad smile on his face, he beamed at her from pale blue eyes.

"Come with me, Miss," he said, bowing slightly toward her. Then, as if certain she would obey, he turned and strode toward the double doors leading into the heart of the workings he supervised, reaching without looking to take the application which the clerk had frantically been trying to smooth out since being commanded to hand it over, for he had begun to crinkle it between his fingers as soon as Madeleine had walked resolutely toward the outer office entrance. One of Buenig's assistants took the form from the clerk and tried to further erase the evidence of the crinkled paper, but had to pass it over to Buenig as he walked toward the doors, one of which the second assistant held open. The first assistant hurried to open the remaining door.

As their boss went through the exact center of the portal of the double doors, he said to the two young men who were looking out of the corners of their eyes at Madeleine trying to keep up with the tall, broad-shouldered man, "You boys get on to the office and straighten up anything that needs it. One of you go to the kitchen and bring in tea service, the other is to tell Mister Waldon I want to see him in about thirty minutes or so."

Behind Buenig, Madeleine was busy looking around as much as she could without seeming too much of a novice. She had never been in such a place as this. It was a large room with a white ceiling and white walls descending to wainscoting of pine paneling painted brown. The room was divided by the arrangement of roll-top desks and tables and upright cabinets holding dozens of file drawers. From the ceiling, large globes were suspended on brass rods. Windows along one wall helped these lights illuminate the room. The wooden floor creaked beneath their feet as they walked, and the sound of Buenig's heavy tread seemed to her to be calling attention to them as they moved quickly down a center aisle toward the back wall. Stealing a glance over her shoulder, she saw that the men working at the various desks and tables followed her passage through their domain with furtive glances.

Buenig made a sharp left at the rear wall and proceeded to his office, enclosed by solid panels, in the corner. As he stood holding the door open for her, he smiled graciously.

"Please sit down," he said, walking around the very large desk to sit in his own equally large leather-covered, high-backed chair. She took a seat in a green baize and oak chair which one of the assistants placed there for her.

Through a window, set in a wall paneled in more of the beautiful oak, she could see part of the mining operations. The tin roofed buildings of unpainted timbers and masonry blocks seemed quite harsh to her. She turned her attention to the room's interior. The wood floor was partially covered by a red, oriental rug. The big desk was of a dark burled wood. A tiffany lamp sat at one corner of it. The remainder of the office's furnishings was of the practical metal variety: a small table and several sizes of cabinets.

They had hardly seated themselves when one of the assistants came in with the tea service.

"Put the tray down," Buenig ordered, "and don't forget the message to Mr. Waldon."

When the tea tray had been set before them, one assistant retreated to a smaller, outer office. The other went to do his boss's bidding in regard to the man named Waldon. She began to feel her nerves a bit, but again the big man set her at ease.

As he took the application up and began to read it, he paused to light a cigar. "I hope you don't mind," he said, smiling at her. She smiled back and gave a little shake of her head. "Because, if you do, I won't smoke the thing."

"No, no," she laughed, "please go ahead."

Without changing his expression, he lit the cigar. He noted the lovely tone of her voice and thought to himself that he had been right about her. Beneath those plain clothes and that hat which she so cleverly used to hide her face, was a gem. He sighed with pleasure as he exhaled the smoke. "Thank you," he said, with real gratitude in his voice," I never like to drink good tea without a good cigar to go with it. Now, let's see what you put down on this application which caused Jensen to want to throw it away."

Startled, she looked up at him with widened eyes, "He wanted to throw it away?"

"He was going to. Had already begun to crumple it. Now," he continued, the smile returning at the thought of how much fun he would have with the pimply-faced young clerk over the issue of that crumpled application, "Miss, Madeleine . . . ," then he paused for a moment while reading before voicing her last name, " . . . Murales, let's see about you," and he looked directly at her.

The smile was gone, now. In its place were furrowed eyebrows, made darker than they really were by the silver streaks in his hair and the pale blue of his eyes. His lips were slightly open. "You are not Mexican, are you? Were you perhaps married at one time to a mister Murales?"

She heard the hope in his voice as he asked the question. She silently cursed her failure to use another name. Murales was the name her mother had given her at birth, the name of the man she thought was Madeleine's father. Madeleine realized she should have taken more time to consider the prejudices of the town, which any fool would be well aware of by just looking around at its daily life. She hadn't done that, but then, she was no fool either. She had been anxious about the job. But that was no excuse. And now, she must use some of her skills at deceit; she didn't feel good about doing that with this man.

She glanced at him with almost velvet eyes that, like dark shadows, suggested alluring possibilities. Dropping her chin slightly and looking away, but still holding him in the corner of her vision, she said very distinctly, yet with delicate pronunciation, "I don't know why everybody always thinks that. My mother was plain American, plain as could be. Her husband, my stepfather, was named Murales. I never knew my real father." And she looked straight up at him, then, her lips slightly parted, her eyes wide and filled with pleading.

She had managed to tell the truth in all but the name of her mother's husband. His name had been Pierce, Langdon James Pierce. She would never forget it, or him. She had killed him with an eight inch hatpin after he had strangled her mother, then reeled in a drunken rage toward her as she lay against the back of a small couch where he had flung her when she tried to help her mother. Half-falling, half-lunging toward her, he had not seen the slim length of metal she held between herself and his large body. The hatpin slipped neatly between his ribs and into his heart. She would remember forever the vacant look of surprise in his cold, green eyes as he died on top of her.

Buenig gazed steadily at her while the scene played once again in her mind. She's lying, he thought. That's interesting. But his face showed nothing of what he was thinking. Finally he spoke, though he did not change his expression. His tone was level and unrevealing as well, "Then your name is not really Murales in so far as nationality is concerned?"

"No, Sir."

"It could be anything else?" Here he seemed to look even harder at her.

"Sir, I . . ."

"Morgan, perhaps?"

"Yes, Sir, it could be."

His eyes still steady on her, he raised his voice and spoke to the assistant in the smaller, adjacent office, "Andy!"

The young man hurried into the room and stood by the big desk, struggling hard not to look at Madeleine.

"Yes, Mister Buenig?"

"Go up front and get another job application form from Jensen. This one won't do, it's been all crumpled and some of the writing is hard to read."

The assistant reached for the form which still lay on Buenig's desk, but his boss waved him away.

"That's alright, I'll throw this one in the wastebasket," said Buenig, "And hurry, Miss Morgan here has other errands to run today."

TEN

"You've got a pretty nice little place here, Cyrus." Mike sat in a comfortable chair in a very comfortable three-room apartment on the second floor of what Cyrus had said was once a prominent rooming house. The old building rose between others of like age, if not condition, on the up-slope side of highway 89A as it came into town from the valley.

"Most of the place is now rented out. There's art shops on the first floor and another apartment down the hallway, bigger'n this one. An' there's also a coupla' rooms that ain't got much except trash in 'em, an' my darkroom, of course. We passed the art shops on the way in from the street below. But, yeah, I like the place."

"You sit out on that balcony much?" Mike asked, pointing his chin toward the front window through which he could see the backs of a couple of chairs on the narrow porch.

The old man laughed and shook his head in the affirmative, "Yeah, I do. Especially if it's evenin' and the weather's right. Looks kind of rickety to you don't it?" he grinned. Mike grinned back in answer.

"But, you know, the rules of buyin' this place was that I had to fix it up, bring it to code 'n all. It's plenty sturdy."

"So, Cyrus, when did you come here?"

"Aw, hell, I first come here back in the late forties, all the way from Clarksville, Tennessee; runnin' away from life behind a mule on a farm. I come here hopin' to find a job takin' pictures for a newspaper. But the last paper petered out here sometime in the thirties. I worked drivin' a delivery wagon for a store here for about a year and then left. Lived in California for most of my life. Finally went to work for a newspaper as a photographer and made it my career. Got divorced. Got married again. And when my wife died a few years back, I decided to find a place where I could die myself. I came here fully expectin' to do just that in the early seventies. Tried to become an alcoholic. Most people think I am anyway, but I ain't."

"So, why didn't you?"

"Why didn't I what?"

"Die."

The old man looked at Mike, grinned and shook his head. "Boy, dyin' is somethin' the good Lord is in charge of. At that time this old town was on the verge of a comeback of sorts. The hippies had found it. Them and a few other good people resurrected it. Formed an association, did all the necessary legal stuff, acquired property rights and put places up for sale with the condition that the buyer had to fix 'em up and either live in 'em or rent 'em out. I done both them things. I rent the bottom of this old place out to three shops, rent the large apartment to the owner of one of them, and I use the rest. Cost me ten thousand dollars to get this place ready so I could do all of that. Brought me a lot of hard work besides. Hell, I was too busy to die! And it helped me get over Lilly's death. Here, enough of this interviewin' me. I'm gonna' put on some coffee. Then we'll look at some pictures I happen to have. You game for that? Maybe you'll find somethin' they didn't have down at the archives."

Mike looked through the photographs Cyrus had to show him, hoping he would find one depicting the scene in the dream. The photos were of varying sizes. "How'd you come by these, Cyrus?" he asked.

"When I came back from California, this place was buzzin' with people doin' almost anything they felt like. Hell, you could grow weed in your flower boxes if you wanted to. I found a bunch of them old photographs in an attic over on Giroux Street. Must've belonged to a photographer who lived here. Anyway, if I hadn't taken 'em, they'd a rotted or somebody might have thrown 'em in the trash; either that or this here Preservation Society woulda' got 'em. 'n they already have their share."

Mike continued to look at them, transferring them from one pile to another. When he finally came to a scene that was like his dream, he sat straighter in his chair and gazed intently at the old black and white picture with no indication that he intended to look at any others.

Sitting across from him, Cyrus noticed his interest and grinned. "How about that, eh? Look at them old Fords all lined up along Main Street."

"No vacant spot here, either," said Mike.

The grin left the old man's face, "What?"

The street," said Mike, "it's all here. I mean, that part that's vacant now. It doesn't show vacant in the picture."

"Well, that's because it wasn't always empty like it is now," said Cyrus, a quizzical look on his face. "You don't think the street was always like it is today, do you?"

"No, but what happened there anyway?" asked Mike, his eyes still fixed on the old photograph.

Cyrus took out a cigarette and lit it. He exhaled and then had to cough before he could answer the question. "The mines were greedy. They not only took off the mountain top with them god-awful big steam shovels, but before that they'd honey-combed this ol' hill with tunnels. Here," and he began to shuffle through a pile of pictures he had placed at his feet, intending to eventually show them to Mike, "look at these."

What Cyrus handed Mike were several pictures of that blank section of Main Street before it had become nothing but an empty expanse, with only enough land past the pavement for parking. In the pictures Cyrus had given him, the buildings were still in place.

However, they were no longer arranged in an even line before the sidewalk. Some seemed to be higher in front than in back, others were below the level of the sidewalk in front of them. Large cracks showed in the walls of most of them.

Now, all of this was gone. Beyond the telephone poles laid on the ground to serve as parking curbs, the earth dropped away to the next street below as if it had been shoved by some giant hand. It was a place where the land below the buildings had begun to move. With the buildings no longer safe or useable, the town had bulldozed the site and left it vacant. Tourists parked where sidewalks had once fronted prosperous business establishments, and they also parked on the land below, where a parking lot took the place of the buildings which had once been behind those above.

Cyrus continued with his explanation as to what had happened. "You see, the mines used dynamite to make them tunnels. In one blast they set off over a hundred tons of powder. Anyway, that part of the street you see gone today was like that by 1937. The land beneath the buildin's started to move. The buildin's resting there got big cracks in their walls and foundations. Some sagged downhill right away. Others took time. But eventually that entire section of street was condemned and tore down. Nobody ever built there again."

"Why couldn't they rebuild?" asked Mike.

"Oh, hell, they could've. But there was a fault there accordin' to the big-wig geologists. The damned depression was in full swing." Cyrus went into another coughing spell. Mike watched with interest as he waited for the usual side-snapping.

"Goddammit!" the old man exclaimed, "Ralph would love to've seen that one. Give him another damned excuse to nag at me."

"Why don't you quit them? Ever try?"

The old man glared at Mike. "Now, by-God, don't you start, too. Where was I? The Depression." He looked at Mike out of narrowed eyes and shook his head as he smiled tightly, "You missed that wonderful episode in the exercise of greed and man's inhumanity to man. Hell, when the results of the crash of 1929 settled on this little berg in the thirties, the last thing on people's minds was rebuildin' a few feet of Main Street. I can tell you that just from what little of its aftermath I went through. Here, let me get you some more coffee."

When Cyrus returned with the coffee pot, Mike was still looking at the photographs showing the street with the buildings in place along that section of it that was now empty, the section where the little yellow Volkswagen was parked, buttoned-up and still.

"Is there somethin' special about that stretch of street?" Cyrus asked as he poured fresh coffee into Mike's nearly empty cup.

For an answer, Mike asked, "Cyrus, how are you with dreams?"

"Whatta' y'mean? Asked Cyrus, placing the coffee pot on a side table and sitting down in the chair opposite Mike.

Mike began to tell his new acquaintance then of the dream he had experienced about the old town. Then he went into a bit of background about himself, something he had not done the first time he had met the old man in the bar, nor earlier in the day while they had been at Mac's.

Cyrus listened as Mike told him of his liking for history and historical sites. And he didn't change expression as Mike talked of his strange ability to feel the past in old buildings and old places.

"So, do you think I'm crazy, Cyrus?" Mike asked when he'd finished.

Cyrus Dooley leaned back in his chair and looked through the window, toward the dusk gathering in the final minutes of the day. Beyond the narrow balcony that ran the length of the old building's second story, he could see the dark bulk of what he knew were the San Francisco Peaks at Flagstaff. He smiled when he looked again at Mike sitting on the couch with all the old photos around him, in disarray now.

"No, boy," he chuckled, "you're just a damned romantic is all."

"And?" Mike sensed he had more to say.

"And, so what? I wouldn't be here in this place if I wasn't one, too."

"I didn't tell you all of it," said Mike, and he recounted his experience in the old church. When he finished, there was silence between them for several moments. Then Cyrus said, "Son, you've got me wonderin' myself, now. I've got lots of old pictures of this place. Why would I just happen to pull out a handful that included them old shots of that part of Main Street you dreamed about?"

"I don't know," said Mike, then continuing in the same line of speculation, "Why didn't I find more pictures like that in the Preservation Society's collection? I mean, I found one, but . . ."

"Well, that's easy to figure, "interrupted Cyrus, "you just didn't look long enough, there's an awful lot of them old pictures down in that collection; an' a lot more that the preservation society's got that it ain't even codified yet." Then he seemed to think of something. He turned his head slightly as if listening, and said, "Say, do you mind if I just sort of come along with you while you make your calendar pictures? Maybe I could be a sort of guide." And seeing the look on Mike's face, he hurried to add, "No, no. I don't mean for pay. Hell, thank God I don't need any damned money. It's just that I've got a feelin' about you. I want to see what you turn up in this old place. By the way," he continued, pulling out another cigarette and lighting it, "you mind if I ask you somethin' personal?"

Mike waited as his new acquaintance went through another coughing spell, then, when the old man's system had completed its complaint against the tar and the smoke he assailed it with, and Cyrus was able to take another long drag off the cigarette without coughing, Mike answered, "No, go ahead."

The old man's voice, ragged and weakened by the tobacco smoke, came out in a rasping and fading whisper, "How are you with ghosts?"

ELEVEN

To her it was the color that mattered, that and the grand, floating-on-a-cloud sensation transferred through the soft leather on which she sat, and which was underscored by the deep throb of the engine pulling beneath the long hood that narrowed before them. At a point on this metallic expanse, just above the thin, vertical grille, a silver ornament, elegant in its simplicity of wings folded together in a single, aerodynamic flow of metal, marked the forward part of the beautiful machine.

"Oh, Harry," she said, favoring him with one of her genuine smiles, "it is simply lovely. How far could it take us?"

He smiled himself, almost believing she really wanted to know; hoping she did. He looked at her, then, and seeing that face turned toward him, shining as the sun shone in its own radiant beauty, he was made helpless. "It will take us all the way to forever," he said, "that is, if you really want to go."

She tossed her head and her smile turned a bit impish. "I just want to go somewhere," she said, gaily. "I mean, a car this delicious deserves to be made to go somewhere, doesn't it?"

For reply, he pressed his foot against the accelerator. The big in-line eight responded with hardly an increase in sound, but the car surged forward and the wind-noise intensified as the air billowed around and over the windshield and flowed past the wing-windows.

It was a 1934 La Salle, 350 series, convertible coupe enfolded in five hand-rubbed coats of glossy plum. This almost edible color was played off against four big, white-walled tires, accentuated by full-moon hubcaps and embraced by large fenders sculpted in flowing curves and linear shapes which allowed the big machine to slip through the air as if it were some kind of land-bird, flying on wheels instead of wings.

Fore and aft, a set of chrome bumpers, fashioned into two silver planes and configured with one above and slightly ahead of the other, and just barely bent at center, jutted beyond the fenders to protect the entire width of the car. The body of the automobile began at the high, narrow grille, flared out to accommodate the great engine housed beneath the hood, flared even more as it flowed in metal artistry past the two-person passenger compartment, then reached its maximum width at the rear of the car, where the shiny deck hid another passenger compartment in what was known as a rumble seat; beyond this the metal kept its width, but it curved gracefully toward the earth and blended with the rear fenders and small back-lights to form a perfectly shaped tail; all of which the thin, bi-plane bumper there was meant to keep from harm. In front, the silver nose was flanked by two large headlights, called bowl-headlights, attached to the car on short wing-like structures, nearly at the top of the high, silver grille. Setting off the long front portion of the body, a row of small portholes, five on each side, half covered with chrome slits, ran the length of the engine panels.

Its narrow grille allowed the grand machine to cut through the wind yet, strangely, it did so with an absolutely flat windshield. Beyond this, inside the passenger compartment, all was refined elegance in leather and metal. The dashboard was flat, the dial cases that housed the instruments were round, and everything was white and silver on black. The inside door panels and seats were of white leather. The light-tan canvas top tucked neatly away when it was down, made for a very snug and secure enclosure when raised. There was a radio, and a heater, for this beautiful automotive creation was meant not only to move one from place to place, but to do so while providing luxurious comfort with entertainment as well.

Sitting behind the thin, ivory-colored wheel that was held by four spidery chrome spokes to the rounded, glass and chrome-encased pedestal, emblazoned with a large L and S and positioned exactly where it should be for his control, he felt himself to be the master of all things; of all things he thought, sadly, except her.

They spent four days together. He had come unexpectedly from San Francisco, driving the new car slowly along the narrow street and turning it into the driveway he had once used for the old Cadillac. It was not the sound of his arrival that apprised her of his presence. Neither the low hum of the engine nor the soft thud and click of the car door as he closed it could be heard inside the old house. But she caught a glimpse of movement through a window as she passed from the dining room into the front foyer on her way to the grand staircase. Pausing then, she turned and went to the front door. This great wooden barrier of solid oak was bordered on each side by glass panes rising from waist-level to the heavy transom, ten feet overhead. Dingy, yellowed curtains covered them. She pulled one aside and peered into the front yard. There was nothing on the old brick walkway curving in from the street. But to the far left, she saw the car, shining like some great metal plum, sitting regally in the driveway before the garage. Then she saw him. He was standing near the car, looking toward the rear of the house.

He turned, shook his head, as if to clear it of some thought, and looked up at the Victorian structure rising before him. She knew he had seen the old wreck in the yard behind the garage, where it had been since the day they had hauled it up from the bottom of the canyon. Since that day she had allowed no one to touch it. And it had sat there, scarred and ruined, its metal rusting, its cloth and canvas rotting, its wooden wheel spokes drying in their sockets and its tires deflated and pulling away from their rims. The rain and snow had touched it during the years, the needles from the pine trees, growing close to where she had had the men place the car on that day, had fallen onto it and accumulated in drifts. Weeds grew around it and through it. It was a monument to ugliness, neglect and grief.

She opened the door before he could use the doorbell. At first they each stood silent and in view of the other. Then he spoke.

"I hope you won't send me away, Madeleine. I am on my way to Phoenix, going to live there, now, new job and all. I, uh, I tried not to come, but I couldn't . . . ." he faltered and looked down at his feet. Then, lifting his head again, he added, "I'm sorry, Madeleine, I had a little time before taking the new job and I could not keep myself from driving up here. I'm sorry."

At first, because his tall, still-boyish figure had surprised her, the feelings welling within her mind had been chaotic mixtures of emotion like the swirling colors in an impressionistic painting, all shouting for attention and each for a different reason. But intellect soon took over. He had not lost his ability to dress with flair. He wore an all-white suit, accented with light blue pinstripes. His head bore a similarly colored porkpie cap. Both the suit and the cap seemed out of place, here, in the winter, but he was as handsome as ever.

"Come in, Harry," she said, smiling, "I have no intention of sending you anywhere today."

She stepped aside as the heavy door swung inward and he entered the house he had once known as his own. His head was all movement while he looked around at the place. Not a thing had been changed, he saw.

He looked back at her. She was still as beautiful as he remembered. There was something about her manner that was different, though. He was glad she had not responded to his impromptu arrival by rejecting him. That at least was a good beginning. Maybe his idea to visit the old town wasn't so bad after all.

"I couldn't come here without seeing you, Madeleine."

She ignored the subtle reference to their past relationship, saying instead, "Jobs these days are hard to find, what is this new job of yours?"

He was suddenly embarrassed. He looked at his feet for a moment before answering her. "Oh, it's nothing like what I had here, not that sort of thing at all. It's in accounting, of course. A friend of mine had a friend. It's a small firm which does some kind of business with the Army. Aeroplanes, I think."

"I see," she said. "Well, come into the dining room and I'll get us some tea. Or would you prefer something else?"

He gave her a weak smile, "I'll have whatever you wish," he replied. Then, as she turned and led the way into the next room he said, in an attempt to express the carefree mood seeing her had put him in, he added, "Actually, I left California a few days earlier than I needed to. Nobody knows where I am at this minute except you."

It had been the car that finally got them past the novelty of seeing each other after all the years; they both used it. He, with his, "You've got to see my new car, have a ride in it."

She, with her completely honest response of delight when she did walk out to see it sitting before the old house, "It is beautiful, Harry."

"It's the very last of my money," he said. "I didn't leave everything here with you. I took some with me, you know. And I had the sense to keep a good bit out of the market. Though I did lose most of it. So what you see is all I have to offer. Just me and that car."

She looked earnestly at him then, her smile faded, and her tone became very level, while her eyes took on an almost vacant look, "There is more to life than money, Harry."

"I've learned that, Madeleine," he said quietly. Then, with an uplift of his head and a happier note in his voice he said, "Let's go for a ride, come on."

"Right now? Oh, no, I couldn't, Harry."

"Why not?"

And he had been right. Why not? What mattered anymore? "I'll have to get a hat. And a coat. You've got the top down." She smiled up at him, the phrases coming out as happy bursts of anticipation, as if she were some little girl filled with too much joy at doing an especially wonderful thing she had been waiting to do for a long time.

"I'll put the top up," he said, "It's really nice in the valley. I stopped there and put it down. I uh, I drove around a bit before gathering my courage to drive up here." He looked away from her, then.

She felt a bit of sadness for him momentarily, but she quickly put an end to that emotion. "Keep it down," she smiled, indicating the canvas top, "it isn't so cold, even here. And in the valley it might be pleasant. I'll just get a coat."

She went inside and got a hat and coat. She returned to find him standing with the door open for her, and with a quiet smile she settled into the luxury of the leather seat. The door clicked softly as he shut it. Then she heard his feet crunching on the gravel of the drive as he walked around behind the car and got in on the driver's side. She simply looked across at him and smiled. He smiled back and twisted the key, then pushed the ignition button on the instrument panel. The big motor turned twice, then caught. She felt the life of the great car in the barely discernible vibration of the engine, beating beneath its long hood like a heart. As he backed out of the driveway, neither of them looked at the old, rusted hulk beneath the tree, partially hidden by the garage that had been specially built for it; the machine that had once been, as the 34 La Salle was now, his pride and his happiness.

They had taken that first ride down through the town, past the flatiron district where the last building came to a point. She glanced once at the apartment on the third floor, then they were beyond that part of the town and curving down to the area of the

Hogback, past the buildings there and down, down toward the valley.

Once out of town, the road became gravel. But it didn't matter to the La Salle. It rolled almost as easily, almost as smoothly, and almost as quietly as if on a cloud. The only let down was that a cloud of dust followed them.

He looked across at her and grinned. She grinned back.

"Oh, Harry, it is simply lovely!"

"I had hoped you would like it."

She was astonished at how easily she could hear his voice. Even with the top down, the windshield and the wing windows kept the wind at bay, preventing its roar from penetrating the confines of the two-seat cockpit. And beneath them, the road's surface was muted and smoothed by the undercarriage of the big car, leaving very little for the leather seats to contend with.

She relaxed and reached toward him with her left hand, placing her fingers on his shoulder. She hadn't touched him earlier, not when he had knocked on the door, not even when he had come into the house. "Will it really take us into forever? And she gave him another smile as alluring and commanding, he thought, as he could bear to look at without being totally destroyed emotionally.

His shoulder felt electrified. He was speechless and could not reply for several moments. When he did answer her, he had no notion of what he was going to say. "Do you really think it is delicious?" he asked.

She removed her hand, dropped her chin slightly while looking at the side of the road falling quickly down and away toward the canyon's depths where the road had been built along the nearest edge. Then she turned her face toward him again, and he saw the dark flash of her eyes that he had thought of constantly since it had all happened so tragically, so senselessly, so foolishly almost a decade ago. He had dreamed of that look. He had cried to himself at night because he could not stop remembering that look.

And then it was gone, replaced by an unreadable, neutral smile and eyes of innocence. "Let's go to Clarkdale and have something fun to eat in that little restaurant on the right, just as you come into town," she said with uplifted chin, "maybe a hamburger with raw onions and pickles, and a soft drink."

*   *   *

She rose from her place on the day bed in the corner of the great bedroom, giving off an effluvium of mould and damp, like a ragged old quilt held tenuously together by rotting threads. It had been good seeing him during those last days of winter. They had driven in the beautiful car, mostly in the valley. Once, they had gone to Prescott. It had reminded her of the last time she had gone to that city. That time, he had remained in Jerome. That's when it had started.

With an angry roar, she swept across the room! The sound reverberated between the old walls, shaking the dust free and causing it to swirl around her as she moved in her own storm of hate and regret within the confines of the structure that only her need and her special fate kept her from destroying in hellish throes of violence of which she was easily capable.

She eventually returned quietly to the filthy surface of the day bed, and the memories followed her. There had been only one time when they had stopped in Jerome. The shiny, plum-colored coupe had stood out among the black, square-bodied Fords and Chevrolets on Main Street. He had insisted on buying groceries.

"I'll call and have them delivered," she had said.

"Nonsense," he countered, "Why not stop and pick them up while we're here?"

They had talked about it while sitting at the intersection of Jerome Avenue and Main Street. "You'll have to turn left and go back around," she'd said, "Just let me call."

"It's not a bit of trouble," he said, and he wheeled the car left, heading down Main Street, toward the flatiron district. They'd parked the car among the lesser machines at curbside and gone into a grocery there. He had commented on the condition of the sidewalk and the storefronts. "What's happening to this part of town?"

"We've had some settling," she said, "a lot of heavy blasting in the mines."

TWELVE

It was as good a name as any, Morgan, as good a lie as another. She had accepted it. Anything would do as long as it was not Mexican or Chinese.

"I really only had this one thing to do today," she informed him, "I know of no errands I need to run."

"I'm sorry; I just wanted to get rid of the issue, that's all. You see," he continued, sitting back in his big chair, now, and truly enjoying the cigar, "this town is supposed to be made up of people from all over the world. And it is that. But you will soon learn that everybody knows their place."

She sat as expressionless as possible. He leaned forward suddenly and indicated the tea service. "May I?"

She allowed him to pour her tea. When he motioned toward the cream and sugar she nodded and said, "A portion of each."

He handed her the cup and saucer. Then he leaned back again and waited till she had taken a sip. He noted the look of pleasure she allowed herself to show and then he smiled himself. "I'm glad you like it," he said.

She knew exactly what he had meant when he'd said the people all knew their places. But she thought it would be better if he did not know that she knew. "What do you mean their place? She asked, after taking a second sip of tea.

He smiled at her. She knows damn well what I mean, he thought, holding the smile steady. "If you look around," he said, "which you probably haven't had a chance to do yet, you'll see. Folks work together, and everybody may eat in the same restaurant together, but each group lives with their own. There are unspoken rules. That clerk who was going to throw away your application?" The smile faded.

She understood it was a question. "Yes?"

You didn't see any non-whites working on the floor as we walked through the section, did you?" He continued without waiting for her reply, "Plenty of Mexicans and non-English Europeans working in the mines; Chinese in restaurants; Hell, they own some of them, but other jobs, the kind you just got, they're filled with good, God-fearing Anglo-Saxon Protestants and a few Irish Catholics." He turned the smile back on as he finished.

"I see," she said quietly.

"I'm glad you do," and he paused for just a moment before adding, "Miss Morgan."

It lay between them like a stepping stone in the middle of a stream of things of questionable verity and dependability. It was a true thing, this fact that illuminated the lie of the name he had selected for her. He never questioned her about it afterward, nor did she bring it up to him again. She became Miss Madeleine Morgan from that day on. And she made sure her younger sister knew that this was now to be their new identity. It became fact in all ways.

*   *   *

Usually, powerful men are impatient. They take what they want. If cars are what they like, they have them. If they want railroads, they have them. If it's a mine they desire, they have that, too. And they never count the cost in individuals they use up in fulfilling their greed. For greed it most surely is if they are indeed so powerful as to have such things when they want them. Men like this already have more than they will ever need. And for them, an individual is the easiest thing of all to possess. If a man of such awesome power desires someone, they usually have them one way or another, and they have them when they first want them. But most of the time, because of their insufferable arrogance and impatience, they fail to have all of them—though they are seldom aware of this fact.

B.L. Buenig was a powerful man in his own right. He did not own the Little Daisy mine, was merely an important cog in one of the many wheels which caused the entire operation to work, but he had his circle of influence. He made a nice salary; the two-bedroom flat in the Sturdevant Apartments was some of the nicest quarters in town. Of course, a flat in the new Delacroix Apartment House would have been as good; an even swankier place would be a suite in the Northlands Hotel, and without question the best would be a company house on what was known as mansion row, also called company row. Except for the house, he could easily acquire the other two if he wished. He didn't wish it, though. B.L. was indeed arrogant at times, and he was as selfish as the next man, but like all things over which he exercised control he kept these two vices within the boundaries of acceptance. He knew that position in society is always relevant. And he was aware of his position in Jerome and quite satisfied with it. He managed to have time away from his job to take the train to San Francisco once in a while. He dressed well. And he commanded men. Only one other person stood between him and the highest levels in the mine's hierarchy. That man was chief of another of the mine's administrative sections. B.L. made sure their relationship always rested on mutual respect. He did not covet the man's more powerful position, seeing in the fact that there was someone above him to act as a buffer, a very good thing. He took pains to assure the man that he was content to be where he was.

As for the relationships between himself and his own subordinates, he was always fair but never naïve. He punished disloyalty and deceit above all else. Honest mistakes he would allow to slide—to a point. But lies which could result in damage to his own position were dangerous things, and so he punished all liars who were responsible to him according to the lies they told and the situation they were in.

He knew that she had not been totally truthful with him. But he understood her position. He saw her acceptance of the fabrication he had offered as the only choice she had open to her. It was part of the rules of the game as far as B.L. Buenig was concerned. Afterwards, should she break those rules, well, that would be another story.

Of course he wanted her. But he would not take her. There was no fun in that sort of thing. He could take the best whore the town had to offer any night of the week. In fact, he usually did. But the whore was involved in a game with rules that allowed this. Madeleine Morgan was not playing that kind of game. And in so far as she was concerned, neither was he. But they were playing a game. She had accepted that fact the moment she accepted the name he had offered her. They both knew it. As a man who played many games, usually at the same time, and who always won more than he lost, B.L. Buenig knew that patience and keen observation were key qualities to success. In time he would have her. And if she came willingly, he would have all of her, or so he was convinced. And in that case, they both would be winners, and that would mean they had played the very best game of all.

THIRTEEN

Her name was Annie. It was really Annabelle Ruth Pierce, but she thought of herself as Annie. The one thing in life she looked out for was herself. The one person in life she cared almost as much about was her older sister, Madeleine.

They moved from the hotel room to an apartment across the street. A man came from the mine office to help them with their things. The largest item he had to carry was a trunk. The two sisters carried the rest. They trooped down from the upstairs hallway into the lobby of the hotel where Madeleine stopped at the front desk.

"Your bill has been taken care of, Ma'am," said the clerk.

Madeleine was only partly surprised. Still, it angered her. It meant that she would have another problem to deal with. But that would come later. She put on a good show to hide her feelings. "Well, I uh, how could it be paid?"

The clerk pursed his lips and managed to prevent the smile behind them from coming out. "It has been taken care of, Ma'am."

"Well, could I see the record I mean . . ."

The clerk faced her in silence and with an air of servility that was just the slightest bit haughty, but he made no move to show her anything, or to provide any further information. Madeleine turned away from the desk and dropped a subdued "Thank you" somewhere behind her as she led Annie and the man carrying the trunk out of the lobby and into the street.

They stood together on the curb for a moment, for the street there was made dangerous due to the difficulty of traffic coming down Main into the one-way flow going up-hill on Hull Avenue.

Their destination was the building rising three stories at the very end of the block where these two streets came together. The third floor of this building contained a two-room flat, a tiny place with its own bath. It was the same building they had viewed earlier from the hotel room. Madeleine looked up at it and the remaining buildings running back and away from it along the two streets and thought as she always would of a ship standing out to sea.

The citizens of Jerome were more practical in their imagery than Madeleine, they called that area of town the flatiron. It was a very busy part of town. Above it, to the north, lay the theatres, the bars, and the places of recreation frequented by most of the single men who lived and worked in the town. The flatiron held grocery stores, furniture stores, clothing stores, restaurants, a theatre, a bowling alley and a shooting gallery, a drugstore, a Chinese laundry, two law offices, a hardware store, a mechanic's garage, a surveyor's office, a dentist's office, a doctor's office, and a house of prostitution. In addition, there were rooms for rent, three hotels and a large apartment house. All of this contained in a two-block section of Hull Avenue, running one-way north, and on both sides of Main Street, coming south and downhill to finally become highway 89A on its way to the Verde Valley.

Madeleine did not like the commercial character of the area. It was not suitable for quiet living or for the raising of a child. Yet it was no different in this regard from what she and Annabelle had always known. In fact, what they had always known was far worse. But Madeleine had hoped they could improve their condition by finding a place in a residential neighborhood. It had always been a dream of hers that her sister would grow up in a normal setting. She thought of the little apartment as a temporary arrangement, even though she was beginning to understand that one of the real problems a person living in Jerome faced was housing. She was not ungrateful to Buenig for securing the place for her and Annabelle, but she intended to pay him back for the influence he had exerted. And she meant the repayment to be in money.

In their little third-floor rooms, she and Annabelle could lock themselves away from the actual events of the town, and like a craft at sea indeed, ride above the ocean of sounds made from the feet of horses and mules, the grinding of gears in the Fords, the hum of people coming and going, and finally, in the early morning hours, the gunshots and the drunken voices that seemed loudest of all the sounds coming from the streets below.

It only ceased at morning, then rose steadily until early afternoon, then increased until some few hours after midnight. It was the accumulated hum of hundreds of men, mostly single, who worked and lived in the twenty-four hour mix of humanity that was Jerome; at one time called the billion dollar copper camp by its proudest inhabitants, my hometown by the few who had been born there, and just plain home by others. But some, those who had known suffering and loss there, called it a hell-place filled with demon-people.

But for Madeleine, the mining town was going to be home. She intended many things to become a reality there for her and her sister, things she had only dreamed of before. Some of these things she would never have for herself, but she was determined to see them become true for Annabelle. A good education was one of them. She had never known most of the normal rites of passage which punctuated childhood: school on a regular basis, graduation from elementary school into high school, school friends, boyfriends, and finally, graduation itself. Annabelle was going to have all of that. Once things at Madeleine's job settled down, once she knew all that she had to know, and once she could see the pathway she had to travel, the stairs she had to climb, she would make sure that they lived better. For right now, the flatiron and the little apartment would have to do.

It was more than enough for Annie. She reveled in it all. The streets below the windows of their little place were entertainment for her. The night sounds beckoned her. She often lay wide-eyed and fully awake beside her sister, listening and wondering.

For Annie, there could never be enough excitement, enough noise, enough people coming and going and shouting and jostling each other on the streets and in the various business establishments. She loved it. Every morning she crossed Main Street and turned left along School Street, which branched off Main and led south, toward the Clark Elementary School. This large, imposing building contained grades one through eight. Although Annie was old enough for high school, she had never attended school regularly. Madeleine entered her in the eighth grade, thinking a year at Clark School would prepare her for high school.

Talk of the night's happenings at school among her classmates was always a magnet that drew Annie's attention. She listened, eyes glistening, a pleased look on her face while tales were told of burglaries, drunken brawls, and "whorehouse rumors" as Madeleine was apt to call some of the stories.

"You're not to listen to such tales, Annabelle," her sister told her sternly. "We're going to be better than what we came from. You remember that. We're going to be better!"

"Are we always going to be Morgan instead of you being Murales and me being Pierce?"

"We are, though with your green eyes you could be anything."

Annabelle smiled impishly as she asked, "What do you think thinned out in me more, the white or the Chinese?" And then, seeing the hurt look on her sister's face, she dropped her eyes and said, "I'm sorry."

But she hadn't been sorry. Annie was never sorry. The fires of poverty and corruption her mother had first put Madeleine through, and then Annabelle, had wrought different patterns in the two girls. Madeleine had suffered, and she vowed to escape into a better life. And while Annabelle had suffered as well, she suffered less because her older sister shielded her. In her, the men coming to their door at all hours, the vulgarity, the drugs and the liquor had not found a soft core to twist into pain and a desire for a goodness that she rarely saw in the people who made up her life; in her it all became a hardened mass of what she already was, and her feelings of tenderness were only creations projected for others to see, they were not real. Annie knew excitement as joy; she saw every means as an end to some desire. Her sister's views were not a mystery to her. She was aware of them. She knew how to mimic them. But she did not share them. For Annie, except for the feelings she reserved for Madeleine, tenderness and true caring for others was something life still held from her.

Unlike Madeleine, whose beauty was almost painful in its realization, Annabelle was only pretty. Not as dark as her sister, she was attractive, but not stunning, although there was mystery and allure in her green eyes which had an effect on people that was often mistaken for beauty. But she did not project a glow that subtly spoke of divinity, an aura which frequently created a barrier beyond which the admirer would not, could not cross. Annabelle at thirteen was not angelic. Instead, she was growing early into a young woman. Unlike the result of Madeleine's attraction, what men would soon begin to feel for her would never be higher emotions than those of arousal and lust. She showed potential for beauty, but a beauty only for the incitement of appetite. There was a goodness in Madeleine's inner core which Annie was never to harbor; even when Madeleine had given herself for money, even when she had felt the long steel needle that was the hatpin meet resistance before it slipped all the way through the heart of the man who had beaten her mother to death and had then tried to do the same thing to her, she had seemed somehow above it all.

What Annie wanted was to be a part of it, not apart from it. She had witnessed the violence of her father's death at the hands of her sister with the same wet-eyed excitement she felt while listening to the tales of carnality and greed her classmates brought to school. But nobody saw the light of passion flickering in her eyes. She kept them concealed, shadowed. Her body was growing into one of simple, musky allure with its long legs, flared hips and beginnings of a complete bosom; all accentuated by a wide mouth and green-eyed glances. And her mind had already achieved a level of intellect and cunning far beyond that of many adults. It was a fact B.L. Buenig was to learn.

FOURTEEN

"I do not appreciate being bought, Mr. Buenig." Madeleine stood before the beautiful wood desk. Buenig had been writing figures on a sheet of paper. He looked up as she spoke. Both of his assistants were in Clemenceau for the day and he had not known it was she who had walked softly into his office. He was startled, but like the player he was, he immediately held any revelation of his surprise in check.

"What do you mean?" His blue eyes twinkled, and a tiny smile played on his lips.

"For two months, now, someone has paid the rent on my flat." She held a stern expression in place on her face.

He leaned back in his chair and the smile widened. "Well, maybe that's why they haven't kicked you out."

"Sir, you have been paying my rent."

"You couldn't live there on what you make here," he said.

"Then my sister and I will move."

"Where?"

She opened her mouth and scooped in a quick breath, then clamped her jaws shut as a cloud of anger settled into her lovely, dark eyes.

"Now, wait a minute," he said, suddenly standing and indicating the baize chair with his left hand, "sit down and let's talk about this thing."

The muscles in her face twitched once more against the anger still held behind her clenched teeth.

"Please," he said, softening what he realized had sounded like a command, "please, sit. We'll talk."

"I'm not going to become your whore," she declared, still standing. "Annabelle and I are going to have a better life than that. At least, she is." She stood there, before him, her anger showing in the rigidity of her body and the tightness of her face. But inside her mind, fear had been loosed, and it ran frantically from thought to thought. They could not give up now. The flat was no place of luxury, but it was adequate. Annabelle was in school. Oh, she had been a fool not to clarify the arrangements the first day. She had seen some of the shacks people lived in here, the children who played near them. Must Annabelle endure the same? As for her, she had grown up in squalor that was no better. She closed her eyes against any possibility of tears. Then she felt herself swaying, and his hands gripped her shoulders as he guided her into the chair.

"Now you sit still for a minute," he said, his voice close to her ear. It was strong, and she noticed the heavy modulations of it which were at the same time soothingly gentle, like a thick bass viol throbbing softly beneath the lighter instruments of an orchestra, hidden beneath them, supporting them.

He left the room. She did not watch him go, but she heard his quick stride and the clicking of the door which shut her off from intrusion. She sat as he had left her for several minutes, trying to gain control of her emotions. Finally, she opened her eyes and began to peer around the office, which she had only been in once before, the day he had hired her. It was a very masculine place with its woods and its greens, its odor of cigar smoke. The Tiffany lamp on the corner of the big desk seemed to hold a presence—aware of itself.

She studied the surface of the desk as the minutes passed. It was uncluttered, yet the opened case containing a beautiful black and gold pen set; the bottle of ink, the papers laid out, all on a green pad trimmed in dark leather, indicated that here was an industrious soul with a sense of purpose. Since she had begun working in the mine office, not once had he given her cause to distrust his motives. But she was convinced she knew them just the same. Still, what would she and Annabelle do if they were suddenly faced with the need to find another place to live? He was right, it would strain her to the limit to pay for the rent on the flat and still have anything left. What had she been thinking when she came striding in to state her position with such nobility anyway?

Her thoughts came to a halt as the door opened to reveal him standing there, holding a tray with tea service, a broad smile on his face. "You liked it the first time," he said, "I hope you will have some more."

She couldn't stop herself from smiling in acceptance, "Aren't you something other than what is required for serving tea?" she asked. For, in his shirt sleeves, rolled midway up his muscular forearms, his tie loosened with collar button unfastened and his vest completely opened, he looked nothing like a servant.

"Miss Morgan," he began, as he moved gracefully past her with the tray and set it on a small table, shoving a book aside as he did so, "I wasn't always such a big man on campus. In fact, I never even went to college so that I could be on a campus."

She looked up at him standing before her. "And," he continued, "since we are being honest here, you've stated that you do not intend to be my whore. Let me say this to you, I never wanted you to become my whore. But should you think that there is anything in that bit of information to be used against whores and against me, let me also say to you that I feel the world needs whores just as much as it needs anything else. And, furthermore, there are whores in this very town whom I know well and some of whom I consider my friends."

It was all too out-of-place for her; his stance, his serious manner, and above all his nearly perfect English. She began to laugh. Finally, she said, "Well, for someone who never went to college and who looks and sounds like a blue-assed business major from Harvard to boot, you've got me fooled."

They exploded into more laughter together. When they finished, and he had retreated to the big leather chair behind his desk, the talk that he had suggested earlier began with the tea and cakes on the tray and from there into the liquor cabinet, where he kept a variety of good whiskies.

When they left his office some time later, he noted that she held her liquor much better than he did. It was afternoon, and he suggested that she allow him to take her home and after that, accompany both her and her young charge to dinner.

"It'll be my way of apologizing," he said.

She hesitated. She had meant what she said about not becoming his whore. But during their more than an hour long talk she had realized that she liked this man, and she knew she did not often feel that emotion for such men as he, powerful men in high positions. She had serviced too many of them in her life before coming to Jerome, and she felt she knew them well.

He noted her hesitation. "It's a perfectly honest thing to do, you know. And you won't get into any kind of trouble for it. Nobody will say a thing. At least, not to your face," and he gave her a broad smile. "Besides, if you think our afternoon in my office went unnoticed you are not as smart a lady as I think you are.

FIFTEEN

"Ghosts! Well, he figured you out quick, didn't he?" They stood on Clark St., in front of the old Delacroix Apartment building. The evening air was cool. Before them, the lights of the town, in the stores and the shops, were sparse. There were several cars parked in the big lot on Hull Avenue below the site where the buildings had once slid downhill. Tourists still shuffled along the old streets, but there were only a few for it was mid-week, and the weather had changed. Jerome was alone with its permanent residents.

Down 89A, headlights, like glistening drops sliding along a string, slipped silently on their way from the little town on Cleopatra Hill into the vibrancy and activity of the more populous lowlands, where the lights of Clarkdale and Cottonwood outlined streets and commercial buildings and told of houses there, far below, in the blue of the early evening.

He chuckled at her comment. He wanted to ignore any implication about ghosts. People never took you seriously when you talked about ghosts. Besides, while he had a thing for the past and old buildings, and while he dreamed his own brand of dreams, he'd never seen a ghost. He'd never had anything to do with ghosts and he wasn't hopeful of changing any of that.

"You know my dreams have nothing to do with spirits," he told her.

"Oh, is that how you look at it?" she answered.

"It is. If Cyrus Dooley wants to put that kind of a spin on it that's his business. Anyway, maybe he can be of some help. Add some local "color" to the pictures I take. Might make 'em better."

She laughed. "Do you realize that you just said some kind of spoonerism thing or something?"

"You mean the local color and the picture thing?"

"Yeah."

"That's really an example of a pun instead of a . . ." He didn't finish. Behind them there was a sudden rush of wind. They both turned. A vortex spun past the corner of the old apartment building and out into the street. It was the dust and scraps of paper which the thing picked up that allowed them to locate it. They watched it spin itself beyond the edge of the guard railing they had been leaning on. It swept a paper cup and another piece of litter high above the little park area set between Clark and Main. The trash flew above the buildings there and swirled out into the void toward Bitter Creek Gulch.

"What was that?" Julia exclaimed in the form of a question.

"Damned if I know, I've seen those little dust devils before, but never at this time of day."

"Oh, I'm cold. Are you cold?" She pressed closer to him.

"No, no, I'm not," he lied. "Hell, it's the middle of August. Let's have a cup of coffee."

They started walking then; he, with both hands in his pockets and his shoulders hunched.

"Thought you weren't cold," she grinned up at him.

"Maybe we can get some coffee in that little pizza place. It stays open later than the other joints, I think. If not, we can get some at Mac's"

They ended up at Mac's. And they drank beer instead of coffee. He introduced her to the Ruby Duo. They danced on the tiny floor there in company with two other couples.

"Uum," she said, her cheek snug against his, "this is nice."

Sitting at the table in Mac's with the hum of talk all around, the clink of glasses and the country licks and tunes of the Ruby Duo coming at them steadily from the electric amplifiers, it was hard to feel the old town's past. Yet they occupied the place where much of its hell had been raised and a lot of its sin had been committed. The very floor they danced on had known the weight of men and women with murder to their credit, lust and its assuagement as their forte, and power as their natural possession. In the street fronting the brick building, below the tar and asphalt, and the cobblestones, there still remained dirt that had felt the stride and imprint of the men and women who had created Jerome. And only one block south of the intersection of Jerome Avenue and Hull, streets that had once led to that area known as the Cribs, where the ladies of the night did their thing, in the interstices between the stones used for pavement before the asphalt had come, could be found, by using the genius and technology this new age of science possessed, several broken teeth with traces of blood on them of one of Jerome's most powerful and honorable men.

A lull in the music, and the announcement that the Ruby Duo would take a short break, allowed for a change of pace in the bar. Mike looked across at Julia and asked through a grin, "Havin' fun? This better'n slingin' hash at Roosters?"

She repaid his grin with one of her own. "It's good to get out once in a while."

"By-God, Son, she's soundin' like a wife. You'd better take a long look at her 'cause she's got her sights set on a target you might not know about."

They both looked up instantly. Julia knew that she was probably looking at the old man Mike had told her of.

"You must be Cyrus," she said with a friendly smile. Then she turned an expectant face toward Mike.

After Mike made the introductions, Cyrus pulled out a chair and sat at the table with them without asking.

"Well, damn," he began, pawing at the pack of cigarettes in his shirt pocket, "it's a good thing I got thirsty after supper." Then he sent a gap-toothed grin across the table toward Julia. "You are even prettier than this young man said you were, Miss Julia."

*   *   *

In the graveyard, the warm night belied the anguish that lay cold in her heart. The memories; she must be true to all of them. She could not slight the painful ones. But, oh, how hard it was. It was her burden to remember only special events related to her past, things which she had done, and things which others had done. She saw each memory with the clarity of detail present in the capabilities of a fine camera, heard the sounds attached to them, from the lightest whisper to the loudest wail; of either human voice or tortured metal. She smelled the evening airs, the morning dews, the stench of terror. Nothing was left out, nothing missed. She could only hurry the process. This helped. But it was a surcease of sorrow which she eventually paid for. Past scenes shortened in this way were relived another time. She could only forestall the pain. But in the young one she had sensed an ability. Perhaps there was an opportunity there. Perhaps.

In ethereal form, she hovered in dark misery above the sunken ground as the dim scenes from the past swirled around her like mists in the evening, down-slope from the lights of the old town.

*   *   *

It had been the car which had presented the answer. The second evening of his stay, she had asked him to park it in the garage. The old doors had not been opened in years, and they resisted. When he finally managed them and came into the house, he was grinning like a little boy who had done something he thought everyone should be as proud of as he.

"I'll put some oil on those hinges," he said, "but first I have to replace the old bulb. It's burned out."

When she found a new bulb and handed it to him, he said with a smile,"You know, she's gonna' look right at home in there."

She answered him with a tilt of her head and a touch of sarcasm, "Really?"

"Yes," he replied, "and, Madeleine, I'd make it so if only . . ."

She stopped him with a look as hard as steel, "Don't say it, Harry, don't say anything like it." And then, because she wanted no bleak cloud of melancholy to interfere with her, she added in a lighter tone, "Oh, go on out while I get something to wear." She started to leave the room, then stopped and smiled broadly at the bewilderment on his face. "Well, do I have to ask? Aren't you going to teach me to drive it?"

"But I just put it up," he said, his palms open to her and the smile in his eyes now turned into a question.

"It doesn't matter," she waved a hand and shook her head negatively, a humorous quirk on her lips, "we'll just go through everything without turning on the motor." Then she hurried to get a wrap to wear, for there was no heat in the garage.

He went outside and stood between the garage and the house. He had built it detached from the house because the style of building a garage as part of one's residence had not been invented then. Coming into his own at the United Verde had given him more than just extra money; it had given him status. Not that he hadn't had that before, but there was nothing like the weight he carried with the new position.

Death had come to the old man and caused a lot of changes in 1925. But it wasn't just the death of William Clark who owned the United Verde Mine that had put him where he finally came to be; it was a result as well of his own machinations. He'd told himself that, and he'd reminded himself that he must remember to give himself the credit he deserved. No more of that down-in-the-mouth demeanor. Not since he had gotten the promotion and the money and the right to the house on mansion row . . . but that had been a long time ago.

He sighed as he walked out onto the path of bricks between the house and the garage. The Cadillac had been important to him. He took a few steps toward the useless metal mass that it had become since then. Once, it had been a source of pride, now it was only a memory of a terrible mistake, a mistake which he had made, one that had ruined everything. Behind him he heard the door open. He turned and looked at her, his thoughts, still on his face, showing in the light from the doorway.

"Oh, don't look at that old thing, now. Forget it. I have," she said. "It's the only way you can survive, you know. Think of the good times, forget the things that hold only sadness and hurt."

"I can't forget it," he said in a flat, joyless tone, "it stands for the worst thing I ever did in my life."

She walked toward him, then, with a lilt in her step as well as in her voice. She wanted to dispel this sudden sadness that had fallen over him. She reached him and stood very close, looking up at his face. "I kept the thing at first because of grief. Then it just sort of rested there, rusting until it became a part of the earth and this place," and she turned slightly and waved her hand in a half-arc to take in the house and the yard with the old car and the garage to the side. She turned back to him, a look of tenderness and concern enveloping her face, "Harry, it wasn't all your fault . . ."

He cut in, "I shouldn't have . . ."

She put a finger to his lips. "Hush, haven't we both paid enough for it? Let it go."

He looked quietly at her, thinking of all the years he had wasted if it didn't matter so much now.

Looking back at him, the smile and the tenderness left her face momentarily. When the smile returned she said, "Besides, you're wrong. If it were the worst thing you ever did, I wouldn't ask you to do it again. Now, come on, show me how to drive this beautiful creation sitting behind those old boards."

He followed her into the garage and paused in the doorway as she groped against the wall. The single bulb hanging in the middle of the garage came on when she found the switch. Below its weak light the La Salle sat like something beneath a magician's velvet cloth, waiting to be revealed by its sudden removal. He looked at the car without seeing it, wondering what she had meant by saying it wasn't the worst thing he had ever done in his life.

As she approached the driver's door of the car she said, "Oh, it is pretty all right." She was already far beyond the thoughts she had just moments ago explored so deftly, while he still stumbled across the ruts in their past.

"Come on, Harry, I'll sit behind the wheel and you sit in the passenger's seat and show me. Come on."

He opened the door, then shut it after she got in. The lock clicked softly and surely. Then he walked around to the other side and got in himself.

Sitting behind the wheel, holding it in both hands and grinning at him, she bounced on the leather seat as if to pretend the car was moving. "So, teach me," she commanded.

He began to instruct her about the car, going over the instrument panel, then the clutch pedal, the gear shift, the brakes and the emergency brake, the radio. It was very familiar. Then he remembered that he had done it all before, with Annie. And the irony of Madeleine's demeanor now, her bouncing and the almost girlish giggle in her voice, fell upon his senses so that he was virtually blinded by it and could see only darkness, as if he were in a room with the door being slowly shut against the only source of light.

He regained control of himself while she went through several times of shifting all the gears. He pointed out each of the gauges and told its purpose: the heat guage, the amp guage, the oil pressure guage. She exclaimed at the speedometer, "It will go a hundred miles an hour?"

"Supposedly, though I doubt it," he said, "Uh, do you want to take it outside and actually drive it?"

"No, not yet. Is the rumble seat as nice as this part of the car?"

"Yes."

"Can we get in it?"

With the top in the down position, it was easy to reach the silver handle on the sloping rear deck of the car. He unlocked the door and raised it so that it formed the backrest of what was a very comfortable leather-upholstered nest; just right for holding two adults with plenty of room for their legs and feet and some luggage besides.

Already climbing into it, she said as she gathered her skirts and sat on the leather seat, patting it with a hand, "Come, Harry, sit with me."

Feeling strange as he complied, he said off-handedly, "Say, Madeleine, do you still have that little book of poetry I gave you?"

*   *   *

"Aargghh!" Her cry ripped into the warmth of the night. It was enough. More could be done later, but this was enough, now. Near her, the old grave lay silent. Never had she heard or seen evidence of anything but death in conjunction with it. She came to it in sorrow and agony. She could remember the importance to her that its contents once held. She knew of the love she had for the once-living owner of those remains. She was cut off from the person they had once been for all time. Oh, Harry Waldon had hurt her those many years ago. The book? She had flung the thing from her bedroom window in a fit of anger.

Moaning, she rose in a filmy spiral and moved toward the town on the hill, her moaning changed to a shriek that lashed the slopes of the town, reverberating back and downward, slicing through the dark surrounding the cemetery; nothing new to the place.

SIXTEEN

Harold Waldon had come to Jerome in the winter of 1922 from New York City, where he had been employed in the accounting firm of Peabody and Greene. He came with good references from P&G, he had forged them himself. He saw nothing wrong in this deception. He was a good accountant. And he felt that as a human being he deserved a fresh start somewhere. When he first saw the little mining town on the side of Cleopatra Hill, he wasn't so sure he had done the right thing by choosing the West for a new beginning. But he was resilient, and he soon found the needed niche downslope from Jerome, in Bittercreek Gulch.

His first real job in Jerome was with the United Verde Extension. He obtained a position with its payroll and employment division in the spring of 1923. B.L. Buenig became his boss. He had met one or two men like Buenig before. His opinion of such men was that they destroyed themselves with their own strength. Waldon felt that men of such iron-like values, who possessed a determination to keep to themselves and do all they could without help from others, were bound to burn out and fall, like a comet streaking across the heavens in a fiery but lonely descent toward the Earth's surface. But while aloft, such a thing was power, and always evoked either admiration or fear. To the credit of his judgement, Waldon admired Buenig. To the credit of his intelligence, he feared him as well. But to the detriment of his character he was jealous of Buenig's power and position; he set himself to be alert to any opportunity to either unseat him or use him to elevate himself in whatever way he could. Harry Waldon was a man who sought opportunity.

B.L. Buenig was soon able to make his own judgements about his new employee from the East. He recognized a common philosophical line in Waldon. Most men were interested in bettering their own positions. That was not a new trait. He would have seen it as a fault in Waldon were it absent. As well, B.L. knew himself, and he was not unaware of the effect he had on lesser men. To his credit he tried to prevent their deference from coloring his feelings about them. It depended on their style. If they maintained their own sense of self-worth while acknowledging who he was, he respected them in turn. And so far, he found that he could respect Waldon. Besides, he had his own figures of speech and, as they applied to Waldon, they were graphic and typical of Buenig; when weeds grew where they were unwanted, you cut them down. If Waldon became a weed, Buenig would do what became necessary.

In addition to his abilities as an accountant, Harold Waldon was very pleasant to be around. Women liked him. He was handsome, just the right age—closer to forty than thirty, and he gave out all the right signals as to what he thought about the politics of the day. He wasn't sure how he felt about feminism, but he certainly wanted to see justice done. Of course, America should remain free of further entanglements in Europe. Commerce and industry were the real business of democracy. And as for prohibition, and those things very close to home, such as the re-naming of saloons as pool halls, and accommodating the drinking customer with set-ups of ice and mixers just so the owners could continue to operate with whiskey made by local bootleggers, whiskey brought along by the customer—well, it all spoke for itself, didn't it? And while on the subject, the continued presence of those "ladies of the evening" was outrageous, but heaven only knew what the poor things would do otherwise. Finally, the working man deserved a better deal if America was ever to take her place in history, but were unions the answer? He really didn't know.

Of course he modified this line of talk whenever circumstances made it necessary. The commerce and industrial references got a big boost if bosses or owners were part of the audience. And if in a poker game at the far end of the Fashion Saloon, or some other local hideaway for men, he never mentioned feminism, nor did he bring up anything about prohibition; but he drank the whiskey that was always present at such occasions. And if there was one thing he dearly enjoyed about the tough little town on the flanks of Mingus Mountain, it was the delectable pleasure afforded by the so-called ladies of the evening.

Harold Waldon had worked for B.L. Buenig for nearly a year and a half when he was called into his boss's office and told to shut the door and sit down. He did as he was told.

As usual, Buenig had been busy writing at his desk. "I'll just finish up here, first, if you don't mind," he said, before lowering his head and taking up his pen once again.

Waldon did not reply. By this time he had changed the standard address of "Mr. Buenig, Sir" to an occasional "B.L." He had begun to feel more at ease around the big man than he had ever thought he would. But this summons into his office, when Waldon believed there was no reason for it, at least not anything having to do with his work or the operation of the division, unnerved him. And so, he sat in silence. It was not something he would ordinarily have done. At the least, he would have made some sort of friendly remark.

With a sigh of satisfaction, Buenig screwed the cap onto his pen and placed it on the desk. He leaned forward and looked at Waldon. "I know you've already been given a yearly written review, Harold. You do good work for me and the division."

Waldon nodded his head and forced a weak smile. "Thank you, Sir." Alarm surged through his mind. So it is about me, he thought. The smile he tried to hold in place began to deteriorate. Buenig did not fail to note this.

"I didn't call you in here to fire you, Harold," he said, "you can relax."

Waldon felt better after the comment, but he was still apprehensive. Something was amiss. If not his job in jeopardy, then what? Could it have anything to do with that saucy bit of fluff he had seen Buenig with earlier?

Buenig reached into a box of cigars on his desk. "Like a smoke, Harold?"

"Uh, no, no, Sir."

Buenig jammed a cigar between his teeth, raked a wooden match along the back of the desk and put the match, flaming brightly, to the end of the cigar while asking, as he drew the smoke into his lungs and exhaled it, "You mind if I have one?"

Waldon declined to answer. What the hell is this about, he thought, annoyance beginning to mix with the already present fear.

Buenig leaned back in his chair, making the leather and fittings creak in an odd harmony. He put one foot up on the edge of the heavy desk that divided the space between them. Waldon noted the shoe type: dark brown, highly buffed leather boots; not cowboy boots with those ridiculous high heels and pointed toes that some of the professional men in Jerome wore, but flat soled and heeled; walking boots with a rounded toe.

The deep voice sounded again. "You like whores, Harold?"

Waldon shook slightly, and almost lurched backward. But he caught himself. Still, Buenig noticed the reaction and smiled inwardly.

"I beg pardon, Sir," said Waldon.

"Whores," said Buenig, giving the word a pronunciation and modulation that made it sound like something religious, "harlots, or as some say here-a-bouts, ladies of the evening. Do you like them?"

A nervous laugh, followed quickly by a cough preceded Waldon's reply. He sat straight in his chair, shifted his weight backward a bit and asked, "Why, Mr. Buenig, would you have cause to ask me that?"

Buenig hadn't moved. He still sat with one long leg stretched across the corner of his desk, he was thoroughly enjoying both his cigar and Waldon's reaction. "Well, Harold, I like whores myself, and I know how I'd feel if I couldn't have the pleasure of their company from time to time. I know I wouldn't like it if something happened to end my visitin' rights. That's why I asked you that question. You do like them, don't you, Harold?"

Waldon had a grip on himself, now. He answered in a level voice, "I'm not following you, Sir."

Buenig drew smoke from the cigar and exhaled it slowly. "The other night, at Becky's place, you had a little too much to drink. You let your mouth run over-time, remember?"

Waldon did remember that he had been to the little house just at the end of Rich Street where the woman called Becky did her own special business for select clientele only, away from the larger houses of the town. He remembered that he had been there, but for the first time in his life when he had gotten drunk, he couldn't remember any of the details of that evening. He looked at Buenig with pleading eyes; all the will to resist, the deception, faded from them.

"Honest, Mr. Buenig, I must have gotten some bad stuff to drink that night. I, I remember being there, but that's all. Honest, Sir."

The big man looked long and hard at Waldon. Then he sat up in the large leather backed chair and leaned forward. "I believe you, Harold. And for what it's worth, you need to be careful about where you get your liquor around here. It's all bootleg, and some of it's real bad."

Waldon nodded, and said almost meekly, "Yes, Sir."

Then, still leaning forward, Buenig continued. "And you need to be careful about what you say and who you say it to." The cigar had become an irritant to him, and he put it out in the heavy glass ashtray sitting on his desk. Then he stood.

To Waldon, in the chair across from him, B.L. Buenig seemed to tower in the room. He wanted to look away, but the ice in Buenig's blue eyes, the measured flow of words and the deep bass tones of his voice held him in the chair, kept his face flat in expression and his head lifted so his eyes could meet those of Buenig's.

Buenig continued, "I like my position with the United Verde Extension, Harold. It keeps me in clothes to wear, provides me with leisure time." He walked a few paces away from his desk. Waldon watched with a fascination he could not control. Then the big man stopped and turned toward him. "As I said, Harold, you do good work for me. But that phrase is the key. You do it for me. For me, Harold. You don't like your place in line, you find another line to stand in. I'll even help you. But you aren't about to climb over me." Buenig turned away then and moved back behind his desk where, still standing, he looked once more at Waldon and said in measured words and a steady tone, "You've got a choice. Work for me and like it or have your resignation on my desk by tomorrow morning. That's all."

Without saying a word, Waldon rose and left Buenig's office. He never did know what he had said that made the big man front him in that way. To him, it had been a brutal thing. He was used to more subtle applications of power and authority. It was like one of the poker games he had begun to sit in on.

No matter what else it was, Jerome was as western in its basic nature as any other town west of the Mississippi. At some time all the lying and the bluffing came down to one word, call. When that word was uttered, it was time to put up or shut up. He had been called, and since the hand he held was weak, he put his cards face-down on the table and left the game. A month later, he was no longer in the employ of the United Verde Extension.

His meeting with Buenig had occurred on the day Madeleine had visited the office looking for a job. He was one of the men who had waited till she and Buenig passed them that day in the division so they might look at the woman their boss was leading between the rows of desks and file cabinets.

Madeleine had only been a curiosity to him then. He was more interested at that time in his career. Long before the confrontation with Buenig, he had been working to improve his circumstances. He had managed to build a small network of friends and confidants. He was very fortunate in that soon after Buenig had given him his ultimatum, this networking resulted in a position with the Little Daisy's competitor, the original mine on Mingus Mountain, the reason the town was there on Cleopatra Hill in the first place. He was to be an accountant with the United Verde. But he made sure he left Buenig's authority with only amicability lying between himself and the big man.

Exactly a year later, almost to the day after he had landed the new position, he took over the division he worked in and became its head, answering only to the chief accountant. That was when he moved into the large Victorian house on the heights above the town. He threw a party in celebration. He would never forget the evening. Buenig, who, characteristically, held no grudges against Waldon, had come and had brought Madeleine. The beauty she radiated had completely captivated Waldon.

*   *   *

After the celebration in his new house, Harold got down to work. It was his intention to become even more important in the professional and social circles of Jerome. He especially wanted to become more important than B.L. Buenig. He looked around from his new perspective and made an intense effort to see where he could forge ahead of his predecessor, build new ground, add to the prestige of the office.

One thing that helped him was the fact that when old man Clark Himself died, one of his several sons stepped into his place. Death changes all things. In some ways policies stiffened and practices were honed sharper. In other ways just the opposite took place. Harold Waldon seemed to have a clear track ahead. It elated him.

Sitting in his Clarkdale office, one of many in the mine's headquarters, he was in an expansive mood. There were some things which bothered him, one of them was that Madeleine still lived in the best suite of rooms the Sturdevant Apartments had to offer, the suite rented by B.L. Buenig. The other irritant was that he had just been apprised of new duties which he had been assigned; the mine's hospital was not able to continue meeting the needs of the town. He had been put in charge of a committee to look into the situation and arrive at a solution. It meant many late-night hours of study and work. Still, life was good. His stocks were doing well on Wall Street. And any woes closer to home that he might have were offset by his recent purchase of his own personal automobile. From now on he would ride in solitary splendor every morning as he left the big Victorian house on the slopes above Jerome and wended his way through town and then down the mountain to his office in Clarkdale.

The car was a 1916 Cadillac, canvas top. A big touring car. He'd got it cheap, when new it would have cost in the range of two thousand dollars. He'd bought this one for seven hundred. It was in excellent condition. A dark green with cream-yellow pin-striping. He was sure it would stand out among all the Fords which, like so many identical insects, chugged along the up and down streets of Jerome. The Cadillac would certainly be more difficult to drive there, considering the tight turns and the narrow streets. He'd have to build a garage for it. There was room enough at the south side of the house, he had already checked on that detail.

As he sat day-dreaming behind his large mahogany desk, looking through the window from his office at Jerome four miles away on the slopes of Mingus Mountain, he was brought back to the daily tasks of work by his secretary's voice on the inter-office communication system.

"Sir, a gentleman to see you."

"Who is it, Grace?" Then, before she could answer, he remembered that he was to meet with a man named Gilmour, someone he had met a week ago while dining late at the Fashion Saloon. Before his secretary could reply, he said into the device on his desk, "Never mind, send him in."

The man named Gilmour was all smiles as he was shown into Waldon's office. He was dressed in a dark suit, and carried a brown leather folder with the word, investments, inscribed in gold lettering on it.

He took the seat Waldon indicated and sat down. "It's good to meet you again, Mr. Waldon," he said.

Harold nodded, and favored the man with a brief smile. He looked at him closely. He was shorter than Waldon, about five feet six; reddish, sandy hair, thinning. Though he was well dressed and manicured, he didn't seem to fit his appearance.

Waldon spoke. "You have heard, I imagine, of that awful event of yesterday, I believe it happened about mid-morning?"

He referred to an explosion in one of the rooming houses in Bitter Creek Gulch which had resulted in a fire and the death of two people.

Gilmour shook his head and smiled, saying, "Yes, if it weren't almost commonplace these days it would be big news. I'm glad I have no connections to such blundering idiots, aren't you?"

Harold tapped the top of his desk with a forefinger. Ignoring the question, he said, "Seems they had been operating there for over six months, right there in the gulch below the hotel."

Gilmour broke into a grin, "Making whiskey is a mighty attractive business these days."

"Well, if destroying houses and killing people is what it comes down to, it isn't attractive to me."

"Me, either, Mr. Waldon. What I say, and what I've always said is that if you're going to do something, you have to do it right. Now, as to the enterprise we spoke of last week," and he put the leather folder aside and leaned toward the big desk.

SEVENTEEN

Despite her brave resolutions, Madeleine eventually moved herself and Annabelle from the little two-room flat across the street and into the suite of rooms B.L. occupied in the Sturdevant apartment house. She was disappointed with the utterly masculine décor of the rooms, but she was delighted in their spaciousness and in the quality of their furnishings. She was also happy with the ease Buenig brought to the change in their lives. When Madeleine thought of they, or them, she meant her sister and herself. Mostly, she was concerned about Annie.

She had not expected anything beyond the fondness she had begun to feel for Buenig shortly after the long talk they'd had in his office. But fortunately, for her and the man she had spoken to so angrily on that day, the day she declared she did not intend to become his kept woman, her feelings began to move past the mark of casual respect and liking. Madeleine had never known love for anyone except her mother and her sister. Now, she realized she could have such feelings for someone else. She had, however, not moved from the little flat into the large apartment for her sake. She had moved for Annie's.

"You're just a different kind of whore, now," Annie said to her shortly after they had made the move.

They were sitting in the largest of the rooms, the parlor. Books filled a shelf along one wall. The scent of stale cigar smoke lay everywhere. Buenig had gone out for the evening. To play some cards, he had said.

Annie's remark hurt Madeleine, but it was true. "I had to do something, Annie. I couldn't go on taking his help for the rent and give nothing in return. Besides, you have your own room here. Don't you like that?"

Annie pulled at a stuffed pillow on the couch and placed it beneath her head. "Just an overgrown closet, that's what he said he'd been using it for," she stated sullenly.

For Annie, the move was not a welcome thing. She had liked the freedom of the little flat. Here, though there was paradise in comparison, it was a controlled one. Madeleine had not hesitated to order her to stay inside. She did not feel Annie was being as deprived as she would have been in the little apartment on the third floor of the building for which the Flatiron district was named. In Buenig's apartment, there were four rooms, counting Annie's. And two of them, except Annie's and the main bedroom, looked out at the street below. B.L. had a nice collection of books and magazines. He had a beautiful upright radio. There was no need for Annie to "run the streets" anymore. She could stay at home after school and tend to her after-school studies. Then, when Madeleine came home from work, she could stay and talk while they prepared dinner together. That's how proper people lived, and that was the way it was going to be from now on.

B.L. had heard these statements expressed in one way or the other several times. He stayed out of the struggle between the two sisters. But he observed very closely. He was interested, of course, more in Madeleine than her sister. Some of what he learned he had already surmised, but some of it was a surprise to him.

Madeleine had that romanticism which women who are forced into doing difficult things often fall back on in time of need. She believed in the strength of her feelings. And though she was quite aware that she did not follow all of her religion's teachings, she was a devout Catholic. She had come here to this damned little town, which was filled with evil and good in concentrated form, on a whim—she had told him this—and decided after the fact that it was a thing meant to be for her and her sister. She was able to cloak its smoke-filled air with aromas and scents of her own imagination. And while she knew people to the same degree as a businessman knew his customers, or even better, as a doctor knew his patients, she had not—and she had told him this too—any continuing interest in people as things for study, for subsequent use; nor did she have in her the desire to help, to cure, to care for them as a physician might have; except for Annie. Toward Annie all of her tenderness was applied. For Annie was all her care reserved.

Annie noted B. L. Buenig's quiet observations of herself and her sister. She was as sure of his perceptions about the two of them as she was her own. He must see, of course, how insufferable Madeleine's attitude was about important things. Annie wondered if he ever had a notion of what she sometimes thought about in relation to him and herself. Sometimes she had rather unusual ideas running through her mind. One thing was sure, she would not follow her older sister's orders to remain in the rooms once she came home from school. Life outside, on the streets of the compact town, was too interesting. She had friends everywhere. People knew who she was. Her sister's fear that she might somehow come to harm was not something she felt at all.

She had one problem, however, that even she was concerned about. She did not look like a child who was enrolled in grammar school. Her body was well along in its betrayal of her innocence. As a boy, she would have been given at least two additional years to run and play at looking and seeing and meeting people before being expected to act more like an adult. But as a girl, unthinkingly skipping across a street or running her hands along the wrought-iron gratings of the bank's windows as she walked past, she attracted glances that were not always those of an amused adult watching a child be a child.

She knew of these glances, for she was growing up inside as well. And no one who had lived as she had for the first twelve years of her life could be without an understanding of certain things—even if it was an incomplete understanding. She knew something of what lay on the minds of men who watched her guardedly—looking away when she looked back at them, there were no uncertainties in her mind about them or how she might handle them if the need arose. What she didn't expect was that word would get back to B.L. Buenig.

It caused a blow-up between Annie and Madeleine. And once it started, B.L. quietly exited the door to the apartment, moved down the staircase, into the lobby, and out onto the street. He went to the Fashion Saloon and spent some time with acquaintances there, then he took a walk up to the next street level, and stood on the sidewalk just across the street from the Delacroix apartment house, looking out past the town below and into the valley.

It was just after dusk, and lights were coming on around him and in houses down the slopes before him. The yellow glow in windows, on store signs, and in the lights of cars on the streets seemed to struggle against the heavy atmosphere. God, he thought. Even with the damned smelters both down there, the smoke and the fumes crawled up the slopes and enveloped everything: trees, bushes, buildings; everything in its yellow-gray self ! Killed the growing stuff, dimmed the lights.

He pulled a cigar from his coat pocket and lit it, inhaling the smoke with a deep sense of pleasure. Then he grunted and laughed at the irony. The smelter fumes probably killed people too. He was sure the cigars didn't do him any good. He wasn't young any more. He grunted again at this sudden introspection. He couldn't do the things he had always been able to do nearly so well anymore. But, he rationalized, I can still do everything I used to do, just can't do it as long. He prided himself on his physical abilities, but took his mental strengths for granted. Hell, he couldn't imagine not being smart, or informed. But at forty-eight, men he knew as his contemporaries were beginning to act old. Not him. He shot out his left arm playfully. Not many people knew he had been in the ring for a short while. That's where he had learned that a body needed building. Even if you came into this world big and strong, you could still make yourself stronger. He noted that the left jab did not snap out and back as it once had. Still pretty damned good, though, he thought, a pleased smile on his face. He considered his habit of walking these streets alone in the evenings, of going into the various night spots by himself. Nothing special, most of the men who worked in the mines did the very same thing without thinking about it. But he dressed too well, and was known to be one of the elite. Men of his position had their own places in the town. But B.L. Buenig came and went as he pleased, and everyone knew it. And those who didn't soon learned it from their friends or someone who warned them. They were lucky if they didn't learn it from B.L. himself.

"I seen him hit a man wunst," said a miner, sitting at a small table with a younger man he had only known since the end of their shift that day, "and I know for a fact that he carries a little .32 Smith on him. B'sides that, 'B.L. is alright."

The younger man leaned toward the speaker whose voice rose higher in an effort to cover the loud piano music and the sounds from all the other voices in the room. At the end of his new acquaintance's speech, the listener asked, "Is 'at what you call 'im, B.L.?"

"Hell, naw, boy. Not to his face. 'At's Mister Buenig. Sheeyut! He's one of them bigwigs at the Lil' Daisy. An' it don't matter whether you work for the Clarks or ol' man Douglas, you mess with B.L. an' he'll get your ass in trouble. An' if so, you ort to hope the trouble don't come straight from the man hisself."

"Well," said the younger man, "if he's such a hardass, why do you like him?"

The other speaker gestured with his glass, sloshing some of the bootleg whiskey it contained onto the dirty wood floor, "Look around, son. You don't see any of the other high-falutin' sons-a-bitches in this place do you?"

"Who's 'at over yonder?" asked the younger man, pointing with his chin.

His new friend craned his neck in the direction indicated. A dark haired man in a pin-striped coat and a small-brimmed Stetson had just gone through a curtained door into the back rooms. "At's Harry Waldon."

"He a bigwig?"

"Some say he is, I don't know."

"Whatta' ya' mean?"

The other man looked down at his hand holding the glass. "He works at the mine offices in Clarkdale. Used to work for Buenig at the Daisy, some says he has business of his own."

"Like what?"

The man drained his glass and set it on the table. He looked hard at his companion, squinted and said, "You never did tell me where you was from, nor how long you been in Jerome?"

EIGHTEEN

She had been able to start the engine in the big car, back it out of the garage, and into the street all by herself. He had stood and watched her and had not said a word.

"But you'd better let me get us out of town and down the hill," he said, as he came to the car after shutting the garage doors. She slid over and he got in on the driver's side.

"Where shall we go, Madeleine?"

She was silent for a moment, then she said as flatly as she could, hiding the nervousness in her voice by an iron will to make this thing work, "Let's not go into the valley. I want to go up the mountain instead, up to the meadows where we can park."

It had to work as smoothly as the machine she was sitting in, she thought, as they rolled down-hill and turned to go south through town. She tried to sit as still and as far back against the seat as she could. Out of the corner of her eye she caught sight of the Sheriff about to enter the door to the Fashion Saloon. He seemed to pause and look upward toward the Delacroix building just as they rolled past it on Clark St. The top was up on the car. The cold had finally become too much. But Harry's white suit would be visible behind the wheel. She hoped the lawman had got a good look.

She let Harry drive until they had passed out of town on the road running south along the canyon which widened behind them · to the northeast and became known there as Deception gulch. The brakes squeaked some as he slowed, pulling over into a small turn-around area so they could exchange seats.

"Be careful of the canyon on your side," she said as he got out to walk around. He didn't answer. She slid over and waited for him to get in.

When he did, she let out the emergency brake, pushed in the clutch and shifted the car into first gear. With her foot trembling in an effort to reach the foot pedal and let it out in an easy motion, she started the big car once more up the hill. Because of the incline, shifting into a higher gear was not easy, but she managed. When the La Salle rolled upward with authority, she sat back and sighed in a release of tension. Then she looked at him and grinned. "I knew I could do it," she exclaimed happily.

"Just don't let her lug down," he said.

"What's that mean?"

"It's when you go too slow in a high gear and the motor begins to stall."

"That's right, I remember that from before."

They wound along the road that eventually reached the high meadows near the summit of the mountain. He rolled his window down and stuck out a hand. "Pretty cold out there," he said.

"Maybe we should go down the other side a ways," she said in reply, "there are some nice, level places not too far."

When the big tires rolled along a relatively flat stretch of road, she stepped on the accelerator. The car leaped ahead into the night, its headlights cutting the darkness. There was no other traffic meeting them. None seemed to follow.

"I want to see how she does on a good, straight road," she said, glancing over at him.

She couldn't see his face in the dark, but she knew him well, and by the way he answered she knew he had smiled. "She'll do just fine," he said.

And the La Salle did. Madeleine found herself almost too interested in the pleasure of driving to concentrate on the real reason she had brought them out in the Arizona evening. She was glad it was cold. She didn't want to put the top down, not tonight.

"Did you and Annie ever drive this way?"

He was jolted by the question. He did not like to talk about Annie and himself, and he had thought she felt the same. He had spent years trying to forget anything he and Annie had ever done together. She haunted him or, rather, what he had allowed himself to succumb to in regard to her haunted him. Like a darkness that was always there in his mind, a filmy, fabric-like shadow of unwanted remembrance, his past-association with Annie was never far from awareness.

The low roar the big tires made on the gravel beneath them seemed louder to him than normal. He looked to his right, from the window on that side of the car he could see nothing in the dark. The lights from the dashboard were a dim glow. He looked at them, and then up at her face as she gazed ahead past the long hood at the road in the headlights. "I told you about me and Annie years ago," he said, "I told you I regretted teaching her to drive. You don't know how hard it has been to know that something I did killed her."

She didn't offer an answer to his remarks. She understood how he felt about her sister, long dead now. She drove on in silence for a few more miles, until they dropped down the flanks of the south side of the mountain and the road sank into the foothills.

A side road presented itself and she slowed in an effort to turn into it. The car began to shudder.

"Drop her down into the next gear," he said.

She was confused. The big engine seemed to want to leap from beneath the long hood.

"Here," he said, leaning over and taking the gear shift in his hand, "push in on the clutch. Push it in. that's right." And he shifted the car into another gear. Immediately the shuddering stopped. But, now, with her foot on the accelerator, the engine began to roar, and the car surged ahead. He told her to push in on the clutch again, and when she did, he shifted the car into a higher gear. Suddenly, it was quiet beneath the hood, and the car rolled along smoothly as before.

She drove on with relief, even though they had missed the side road. They talked small talk for a while. Inwardly, she reflected on how useful a man could be at times. He had been useful. She and Annie had lived better with him than they ever had before. But she made herself stop thinking along that line and drove on in silence.

Finally, in the lights she saw a sign that marked a parking space at the edge of the road. The space, partially hidden from the road by a ring of trees and brush, contained a roadside table. She allowed the powerful engine to slow and turned the La Salle off the road just past the sign. She braked to a halt, pushed in on the clutch and shifted to reverse. She backed the few feet to the turn-off into the rest area, then she pulled on the steering wheel and drove into the dark little grove near the table. The car came to a halt when she pushed on the brake pedal. She switched the engine off and swiveled her shoulders so she could look directly at him. "I want us to sit in the rumble seat," she said.

He looked at her in amazement and laughed, "The rumble seat, again? It's chilly out there, you know."

"I know, but we can sit out there and see the stars. Then, when we're ready to go, we can just close it up and drive away. It will be less trouble than taking the top down and putting it back up again."

"You wanta' sit and look at the stars?"

"Yes."

She stood near the back of the car while he opened the door to the rumble seat. He pulled it up and locked it into position. She stepped onto the little places made for feet in the fender of the La Salle and climbed into the leather upholstered seat that the opened door now made in the rear deck of the big car. He got in beside her.

"This is kinda' silly," he said.

She only smiled. Then, with a turn of her head, a slight opening of her mouth, she invited him to kiss her for the first time since he had come back.

The kiss was a long one. When it was over, and they both leaned into the leather seat with heads tilted to the glory of the sky revealed in the cold, evening air, he was the first to speak.

"Oh, God, Madeleine, you don't know how much I've missed you. I wanted to call you, then I thought I should write you, but I could do neither. I'm so sorry, so sorry everything came to nothing, all my fault, but I swear I never meant it to be that way."

She looked at him with an expressionless face. She knew he was sorry. A part of her was sorry for him. She remembered the night, would never forget it.

"You don't know how I've suffered trying to forget it all," he continued.

"You could have stayed, Harry. We would have worked through it. You didn't have to go."

"No," he said, shaking his head from side to side, "no, I had to go, had to."

"Why?" she asked, "I lost my little sister, my child actually, I didn't need to lose you, too."

"But I was the reason you lost her," he said, "If I hadn't begun teaching her to drive the damned car, none of it would have happened. I couldn't remain and bear the guilt of all that. I, I couldn't face you; not any place, and certainly not in the bedroom." He turned to her then with his mouth twisted and his eyes tightened like a little boy begging for one more story to be read before the lights went out and the door to his room was shut for the night. "I had to go, Madeleine, I had to."

"I've always wondered why you allowed her to touch the car in the first place," she said, a bit of the old resentment in her voice, "I remember when I wanted to learn to drive it that you always had some excuse. I finally had to force you to teach me." She seemed to change suddenly in her mood, and he pulled back from her.

"It was just that she, well, you know how she could be," he

began, "She kept after me and I did it. I just did. I never should have walked into her room that time. I . . ." He paused, like someone crossing a stream who, leaping from rock to rock, had suddenly lost his way and didn't know where to leap next. She noted his hesitation.

"What are you talking about? What do you mean?" She leaned toward him, now.

A sudden layer of cold air shifted past the car and became a breeze that lasted for a moment or two. He shuddered, but it wasn't the wind that made him do so.

"I'm not talking about anything," he said, "just that it hurts me to think back all those years to her death and my leaving, it was all so horrible." Absently, he moved his hand to stroke her head. He encountered something hard there, and in touching it he pulled at her hair. She laughed at him as he jerked his hand away.

"I'm sorry," he said, "what is it?"

"Just something to hold my hair in place," she said, laughing softly, "I've always needed something to keep it in place." Then, she shivered slightly and said, "Ooh, it's cold."

He moved closer at the subtle invitation. They kissed again. This time when he stopped, he did not pull away. Instead, he moved his hands on her body. She came to him suddenly.

"Oh, Harry, it's been so long, so long."

His hand slid along one leg and he touched her. She inhaled sharply. He jerked his hand back as if he had laid it on a hot iron instead of the outline of her vulva.

"I, I'm, sorry, Madeleine, I don't know what came over me, I . . ." His voice crawled from his chest in a hollow moaning, he could hardly control his breathing.

"Don't be, Harry," she said softly. Then she reached for the hand he had withdrawn and pulled it back to lie against the silken place he had found. She pulled against each finger, flattening the hand so that she could place his palm there. Then she held his hand and moved her body against it, a smile lay on her lips and her eyelids were closed. "Ooh," she breathed, "ooh, Harry."

It was all too much like another time for him, and he thought that the night around them no longer seemed real. Madeleine was no longer real, and with a dark moan he fell into the depths of memory. He wasn't in the La Salle, he was in Annie's bedroom on that pivotal day in his life when Madeleine had gone to Prescott and he had stumbled onto the girl as she lay on her bed with the door to her room open.

He had walked in and sat on the bed and put his hand on her. He should have gotten out of the room then. In the back of his head a voice screamed for him to do that. But he could not. Instead, he crawled onto the bed and began to kiss her along the soft insides of her legs and around the edges of the mound that lay like a damp mouth which she moved in ecstasy so that his lips found it and he laved it and kissed it while she held his head there with her two hands and cried softly.

Oh, God, he screamed inwardly, as the hard surfaces of the rumbleseat against his body and the gusting wind caused the illusion to dissipate. The realization that he was on a dangerous path clouded the old memories long enough for him to steel himself against them and concentrate on the present. He made himself feel the warmth of Madeleine's body beneath his hands.

"Madeleine, oh, my lovely, you don't know of the times I have imagined just this very moment with you. I even wrote poems about it."

"Umm," she said, thinking she had never known him to be interested in poetry, except when he had given her the book of verses.

"I have one I meant to send you, but of course, I never did. It's in my coat. Oh, Madeleine, I need to tell you . . ."

"You can tell me anything, Harry, you know that," she breathed.

He had moved onto her, now, and with one hand, was fumbling with the buttons on his trousers. He tried to continue talking, but his state of arousal had returned and caused him to falter in expressing his thoughts, themselves now in the throes of sexual heat. What he did manage to say came out in heavy whispers, at times unintelligible. Finally, he rose above her and breathed her name in ecstasy as he entered her, "I said it would take us into forever, but this is far enough for me."

"I'm so glad, so glad, she breathed in return. She had pulled the hatpin from the heavy waves of her hair. Now, she placed the point where she thought it would pass between his ribs and into his heart, and then she pulled him down upon her. He made no sound at all, and she began to sob in heavy, uncontrollable waves of grief. About her, now, she could feel the cold that heretofore, she had held at bay.

NINETEEN

They left Cyrus's place at ten minutes after midnight and walked unsteadily up the hill toward the flatiron building. Giggling, she had to help him climb the six feet of steps leading from Hull Street up to the level of Main, right at the point where, had the old building really been a ship, the toe of the bow would have cut into the water at least two fathoms below the surface.

She continued to giggle. As they made their way up the narrow stairway inside the building, the old wood creaked beneath them, and they thumped their elbows against the wall. He turned once and tried to make her hush, but it was no good, and he broke into laughter himself. Finally, they opened the door to their rooms and, together, almost fell inside.

"I'm going to jus' sleep like 'is on the damned bed," he declared as he fell across it.

"No," she protested, "we have to get into it right," and she began hauling at him and laughing until he sat up and pulled at the buttons of his shirt.

"Now, don' tear th' buttons off like that," she ordered.

Well, then, h . . . help me."

When they did get undressed and into bed, finally, they turned toward each other and flopped their arms and legs into a tangle.

She laughed quietly at the idea of making love. But he was already asleep, and she could not keep herself from drifting away into slumber too.

*   *   *

The next morning, the town was aglow in sunlight. With its greenery, its stucco walls glaring white as the sun struck them, and the vari-colored paints a few of its new residents had chosen for some of the old buildings, the place resembled a European village high on a hill. Its narrow streets were nearly empty except for some campers and cars and one or two Harley Davidson motorcycles parked among them. Few people were out. It was too early in the morning. Along with this visual peace and the emptiness of the streets, there was a silence that was itself a joy.

In the little flat, the sun streamed through the windows. A sweet, fresh draft flowed through the bottom of the large window at the point of the bedroom. He had gotten up in the night and lifted the old frame in order for a breeze to come in. After getting back into bed, he found her again so that their bodies were still in a tangle when morning came. But their posture was unusual. He was turned away from her, on his left side, his arms reaching out and hanging over the edge of the bed. His legs, if they had been able to move, would have been pumping furiously in a running motion. She held onto his shoulder and her legs were entwined with his.

Suddenly, he screamed and sat up. She slid from him in a single abrupt motion and came awake as she fell onto her back and looked up at him sitting with face contorted, jaws stretched apart, and eyes widened. Echoes of his scream were still in the room.

He almost screamed again, but he caught himself as he recognized the outline of the little room and saw her on the bed beside him. He thought the expression on her face was exactly the way he felt inside.

He took a deep breath, then he reached out to her and smiled weakly, "It's alright, Babe," he said, "just a dream."

She sat up and ran a hand through the long black waves of her hair. Then, almost stuttering, she asked, "What . . . kind . . . of a damned just-a-dream was it?"

He laughed with embarrassment, partly because of her manner of questioning him, and partly because he could view it as a dream— now. It had been, like the other dream, very real. Still, it was some time before he could talk in an even and calm way.

"Do you remember, Julia, how you felt when we first drove into this place?"

She looked at him and said grimly, "You mean about how one wrong move of the steering wheel and we could have left this world for good?"

"Yeah," he said, with a nod of his head, "yeah, something like that."

"You dreamed you went over the side?"

He took another deep breath and thought for a moment. That's what had happened in the dream, he had gone over the side, but instead of answering her question, he got out of bed and went to the old dresser. He pulled out a drawer. Inside, he found some brown wrapping paper. From the top of the dresser he picked up a pen. He took the paper and the pen back to bed while she watched silently.

"What are you doing?" she asked, when he settled himself.

"Something's happening here," he said, "I want to get all of the details down as much as I can before I forget them. Here, you write and I'll start talking about it. Come on, don't look at me that way. Just do it, Babe."

The road had been different, somehow. It wasn't paved, not with asphalt or concrete. It was a gravel road. He knew the sound a gravel road made as a car's wheels rolled over it. Big wheels! It had big wheels. Something else; it was a great, long thing, and the steering wheel was made of real wood and it had been hard to turn. The floor pedals were strange. They seemed to go in a long way before engaging anything. And the motor was loud. Somehow, though he wasn't driving the car, he knew these things about it. And the wind; it had blown hard, it had roared. No top. The car had no top. No, wait, it had a top. But the windows were all down. No. There were no windows. Color? It had been at night, and it was raining. That was another thing, the headlights seemed awful weak. And the damned thing was going too fast. He could feel it every time they came to a curve. He knew it was going too fast. They? Was he alone? No, someone else was with him. Who? What did they look like? Couldn't tell. He was screaming at somebody in the car. Him? No. someone else, then? Yes. I guess so. Then he . . . What? Just as the thing went over the side. Oh, God!

And he screamed as she sat, stunned, holding the pen with which she had tried to keep up while the words poured from his mouth.

He caught himself, stopped screaming and looked at her. He breathed as if he had just finished a footrace.

"You alright?" she asked with concern.

"I'm o.k.," he said, "It went over the side. I could see the rocks, the canyon, and the curves of the road. It was here, Julia. I dreamed about an accident that happened here, past the south end of town on the road coming down the mountain from Prescott."

An hour later, while Julia worked nervously behind the counter at Rooster's, he told the thing to Cyrus. Julia had long since removed the breakfast plates from between the two men. Now, only their coffee cups occupied the counter as they leaned toward each other and talked quietly.

"Did you go over all the way?" asked Cyrus.

"It went down and down through blackness, past heavier pieces of black . . ."

Cyrus interrupted, "Were those the places on the canyon wall that stuck out?" he asked.

"Could've been," Mike replied, "It hit one, and there was a hell of a crunching, tearing noise and I fell screaming into darkness."

"And that was it?" asked Cyrus, "no names, nothing to identify anything?" Then, before Mike could answer, the old man went on, "You know what we gotta' do now, doncha'?"

Julia, who had been listening as best she could while walking past the two men to wait on her customers, suddenly stopped as she heard that last remark. "Wait a minute," she said. Both men looked up at her, their faces still carrying the expressions they'd had from seconds before.

"Yeah?" queried Mike.

"When you woke up this morning, you said something about jumping out before the thing went over the side."

Mike looked down quickly at the surface of the counter and then back at Julia. "Yeah?"

Cyrus looked at Mike and then quickly up at Julia.

"Well," continued Julia, "How could you have still been in the seat when this car or truck, whatever it was, hit the side of the canyon if you'd already jumped out just as it left the road?"

Suddenly, as if he had lost control of his voice, Mike blurted out, "No, she didn't jump out, he did."

Both Cyrus and Julia looked at him as if he weren't there, as if he were someone else.

"Oh," breathed Julia, looking at Cyrus, "Oh, my-god. Now we know there was a he and a she. Either that or you're going crazy, Mike." And she left them then, walking slowly and without her usual happy flair toward a customer who had just slid onto a seat at the far end of the counter.

The two men turned to look at each other. Cyrus spoke first, "What's it all about, son?"

"I don't know, man," said Mike.

TWENTY

The sunlight fell across the faded, paint-peeled walls of the big house on the hill just as it bathed the rest of the little town. She lay in her place. Like rain on the roof, the man's thoughts had fallen across her awareness, and she had felt his terror as he tossed in the little room in the flatiron building.

Her quiet manner concealed the fury seething within her being. She knew all of the sad things! She had felt them over and over for too many years. Would all of eternity not pay her some homage and at least allow her a small portion of peace? Oh, if any had deserved death, he had for what he had done. He could have prevented most of the pain she felt. Instead, he chose to follow greed and lust. Was she to bear all of the blame?

She had swept up the mountainside from the old burial ground and had heard the man's dream. In hate-encrusted anger she continued upward past the walls of the old house where she sank into the thing that lay waiting for her in the filth of the small cot that contained it.

Like a pit of spiders, her feelings crawled among themselves until it was late in the day; more misery for her, more heartache in the long fated seconds and minutes and hours of eternal heartache that awaited her. She had only hoped that from the man's seemingly special abilities, perhaps not abilities at all, but surely he had shown a willingness to feel things that most people could not or would not let themselves feel, she had wanted only that he be allowed to dream a few of the good times; just a few. But all he had dreamed so far were the events of the bad times.

She rose in hatred and uttered a grinding, gritty howl that shook the old walls and caused a bird sitting outside a broken window to fling itself into the air and fly straight out over the slopes that fell toward the town below.

In all the years she had been alone, not ever had she encountered any evidence of the others. She had assumed they had gone on, and she had accepted the misery she had been left to, assuming it was her lot from some great hand of power. She had found herself boxed in, as if she walked a street leading to nowhere. She was in a hard place. She had come to herself as she was now and had learned to be what she had always felt was a punishment. Willingly, she took up the burden she had been given, but it had not been easy. And when this young man had come, she had thought to have just a dream or two. She wanted to dream of B.L. Was it too much?

TWENTY ONE

"Hell, boy, we can take some pictures, now. Where do you wanta' go first?"

Mike and Cyrus were walking up Main Street. It was a beautiful day, a Thursday. Mike reflected that he and Julia had been in Jerome the better part of a week.

"You know, Cyrus, I haven't even taken my first roll yet. I know I want some of the theatre front, and the old Catholic church up there on the hill. And for sure I want some of those old Victorian ladies up there, too. But, to tell you the truth, right now I'm just fishin'."

"Well," said the old man, walking easily beside Mike, "that's sometimes the best thing to do."

Mike looked at Cyrus who had a canvas bag hanging from one shoulder. He thought the old man did alright, considering his age and the fact that he smoked—that and the fact that when he did light up he went through such agony for the first few puffs. Mike wanted to say something to that effect, but he decided he didn't know Cyrus well enough yet to tease him. He thought the old fella would indeed be of some help to him after all. There were the pictures in Cyrus's own collection to consider, and then there was his knowledge of the old town that went back to his earlier life there, before he left for California. Finally, Cyrus knew the current residents.

"What you got in the pack, Cyrus?"

Cyrus looked at Mike and grinned, "Got us a coupla' cold ones in a special little bag to keep 'em that way. Got a little thermos of coffee, too, just in case we, more probably, you, want it instead. To go with it is some doughnuts I had your sweet little Julia put in 'cause she said you might need something to munch on. An' I got a good set of b'noculars. That an' plus my reg'lar things."

"What might they be?" asked Mike, a look of pleasure on his face at mention of the doughnuts.

"Oh, just my all-purpose tool, a little flashlight, and a coupla' screwdrivers. Things like that."

"Cyrus," Mike was suddenly concerned, "We aren't going to have to force our way in anywhere are we? I mean, I don't intend to break any law or anything."

The old man looked at him with opened mouth and widened eyes, "Now, you don't think I would do any such thing, do you?" he asked. Then, looking quickly away and then back at Mike, this time with a twinkle in his eyes and a tiny touch of a smile on his lips, he said, "However, we might have to open up an old mine entrance door, or a shed door, or something like that."

Seeing the worried look still on Mike's face, Cyrus patted him on the shoulder reassuringly. "Don't worry. The best thing for you that I'm bringin' is me, myself. Folks around here are mighty touchy about strangers—outsiders—more to the point, what they consider a tourist—pokin' around in private places with a camera."

"This sure isn't a private setting," said Mike, looking around. They were opposite an old hotel which was now a crumbling shell, its main floor long since gone, leaving the below-ground level floor visible. Beyond this the old building's walls managed still to stand, showing that at one time the hotel had been somewhat grand. Its remains invited the touch of the hand, the weight of feet across the old floors and down interesting hallways into rooms still shouting life to those who could hear, but everything had been fenced off from the public. They could only look. An old outhouse sat on the floor of what appeared to be a basement with a sign asking for donations in the form of change to be pitched from the sidewalk above into its one-hole interior. A metal plaque informed anyone who wished to know that the ruin had once been the Bartlett Hotel and that the old toilet sat in what had actually been the lobby.

It was hardly past eight-thirty in the morning, but already tourists were on the sidewalk, coming and going, and two different couples were engaged in pitching pennies into the old toilet.

"Well, this," said Cyrus, jerking his head toward the people, "is exactly what I was referrin' to. Hell, you are goin to do bettern' the run of the mill tourist with an autymatic 35 millymeter hangin' off his neck, ain't ya'?"

Mike nodded his head in the affirmative. "Yeah," he began, looking around at the people on the sidewalk, and at the cars already moving in the circle that began at the juncture of Main and Hull and moved up Hull to Jerome Avenue and back down the hill again, as drivers tried to find suitable parking spots.

"Let's go down this way," Mike said to Cyrus, heading east along the sidewalk that paralleled First Avenue, a short street running from Main down to Hull.

"Good choice," said Cyrus.

They walked along the old sidewalk past what had once been a row of shops and businesses set in rooms of the building that began at Main St. and ran most of the block down hill to Hull. But the blocks in Jerome were not to be equated with those of any other city. They were not all uniform in size nor shape. The distance past the old building, including the two others which completed the block, was hardly greater than a hundred and fifty feet, making the building itself nearly a hundred feet in length. Still, for a little town on the side of a hill, a one hundred foot long building was quite an edifice.

And Mike could see that it had been. Made of brick and trimmed with granite at its doorways and along its cornices, the old building was impressive even in decay. In its time of use it must have been a proud sight, he thought.

As they continued walking, they passed one broad and fancy entryway, then doors and windows to other chambers on that side of the building. Each walled space seemed to be separate and sufficient to itself. One or two were made of more than a single room.

"What were these, Cyrus?" Mike asked, indicating the rooms with a wave of his hand.

"Well, you see, this old buildin' was a hotel. The lobby was where those people was throwin' pennies into the old toilet. There was a bank located there. Most of the place was for the hotel rooms, but along the sides here there were stores. One I believe was a jewelry store, one was a dress shop for ladies. Anyway, that's what all these various rooms was once used for along here."

Mike stopped and looked into one room that now had its floor filled with trash. The ceiling above it had long since fallen in. Part of a brick wall was down, and he could see into the rest of the building until the darkness there shut out the light. He looked down at the pitted concrete of the sidewalk. It was obviously the original. He thought of all the people from the town's past who had walked on this same surface. It was damp, and grass grew in the cracks of it. It felt only the tread of tourists now, but once, it had been alive with the weight of the people who had made this town work. The businesses that it fronted, that it allowed access to, that it supported as men and women and children walked along its surface, had been as vibrant and important at one time as businesses in any city of the world.

He turned and looked out across the floor of the great valley below, then back to the old gas station that still sat at the corner of Hull and First Avenue, on a hill, no less. The gas pumps, the old bubble-head style, with the letter E in red on the white globe of one, the other globe having been broken, stood in front of the old wooden building which was an antique store, now. But anybody looking at it knew what it had once been.

Mike shook his head and smiled, "I'd hate to have to stop on the up-hill like that to get gas," he said to Cyrus.

The old man laughed with him, "Yep, you needed a good

emergency brake for that one," then more seriously, "However, they had a wheel chock the attendant threw under the back wheels whenever a customer pulled in."

"Pulled in?" Mike remarked incredulously, "Hell, there isn't much room between the street and the space needed alongside the fuel pumps. Stopped-next-to is more like it."

"Yeah," agreed Cyrus, "there wasn't any room to spare," then, looking more to their right so that his gaze fell on the open space below Main where the buildings had at one time slid downhill, and where there was now a large parking lot where the rubble had been, he said, "Man, look at that place fillin' up. I can see this is goin' to be a busy day in ol' Jerome."

"Let's get the jump on them, then," said Mike.

"Alright, Boss, you say which way. But I hope it ain't that old fillin' station. Everybody goes there. He has a lot of stuff that they want to see."

"No," said Mike, already striding down the sidewalk, "let's go back over in there."

"Where?"

Mike pointed to an area ahead and to their right, a location one street past Hull and slightly south of the line made by First Avenue as it ran toward the east.

"Why, that's . . ."

"What? What is it?" asked Mike, looking querulously at the old man and wondering at his hesitation.

Cyrus was grinning, "Boy, you either have luck or instinct. You go on, I'll follow. I'll tell you when and if we get there. Go on."

They stood finally on a street which ran no more than three blocks in its entirety. All around them were broken foundations where buildings had once been. Wherever there was a patch of bare earth, spindly chinaberry saplings grew in tight bunches. Wild grass sprouted in the damp soil and from cracks in the paving. As well, there rose above the street and the forsaken lots several great trees, their shade was responsible for the dampness in the ground.

It was a quiet place. Here, there were no large buildings, no stores with flashy fronts advertising art or western wear or Indian artifacts.

After walking around in the area, Mike and Cyrus eventually came to stand before the remains of two houses. The walls of one, above an entryway that itself stood a level above the street, required climbing in order to reach the door. Mike looked at it and wondered; then he turned to the other ruin. It still had most of its walls and a part of its roof.

He turned back to the first house. There was yellow tape around it warning passersby not to enter it, obviously because of a danger of being injured. But he knew he could walk around in the old structure if he wished. Nobody would stop him. Still, it was not this building which drew him. And that was odd. It was decidedly the more interesting of the two; it was larger and had a more complicated room arrangement. He looked longingly back at the other house. It was a square little thing made of wood and stucco. It had once been painted green and white. He could see the outline of its small yard. A path of bricks still led through an old gate and up to the front door. In the blank spaces that had once been windows, he could imagine lace curtains moving gently as the breeze blew past the little structure. The ever-present saplings crowded it now on all but one side.

Standing slightly off from him, Cyrus Dooley watched closely. Finally, Mike turned to him.

"You know anything about either of these two places, Cyrus?"

"Which one you interested in?"

"The small one," said Mike, pointing.

Cyrus grinned broadly and shook his head. Then he said, "Boy, I do believe it's your instinct, I surely do."

"Whatta' y'mean?" asked Mike.

"That house," said Cyrus, ignoring the question, "happens to be rather famous. In about another hour or two, after that little information booth up yonder near the old gas station opens, people will be walkin' all over this place, takin' pictures, droppin' trash on the ground, and most of 'em will ignore that yeller tape over yonder which shows that it's dangerous to be walkin' about in them old ruins. It'll make the man that put it up maddern' hell-on-Sunday."

"So, what's so important about this little house, Cyrus?" asked Mike, looking at the old ruins lying in the warmth of the sunshine passing through the trees. He was in the process of framing the scene in the lens of his camera and thinking what a beautiful day it was when his companion finally answered the question.

"Well, this little house belonged to a woman named Becky Noble," Cyrus said, "I'll show you what she looked like when we get back to my place. Anyway, she was one of, possibly the only one, to tell the truth . . ." Cyrus stopped talking and took out his pack of cigarettes, "anyway, she was what you might call the queen of the whores. And that was her place." He shook out a cigarette and shoved it into his mouth.

Mike had the shot of the old place that he wanted. He pressed a button on the top of the camera and it clicked softly. "So," he asked, "is that all that makes this little pile of sagging walls and old roofing famous?"

Behind him, Cyrus began to cough. When he finished, he said, "No, no, it was some of the people she associated with, that and the fact that a murder took place here, her own. And it was never solved. That all made this little old wreck of a house and this neighborhood important—if you know what I mean."

TWENTY TWO

B.L. Buenig had known about Waldon's involvement in the bootleg whiskey business almost from the start. He didn't know the details: who the suppliers were, the storage location, the delivery schedules, but he did know some of the people Waldon, despite his efforts to be discreet, had been seen with. A few were as bad as Buenig had ever known such men to be. And because of these facts, he could have told Waldon that his association with the man named R. Lloyd Gilmour was a bigger mistake than engaging in the illegal activity itself; which so many in Jerome already were doing to their benefit one way or the other.

The bars in town certainly did not wish to see the bootleggers go out of business. In fact, in Jerome, the age of prohibition hardly made a rough spot in the road. Not even the police were concerned about the source of illegal alcohol there. Of course, there were arrests. Stills were found and destroyed. But the truth was, in Jerome a man who wanted a drink could have one. And he could have it, for the most part, in the same old watering holes which had always dispensed it there.

What Buenig and others were concerned about was the crime which some of the men and women engaged in making and selling moonshine liquor in Jerome seemed to engender. An example was the fire that had killed two and almost got out ahead of the firefighters in the rooming house in Bitter Creek Gulch. And, of course, there was the violence which seemed to follow drunks like their very own shadows. The police were interested in that, and so were the prostitutes for they were often the victims of it. But, except for the religious elements of the town, and the many good wives and mothers who saw liquor as a threat to their families, few people wanted to see a total halt to the flow of alcohol in Jerome.

Whiskey wasn't the enemy. Hell, where would anybody in the West, or anywhere else for that matter, be without a dependable supply of good whiskey. What was wanted were sensible men, men with common decency and some apportionment of intelligence to make the stuff and sell it, or bring it in from elsewhere. But what Jerome did not need were hardened criminals; people without any respect for the town or its citizens. In other words, incompetents and outsiders would not be allowed to flourish in the business, for they either did damage through stupidity—the fire for example—or they brought about general injury due to a lack of loyalty toward the town.

It was this attitude on the part of the town leadership which, along with something else, had caused Gilmour to approach Waldon with a proposal of partnership. Gilmour needed Waldon's name and identity. Otherwise, he would not be allowed to do business in Jerome.

Gilmour was a transplant from Chicago. A minor player in crime there, in Jerome he intended to become what was known as a big frog in a little pond. He had secured a job in the Fountain Theatre as projectionist. And it was there in the dark little booth that he conducted meetings with people who eventually agreed to work for him: deliverymen, truck drivers and buyers who made the trips to Phoenix and Tucson. He did not intend to buy from local stills. He wanted few leads to himself or his operation, and he knew that sooner or later, association with small-time makers of illegal booze would result in mistakes; and mistakes meant eventual failure. Shrewd and experienced, he had learned well in Chicago.

*   *   *

Harry Waldon might have thought that Gilmour was the principal controller of a legitimate investments business located somewhere other than Jerome, and that he only brokered whiskey as a sideline, an activity he called his special enterprise. But Waldon would have been wrong. Gilmour allowed him this fantasy, and he made sure that Waldon was unaware of his job at the theatre. This was easy to do.

Gilmour always met with Waldon at his office in Clarkdale. And in Jerome, he played it safe and stayed indoors as much as possible. To this end, he rented one of the smaller apartments in the Delacroix apartment house. He managed this feat in the overcrowded little town by watching carefully for months until a vacancy in the popular building was rumored. Then, he contacted one of his Chicago friends who sent a letter of inquiry on very impressive looking stationery to the manager of the place. He moved like a rat one night from a single little room in a shack in Bitter Creek Gulch into his new quarters. One of his minions, he had several working for him by this time, holed up in a room close to the Fountain, and, when he needed to, Gilmour slipped inside there.

He hid in this way from the people of the town. He made no friends. He didn't want anyone interested in him. But he had failed to take note of the one group in Jerome which, more than any other, was visited by boredom on a daily, even an hourly, basis. Those in this group, during quick breaks to smoke or drink at an outside corner, or by gazing longingly through curtained windows open to the freedom of the breezes, or on a second floor porch high above those walking the streets and moving through the alleyways, sooner or later observed Gilmour's entrances and exits at his lackey's little room.

The ladies of the evening saw through Gilmour, but they were more than wise to the dangers of spreading gossip about the men who might use them with even a bit of delicacy one night and shoot them or cut their throats the next. Still, the word got to a few people that there was something odd about the man named Gilmour. B.L. Buenig was one person in the know.

At first, Gilmour had needed the job at the Fountain for the money it provided. Once his plans for selling liquor took shape, and he and those he had aligned himself with began to realize income, he intended to quit the job. But before things came together that way, he stumbled onto something of possible advantage to his illegal activity. Suddenly, he needed the job more than ever before.

It was after Gilmour had made his find, as he called it, that Waldon's importance to him increased. Now, he needed him for his association with the mines as well as for his ability to launder Gilmour's status in the town. There was a mining shaft, a very old one, which at one point ran within a yard of the cellar beneath the theatre. True, it had never been completely developed. But it was there, and at its deepest, had been expanded into several exploratory tunnels, all of which ended in dead-ends. At some point in the past, someone had broken into the old shaft from the cellar. The hole was masked by old lumber and broken theatre seats. This was what Gilmour referred to as his find.

In his projectionist booth, which, oddly, was at the north end of the building housing the theatre, so that films were projected onto a screen rising at the entrance of the building, Gilmour sat and schemed. He would become the principal supplier of illegal alcohol in town. He would operate right in its very heart ! He would use the cellar as his operations center and the old mine shaft as his warehouse.

*   *   *

It was in the little booth filled with muted light and heavy shadows that Annie first met Gilmour. She had opened the door to the little room and brazenly pushed herself into its narrow space. She then introduced herself and said she had wondered how everything worked in the booth which she had always seen as a bright hole in the darkness over her shoulder while she watched the big screen.

But Annie had been in the booth before. She had made a

similar introduction of herself to the projectionist who had held the job prior to Gilmour's coming. She had found out all she wanted to know about this man and decided he wasn't worth her interest. He certainly was not able to keep his job, for he was eventually fired. Then Gilmour came. It was the little Irishman and not the inner workings of the projector that Annie was curious about.

In answer to her question, while just a bit taken aback by her forward manner, Gilmour quickly offered a hurried explanation of the operations of the projector to her and then asked her to leave because it was against the rules of the owners for her to be there. Annie thanked him and left after a few minutes.

But, as with Annie in all things, if something or someone interested her, she was not satisfied with a single examination. She returned to the darkened little booth, and Gilmour allowed her to stay for a while. A few days later, after another visit, he learned of her connection with B.L. Buenig, knowledge, which, he thought, might eventually be put to use.

TWENTY THREE

They worked in Cyrus's darkroom in the afternoon. Mike had shot four rolls of film. To do it, they had walked over nearly the entire town. Cyrus was showing his age by the time they limped into Rooster's at two o'clock and sat at the counter for a cold drink. They had long since drained the two beers he had brought in his bag that morning. After Julia delivered a coke for Mike and an iced tea for the old man, they drank and rested while she queried them about what they had done earlier in the day. Finally, they left to go down the street to Cyrus's place. Julia was to join them there when she got off work.

They lost little time in developing the film from Mike's camera. It took them a while before they got any inkling of what was on it. The pictures appeared good, but there were too many of them to look at during the developing process. They finished with the work and left the prints hanging to dry. Then they each took a bottle of beer and sat on the veranda, high above 89A, watching the vehicles crawl up and down, in and out of town.

Mike leaned back in his chair, glad for the beer and the serenity. It was like watching the flow of water in a streambed.

"It's very nice, Cyrus, I can see where you'd appreciate this."

"You shoulda' seen it when it was a real town," Cyrus replied.

"More traffic? Mike asked.

"Nah, not so much as far as cars go. People walked more in them days; used horses an' wagons to deliver things around town. Trains hauled away the ore an' brought in the heavy stuff-stuff that trucks couldn't handle. An' most people used the train for long trips back then, too. Folks had more purpose to where they was goin'; not like everybody was headin' for a picnic, on a vacation. You could tell that work was happening here. It was alive then. This . . ." and he made a motion to take in the street below, "this is a lot of movement, but it's artificial; y'know what I mean?"

Mike did not reply. He knew what Cyrus meant, alright. This old place was just a toy now. If he were such a thing as a tough old mining town, as western as western ever got, would he want to become a bauble for adults with childish minds, or childish intentions at least, to gawk at and fumble with like a kid with some plaything? He grunted and shook his head at the thought. Below them, a group of three Harleys rumbled by slowly, headed downhill.

"They're going the wrong way," said Mike.

"Oh, they'll be back," replied Cyrus in a sour tone.

The riders were all men who appeared to be past forty, in black leather jackets, no helmets, guns in evidence, one with an ugly looking knife the size of a machete in a sheath attached to the bike itself. One's long hair was mixed, black and silver. Another covered his balding head with a red bandana. They all wore dark glasses.

"Look tough, don't they?" said Cyrus.

"Yep, they sure do," said Mike, "especially with those guns."

"Well, that's Arizona for you," said Cyrus, "it's legal here. One good thing about it, you'n me are free to arm ourselves, too. Some other places I know, the thugs'd still have the guns, just concealed. But you'n me, we'd have to go bare-handed; on account of the law, y'see. Here, at least the law's on our side."

"I wonder how they'd stack up against some real rowdies from times past in this old burg? Mike remarked.

Cyrus chuckled, "Meanin' them boys on the motorcycles?"

"Yeah," said Mike.

"Let's go crop them pictures and see what we got," Cyrus said.

On the way to the darkroom, the old man expressed himself about the idea Mike had raised. "You've seen that picture where the hero pulls out his .44 and shoots the driver in a get-a-way car an' causes the car to crash?"

Mike replied that he had.

"Well, these boys on these here motorcycles are a hell of a lot of show."

"Yeah?"

"Yeah," said Cyrus, "They may be bad, but they damn sure want you to think they are too. That's why they dress the way they do and carry them big knives an' guns like that."

Mike remained silent and Cyrus continued.

"There was a sheriff here who carried his gun in his coat pocket. Didn't wear no big holster with bullets in his belt. By lookin' at him you wouldn't think he was any different than any of the other men around him. But, by-God he was. There was a robbery here one time. On up the hill. A bank robbery. This old man, he was old by that time, retired, actually; anyway, he was comin' off duty from a night job when he seen the crooks runnin' and shootin' behind them as they jumped into their car."

Mike stopped and turned to look at Cyrus. The old man grinned and shook his head once, nodded to emphasize his point. Then, eyes twinkling, he continued, "The old sheriff stepped out into the street in front of the car and reached into his coat pocket, pulled out his .45 Colt an' hit the driver right smack-dab between the eyes with a single shot. The car swerved and ran into a power pole and stopped. By the time the regular law got there, the old man had the other crook sittin' nice an' still at the end of his pistol barrel."

Mike grinned at Cyrus and Cyrus returned the sentiment with a wide grin of his own, eyes lit up in the joy of good triumphing over evil as his story implied. "I see what you mean," said Mike, "but I still wouldn't want to have trouble with those guys on the Harleys."

*   *   *

They were sitting in Cyrus's living room looking through the photographs when Julia knocked on the door. Cyrus let her in with his usual air of delight where she was concerned. He asked her if she wanted anything, a cup of coffee, perhaps? She declined with a shake of her head and a wry comment about seeing enough food and drink for one day. She was interested in the pictures—that and just getting a chance to sit down. She was tired.

"Hi, Babe," said Mike. He was looking at a shot of the little house they had seen that morning.

Julia sat down and reached for a stack of proofs. She began flipping through them. Watching her, Mike shook his head and smiled to himself. She noticed the gesture.

"What?" she asked.

He chuckled, "Nothing. It's just that you take so much time to admire my work."

"I see them," she said defensively, "You always take good pictures. You know that. I've told you that before."

He laughed softly, still shaking his head.

She put her hands in her lap and looked directly at him. "Michael, what do you want me to say, that you're another Robert Capa? I mean, you're pretty good. So, lighten up a little."

Cyrus regarded her with a very serious expression. "You know about Capa?" he asked.

"Yes," she said, "Robert Capa, the photographer from the 30's who did so much to frame that era."

Mike's mouth opened and his eyebrows rose, as if he needed all the light he could get into his eyes.

She looked back at him. "I do know some things, even if you don't think so," then, with an impish grin, she continued, "Oh, alright, I heard you say that to someone once."

Both men looked at each other, grinning and shaking their heads in recognition of the humor involved. Then things became serious. Holding a picture up so they could each see it, she asked, "Who's the babe standing by the old car? You never told me you ran into anything like this."

"Let me see," said Mike, reaching for the photograph.

The paper felt cold in his hand. He looked at the photograph through a haze of confusion, holding it in front of his eyes as if it were some unknown thing, some strange object never seen before by himself or anyone else. The expression on his face and the silence that ensued caused both Cyrus and Julia to glance at each other. Then Julia spoke, "What is it, Mike? What's wrong?"

His voice was heavy and labored as he answered her, "I never took this picture, I mean, when I took it there was no girl there."

"Wait, let me see!" exclaimed Julia.

But Mike held onto the photo. In it, the old car was shown just as he remembered it. Part of the garage appeared in the background as well. He had purposefully avoided the house. However, standing near the front of the rusted wreck was a girl. He guessed she was in her teens. The colors in the print were wrong, somehow. Her dark hair looked right, but her long dress and the dark stockings she was wearing were faded and her face was washed out, except for her eyes. Something was unusual about the color of her eyes.

"Cyrus, do you have a magnifying glass?" he asked. Then he remembered that he had recently bought one himself. "Never mind," he said as he hurriedly checked his pockets. "Damn!" he exclaimed, "I must have left the thing somewhere."

"I've got one here, someplace," Said Cyrus, as he rose and walked across the room to the large bookcase running along the wall there.

"Here. I knew I did." He turned and walked back to Mike.

Almost snatching the glass from Cyrus's hand, Mike held it above the picture. The girl's face enlarged. He saw that her image was not like anything else in the photo. It was as if it had been layered over the surface of the film. Though it was no clearer beneath the magnification of the glass, the question he had about the eyes was answered for him.

"She has green eyes," he said. Then he put the photograph in his lap along with the magnifying glass. He looked at Julia, whose face held a wondering, quizzical expression. Mike turned toward his newly made friend and said, "Cyrus, I think we had better get busy doing something with pictures besides taking them."

"Whatta' y' mean, son?" breathed the old man.

"We better look at every old picture of the past we can find in this town, that's what I mean. This girl not only wasn't in the viewfinder when I took the picture, she's not wearing anything for clothes that a girl her age would wear today."

"So, what does that mean?" asked Julia, her own voice and manner as indicative of confusion as was Cyrus's.

"It means," said Mike, "that at the very least we have some answers to find. Colors don't have minds of their own; not on film they don't."

Cyrus had a glazed look in his eyes as he breathed the question, "The dream, could this have somethin' to do with the dream?"

Mike stared at him. He hadn't thought of the damned dream.

Julia clutched her hands together in her lap, her face showing frustration, which was only an extension of the unease she was beginning to feel. "Mike, tell me what you're talking about. What answers? You have to ask questions before you get answers. What are you getting at?"

Outside, heavy thunder rolled suddenly from the heights of the mountain behind them.

"By-God," said Cyrus as he moved slowly over to a window and looked out, "I was beginnin' to wonder if the other night was a fluke or not."

*   *   *

Julia's questions came back to Mike nearly eight hours later as he trudged wearily up-hill toward the building where their apartment was, visible to him as a dark bulk in the rain that had finally begun in the late evening and now fell as a drizzle in the early dawn. He and Cyrus had pored over every photograph the old man had in his possession. He had learned a lot about the old town. But they had found nothing to help with the questions which Julia had implied needed to be asked.

Mike had asked them, though; in his own mind he had asked them. He was certain, as he had told Cyrus, there had been no accident with the camera. He hadn't made a double-exposure.

They had been sitting on the verandah, delighting in the rain and staring out over the valley which was about to awaken to another day. To the east there was that quality morning has just before sunrise, darker than usual because of the weather, but still there. Below them, where earlier traffic had rolled up 89A into town, the empty street caught the rain and funneled it away. Mike and Cyrus spoke quietly, but in the utter silence of the hour their voices held substance and pierced the dark before them like shafts hurled with purpose and intent.

"In all my years," Cyrus was saying, "I have never seen one. I'm not even sure I ever really believed in them, either. I mean, oh, I talked about the subject; said I believed. But I ain't sure I ever did."

"You'd think I would," said Mike, "the way I imagine myself going back into the past. But, dammit, Cyrus, I do and I don't!"

The old man looked over at Mike sitting beside him in the dark of the early morning. They had not only sat up most of the night thumbing through his collection of old pictures, but Cyrus had made his young friend re-tell about his experience in the church, and the dreams he'd had while sleeping in the little apartment.

He spoke to Mike, a hint of annoyance in his voice, "Then, why did we just spend the whole damned evenin' and the best part of the mornin' for sleeping lookin' at them old pictures? Hell, it could be a double-exposure; could be some other things, one or two anyway. Maybe I had the image of the girl on one of the sheets of developing paper we used, or maybe a light comin' from somewhere an' shinin' through a glass or somethin', maybe off of a picture, some kind of reflection that way. Hell, I don't know. But if it wasn't one of them things, then . . . what was it?"

Mike answered, "I don't know, Cyrus. It doesn't make sense."

"Well, you'd better ask yourself some different questions, boy."

"I know. It's just that, well, I think I expected something more, you know?"

"Whatta' y'mean, son? How could it be more than it is?"

"That's the problem, Cyrus. I guess I was thinking along the lines of wispy smoky shapes. Ethereal stuff. I mean, dammit! She was right there in the picture, arms and legs and hair and those green eyes for god's sake!"

"I don't get the green-eyes thing," said Cyrus, "What's so important about the color of her eyes?"

"They are in vivid color, Cyrus. Everything else is faded and washed-out. Pretty unusual for some kind of mistake in film development or accidental exposure, don't you think?"

Around them in the damp dark of the coming dawn, a huge silence seemed to settle. It was as if the mountain rising behind them, the buildings and even the streets, wet and glistening from the rain, had paused to listen in on their conversation as they sat on the narrow porch above 89A. The highway itself was visible to their left and for a few yards down-hill where it looped upward from a curve at the beginning of the hogback and came toward them, not only out of the darkness there, but out of the shades of the past as well.

Cyrus spoke in the quiet, "Well, by-god I hadn't thought of that. Of course you're right." Then, he began to chuckle, "Shit, son, you're scared," he declared, and went on laughing softly.

"Yeah," agreed Mike, nodding his head.

"Tell me somethin'," asked Cyrus, "were you scared in the old church the other day? Is that why you didn't take any pictures of it? I did wonder at that when you said you didn't—take any shots inside, I mean, because most people would've."

Mike thought back on his feelings of that day. He had been

flustered some by the trance-like experience he'd had in the confessional. He remembered when he'd talked about it with Julia that he had told her he felt as if he'd encountered a kind of evil.

Cyrus interrupted his thoughts with a comment. "I suppose," the old man began, "that people like to put things into their own little boxes of interpretation."

"Such as?" queried Mike.

"Such as you an' this, whatever it is, in the picture. You want to think that these things . . ."

It was Mike's turn to laugh at Cyrus. "The word is ghosts."

"Alright, then, ghosts. I think people have their own ideas about them. An' when they don't fit, well . . ."

"You mean me, of course" said Mike.

"Like you, yes sir, I mean like you. You see, as long as the things you think of as ghosts are made of air an' smoke an' vapor, you feel alright about them. But when they seem to be a little more substantial, you shy away from the idea that they might exist."

Below them, in the valley, a few lights came on. The sun was just about to break into the eastern sky. And as if they were linked somehow to the lights far below and the bright edge of the morning about to show itself, one or two lights came on in houses on the slopes of Cleopatra Hill.

Mike leaned forward, toward the railing that protected them from the street twenty feet beneath them. "Well, now, I think you're wrong about that, Cyrus."

"Could be," the old man replied, his mouth opening wide and his lungs pulling in a deep breath.

It made Mike suddenly yearn for bed. It was late, but he could get in a bit of sleep before Julia left for work. Thinking of her, and considering the content of his conversation with Cyrus over the last few minutes, he chuckled as he pictured her in the little apartment. She had walked to it earlier in the evening by herself. Luckily, it had been during a lull in the rain. But before leaving she had made it clear that she was not ready to accept any hair-brained superstition about spirits. For once, he had appreciated her skepticism.

He gathered his feet and rose, with a hand on the railing to steady himself. "I gotta' get to bed, Cyrus," he said, "Hell, as it is I won't be rested before noon. I'll see you then."

The old man had one final thing to say before Mike left. "They have been known to move chairs and cause things to fly through the air, you know."

"Ghosts? Are you referring to ghosts, Cyrus?"

"Ain't that what we been talkin' about?" answered the old man.

TWENTY FOUR

I ndeed, they had been talking about ghosts, but as Mike walked up the stairs to the little apartment, he wanted only to sleep. Opening the door that led into the small kitchen, he expected to hear nothing except the quiet breathing of Julia asleep on the bed. Instead, the melody of the rain came clearly through the open window, while her voice greeted him from the darkness.

"God, I thought you'd never come home," she said.

He stepped to the dresser and emptied his pockets, then he sat in the green chair to unlace his shoes. "We went over everything one more time," he said, "I'm very tired. I just want to sleep."

She sat up in bed. He could tell that from the sounds she made and the creak of the old headboard as she leaned against it. "I want to leave this place," she said.

He straightened abruptly and sat back against the chair. Her words were like a blow to the chest. He couldn't leave now. There was something going on here.

From the darkness, she spoke again, "You weren't the only one staying up all night. I did too."

"Now, why did you do that," he complained. He was irritated. She had put herself out on her own accord but would, as usual, find a way to make him accountable for it. He relaxed in the comfort of the old chair, leaning his head back and allowing his arms to lie along the padded rests. "I told you, Babe," he said, looking toward where she sat in the darkness, "Even if it is . . ." and he paused, "something we are unfamiliar with, whatever it is, it'll be alright."

"Michael, it isn't anything like that. I don't believe in ghosts. I wasn't raised to believe in such things. My people were not superstitious . . . we were not from the South! Besides, it isn't anything that might or might not be here that worries me."

"Then what does?"

"It's what might be happening to you."

He tensed up again and sat forward in the chair. "Now, that doesn't make sense, Julia, I haven't . . ."

"Yes you have!" she cut him off. "All that stuff about evil in the old church. Now you have images on your film that shouldn't be there. Well, I know why that girl is in that picture. She's not a ghost, Michael."

He let silence fall between them before he asked, "What are you talking about?"

She chuckled condescendingly from the bed. "Mike, don't you remember those people we met in Ruby?"

"The old ghost town? The one we went to first?"

"Yes, that one."

"Well?"

"The family living there in the motorhome, the ones you said looked like something out of The Grapes of Wrath."

"And?"

"Mike! Remember? They had a teenage daughter. You took pictures of them. Don't you see? That's where your double-exposure came from."

He was relieved. Of course, that had to be it, although he didn't see how. It didn't explain the coloration of the photograph, but it offered a lead toward an explanation, one he was sure he would eventually find. He had forgotten about those people at Ruby. Usually, he sent everything good back to the agent in

Oklahoma and threw the rest of his film away. But, maybe he'd kept some of it this time. He'd have to look tomorrow and see. Right now, he needed sleep.

But, crawling into bed beside her, he couldn't keep from talking to her. "Alright, so if you've got it figured out about the image in the shot of the old car, why talk about leaving?"

She remained quiet. Finally, she sighed heavily and said, "I read that book of poetry you got from the library. It's pretty much marked up."

"And? Marking in books is something quite normal to some folks, Julia. What do the markings in the book have to do with your wanting to leave?"

The morning light had just found the window and he could see her turn toward him. He knew by the tone of her voice that she had a sardonic smile on her face. "You haven't seen it yet, have you?"

It was his turn to show frustration. "Seen what?"

She got out of bed, drew the shades against the light that was gaining strength by the minute, and began her morning routine of preparing for work. She talked while he lay in bed, eyes closed, listening and fighting the urge to sleep.

"I might as well tell you about it," she began, "You need to know about it anyway, especially now."

"What are you talking about, Julia?" His voice carried more irritation.

"Anagrams, they're called anagrams. I remember them from a story we had to read in high school. It's where you make special marks beneath letters and words in a book—in a letter or something already written. It's a way of concealing a hidden message. And that book of yours is full of secret messages." She was in the bathroom now. Her voice took on a distant tone, but he could still hear her. "And what really surprises me," she went on, "is that you haven't found them."

His feet hit the floor with her last comment. He had been aware of the markings in the book. There were underlined passages, could be something there; the doodles, the words in the margin in reference to the text itself, he hadn't seen any clues to a message in them. There was the one thing which had interested him the most, the inscription that contained the identities M and Me. He had already determined that there were two writers at work there. But none of this constituted an anagram. It could be a code, though. What in hell had he overlooked?

His hands closed on the book where she had left it and he took it back to bed. He switched on the lamp, fluffed the pillows behind his head so he could be more comfortable, and opened Spoon River Anthology. Julia came back into the room and smiled at him as she began to dress herself.

He looked up, His face was blank, in its serious mode. "So, tell me, Miss-wonderful-I-got-it-before-you-did, what's in this book that you know about and I don't, and why would it make you want to leave so suddenly?"

She came to lean over the foot of the bed where she looked at him through an expression he called her sweet and sour face. It meant that she was of two minds. It was a look he usually saw when she couldn't make a decision about something. She wanted something but didn't want it, she felt one way but also another.

"You're right," she began, "something did happen in this old town once upon a time. And you may be right that something strange is going on now. I don't know. I do know that I liked things the way they were before we got here. And I know you. I just don't want to be stuck here forever, and I think maybe we will be if you get involved in something real heavy."

"You're afraid," he said.

She glared at him, "No, I'm not." She turned from him abruptly and walked toward the kitchen and the entrance to the little apartment. "I'm going to work," she said over her shoulder, "I'll see you at lunch."

She closed the door, and he listened to her feet on the stairway as she descended to the street. For a moment he imagined her hurrying along in the rain toward Rooster's. He thought of breakfast for himself, but he was too tired. He was even too tired to read much in the book, and before Julia reached the front door of the little restaurant that was in what was once the lobby of the Sturdevant Apartments, he was asleep.

The book had fallen from his grasp onto the floor near the bed and lay open there. Though the drawn shades kept out the ever-strengthening morning light, the sounds of the coming day filtered through the open windows. Part of those sounds were made by the three big Harley Davidson motorcycles growling up the street until their sodden riders, eager for the first available refuge from the rain, turned them to the curb in front of Rooster's.

TWENTY FIVE

D own-hill from them, in the old graveyard, she had caught their voices on the wind as Mike and Cyrus sat talking on the narrow porch. She only had to send her self-tendrils upward to feel their moods as well. A last bit of thunder complained from across the mountain flanks southeast of town. The rain would cease soon. She would have to go. The thing she was in this day was not as swift or as able as the forms she sometimes used. Oh, but she was reluctant. In the casket below the sunken surface, a surface she had seen mounded new and fresh once, lay one that she had loved. Being here each day was the only respite she had from the task given her when she herself had ceased to be as she was before. She began to climb the hill, hidden in the dying storm and the abhorrent anguish of remembering.

She reached 89A just as the three bikers wheeled past, for a moment she felt of them. These fools saw themselves as hard men. She had known a few truly hard men. These fat bullies did not impress her. She would like to show them some authentic evil. But she must be careful. It was not for her to meddle with the people of this town, the town which had once been hers as it now was theirs. Still, she had taken liberties before.

She turned toward the apartment as she moved across the street and upward against the incline. He was there, alone. The stairs were empty. The thought that she had once used those same stairs touched her for an instant with a sadness that draped across her like a cloak, pulling heavily on her with the weight of regret and grief. But she fought off the feeling. She was weary of all that was sad. She would use those stairs this day, even though the thing she sometimes dwelled in, and was in now, would find that a hard task. She had other powers, but sometimes like a battery's energy they waned. She would be niggardly with them. They were needed for an unusual purpose this day. Using the stairs would be a good way to start the making of the dream he would dream for her to share. She would make sure. She would cause him to open that special door, to find the seam and go within.

A sudden gathering of rain and wind shielded her from view as the bikers revved their motors one final time in the glory of self-indulgence while wheeling in to park at the curb in front of Rooster's. And with an audible slushing, as if the entrance to the stairs had sucked her presence inward, rain and all, she entered the flatiron building.

Not in all the many days that had opened and closed like bright flowers in the gray and the rain and the smelter smoke of the old town, not since she had moved across the street to live with B.L., in that first year when she had come to Jerome, had she been inside the walls of what had once been her refuge. She had wanted to hear happy memories from those times, but such was denied. She moved upward in the damp of the rain she had brought with her. She could have sifted her senses through the closed door with little trouble, like a shadow into a shadow, but it was more than her senses that she wanted to be within. It was her entire self she wanted inside, the living death which fate had decreed she must bear, a death-life filled only with misery, a thing to be endured forever. Yes, she hissed in seething hatred, indeed, it had taken them into forever!

The door opened with the force she directed against it and she stood inside the little kitchen. Beyond, she saw the bed in the small, semi-darkened room. Then she saw the book on the floor.

Ah! It had been so long since she had seen it, so long since she had flung it away in the heat of her anger, anger that she must not allow herself to feel now.

She moved to the bed and looked down. She examined him as he slept. He would do. A soft cackle escaped her. He turned on his side. She moved away from the bed and stood before the mirror of the old dresser. It was the only piece of furniture in the little apartment that she knew. She had seen her image in it many times. But, oh, never like this. She twisted away in rage at what she saw now. It was one reason she avoided certain places in the old house on the hill, one reason she always hurried to pass windows which might reflect, puddles of water that might show herself to herself. Oh, she knew, she knew; but she could do nothing except bear it.

She hardened herself against these thoughts. She must do this thing she had come to do. Resolutely, she turned back to the glass. A dark, gray misting lay there; a shadow she had caused to form as a matrix for her intentions. One red orb that was her remaining eye lay within it. There were also things showing which she knew were bones. Something hung from them in ropy strings. That was her flesh. A chittering emanated from her that would have been sobbing once, long ago. Then she thought of what the man on the bed might be induced to dream. It helped to stop the lamentation, to quell the heavy regret that lay within her mind. With effort she created the illusion in her own thoughts which she would cause him to see in his. Three times she did it, for each time, on seeing what she had once been, the chittering that was her crying returned and the image in the mirror shattered into rotted flesh and yellowed bones shrouded in the mist through which the hellish red orb burned. Oh, God! Will this be the forever into which he sent us both? Was he not the reason for it all? The thought was accompanied by a gurgling, choking groan. It took all her strength to create the image of her youth in her mind and crawl onto the bottom half of the bed. He awoke briefly, and she caused him to see her dark and beautiful as she had once been; hair falling in waves of ebony, eyes as soft as the shadows of dusk, and a smile that radiated light.

Upon receiving this illusion in his mind, he believed himself to be dreaming, and fell backward where he would not wake until she deemed he could, and where he would indeed dream the dreams she so longed for him to dream. But, when the dreaming had finished, only she would remember them; she would lift them from his mind to treasure for herself, and she would return to them whenever the burden of her own torment became too much.

She moved upon him with a quiet cackling that he would recall as gentle laughter which came from the loveliest, most beautiful voice he had ever heard, nearly all that he would be allowed to keep of the illusion. Oh, she intended to make it a resplendent time for them both. She brushed his lips with the shredded remnants of hers in what he declared thereafter to be an angel's kiss, then his dreaming began.

TWENTY SIX

Regis Gilmour thought he was the master of the situation whenever in Annie's presence. But he was wrong.

"What does this do?" she asked him on one of her visits to the little booth. She peered into the mechanical workings of the projector as it whirred and turned, sending a ray of light into the darkened volume of the theatre, a shaft over the heads of the audience, something that she had often wondered about.

"Well," said Gilmour, moving up to stand near her as she examined the machine, "it simply makes the film run straight through its track as the reels turn. Then the light goes through here . . ."

She felt his hands on her body, then. It was only a slight brush, a quick touch. She ignored it, and he continued with his explanation. When she had finished looking, and they both moved away from the machine, he to a chair before a small table which he used as a desk, and she to stand peering into one corner at movie advertisements stacked there, depicting pictures of actors and actresses she found interesting, she said to him over her shoulder, "If I wanted you to touch me like that I would have told you so. I've seen sneaky moves made by creeps worse than you, Mister!"

At his table-desk, Gilmour lurched from the shock of her remarks. He was made temporarily speechless by them. He wondered at her ability to say such things. He was suddenly aware of fear moving across his mind. He hadn't meant to touch her. By-God he ought to have never let the little bitch into the projection booth in the first place!

But Gilmour knew he had to show another kind of face. He couldn't let her think he was angry with her. He had to get rid of her, yes. But he wanted her to leave with no reason to feel bad toward him.

"I . . . I didn't mean to offend you," he said, facing her with his hands turned palms up, shaking his head and looking directly at her out of wide, open eyes, "It was only a mistake, I didn't intend to brush against you."

Annie moved to the door and paused there, looking back at the little man through the muted light of the booth. "I'll be back," she said coldly, "and I want one of those posters in the corner there." She pointed at the playbills. Then she flounced a bit, hiking a hip toward him and running a hand down her side, "And you had better behave yourself."

*   *   *

Despite her request for the movie posters, Annie's interest in Regis Gilmour lay not in his connections with that far away, golden dreamland most girls her age knew as Hollywood, California. Her interest was not based on anything so grand. Unlike many in her circumstances who sought to overcome the past through fantasy and fame, Annie had no such need. Her perspective did not contain a good and a bad so that she might make comparisons. The only real good she had ever had in her life was embodied in her sister. And she secretly thought Madeleine was a fool. She was convinced that people were not like Madeleine believed them to be.

Annie delighted in all things filled with excitement. She had heard enough talk from Buenig and the community itself to know about some of the illegal things being done in the little town.

There was something about Gilmour which just didn't seem right to her, and it wasn't the bootlegging he was involved in.

While she did not understand the connection between the term and the illegal making and selling of whiskey, she knew what bootlegging was. And it wasn't that which made her curious about the man. Alcohol and the drunks it made of foolish women and even more foolish men had been a part of her life forever. No, the thing she found odd about Gilmour was that he didn't seem to be interested in her femininity. The thought had occurred to her that he might be one of those men who liked other men. But she dismissed that notion. She could usually tell one of those right away. No, whatever was different about this man was not that. But whatever it was, she saw finding out about it to be a challenge.

She was not ignorant of the many avenues men used to reach their single objective with women; all men, all women, all the time. Her sister had shielded her as much as she could, but Annie had been a long-enduring witness to the most basic associations between men and women; she knew more about sex at the age of fourteen than many adults. But it was the act of sex about which she was knowledgeable; she had no great depth of insight into the subject. Sadly, for her, such an early introduction to this part of life had engendered something less than an eagerness for it. She wasn't even abhorrent toward it, she was simply indifferent. Right now, her sexuality was a nuisance to her, for Madeleine was more and more adamant that she should stay in the apartment or go out only when it was appropriate and in a manner which was equally appropriate and only to such places as were also safe for young girls.

But Annie continued to defy her. Getting home after school, a high school now, meant being there alone. Both B.L. and Madeleine were still at work. Of course she should have obeyed her sister. But as precocious as she was in some ways, she was still a child in others. And like a child, she was often drawn to the glitter instead of the substance of things.

The center of Jerome attracted her with its saloons, its restaurants, and its movie houses; the Fountain where she had friends, and the Royal, the theatre which showed the new talking films and which had a manager who had forbidden her to come back after she had been discovered prowling in the office area. Annie had only been exercising her curiosity, and intended no harm. The edict by the manager did not bother her greatly; she was still able to sneak in when she wanted to. Then, there were the many places of prostitution. Everything interested her, and for over a year she had been known by the people who lived and worked in that part of town.

One of these, a middle-aged black piano player, a woman named DeNelle, was especially concerned about Annie's visits to that section of town. DeNelle played the piano at the Fountain. Her talented fingers on the old upright, in a darkened corner near the big screen, added drama to the silent films shown there. She had taken no notice of the girl, whom she knew was called Annie, until after Annie had visited the projection booth again. DeNelle then accosted the little Irish projectionist.

"You might be doin' the wrong thing by havin' that kid in here," she said to Gilmour as they passed each other in the theatre one day.

The little man looked at her for a moment before replying. He knew he must make sure his answer was acceptable. He wanted no suspicious eyes and ears attuned to anything he was doing. "You are certainly correct," he said, "but she just keeps coming back. The first time she came, I showed her how things worked with the machine. I thought that would be the end of it when she left, but then she returned. She's a bit of a nuisance."

"Tell you what," said DeNelle, "nex' time she comes in, send her to me."

At first, Gilmour felt anger surge within him at the impudence the girl had displayed. It took him some time, but he eventually learned all he needed to know about her. He had deduced from her behavior that she was unusual. Gilmour was no stranger to disturbed children. He had been one himself. Poverty and hard times stood out all over the girl. Her name was Annie. Well, he had plans for little miss Annie. He would be ready the next time she came calling.

*   *   *

Waldon sat across from Gilmour and looked at him over steepled fingers, his chin resting on his two thumbs. He had long-since learned that Gilmour worked at the Fountain theatre. It had been with Waldon's help that Gilmour had been able to convince the owners of the theatre to allow him the use of the old cellar. Gilmour had agreed to pay good money for the space, but had never divulged his real reason for wanting it. The contract that Waldon helped Gilmour draw up detailed his leasing of the premises as being for the purpose of storage. Looking at Gilmour on the other side of his desk, Waldon realized for the first time that he resented the little red-haired man. Gilmour had just introduced a proposal which Waldon did not find welcome.

"I told you when we started this thing that I didn't operate that way," he said to Gilmour.

Regis Gilmour smiled and turned his head aside, holding up his two empty hands as if waiting to catch something. "Mister Waldon," he implored, "the man is an irritant. He is undermining me with the forces who run this town. We gotta' begin to discredit him, make him look like a bum."

Harry Waldon took a deep breath and exhaled slowly. His lips were compressed and he shook his head from side to side. "It'll take more than a good beating to make B.L. Buenig look like a bum," he said.

"We'll dump him in some garbage near the cribs, pour whiskey all over him," Gilmour countered.

The two men looked at each other in silence. Waldon sat back in his chair and rubbed his eyes against the knuckles of both hands. "I'm telling you," he said, "it won't shock this town to know that Bartholomew Buenig visits the whores from time to time."

"Hell," Gilmour said, leaning back himself and smiling,

"Mister Waldon, that's only for starters. When we get through with him, the man will be ruined in this town."

Taking another deep breath, Waldon replied, "I just don't see how roughing him up can help us in any way."

Gilmour lifted his open hands again, "Come on, Mister Waldon, do I want to do any of this? I mean, if a polite note would get the man to leave us alone I'd write it and deliver it myself. My boys will slap him around a bit and leave him looking like some drunk who got kicked out of a whore house and told to go home to his wife. He'll look stupid, not so hot after all."

Again, Waldon's expression showed that he wasn't impressed with the idea. Gilmour stopped smiling, then looked straight into Waldon's eyes, "Mister Waldon, we're makin' money. You'll be able to get a new car next time. Maybe one of them big Packards. Hey, we gotta' do this. Think what might happen if he learns where we're storin' the stuff."

Waldon scowled, "It's not my fault you chose that old mine shaft."

"Yeah, well at the time I thought it might belong to the mine you're workin' for."

"Well, it doesn't," said Waldon, "and there's nothing I can do about it."

Gilmour edged forward, extending one hand to rest on the smooth surface of Waldon's desk. "That's why this is a necessary thing which we have to do. Look, we'll let the man know that he's not messin' with a bunch of dummies."

Waldon shook his head to show his skepticism, "When do you intend to do this?" he asked.

"When the opportunity arises," said Gilmour, "We have to wait till he's in the right place at the right time; can't go up to his apartment an' knock on the door, y'know."

"No, you can't," said Waldon, sitting straight in his chair and taking another deep breath. Then he looked with resolution into Gilmour's eyes, "And you won't, "he said quietly, "Not until I give you the go-ahead. It's either that or I'm out of the entire thing."

*   *   *

It was hard for Gilmour to accept the fact that Waldon had refused to agree to take action against Buenig. But he wasn't finished. He intended to work on Waldon until he did agree to it. As for the girl, Annie, her connection with Buenig made her important, now. He allowed himself to get over his anger toward her. When she came back, he would give her some items of movie paraphernalia he would procure for her. That she was a little rebel, a self-encased narcissist, he knew. She had told him that she had no friends at school, no friends her own age. From the talk around that part of town, she ran the streets like some rag-tag orphan with no parental supervision. She was a kid out of place for sure.

On the day that she did once more pay him a visit, as he had been sure she would, instead of sending her away, he let her in the booth. "You know," he said to her, "that lady who plays the piano told me to have you see her the next time you came here. Are you in some kind of trouble?"

Ignoring the question, Annie said, "My sister's stand-in for a husband says you are a bootlegger." She watched as her words seemed to hit the little Irishman with tangible force.

Gilmour's face reddened, and for a moment he could not speak. He turned away from her until he could gather himself. When he did look at her again, he spoke with a will to control himself that almost broke. But he managed to deny her accusation.

She laughed at him.

"How old are you, girl?" he asked, holding his anger in check with great difficulty.

"I'm fourteen."

TWENTY SEVEN

I t was to be the second party Harry Waldon had thrown in the big house on Hill Street since he had gained the right to occupy the place. Light streamed from all windows and doors. Outside, the weather had cooperated as well. It was a beautiful evening. Even the lingering stench of smelter smoke did not seem to detract from the balmy romanticism of the stars in the sky or the lights from other places in town seemingly flung against the dark mountainside like so many diamonds.

The occasion this time was, like the first, a celebration of achievement. The hospital project was on schedule. This was an important thing for the people of the little town. In a little less than two years, by 1927 at the latest, theirs would be on its way to being the best and most modern hospital in the entire state. And it would rank with the very best in the whole southwest. He intended to take as much credit for this as he could.

He had invited everyone who had influence in the town and the general area. The guest list contained only names of the elite. Some had been asked to come because of their money. Others had been invited due to their position in the town's hierarchy of power. All were important to the leadership of Jerome. But as he stood in the large front room, he could see that, though the house was crowded, and people walked along its halls and in and out of its rooms in conversational liquidity, drinks in their hands, affability on their faces, some of the people he had hoped to see there were not present.

B.L. was there, and so was Madeleine. And he saw that they had brought along Madeleine's young sister. They had just entered, had probably walked up from town.

For a moment he wondered what a walk on such an evening with Madeleine might be like.

His mind played with the possibilities suggested by this thought as he approached Buenig and offered his hand. He ceased thinking of Madeleine long enough to steel himself so as not to show the least trace of his former subservience as he and Buenig shook hands. Nor did he perceive anything but good humor and good will from his one-time boss. Madeleine's eyes told him that she remembered her first visit to the house. He smiled brightly at her and then turned his attention to her sister, giving the young girl the standard adult-to-child smile of condescension, not sure whether to shake her hand or pat her on the head. But as he looked at her, his smile changed slightly, and he offered his hand. She took it, smiling back at him.

"This is Mr. Harold Waldon, Annabelle," said Madeleine, introducing them.

The girl gave his hand a faint squeeze and said, "Hello, Mr. Waldon."

Madeleine was pleased with Annie's conduct. "I hope you don't mind, Mr. Waldon," she said, "I so hate to leave her alone in the rooms on such a wonderful evening."

Noticing that B.L. was watching him with what seemed to be amusement, Waldon looked away from the big man, then, allowing his eyes to flick quickly into a far corner of the room before looking once again at the girl, and finally fastening his gaze on Madeleine's face, he said, "Of course, I don't mind at all. In fact, I'm really delighted that she's here. Welcome to my home," and he paused before adding, "for the second time." Then, to B.L., as if he needed something more familiar and ordinary after all that, he said in a voice a little too loud, "Good to see you, B.L., just ask for anything you can't find." And with one final smile at Madeleine and Annie, he slipped into the crowd and disappeared into its low hum of voices, its laughter and the shuffling of feet against the quiet sounds of violins and guitars from the small group of musicians he had hired.

It still might be a wonderful party, Waldon thought as he eased quietly from room to room and level to level of the big house that, by Jerome's standards, was indeed a mansion.

An hour later, he felt as if his optimism for the success of the night's events was on target. He stood on the big staircase in the front room and called on everyone to listen to a few words he had to say. He was delighted to see his guests respond quickly to his request. They turned friendly faces toward him and the room became silent. He welcomed one and all and then began his report on the hospital project.

There was applause at the end of his little speech. Several people made comments that carried above the returning hum of renewed conversation. All of the remarks were in his favor. He glowed as he stood above them on the stairs.

Finally, the musicians once more made their music and individuals began to walk away, while the usual groups formed. Most were simply for the purpose of socializing—which was what parties were for, but a few were for more than that.

Like all such gatherings in such little towns, the men who truly ran things, not those appointed to a particular office necessarily, or those who held down certain jobs and thus were supposedly responsible for outcomes related to these positions, but men who actually caused things to move one way or the other in the town, men who owned interest in banks, who controlled or owned businesses, or held mortgages and financial notes, men who could make or break other men, these men gathered to talk over glasses filled with ice and illegal whiskey, and to use tobacco in all of its forms—depending on their individual habits. They talked about many things, but they talked always about one thing—money. And they did so for only one reason—power.

Waldon was invited into some of these conversational circles, while others seemed to recede in volume as he approached. But he did arrive on the fringes of one little circle before the person talking knew he was at his elbow, and therefore he was able to hear all of what was being said. The subject was clearly illegal whiskey and it was in company with his own name. There was a quick look over the shoulder from the man who had made the remarks, and a red face and a stoic hunching of the man's body as Waldon tried a clever phrase intended to soften the moment and get them both off the hook.

But despite Waldon's smile and discreet departure from the circle, he was embarrassed. He was also furious, for B.L. Buenig had been one of the men in the group. What in hell was wrong with the man, he thought as he hurried away. He, Harold Waldon, was not the only one involved in the business of illegal distribution of booze. In this godforsaken whore infested hell on the side of the bleak mountain, men killed each other over the slightest thing. Even the lawmen themselves usually did nothing about the people they knew who ran gambling dens, sold bootleg whiskey, or supplied opium to the Chinese or anybody else who wanted it. And he knew all about the argument that it wasn't the whiskey or the drug or the gambling itself which the little town's leaders were against. But why was his name a part of the talk in the first place? Was Gilmour doing something he was not aware of? Dammit, if he was, he'd pull out of the whole damned thing and leave the little bastard to get by the best he could!

But aside from the aggravation he felt at the talk he'd overheard, the single thing that ran through the evening for Waldon, like a thread in a tapestry, was the presence of Madeleine. Ah, she was as beautiful as he had ever seen her. He had kept up with her whereabouts since that first time they had met. He knew she was B.L. Buenig's woman. He knew they lived, she and her sister, with Buenig in the Sturdevant Apartment House on Main Street.

But he couldn't keep himself from imagining her in the house on Hill Street, and when the evening stretched itself into later hours, he made sure to be near as B.L. guided Madeleine, along with the young girl, to the front door. Waldon went through it with them, and walked them out toward the curb.

It was a beautiful night for looking at the sky, a summer night. Around them, however, lay the stench of the smelter fumes, even though they came from the valley several miles below. Still, it was better living there on the side of the mountain than it had been before the smelter was moved to the new town of Clarkdale in 1915.

Waldon had tried to beautify the grounds around the big house. On the hillside, perched above the remainder of the town, there was little spare earth for lawns or gardens. But his house had space for that purpose. Roses grew below windows and along walls—in a perpetual state of death, as his housekeeper often put it. There was a small but lovely fenced in garden; a place he had always thought would make a perfect private lounging area. In addition, he had a sizeable back yard and an area of grass with a tree growing from it at one corner of the house. The Cadillac sat at the edge of this lawn.

Gesturing toward the car as he walked beside them toward the street, he said to B.L., as well as to Madeleine and her young sister, "I intend to build a garage there, soon, won't have to worry about freezing the engine block during the winters then, draining the water and all that." Then, suddenly struck with an idea, he added quickly, "Oh, say, let me drive you all home in the car."

B.L. grinned into the darkness. "No," he said, "that would be too much trouble."

"But it would be no trouble at all, B.L., please allow me."

In a voice as soft as starlight, Madeleine said, "No, Mister Waldon . . ."

He interrupted her, "Oh, do please call me Harry."

Continuing as if she had not heard his request, she said, "We like to walk on pleasant evenings such as this."

He was disappointed that she had not used his familiar, first name, but he didn't show it as he asked, "Have you ever ridden in a Cadillac? It is a one-of-a-kind experience." He, too, smiled into the darkness.

They had come to the end of the walkway, now, and they all stopped. Buenig turned toward the big house where light and sound indicated activity still going on. He lifted his chin, nodding in that direction, and said, "You've got a party to attend to, Harold. Better see to your other guests. We'll be fine." And he turned away from Waldon and the house. The three of them then began walking down the street.

Waldon watched as they walked away into the soft shades of the evening. Buenig's large frame was a darker bit of darkness beside Madeleine's. The girl walked to the right, separated from the man and woman. Waldon felt envy then. Tonight was supposed to have been his time to crow. And he had. Yes, indeed. but somehow, the big man who had once made him feel small and inadequate, simply by being who he was, had done it again.

TWENTY EIGHT

It was another evening, one when B.L. saw a need to be away from the two sisters. He had taken to walking more than usual. It was because of Annabelle. He saw through her. She knew it and knew that he knew. It was a situation which made it simply easier for him to get up and declare himself off for a walk and maybe a drink somewhere. He never lied. No point in that. Neither did he make excuses—for himself or for them. Annie was what she was. He had told Madeleine about her once. If Madeleine could not see any value in what he had said, then it was her loss. There was a man somewhere, maybe several men, waiting to fall victim in some way to Annie. He was damned if he was going to be that man. She had at first pleaded with him out of the depths of those great, green eyes. But he would not become her ally against the rules Madeleine had set for her. Then she had tried other tactics. He wondered at how much she understood about what she was doing. When he hadn't responded to her flirtations, she grew hard toward him. Yet, Madeleine could see none of it. He had spoken his piece once. He would say no more.

He decided this night to see an old friend, one he had taken leave of since he and Madeleine had become a pair. He walked up Main toward the crest of the hill where Jerome Avenue ended at the corner occupied by the Fashion Saloon. He thought he might have a drink there and then go on down to Becky's place.

As usual, the Fashion was full. He walked quietly in and took a seat at one end of the first of three long bars in the place. The bartender knew him, and he leaned toward him to ask what his pleasure might be.

"Dammit, Rafe," said Buenig, feeling the inside pocket of his coat for the little flask he always carried, "I don't have a drop on me, so that little set-up you are about to offer me won't do me a lot of good."

The man looked quickly around, then said, "Never mind, Mister Buenig, you just let me know what you want in it and when you drink it, don't be surprised."

"Why, then, Rafe, my friend, I'll have plain water, with a piece or two of ice, and whatever goes well with it."

He accepted the glass from the bartender thinking that he had also come off without the pistol he never failed to slip into the same pocket with the whiskey flask. That little girl and her shenanigans certainly had thrown him off. But what the hell, he rationalized, he had his whiskey anyway, and he could get along without the little .32 for at least one evening on the town.

As he enjoyed his whiskey and water, B.L. looked amiably around at the crowd through the tobacco smoke. The noise of a hundred conversations and the clink of glasses splashed against the backdrop of the piano. He knew many of the men there. He nodded at some of them as their eyes met. They all returned the courtesy. There were some strangers in the place. There always were a few. He looked them over casually and let his mind and his eyes rest on other things. There were a few women present aside from the whores employed to work the crowd for drinks. Some of these were there for dinner, which would be served in the back rooms. He smiled and thought of women in general. The world would be a poor place without them. Tonight he would see Becky. The idea of sleeping with her surfaced briefly in his thoughts, but, no, he wouldn't do that. And she wouldn't ask why, either. They both knew he did not play the game that way. But he sure as hell would talk and enjoy her company.

He finished his drink and set the glass on the bar, sent a thank-you look toward the bartender, left some money near the empty glass, and eased his large frame between the tables as he made his way toward the back of the saloon and the side entrance there. Behind him, two men observed his departure.

"He goin' downstairs or what?" queried one.

"Naw, looks like he's headed for the side door. Yeah, there he goes, maybe goin' down to the cribs."

"The boss said he don't see them whores no more."

"Well," said the other, with some irritation, "they ain't much down that-a-way except whores, now is they?"

B.L. walked casually east on Jerome Avenue, past the American Café which was owned and operated by a Chinaman. He chuckled inwardly at the irony. At the corner, he skipped lightly down from the sidewalk, which was unusually high there, and drifted to the other side of the street as he progressed south on Hull the short distance to First Avenue. He remembered with humor the remark Becky had made about working out of her home. He hoped she was not busy when he walked into the little front parlor she kept lighted so that the light could be seen from the street, but not be too revealing of who might walk up her short path of bricks and knock on the door. If she was busy in one of the back rooms, the person knew to simply enter and wait. Although, if the waiting room was already occupied, most just turned and stood somewhere in the shadows on the street or left the area and returned later. And if Becky had contracted with a customer for an entire evening of pleasure, one which usually ran into a breakfast of eggs, bacon, and the "Best biscuits a whore could cook," to use her own phrase, the little front parlor would be dark. There would be no light in it, dim or otherwise, and whoever had approached the door would know to come back the next day.

At First Avenue he turned and headed toward Rich Street, now only a block away. Nearing Becky's house, he was pleased to see the light in the little front room. He walked up the brick path and knocked on the door. He could see through the window that there was no one waiting. He was just opening the door to walk inside when Becky herself came into the room from the back of the house.

*   *   *

It was three hours later that Buenig put his coffee cup down in Becky's kitchen and said, "I've kept you long enough."

She looked at him fondly and replied, "B.L., it has been good having you. My goodness, get away from that woman more often."

He shook his head, looked briefly down at the clean tablecloth on the small table and then back at her, his lips compressed into a thin line that barely turned up at one corner.

"It isn't her, Becky, it's that sister of hers. Damn, she's a bit to handle."

"I know, Honey," said the woman across from him, returning his wry expression with a grim smile of her own. "I've seen her sashaying her little self all over this part of town. She's goin' to cause somebody a lot of trouble someday. That big sister of hers needs to see the truth."

"Well," he said, "that's not likely to happen. She thinks all the world is in that girl."

Becky directed her eyes downward for a moment. When she lifted her head, B.L. was peering at her with a serious expression on his face. "What is it?" he asked.

His friend faced him then with a touch of sympathy in her smile. She put a hand on his forearm where it rested on the small table. "It's just that I hear stories, that's all. If I had to guess, I'd say that girl is keeping some very bad company."

They talked for another hour. Then, with a heavy groan that brought a quick flash of humor to both their faces, he lifted himself and declared the visit over. She followed him quietly to the front of the house. At the door, he gave her a friendly goodnight kiss.

"Thanks for retaining me for the entire evening," she said, "I can use the rest—either that or the money." They both smiled at the joke. He turned then and walked into the dark.

*   *   *

Things had quieted considerably in town since B.L. had left his own apartment. The streets were almost empty. Most of the hell-raisers were either in their own bunks or sitting in the corner of a bar. And the harlots had taken the edge off the collective need of the off-duty shift. Now, only a few stragglers were out and about.

Still, he decided it would be best to take another route back to the apartment house. The lighting along the way would not be as good but the likelihood of meeting anyone would be less. Absently, his hand brushed against the pocket where he usually carried the .32. Ah, hell, he thought, don't wish for trouble.

It was just as he was about to cross Hull and head west on First Avenue that they stepped out of the darkness to face him. He didn't bother to speak to either of them. He knew immediately what situation he was in. He hit the nearest one with a straight left directly on the point of the chin, knocking him momentarily senseless. But he took a blow himself from the other one at the same time. It sent him reeling out of the shadows and into the street. He shook his head to clear it and tried to hold to his feet. But he couldn't. He sprawled in a heap near the center of the street. Both of them leaped onto him then.

He moved as best he could to avoid the blows and regain his standing position. One of them was hitting him with his fists, the other one used a club. It was the club that had sent him into the street. As he rolled up to rest on his knees, he reached out to the legs in front of him and pulled one of the men down to the pavement. He could feel fists on the back of his head and his neck. Good, he thought, he had the one with the club, he knew he must not let him get back up. He pulled the struggling man toward him and hit him hard in the middle of his face. He hit him again. Suddenly, he felt tired. He knew he had to get it over with quickly.

Again he hit the man and he heard the wooden club fall to the street's cobbled surface. He released his assailant and stood wearily, all the while with the other man raining blows against his back. Then B.L. turned to face that one. But he could not see well, blood ran into his eyes from the gash made on his head from the first blow of the club. And while he stood swaying in the dim illumination of the street light on the corner, the other thug picked up the club dropped by his partner and, leaping at the big man like a skinny hound at a bear it has cornered, hit him a smashing blow on the forehead.

Buenig fell with his head lying toward the intersection, a matter of only twenty feet or so away along the narrow street. The attacker walked to him and struck him viciously in his open and slack-jawed mouth with the club. The man's partner, recovered now from the beating he had received from Buenig's fists, staggered over to where the big man lay and drove a thin-bladed knife into his chest. Then, after peering around into the darkness, he began to rifle Buenig's pockets.

"Boss said make it look like a robbery," he choked, fighting to regain his wind.

"Feel his Goddamned pulse," said the man holding the club, breathing heavily himself from the exertion of the struggle, "We shoulda' shot the bastard 'stead of fightin' him like that. Noise or no damned noise. He nearly broke my Goddamned jaw!"

"Shut up," gasped his partner, ignoring the order, "He busted my nose. We're lucky ain't nobody here what seen us. Now let's git!"

With that, the two thugs hurried away. Behind them, his head twisted at an angle because of the way it had landed against the curb, half of his lower teeth shattered due to the final blow of the club, B.L. Buenig lay dead, his blood running from him in a dark rivulet. There had been no need for the knife, his neck was broken. One of his teeth had dropped into a crack in the stone paving and would never be found.

*   *   *

The investigation was brief, and there was no autopsy, other than a quick external examination. Autopsies were invasive, and not always seen as necessary. And in small towns like Jerome, they were often left out of the process on the basis of clear and decisive evidence. The evidence was plentiful as well as quite plain. Witnesses had seen B.L. at the bar in the Fashion Saloon earlier in the evening. His mistress had said he had decided to go out for a walk and to visit an old friend. That "old friend" had given the time of his departure from her home on Rich St. It was a common case of robbery. The viciousness of it was explained by the facts surrounding B.L. himself; he made good money, he was powerful, he had enemies, and anyone who knew him would guess that he had probably fought like a tiger.

There had been two men. The clues for that were obvious: there were two weapons, a bludgeon of some kind and a knife. There was nothing to lead the sheriff and his deputies to conclude anything more than that. What had happened to Mr. Buenig happened with some frequency in Jerome, though usually more to common folk. Buenig was known to roam the streets at night on his jaunts, as he himself called them. He was an uncommon man in more than one way.

The headlines in the Valley Copper News read: Little Daisy Top Man Found Dead in Red-Light District. It was calculated to cause readers to think the mine's owner, J. Douglas, had met foul play, but subsequent study soon brought Buenig's name to light. Still, he was also a top man in the town, and at the mine, and news of his death was shocking.

TWENTY NINE

Father Jovan Kilryc Katichovic had not minded the transfer all the way from Chicago to the little town in Arizona. To him it was God's will. He had failed once before. He ascribed it to his youth, although he was well past thirty when he came to the priesthood. He vowed not to fail again.

Father Katichovic had difficulty in seeing all things the same way the Holy Roman Catholic Church saw them. He knew this about himself. He had promised himself to hold hard to the Church's views, as an iron rod would hold when placed somewhere for that purpose. He would keep his mind clear of any thoughts or inclinations which might cause him to become subversive.

It was a harsh word, subversive. He had never thought of himself as being that way. But it was what Father Mason, his assigned counselor in Chicago, after the trouble, had said he was.

"Jovan," he had said softly, for he was sympathetic with his younger colleague, "when you do these things or say these words, you are undermining the work of the Church itself, you are being subversive."

When Father Katichovic had replied that he had not intended to do anything bad, Father Mason said that it did not matter what his intentions were. One kept confessions confidential, one acted as a refuge for sinners. One was, afterall, a representative of the Church and not one's own personal views. And he added, anyway, one's views ought not to run counter to those of the Church.

Father Katichovic knew this already. It was his special burden. But he had promised himself that he would succeed in Jerome. He would not be subversive. Still, he thought it strange that men who believed in God and his wrath would sin and ask his forgiveness time after time. It seemed somehow to abet evil and do nothing for those they had sinned against.

But the years settled Father K., as he came to be called, and in time he developed an ability to tolerate this constant sinning and asking for forgiveness that the people seemed to be better at than they were at learning to become righteous. He came to know where many of the bootleg stills were in Jerome and the surrounding area. And the sexual transgressions he had been told about during confessions were too many to count; if he had wished to count them, which he certainly did not. He even knew the answer to an unsolved murder.

It lay heavy with him, all the sin. He wanted to be rid of it. He had almost turned the man in who had confessed responsibility for the murder. He would have if the man had not convinced him that it was accidental, that he had never intended for anyone to die.

Father K. had considered it for a very long time. The dead man had no relatives in Jerome. He himself was a sinner of some proportions. The guilty man was in similar circumstances. In the end, Father K held to the tenet that a plea to the Church for forgiveness was not something to run to the nearest police station with. But it was difficult for him. He urged the man to confess to the authorities. The man said he would consider it, but he never did confess.

Other men came to confession as if they were vegetable peddlers whose carts were filled with rotten produce which they wanted to off-load in order to have an empty cargo bed when next the opportunity came to sin. Father K. always pleaded with them to stop their sinful activities before greater responsibilities were engendered. Often, young girls came to him. They usually told him what he expected to hear; it began with flirtation, then proceeded to more than that. It always ended one way, with pregnancy. It meant an early life of motherhood, perhaps drudgery and more abuse.

Sometimes, providence took care of things for everybody involved. God worked in his own way. One day the girl was there, the next she was gone. Silence, deep and committed silence made an end, a finality of the entire thing. He had always thought it a tragedy that something as precious as the life of a young and beautiful girl could be deemed less important than the reputation and well-being of the man who had fouled her for a few moments of pleasure. But it was often so among the societies of men. Father K.'s only refuge from the pain of this fact lay in another; the end of one chapter in a life often meant the beginning of a new chapter in the life of someone else. There was a price for all to pay.

That was it, wasn't it? At least for Jovan Kilryc Katichovic it was. In the end, the sins of men were totalled and the price was paid. This absolute was as true for life as was the inexorable movement of the sun across the sky; it was a truth underlined for him every time he gave the last rites to a striken miner on the physician's table. It was in the sound the handfuls of dirt made as they struck the casket waiting in the grave before being covered forever.

It was as a doorman, really, that a priest functioned; baptism, marriage, death, and salvation—one hoped. And along the way, forgiveness for a door opened which should always be kept closed. Opened once and then closed forever; this was understood, but opened again and again? Ah, this too was to be tolerated. But it was difficult for him.

*   *   *

Father K. stood looking down on the town from the window high on the side of the old church. It was early evening. Jerome had endured a decrease in mine operations over the past four years.

Only this year, in 1935, had normal mining activities resumed. But there was not the same number of men in the town that ordinarily manned the three shifts the mines ran, and only two shifts were in place now.

It was that time after a shift change when most of the men, tired from their long hours of work, were sleeping, or resting in some manner, and so, the streets were not filled with people.

Father K. could see a few people walking along Main Street, in the area of the saloons and the other night places. Then, at the corner of Giroux and 89A, the roadster came into view. Oh, yes, he had seen it once or twice before. He knew where it went in town.

He turned from the window and moved slowly out of the room. Maybe some good would come from it afterall. It had grown cold in his mind. All the years had helped to make it so. Still, he could resurrect it if he wished.

But he did not wish. Instead, he would prepare for the rest of the evening; a bit of something to eat perhaps, some study, and then to bed. His housekeeper and the man who assisted her in seeing to his needs had long since retired to their own quarters. But he didn't mind that he would have to see to his late snack himself. He was at home.

He had been in this parish now for twenty years. Occasionally he had a letter from friends in other places. A few times he had heard from Father Mason. It had been a while now since he had felt a need or a desire to leave Jerome. It had become his town, his place. The people were his people. Here, he was finally growing old.

He had his small portion of food and then sat in his favorite chair and began to read. It was something in a news magazine about the so-called responsibilities of Catholicism in regard to world-wide freedoms. After a few minutes of reading, his head fell forward and he slept.

Father K. had been asleep for over two hours when, beyond the walls of the rectory, that wooden section built against the brick wall of the church which served as a residence for the priest and his attendants, thunder rolled. In minutes the rain came. It fell heavily for half an hour before reducing itself to a long, steady drizzle. He tried to fight the urge, but eventually it won, and he got to his feet with some effort, put aside the material he had been reading before he had fallen asleep, and walked out of the room toward the front of the church, which was edged by Giroux Street.

He stood on the small front porch of the rectory, where he would be shielded from the wet, and looked into the night. It was what he considered the best kind of night, cool and rainy. He loved the sound of the rain, the feel of it, and best of all, the smell of it. He imagined himself surrounded by a great curtain of anonymity as he stood within the passage of the storm. He felt at peace during rainy nights such as this one.

He noticed that the rain had driven most people inside. There were cars parked along the streets, and a handful of people walked the sidewalks, but for the most part the town was quiet.

Suddenly, a gust of wind swept up the street and he was momentarily chilled. It hadn't been as cold as it normally was at this time of year, but the sharp wind brought reality with it; this was a winter night.

He was about to turn and go back inside, even though he didn't really want to, when a pair of headlights cut around the corner of the Delacroix apartment house and sent their rain-diffused beams along the incline of Giroux.

The big car climbed the street in low gear, its painted contours gleaming darkly in the rain. Father K. strained his eyes to see if the man in the white suit was behind the wheel, but he could not be sure if he was or wasn't. The windows of the car were up. He heard the deep rumble of the motor as the car passed. The rain drops made a tattering sound against the tightly stretched canvas of the top. He knew where it would eventually go. While he waited and listened, the sound of its motor confirmed this. He stood for a few moments in thought and then turned and went inside.

*   *   *

She had driven down the far side of the mountain, then back up and once more into Jerome, more than thirty miles. It was good that it was raining. It had begun to rain as she wound her way down from the crest of the mountain and into the tight turns that offered security in their rock walls to the left and guaranteed death on the right; plummeting there, sometimes, for nearly a thousand feet.

The La Salle coasted along with the big motor hardly whispering. It was the tires which made the greatest sound. They growled against the granite of the roadbed. An occasional loud pop interrupted the steady noise they made as a rock, caught just right between the rubber and the road, was propelled like a bullet, either against something to the left of the heavy machine or into the blank nothingness within the deep canyons to the right. But she did not care about these sounds. Only the rain falling on the tightly stretched canvas roof, and the whine of the gear box below the smooth hush of the engine were real to her.

Her mind was firm against the memories engendered by the night and this road. She watched the headlights strive to penetrate the attacking sheets of rain. The road looped and descended before her. The car, like a mechanical cat, seemed to leap and bound in effortless quiet after it, hurrying along the path revealed by the headlights.

She concentrated hard, holding the steering wheel with both hands while keeping her eyes and mind steady against the slippery surface of the road. Then, as the La Salle turned another curve, she saw the lights of the town. She pushed against the brake pedal, slowing the big car, then shoved in the clutch pedal and with effort shifted into a lower gear. The La Salle lurched as she let out the clutch, but the motor caught itself and continued smoothly on, past the final turn and into town. She did not want to drive too slowly in a high gear, to lug it down. She had already done that once this evening.

She encountered no other cars on this end of town. Looking ahead, with the aid of her own headlights and the lights from houses along the street, she could see that the sidewalks were nearly empty of people. She drove on toward the downtown section where she saw with relief that the brightness of the lights there was somewhat diminished by the rainfall. But the few lights on in the Delacroix apartments seemed garish. It was because she had to pass so near to them, she knew. It was only her fear working against her, but she cringed anyway as they loomed toward her.

The heavy roadster seemed to have a mind of its own. It rolled slowly and powerfully onward. She turned into Giroux and, with only a slight acknowledgement of the effort, the big in-line eight maintained speed as the car climbed the cobbled surface of the street toward the crest of the hill, where it would turn to its left and then back to its right at Hill Street where it would roll quietly along until it arrived at the garage once meant for another machine, as elegant in its time as the La Salle was now.

As the car passed the church, she noticed the dark figure standing on the little porch of the rectory. If he was the only one aware of the plum colored roadster's whereabouts on this rainy night, she needn't worry.

THIRTY

G oing inside with the rain still calling to him, Father K. could not keep the memory of another such night out of his mind. He tried to, but it was relentless. Like a tired soul seeking entrance as protection from the forces of sin and damnation, the memory knocked and he, though reluctantly, allowed it in.

Only she had known for certain what had happened. They, the rest of them in the town, had only conjecture to lead them. But it was not hard, at least for the greater part of it, it wasn't. The car had gone over the side. That was simple enough. And it was irrefutable. For there the thing hung at least two hundred feet down, a great gob of metal dangling from a naturally formed granite hook that held it there for them all to see, goggling and crowding each other up there on the road in the rain and the dark and the flashlights of the police.

The firemen and the ambulance people were there too. So was a wrecker truck. The police shouted at the people to stand back and let the firemen work. It was necessary to somehow get a cable onto the car so it could be winched up to the road. One policeman, the Sheriff, actually, pulled his revolver and held it above his head so it could be seen.

"By-damn you all to hell!" he bellowed, "If you don't get the hell back so these men can do their jobs, I'll shoot any man who refuses to move!" And he fired the .45 double-action three times in a row. Its crashing sound and the red streaks of fire that leapt from its muzzle did get the crowd's attention, and people began to slowly move back from the edge of the road where the canyon dropped off into eight hundred feet of ebon space; a hole that might, for all that were there could tell, and certainly for the car and anyone in it, have gone on forever.

The big Cadillac's tire marks could be seen in the mud at the edge of the road. The car had gone right through the wooden guard rail; which meant the driver had not known the car was headed for the abyss and had failed to apply the brakes, which allowed the vehicle to sail smoothly over the lip of the cliff and out into empty space at a high rate of speed. Perhaps the rain and the night had confused the driver, had masked the road somehow, had tricked the mind into thinking the curve was somewhere ahead and not where it was, until it was too late; and then came the realization that the car was going too fast and that the dreaded drop-off was what was indeed being illuminated by the weak, yellow light of the headlights, and that only death could be the result of it all.

They knew it was the Cadillac. A dozen lights probed the rain and the dark to finally brush against its metal body. Even at two hundred feet down it could be recognized for what it was. The ribbing of the top had been flattened, the cloth ripped to pieces. It draped from the machine like some dark flag of distress, so that when a beam of light touched it, if the wind happened to also catch it at that moment, it moved like a living thing; a hideous illusion abetted by the excitement of the noise and the night and the knowledge of disaster that everyone there felt.

The big machine had flown out and over the cliff like an element of some Rube-Goldberg contraption and had sailed downward in an uninterrupted arc until one of its still-spinning wheels caught at a lip of rock and the nearly two tons of steel that made up the car began to tumble end for end; the sides of the cliff a hundred feet down were just close enough to make contact with the top which brushed past at thirty-two feet per second per second. The cloth top was ripped from its fastenings, and then the bottom of the car came around and the wheels rolled for a tenth of a second along the face of the cliff as they were designed to do before another projection of granite sent the whole thing off to the side, so that it began to rotate along its axis as well as turn in the air nose to tail.

Of course, none of the people could know that, standing on the road looking down at the car hanging by something on the underside of its rear end, probably its axle or more probably a piece of the frame itself. They could only see that it had come to rest after an obvious flight over the cliff. But they knew that very cliff themselves, had driven or ridden along the road on its top, and had looked into the emptiness there. They could imagine what had happened when the car went over the side. Many of them had already made the same imaginary flight innumerable times before, shuddering while they saw it all happening in their mind, and not quite believing it at first when they came back to reality and knew they were safe; the horror of it, real or illusory, was too much to accept.

"Get that chain wrapped around something good enough to hold her!" This from between hands cupped together to form a trumpet, the speaker stood at the edge of the road, looking down into the dark where two men worked there on the car. It was not the Fire Chief or the Sheriff.

A voice came back in a high scream which seemed far away from two hundred feet down in the rain and the dark, "We got her on the drive shaft and the frame, Manny, but for God's sake let us get up before you give her a try, else she's liable to swing on both of us, Manny? You hear us? For God's sake, Manny!" The fear in the voice matched the misery of the night with its rain still falling hard.

Again the voice spoke through cupped hands, "We're pullin' you up! Kick away from the car." Then, stepping back from the edge, and turning to the men there, "Alright, Sheriff, keep 'em back. Soon's we get Al and Belcher up we're gonna' haul on the cable. It'll be tricky."

"What about anybody in the thing, Manny?" It was the Sheriff. He had one arm around Madeleine Morgan. She looked on in silence, but her empty expression, instead of masking her fear, only told of the exertion she was applying in order to maintain control. Beside her stood Harry Waldon, behind him stood Father K.

Getting no answer from Manny, who had attention only for his men and the job at hand, the Sheriff leaned across in front of Madeleine and addressed Waldon, the rain gathered in the brim of his hat ran off in a rush as he tilted his head.

"Dammit, Harry, you think it's her? How in hell did she get it in the first place? I didn't even know she could drive the damned thing."

The answer to his last question came from Waldon as if from a dead man himself, for that is what he wanted to be at the time, "I taught her to drive it," he said. "She insisted that we keep it a secret." He wanted to look at Madeleine, to see what her reaction was to this statement from him, but he hadn't the courage.

Father K. heard the anguish in his voice and decided it was genuine, but he held final judgement on that. He would know, eventually, he would know. It would be another scene reflecting improper choice, another setting for man's failures; another kind of cliffside into the hell of man's sins, with its own wrecker truck ready to winch things back to a level of safety, at least a level for a new beginning. He was thinking of the confessional. He wondered, was he the truck, or the cable.

Like some great beast fished from the deeps of the ocean, the car came slowly up to the level of the road, its rain-streaked metal, battered and scraped, shining in the lights there. The cable holding it was as taut and precise as a line drawn between stars in a Mercator projection of the night sky. Indeed, the winch-arm of the wrecker rising in dark substance against the space above the canyon, with the cable running from it down to the shiny bulk of the car lying against the cliffside, made a kind of constellation of its own. The growling of the big motor of the wrecker, in accompaniment with the squealing and the grinding of the metal parts in the winch, provided a dirge of sound for the tragedy of probable death in the rainy night that must surely be an answer of some kind. Father K. thought that it might just be an answer.

But when they drug the hulk of the machine onto the surface of the road and looked inside, they found life. Wedged with her shoulders and head between the floorboards and the bent shaft of the steering wheel, Annabelle Morgan lay, barely breathing.

They took her out and placed her in the ambulance. It was an irony that the machines of the ordinary citizen, built by one of the richest men in the world, were used by the caretakers of those who drove the more expensive cars of his competitors and that the wealthy would stand on common ground in places of tragedy like this cold cliffside and watch as their loved ones were taken from the Cadillacs and the Chryslers, the Packard's and the other, more expensive, automobiles where they had come to know terror and horrible violence, and be placed in final safety inside a Ford. The Sheriff, too, and the other officers of the law left the scene of the accident in Fords. Only the firetruck and the wrecker were different; each of them was a Reo.

The operating room of the hospital, under assault from construction crews working to complete the hospital's final floor, was filled with light. It was a place where eye and hand had to work together precisely in harmony of movement and intent upon the canvas of the human body in the state of mutilation. The hospital stood as an achievement of many men. One of them was Harry Waldon. But had he known that the thing he took so much pride in was also that which was to stand for his greatest blunder in life he would not have begun to work for its existence. And were that always the case, civilization itself would not be possible, for one thing feeds off another in life. If men knew what dangers lay ahead, they would always change their way.

They put Harry and Madeleine into a small waiting room with newspapers and magazines to read. But no event related in print could measure up to the one they each faced now. No robbery, no crime, no social catastrophe could be of interest to them as they waited in that dismal little place. No story could arrest them long enough to numb their awareness of the moment. Theirs was a double agony. Annie was hurt badly. They each wondered if she would make it through. In addition, Madeleine wondered, now, about his keeping a secret with Annie. He wondered if she might think there were other secrets.

Inside the operating theatre, on the table flooded with light from overhead, Annie's body presented its own need for wonder. Externally, except for scrapes and bruises, it appeared to be alright. But internally it was barely functioning. Already the liver and the kidneys were shutting down. The spleen was ruptured. The ribs were cracked; not broken, but cracked in that way an egg is cracked that has been boiled, then prepared for removal from the shell. It is a kind of cracking which requires an even battering all over. And that was what she had sustained. When the big car first shot out over the edge of the cliff, like a rider on horseback who has lost contact with the saddle, she was hurled by her own momentum from the seat and into the dashboard. For a moment she was able to keep her awareness of what was happening, and she clawed at the steering wheel in order to have something to hold to as the body of the car described the arc that took it downward alongside the face of the cliff.

When it struck the cliff's face for the first time she was sent heavily against the floorboards and wedged there between the clutch and brake pedals and the steering wheel, then the car began to flip end over end. As it encountered the cliff with its top, the windshield was shattered and the steering wheel was bent downward toward her, holding her in place by her head and one shoulder. The car went into its series of rotations along its axis then, its side panels and its doors were battered against the rocks, and she was beaten against the pedals and the steering wheel until her insides became jelly.

She breathed her final breath on the operating table beneath the white lights designed to show the gifted surgeons where to place their hands and their tools. Artists of the scalpel and suture, they stood ready to protect her from death through the medium of their perceptions and the administration of their skills, but they found themselves looking at a surface on which fate had already applied itself, one on which the colors all ran together in surreal and macabre absurdity in the common answer to life's struggles and choices.

That is when they brought Father K. into the operating theatre. As he bent over the lifeless body, resting with one knee on the floor and said what he had to say, prayed the prayer he had to pray, he uttered a prayer of his own. He knew this girl's burdens. He was aware of her arrogance. He felt regret for her. There, in the glaring lights that lit her passage into darkness, he asked God to give her a better role to play in whatever awaited her beyond the life she had just relinquished. Finally, he rose from his kneeling position. He heard the agonized sound that Madeleine Morgan made a single time before they led her, walking slowly, for she was like a stick figure, into the white glare of death. He stood beside the body and looked at her. She did not see him.

It had all been so long ago, on a rainy night, just like the one tonight.

THIRTY ONE

J ulia heard the motorcycle engines as the machines wheeled to the curb in front of Rooster's. She did not even look up as the three men entered the small restaurant, filling it with their loud voices and heavy feet. When she turned toward where they sat in a row along the counter, she saw exactly what she had expected to see: big men, mostly fat, in levis and leather, with leering grins on their faces. But she flinched not the least at this, nor did she allow any sign that she was bothered by their words and manners to show.

One of them said, "Hey, honey, what you doin' here when you could be ridin' with us, huh?" He exchanged looks with the other two, grinning as if he had won a prize. They both rewarded him with grins of encouragement and reassurance.

"Honey, don' lissen to him," said another, "what does he know? His hair's all gone, see?" Then the quick grasp at the bandana tied tightly around the big skull, the just-as-quick blocking arm and bit of defensive repartee, "What you talkin', man? She ain't lookin' to be wit' you neither, hey?"

It was all as predictable as the glisten on the Harleys' pampered surfaces as they sat cooling in the rain that had begun to fall again.

Rooster, who did not like the type of clientele the bikers represented, nevertheless had kept his "smiley-face" in place as the men lumbered inside, bringing their rude manners and heavy-handed style along with them. He knew that sometimes people would go to another restaurant if they saw too many motorcycles parked out front; families, old people. He could see the bikers through the little window past the silver wheel that held Julia's tickets. He listened to them flirting with her and waited for their orders to come. Their money was good. And judging from the fat on them, they would probably eat large breakfasts.

They did. One ordered steak and eggs in addition to a full order of pancakes. Once the food was placed before them, the talking stopped. Outside, the rain increased.

It was still early in the morning. Even so, other than one or two customers who had been out walking, the restaurant was getting off to a slow start. Julia found herself thinking about the night's events. She really did feel a sense of uneasiness. She and Mike? Well, that was a thought, wasn't it. They had been together for several months now. She liked him a lot. Maybe she even loved the jerk, for god's sake. But one thing was true, she knew him well. He might decide to stay here for a long time.

Julia didn't like being in one place for very long. She liked the going. It was one reason she had teamed up with Michael to begin with. New things and new places kept her interest peaked. If she had to stay at Rooster's for longer than a month or two she would become unhappy. And this thing with double-exposures and stories from the past in this town could be enough to hold Mike. She knew that the time would come when she would want to get in the little yellow car, put the top down, and feel the wind in her hair. Besides, no matter what she had told him about how she felt in regard to the supernatural, things were getting just too weird for her. Sure, she was never bothered about such things. But the truth was, she never allowed them to become a part of her life anyway. She suddenly wished she had not told him about the codes she had found in the poem book.

The bikers remained at the counter in Rooster's for nearly an hour. Then the rain began to slow. They left Julia a good tip. As she rang their tickets up on the register, she thanked each of them and smiled at their parting remarks, then she went back to clean up the mess they had left. Still, the little place was not busy.

When the last biker had lumbered out the front door, rooster looked through the little window and said, "Maybe now we'll get some bizness in heah."

Outside, the three men removed the covers from their seats and straddled their bikes. They started the motors and, with the engines rumbling, worked the heavy machines away from the curb enough to turn into the street so they could head out. They had broken the law earlier by coming up Main against its down-hill, one-way direction. The early hour, and the absence of traffic had made this easy to do. But, now, they must ride back down to where Main and Hull Avenue met before they could turn and go uphill into town again.

Julia, who had a love of motorcycles herself, moved to the front of the restaurant to watch the bikes as they pulled away. The bikers saw her through the glass front and grinned at her and waved. She smiled and waved back, stepping just outside the entrance in order to watch them move off down the street. It called for some showboating on their part, so the bikers revved up their big motors and rolled down the hill in a combined roar, three abreast.

It was just as they passed the doorway leading to the stairs going up to the flat Julia and Mike rented that they encountered what appeared to be a twisting and whirling cloud of gray, a sudden whipping of wind and rain that caused one rider to swerve into the others and put all three chromed and lacquered motorcycles into a slide along the harsh surface of the street in a shower of sparks and a sickening grinding of metal. In an instant, they all came together in a pile at the declining apex of Main and Hull.

As they struggled to shut off their motors and stand, the men groaned in pain. They had not been moving fast enough for serious injury. Still, their beautiful machines had been scraped and bent. They themselves had been bloodied. One had a broken thumb. And one, the one with the bandana, had the skin of the entire left side of his skull lacerated and cut to the bone where his head had met with the curb. It was something a helmet would have prevented, but helmets were so un-cool.

Across the street from the men and their bikes, the whirling mass of rain moved uphill toward the highest parts of town. Somewhere within it, it seemed to them, they heard a clicking sound, as if someone were running past a picket fence and trailing a stick alongside it.

Julia had been quick to react to the accident. With a shout over her shoulder to Rooster, she informed him of it. Then she ran down the street toward the pile of men and motorcycles. She, too, had heard the odd sound, and she had also seen something strange, something which bothered her very much in light of all that she and Mike and their friend Cyrus had been engaged in of late; she put it in the back of her mind as she came upon the injured motorcycle riders. Behind her, she heard footsteps as Rooster and his two customers ran down to the scene too.

Three streets above the location of the accident, and several hundred yards to the east, the building that had once housed the finest hospital for hundreds of miles in all directions sat unaffected in its current role as hotel. It was to it in earlier times that such events playing on Jerome's streets usually came for their final acts. Its doctors and nurses had brought children into the world there on the mountain. It had seen men who had been torn and rent in terrible ways put back together, so that their lives might continue in some fashion if not exactly as before. It had housed death in all its forms. And it had been the place where those dead sometimes lay until they could be interred in the rocky soil on the slopes below or turned to ash in the white heat of the hospital's crematorium. For, while there were enough morticians, called undertakers then, in Jerome, no funeral establishment could vie with the great hospital's up-to-date facilities. They were often used for autopsy, as a morgue, or for cremation.

But the little pile of men and metal in the heart of the flatiron district in the Jerome that had been reborn as a tourist attraction, and an artists' haven, would not disturb the grounds of the once superb medical institution on the hill above them. They needed what the old building could no longer give.

Jerome had its own squad of volunteer paramedics to handle the situation. When they arrived on the scene, they took over in that way such people in small towns have of taking the opportunity to show off their skills and circumstantial authority, while at the same time trying to appear solemn and matter-of-fact.

Julia saw that the bikers were being attended to, then she found Rooster at the edge of what was becoming a small crowd. The little man had a strange expression on his face. He didn't look at Julia as she tugged on his sleeve and called his name, but he said to her as she tried to get his attention, "Shua did mix 'em up, like scrambled eggs."

"Rooster," Julia said, "I need a couple of minutes. I want to check on Mike."

"Go on, Julie," he said, not taking his eyes off the scene before him.

THIRTY TWO

It was an old story to Father K., "Forgive me, Father, for I have sinned."

He had heard the words so often that now they ran together in his mind like part of a foreign language. He knew what the meaning was, the tone told him that, but the syllables, the consonants and vowels, were all one. It was all about the unflagging continuation of mankind's fall.

A man looking at a woman and lusting; his mind touching her body like invisible fingers, lifting the very cloth of her garments and running his thoughts across her flesh like hands, taking her imaginatively; secretly and silently sinning while wrapped and hidden in his thoughts; a woman, silently cursing her drunk husband as he took her, and afterwards, feeling that she was no longer a good wife; a person taking a bit of something from a merchant's shelves; these, these were sins he could help to send away. These were things he could smooth over. He almost laughed at the parishioners who made such confessions. How good indeed were such people. Heaven was safe in their hands.

But the others, the real sinners, had been long with him. They bent the iron rod he had planted in his own resolve all those years ago. He had been well past youth then. Now he was old. Now the sins of such people seemed like heavy lumps of filth that lay like an infection of the blood in painful carbuncles, and over time oozed out more filth through the medium of mind and memory. And when again and again these men and women arrived with mouths asking deliverance from having committed their foul deeds, after having infected others like streptococcal pieces of evil by crawling from one skin to another and sinking into the host bloodstream, their wails of torment to be forgiven always seemed to carry the same ring, and he knew when they spoke that phrase asking formally for his hand to be applied to the filthy sore of their life that their transgression was serious. He always knew.

But this time, he felt the rod breaking. It had been imbedded so long in the damp and the rot of sins which he had been forced to enfold that its middle had been eaten away. His voice was weary and thickened as he asked her, "Why do you bring this to me?"

It stunned her. Here was supposed to be an end to the pain. At least, a beginning to an end. She had not always known everything at once. But she remembered thinking, when she learned how much he had known before her, that somehow it was different. His knowing was not to be confused with the fact that she did not know. She had kept her resentment of this away from him, from thoughts of him. Now, she realized she had kept it even from herself.

She answered his question with a question of her own, "You did not bring the other to me when you could have. I should ask you, why?"

"Confessions to a priest are not like little secrets between children."

"The other was about a child."

"A child's soul is no less than an adult's."

"I was the adult responsible for her, Father."

"It is the way of the Church." Their voices were flat and quiet, as if they were intoning a ritualistic dialogue.

She folded her hands and hung her head. The words came from her mouth, then, coated in the misery she felt. "My sister did not go over the side in that damned thing alone. She was pregnant. Knowing who the father was would have changed everything. It would have pointed the finger at him, and you knew it!"

He was silent, but his thoughts were not. The girl had never actually named the man. He had only surmised who it was. Ah, but he was certain. Still, he could say that, he could deny, and truthfully so, that he knew the identity of the man who had made the girl pregnant. But it would be sophistry to do this. And he couldn't lie that way. It was lying enough, was it not, to absorb their sins while they continued to commit them over and over in the safety of their knowledge of his intercession?

She could barely recognize any sound coming from his side of the confessional. Then, in the quiet, she located his slow breathing. She heard the soft rasp of his tongue administering to his lips as he licked at their dryness. She could picture him sitting calmly with his eyes closed. It was intolerable to her; the ever-present ritual and the insufferable act of forgiveness which had covered it all up in the first place. In a fury, she lashed out at the little screen between them, hit it with the bottom of her clenched hand. Beyond it, the silhouette of his head did not move.

She began to sob. She had hoped she wouldn't, but she found herself doing it anyway. She cried heavily. For the first time since it had all happened, she felt a sense of release. She had not cried for her mother. She had not cried for B.L. She had not always known how much she loved him.

Oh, it was hard. None of it had worked out. She had wanted so much for Annie. She had intended that they would be something better than what fate had selected for them. She had thought that this place, this town, would finally be the answer. But it had brought her more unhappiness than she had ever known before.

In the opposite cubicle, Father Jovan Kilryc Katichovic sat and listened to her anguish. He felt it, too. But she would not believe him if he told her that. Still, he had to give her something. To sit and do nothing would make his own suffering harder, and he knew that his time of suffering would surely come. She was about to hand him her personal sinning to keep. Once he took it, she would be free of it, at least she would feel some relief from it. He must create a bulwark against the future pain he knew he would know. Like an antiseptic which kills the germs, causes them to shrivel and die, curl and become harmless in whatever death agonies they endured, he would take her sin from her. Ah, but would it, even shrunken and dormant in death, would it not stink in its own decay? Would not the noxious fumes of its evil odors have to be endured by him, just as the antiseptic, even if thrown away, flushed away down some drain, carried in itself the dead and filthy bodies of the germs? And, dear God, he hoped he was not to be flushed away, at least not yet. Had his life been of so little use as to be merely a medication to be used and tossed aside?

He wrenched himself away from these thoughts and said in a heavy whisper, "He was a man who wished for power. He never really meant to do evil."

In the little booth the crying continued, but he could tell from a slight change in it that she had heard. He went on, "It was the whiskey and the money it brought. It was the power he craved. He wanted what he saw. He saw you, he saw her."

The crying stopped. "But you knew all this," she said, "You could have told me. I would have acted." Then she began crying again. She continued for a few more moments, then spoke, "I found it in a book that he gave to me. She put it there. A message. She meant for me to know, she just couldn't tell me herself. Why didn't you tell me?"

"I wanted to tell," he said, "When . . . Mr. Buenig was . . . I wanted to but I couldn't."

Across from him there was a quick intake of her breath. A rush of emotion filled her head, then the ice-cold inference cleared her thoughts of all else. "W-what? What do you mean? Tell me! What do you mean?"

He sat silent across from her. His mind journeyed back to the day of the funeral. He hadn't known anything then. Nobody had.

The police, and the murderers of course, things were known to them. But the rest of the town knew nothing. They stood placidly and watched the line of vehicles following the hearse and the company cars down through the narrow streets to the cemetery lying on the descending slopes of the town.

Most of the people came in black, square-bodied Fords and Chevrolets; somber in color if not anything else. The conveyances of people above average, perhaps, but certainly not people who were much beyond that. The majority of the cars were in fair condition, but here and there one would be without its fenders, another might have been converted from a sedan to a truck. One or two were hardly more than motorized buckboards. And there were real trucks in the line, and real buckboards pulled by horses, that had come to the cemetery that day. B.L. Buenig was a man whose friendships and lines of acquaintance had reached into all levels of Jerome's society.

The casket had lain in Father K.'s church, and he had conducted the services. He had done it for her sake. Buenig was not known to be a Catholic, but he was not known to be anything else, either.

He remembered that she had not cried. At the time, it was no mystery to him. Buenig had taken her and her sister in, had provided for them. In turn, she had provided for him. It is love that brings grief in the end. Other emotions might cause tears to well in the eyes, perhaps flow down the face, but only real love will engender true grief. She had not shown any of that, according to his memory.

He did remember being relieved to learn a few weeks later that she had found help in the person of the other man. This eventually became an arrangement somewhat like the one she had had with Buenig. In time, she and the girl and Harry Waldon had made a kind of family at his church. Father K. was happy about that. And she seemed to display a better sense of well-being herself; perhaps a recovery from Buenig's death. For a while it all went well.

But life is a thing of contrasts, and shadows always accompany sunlight. It was later, when he heard Waldon's confession, that he was dismayed by the position he was in because of his priesthood.

Long hours of agony followed him after that. Should he tell? What would it accomplish?

In the end, he did what he had been trained to do, follow the line of least destruction in the lives of his people, seek the good that is always there somewhere along with the bad. Penitence led the way. Seek it and offer forgiveness in return. He had done so. And only he held the fiery cup of guilt then. It was as it always was with him.

In the booth opposite him, there was more sobbing from her, but it carried a different tone, now. She rose and stepped out of the booth's confinement, trembling from the new wound he had given her.

She moved closer to his side of the double compartment and with a slash of her arm pulled back the curtain from the entrance to the booth where he sat, head bowed, just beyond the tiny wire mesh window that allowed two people, repentant parishioner and forgiving priest, to make the ritual transfer of whatever sin the one had placed before the other.

He looked up at her, then. In his eyes was a plea for his own forgiveness, a forgiveness he seemed to be asking of her. But she could not, would not give it. With a shriek of fury she reached in and grasped him as if to pull him erect, as if to bring him into her own painful reality. He rose to a standing position within the close walls of the booth, while she screamed at him to tell her what he had meant by referring to B.L. Buenig.

And then, half-standing himself, half-held by her, his own frail arms clawing at the curtain for support, his face contorted, he clutched at his chest. A short cry, then a gurgle, came from his mouth. His eyes widened and he broke away from her, stumbling across the room to lurch against a chair near the wall. His body sent the chair skittering along the polished hardwood floor. Then he fell and lay on his back, pawing at his chest and breathing heavily. "Get help," he said in a rasping voice. His eyes pleaded with her. But she only moved backward and away from him.

"Please," he implored her, "I'm a priest, don't do this . . . to yourself." He continued to beg her with his eyes, but his voice remained silent and his body lay still.

She ran from the room, then, out of the church and into the street, where she blended into the ordinary surroundings there.

THIRTY THREE

Julia noticed it the moment she opened the door at street level and started up the stairway; the smell. It was faint at first, then it became stronger. By the time she reached the top of the stairs, she knew it was coming from the apartment itself. Almost gagging, she held her hand over her mouth and nose and entered the little kitchen. Beyond, the darkened bedroom was as she had left it. She could see Mike on the bed. She thought he must have been having another of those dreams because the sheets were twisted around one leg and he lay half on his back and half on his side.

As she moved nearer, she saw that he had somehow managed to pull his underwear off one leg. At any other time she would have smiled to herself at the semi-erect condition of his penis, but the fetid odor of rot seemed to be everywhere, and she could hardly breathe.

She moved quickly to the large front window and pulled the string which allowed the blinds to open. She pulled back the curtains. Turning toward the bed once again, she could see by the additional light that the sheets were streaked with a dark stain. The stench was so strong that she had to stick her head close to the open window to breathe fresh air.

God! What was it? She felt that somewhere in her memory she knew. She had encountered such a smell before. Back in her childhood in Liberal, Kansas, a town which had not been very liberal at all, a town which she had vowed to leave for the very fact of its mundane traditionalism, one which always elicited snide comment due to its name, but a town nonetheless which had succored her family and had shaded her from the worldly sun of other, more sophisticated, places while she grew to the age of sixteen. It had been her idea to leave then. The law said eighteen. She made it two years earlier. Now it didn't matter. God! The smell!

Then the memory returned and she suddenly knew what the stench was that floated in the air of the little flat, but which was concentrated most on the twisted, sweat-soaked and stained sheets. With a sense of shock she realized that it must be as well on the naked, semen-besmeared genitalia of the man she had made love to so many times she could not remember.

She shook herself. This had to stop. She lived in a rational world because she was a rational person. With a determined stride toward the bed, she reached out and whipped the soiled sheets off Mike and from beneath the mattress where they were partially tucked in.

"Mike, get up!" she ordered. She had to repeat this before he began to emerge from the deep sleep he had been in. He rolled over onto his back and his eyes opened. He looked blankly at the ceiling for a moment or two before turning his head and seeing her standing above him at the side of the bed.

"Julia," he breathed. I must have slept all day. I, I had this dream, the strangest of all. I have to tell you about it." And then, as he became fully aware, "Oh, God, what is that awful smell?"

*　*　*

In the large bedroom in the old house high on the hill, she lay on the daybed which was her place. Ah, he had been her one love. They had found something together that had surprised them both.

Love for her had not been a goal when she had decided to come to Jerome. She had been fleeing possible arrest for murder, then. But time passed and no lawmen came knocking on her door.

She had never told B.L. about that episode in her life. How easy the hatpin had gone in; eight inches of steel, hardly larger than a wire. It did the job as well as anything else. Her stepfather had died with a wide-eyed look of incredulity on his face. Could the pain of the hatpin's entry have been as subtle as the use of the hatpin itself?

It made her think of other things. She had long ago forgotten about her stepfather. And she did not want to think of Harry Waldon; going into forever, into forever. Agghkk! She rose from the dust and filth of the daybed. Could she not have a little peace?

But as her form moved within the darkened room, the grating sounds that were hers, now, blended with the cracking, the creaking, and the groaning of the old timbers of the house, and the memories came back in a tumble—all mixed together, and all against her will in total defiance of her ability to modify them.

B.L. had told her of what Annie had been doing . . . *She's running with some bad people, Madeleine* . . . Just how do you know that? This in anger, for she so hated to hear ill of Annie . . . *I have my sources* . . . One of your celebrated whores, I suppose . . . He laughed . . . *No, you are my only celebrated whore. This source is a piano player* . . . He ducked and laughed even louder as she threw a pillow at him . . . *Here, here is a gift of poetry I hope you will like* . . . She had looked up at him and smiled. She knew he was trying hard . . . Harry, she had said . . . I hope you understand, I get in these moods and it is difficult to come out of them . . . *I know he was a wonderful man, but, Madeleine, I want to take care of you and Annie. You know that, don't you? Someday, perhaps, you will sit and long for me, here, in this grand old house, your eyes wistful and sad just the way they are now . . . the photograph is wonderful, please say I may have it made into a portrait . . . we can hang it in the* . . . Oh, Harry. First of all, I am fond of you. And I know your heart is in the right place. Yes, yes you may do so if it makes you happy. And as for me doubting your true feelings, don't even think it. B.L. is gone, gone forever. And it hurts. How can you even think I might not . . . It had been on a sunny day in September, and fall was in its Indian summer stage . . . *Miss Madeleine* . . . she had decided to stroll down to the center of town and so some shopping. She needed nothing, it was the walk that interested her, that and the prettiness of the day. Since B.L. had died and she and Annie had come to live in the big house on Hill Street, she had quit working. She had found her new freedom a thing which was both good and bad. She knew she was something of an item as far as gossip among the so-called ladies, the good wives of the town, was concerned. But it was the Twenties, women did walk on the streets alone these days.

It had been in a small shop on First Avenue. The voice plucked at her attention even as the woman's hand pulled slightly on Madeleine's sleeve. She had answered the plea with a "hello" which was as much a question as a greeting . . . *You don' know me. I was one of Mister Buenig's friends* . . . this last said with a smile which Madeleine returned, Who are you? . . . *My name's DeNelle. I was one of his friends. He was a wonderful man* . . . Madeleine nodded in affirmation of this statement, the smile had left her face at the thought of B.L. A touch of sadness took its place. The woman before her was a Negro. Madeleine paused but only for a moment in her thoughts before the name registered in her mind . . . Why, yes, she said, the smile returning, he spoke of you once, DeNelle . . . *That's nice to know* . . . then, taking Madeleine's arm, she asked, as if inquiring about someone on the verge of dying from a bad disease . . . *How is your sister Annie, how is she doin' Miss Madeleine?* Madeleine's mind shifted, pulled inward on itself as if to get away . . . *He's my friend and I will see him if I want to!* You will not, young lady. He is at least twenty years your senior. And, besides, I want more for you than some little Irish bootlegger who hardly stands above your own earlobes . . . *And how did we get so high and mighty all of a sudden? You really are a whore. First with B.L. and now Harry Waldon* . . . To keep you in clothes and under a roof! Then, after a pause, Alright, maybe I am, but if I lie on my back and give myself up it is for your sake, it always has been! *What? You don't like this big old house with your picture on the wall, and that Cadillac, and all the parties you and Harry give now that the two of you are together?*

Aarrggh! They were too much! The memories were like people, personalities in themselves. With a roar she left the old room and swept along in ethereal form down the large hallway. She had few choices in the hell that had become hers since that day she had driven the big car through the rain and into the garage for good. Never could she forget the memories. They were her duty. She could speed them up or put them off, but eventually she must re-live them, down to the smallest particle of occurrence they contained. In a way that was a kind of choice. She had chosen to visit the grave every evening. It had been allowed. And the other thing, especially now in these later years, when all things physical were far past being what they once were, was her mode of coming and going. It was left for her to decide. At least, for the most part it was.

Sometimes, when she wanted to move from place to place with the ease and subtlety of a drifting shadow or a burst of wind, she found herself imprisoned in the foul thing that she had once been. Only with effort could she move it along, even then it was slow and clumsy; something akin to dragging a heavy burden up the stairs in order to jump from the landing and feel free, but only momentarily. She had long ago ceased leaving the old house with it. If it would not lie in its own filth on the daybed, she would remain with it in seething anger. But always, if her intent was to visit the grave, she would be allowed to go sooner or later.

There was no stealth with it along. The coyotes had been the first to apprise her of its telltale qualities. Once, in deep sadness at the grave, she had become alerted to the presence of not one lurking about the old cemetery, but an entire pack. They sat on their flea-ridden haunches in the shadows, eyeing her dark form in its tattered rags as if she were the rank carcass of some kill lying on the cold ground, awaiting their savage rending of her putrid flesh. But her means of sending hellish hate outward from herself in such palpable form that the very air crackled and split in heat and sound, as if lightning bolts were suddenly descending, had sent them scurrying off into the darkness of the night, terrified as they had never been before, for she had lifted the very dust of the ground and hurled it after them!

Since then, she had begun to leave her corporeal being behind when she could. But it had been necessary to take it along the morning she had visited the man in the old flat. She had a use for it then. Its substance, no matter how changed, was required. She needed just the slightest bit of touching to help with the dreaming she had induced in his mind.

And now, merely a shadow in the stale air, she swept past the room which had been Annie's, then down the broad staircase. Like an angry storm she surged within the environs of the old house, whirling through rooms that had not been entered in years, except by an errant beam of sunlight or a sudden breath of air as somewhere in the carcass of the grand old residence something shifted enough to cause movement in its dank atmosphere.

*   *   *

In the apartment, Julia had finally gotten Mike to wake up.

"It smells like something dead in here!"

"Mike, get up and get in the shower. We are leaving this place right now!"

He looked at her in confusion. "What do you mean? What the hell is this all about? And what in God's name is that stink? It's awful!"

"Come on, Mike, we're going to Cyrus's place. Now get in the shower. God! I can hardly stand to be in the same room with you."

THIRTY FOUR

Annie had not mourned the loss of B.L. Buenig from their lives. After Madeleine had agreed to live with Harry Waldon in the big house above the town, Annie almost came to be glad that Buenig had arrived at a bad end. A bad end is what people around the town called it. Annie had even more freedom to come and go, now. So she knew the scuttlebutt as Gilmour said about things sometimes, down to a T.

"What's down to a T mean, anyway," she asked the little man one day as he worked in his office in the cellar beneath the theatre. Gilmour had long since seen to it that someone else had taken his place as projectionist. He devoted all of his time now to running his liquor business out of the cellar, which he had made into a passable office.

Despite DeNelle's warnings to Gilmour, he had continued to allow the girl access to himself. The truth of it was that the little Irishman felt quite safe now that Buenig was no longer a threat. As for Harry Waldon, he was simply a front for Gilmour's business of bringing whiskey to the town and distributing it among the large population of miners. Besides that, Gilmour was in somewhat of a dilemma about the girl. He had made no overtures of any kind toward her, nothing had been offered by him that would serve to keep a young person, especially a girl, coming around someone like himself. At first, he had wanted her to visit so he could learn things about Buenig. Then, he had decided she might serve as a similar pipeline of information about Waldon. But he had since learned that Harry Waldon was easier to control than he had at first thought he might be. He needed no special strings in order to handle him.

The thought that he was taking a chance by allowing a kid such as her to hang around the operation was not a new notion to Gilmour. But he had let her in in the first place, and then he had continued to let her in. He was at the point now where he was reluctant to take the necessary measures to stop her from coming around. So far, none of his associates had made any inquiries about her. He had managed to keep her away on days when he attended to business involving face-to-face meetings with his people. But if it became a topic of concern with any of them, well, his hands would be tied as to what happened next.

The little man leaned back in the large leather covered chair he had brought in to complement the equally expensive desk. He looked at the girl while he held both hands behind his head. "You know, kid, I used to wonder about you when you came into the booth. Now you're stickin' your nose into my business down here. I wouldn't like it if you turned out to be some kind of spy or somethin' like that."

"Ha!" she said through a grin, "People all know you sell whiskey."

"People only suspect," he countered, "they don't know whether I do it or not, and neither do you. Anyway, don't change the subject, what keeps you comin' around, huh?" It was a direct question. One he had wanted to ask for a long time.

"School's not the real world. Anyway, not like I know it to be," she began.

He took a deep breath and folded his hands in his lap, sensing that she was about to reveal more of herself to him.

She walked over to a nearby chair and sat, almost shyly, before him. For the first time, she thought, he seemed really interested in her. She continued talking, "You know, my sister and me, well, we grew up different. She tries to hide it, I mean, she wants to forget it, but I, well I thought it was alright in some ways," she looked down at the floor and then back in his direction, but not at him, a smile played at the corners of her mouth. "I don't know, I just like to be where people are different. You're different. Besides, I don't just hang around here." Then she laughed, "Sometimes I go to the cribs and see what's going on down there."

There was an intake of breath as he heard this. "That's no place for a girl like you," he declared.

"How do you know? Do you ever go there?" She looked up at him from beneath her eyelashes then and gave him an impish grin, "Or is there something wrong with you?"

The barb stung him. Small of stature, red-headed, freckled, he had not had a good adolescence where girls were concerned. The experience had left its taste in his mouth well into adulthood. Of course he went to the cribs. That was the easy way. You went in, made your choice, had what you wanted, paid for it and left. No strings. No responsibilities. No tests to pass, nobody to win over. Everything got taken care of and you went back to business until the next time you needed the same thing.

But what the hell! How dare this little bitch ask such a question. What had he been thinking of, letting her touch his life. By-God, she was becoming a nuisance! I should have stopped it right at the start, he thought. Now, I'll have to do something hard, something I don't want to do. Dammit!

She watched him closely as he searched for the answer to her question. She knew something of his thoughts. As always, he felt he was in control. But her years in company with her mother and her sister had allowed her to see all the human plots in all the human dramas over and over until she knew them by heart. As simple as Regis Gilmour found Harry Waldon, as easy to handle as he thought he was, Annie believed Gilmour to be even simpler and even easier, and she intended to take advantage of that perception.

"Listen," he began, as she stood up from the chair she had been sitting in and moved a bit closer to the big desk, "listen, I, there's nothing wrong with me. It's just that," and she began walking toward him. He waited until she stood by his chair at his right side before continuing to speak. He didn't notice that his voice sounded strangely different in tone and strength, that it was almost at the level of a whisper, "I'm a grown man. You're too young. You, you could get me lynched." It was all he said.

But she continued to stand near him. He would reveal himself to her this day. He would become hers to control this day. The excitement of the mere thought thrilled her, carried her to an ecstasy far beyond anything sexual. She had been aware of her own sexuality since the age of eleven, and though resenting the inconvenience it sometimes caused, she was not above using it for her own purposes.

But, sensing the danger that lay beyond the next moment, Gilmour shook himself out of the spell that had come over him. He surged forward in his seat, shoving her rudely away from him. "Go on, get out of here. Find some kid like yourself to spend time with. I got work to do. And by the way," he continued as she stood, stunned into silence by his rough manner, "don't keep comin' in here like you own the place. 'Cause you don't. Go see that lady, that DeNelle. Go on," and he turned away from her.

Annie remained quiet for a few moments. Then, with emotions of anger and a sense of confusion, she turned to walk out of the door.

Behind the double doors Gilmour had made for the entrance to the depths below the cellar, another pair of eyes viewed the scene from the darkness there. It was the younger of the two thugs who worked for Regis Gilmour. A leer draped his face as he listened to the last bit of dialogue between Gilmour and Annie. Hell yes, he breathed to himself, get your little ass on out of our business. Regis shoulda' done sent you packin' when you first come around.

As the door closed behind Annie, Gilmour sighed and raised himself from the papers he had pretended to be working on. He was aware of the man at the double doors leading to the tunnels below the basement. He called to him.

"Faro, come in here."

The lanky man slouched into the room and looked in the direction of the desk. "Yeah, Boss?"

"You see that kid hangin' 'round here again you send her away, you hear?"

A grin uncovered a double row of yellowed and broken teeth in the face of the man called Faro. He shook his head in affirmation that he had heard and understood. "I'll do it, Boss."

"Now, you listen," Gilmour's right index finger pointed directly at Faro, "No bullshit! We don't want anything to interfere with what we're doin' in our business. Just tell her to leave. No rough stuff. You know she's connected with Waldon. Her sister's shackin' with him."

Faro just smiled back at his boss.

"Ain't you got somethin' to do," said Gilmour, sourly.

"Yeah," said the thug, "I gotta check with Burt over at the Fashion."

Gilmour leaned back and allowed his face to adopt an even darker expression. He was of the school which said a boss should always appear to be grim. He was not in any doubt as to the level of Faro's intelligence. As a ruffian he was valuable. But he was little more than a paid bully. It was best that he always see Gilmour as unhappy, displeased. But the mention of the Fashion Saloon meant more whiskey leaving the tunnels below and more money coming into Gilmour's pockets. Such thoughts always brought pleasure to the little Irishman's mind.

"You make sure to keep those orders straight, Faro! You an' Burt had better damn well agree on what's what at tally time."

Gilmour laughed to himself because of the concern his remarks brought to Faro's face. He watched him move through the door, nodding his head to reassure his boss of his careful attention to what he was doing. Gilmour wasn't worried. He had a man watching Faro and another watching that man. There was someone watching Burt, as well, to make sure his hands didn't get sticky and lift money from the cash drawer that didn't belong to him. It was the way you had to run things.

THIRTY FIVE

"It's the craziest damn thing I ever heard," said Cyrus Dooley. They were all three sitting on the narrow balcony fronting his apartment on the second floor above 89A coming up into Jerome. The day was just ending, and the scene before them was a natural delight. The buildings lining the street there were all in one state or another of restoration and repair. The colors were varied on the old walls. Flower pots were in evidence everywhere, and across the street, the land sloped away in folds of green and rust toward the great valley below. A breeze wafted past, but only enough to take the edge of heat off the dying afternoon.

Mike sat silent, not replying to the comment by his new-found friend. It was Julia who spoke next. All day she had been thinking of the events they had experienced in the old town over the last few days. Less than a week had come and gone since they had first rolled carefree and happy into the upper end of town and finally down into its heart. Now, the entire character of the place had changed. At least, her perception of it had. She had resisted, at first, the notion of strange and unusual things—ghosts, for instance—as being at the bottom of Mike's dreams: the unexplained double-exposure on the film in his camera, and the experience he said he'd had in the old church. She had been with Michael long enough to know that he was a romantic, a believer. But the smell in the apartment, and all over the sheets, had been too much for her to explain away. She thought something here was different from anything she knew about—at least in the world she thought existed. And then her own past had come to her rescue.

She leaned slightly forward as she spoke in reply to Cyrus's comment, "You know, that smell, I've smelled it before. And so have both of you."

"What do you mean?" asked Cyrus. He looked quickly at Mike who had turned, his face an open question, toward Julia.

"It's the same smell I encountered once when I was a little girl in my hometown in Kansas. I went down a street farther than I was supposed to go one day. I guess the freedom felt good. I should have been afraid, but I wasn't."

Both men looked at her with interest. Cyrus even lit up a new cigarette in anticipation of a story. Julia waited for the usual coughing fit to come and go before she continued.

"Anyway, like I said, I wasn't afraid at first, but I got turned around and became lost. I meandered along until I got into an alley. I didn't know which way to go. That's when I got scared. Walking along in that alley, I began to smell something that didn't smell good. The closer I got the worse it became. Finally, it was so bad that I had to put my hand over my mouth and nose. It was awful and it was everywhere around me, it seemed. I stood still, looking at the walls of the big building that ran all along one side of the alley. Then, I examined the ground beyond the edge of the gravel, where heavy grass grew. But I couldn't see anything that might account for the smell. I was about to run away from that place when I heard this buzzing."

Mike interrupted her, "You heard buzzing, did you say buzzing"

"Yes, it was the noise made by a whole bunch of flies. They were big and green with shiny black on their eyes and legs. The buzzing was coming from a pile of rubbish stacked against the back wall of the building there. I found a stick and pulled back some of the trash in the pile. All I could see was a mound of these

black flies, moving all over something there in the rubbish pile. I
stuck the stick into them and they suddenly flew up and away
from the thing, but they came right back, crawling around on it,
covering it up so it was hard to see what it was. The smell was even
worse than it had been before. I kept poking at whatever it was the
flies were on until suddenly I recognized it. Then I ran, I ran away
from there as fast as I could."

"Well, what was it?" Mike and Cyrus almost spoke in unison.

"It was the half-rotted head of a cow, its eyes were glassy and
half-gone. Its mouth was open and I could see its tongue."

Mike and Cyrus looked at her blankly.

"It was rotting flesh," she said, looking intently back at them,
"and that's what the smell in the apartment was from, rotten meat
of some kind. And, you know what? I saw somebody running away
from that accident those men on the motorcycles had. Somebody
wants us gone and they slipped into that apartment and smeared
Mike all over with it." She did not want to think it was anything
else but that.

"How do you account, then, for the dreams I've had?" asked
Michael as he looked levelly at her.

"Not only them dreams," interjected Cyrus, "but the evidence
of, well," and he seemed embarrassed as he directed himself to
Julia, "didn't you say he looked as if he had been in what you
might call a state of arousal?"

"Oh, hell, Cyrus," said Mike gruffly, but looking away to hide
his own embarrassment, "this ain't no time to pussyfoot around. I
had a hard-on you couldn't dent with a ballpeen hammer."

The two men laughed then. It was the bit of humor they
needed. But Julia was quiet. After a moment she said seriously, "I
wonder why you can't remember much of this latest dream, Mike?"

He was on the defensive immediately. "I don't know, Babe, all
I remember is a beautiful woman with dark hair and eyes, like
yours."

It was Cyrus Dooley who spoke next in an effort to avert what
he sensed might be an argument in the making. "Let's go over all
that we've got so far," he began, "chart it out on a big sheet of

paper. Then, let's figger where we have to go to find the answers. I already have one or two ideas."

"Well, aside from that old church, I don't have a thing," said Mike. He looked at Julia.

She shook her head, almost shuddering, "I think we should just leave," she declared.

"What, and not uncover whatever it is that's goin' on?" asked Cyrus, pulling out another cigarette. When he finished his coughing spell, and shook his head with a slight grin of apology, he said, "I think there's more'n the old church. What about the details of them dreams?"

"Don't forget that poetry book," said Julia, "even though I don't see how it could possibly be connected with any of this."

Mike looked quickly at her. "I picked it at random, not because of the poetry in it."

"You picked it because it had writing in it," she said, "You told me that yourself. Besides, it contains coded messages. I found some of them. They're about M. and Me. and Us. I told you about that, Mike. Didn't you read it?"

"I was tired," said Michael, "I went to sleep after you left for work."

"I think we need to go over that book again," said Cyrus, "Maybe it'll help us. If it don't, I have a possible source that might."

"Well I hope it isn't more messages in poetry," said Mike.

"As a matter of fact," replied the old man, "I don't care for poetry much. But my wife did. She kept some books on it. After she passed on, I got to lookin' into one that I knew was her favorite. Not for the poems in it. Missed her, you know. Anyways, it ain't the poems in that book of yours we need to examine, its them messages Julia was talkin' about, and the possible source I referred to ain't got nothin' to do with poetry."

They both looked at him, waiting for more information. He just grinned back at them.

THIRTY SIX

I t was fun driving the car. The thing was big and it was hard to steer, but it was still fun. They had only gone out in it three or four times before she became able to manage it all by herself. It pleased her to know that she could handle the large machine, and the glow on her face showed this. They were heading up the incline south of town. In the seat opposite her, he did not seem as happy as she was. He directed her to pull over at the next place on the road where people could turn around if they wished, or simply sit and look at the view. She reluctantly complied.

When they pulled in and she had turned off the motor and dutifully left the car in gear so that it would not move, he said to her, "I don't think it's a good thing to keep this from Madeleine, let's tell her."

"And then, should we tell her about all of it? She will make me stop, you know. At least, she will say I shouldn't be doing it. That will make things harder from then on."

"What do you mean, tell her all of it?" he asked in a grim tone, "I told you how sorry I was about that. I told you so and I meant it. I haven't done anything like it since."

She looked across at him with a tiny smile in the corner of her mouth. Before them the mountain opened up in a great gash of rock to reveal the valley in panoramic splendor thousands of feet below and lying miles into the distance.

The car sat perched at the edge of the canyon, and they sat in the car, each with their own thoughts. His were that he wished he had never blundered and put himself at her mercy. She had no business driving this big beast of an automobile on such a bad road. Madeleine would be furious if she knew about it.

Annie's thoughts were more about her pleasure than they were her responsibility for anything else. He was no better. They were both thinking of themselves.

"But you did do it that one time," she said through an impish smile, "and I think you liked it."

He looked away from her in an agony of remorse and regret. In the canyon before him, the spaces fell away into empty halls of air, and he could see a raven flapping along far below. How simple life could be for some creatures; nothing to do but hunt for food; no societal complications. You ate, you slept, you excreted, you mated, you avoided danger. And you did it all as opportunity allowed, and you either lived or you died.

But that wasn't the way it was for people. It mattered how one lived. It made a difference how one found one's food. How one dealt with one's enemies was governed by law. And the simple act of sex was perhaps the most controlled behavior of all. There was religion. There was ethics. Oh, hell! Things were insufferably complicated. Looking at the raven as it wheeled on the currents of up-drafting air in the empty spaces of the canyon, he actually wanted to be that crow bird.

He got out of his side of the car and walked around to the driver's side. All semblance of affability had left his face. "Let's go back, now," he said with his hand on the door handle, "I'll drop you off in town and you can walk up to the house."

*   *   *

Annie knew that she had things her way. If she wanted to drive the car, she could. He would always let her. Even if he had to drive up from his office in Clarkdale to meet her, he would. It was better with him than it had been with B.L. Buenig. Buenig had resisted. He had held onto that seat of power that in the adult world was the wall that separates the *them* from the *us*, which was how she thought of herself.

The only flaw in her world, aside from her sister, was the indifference with which Regis had begun to treat her. She had been met by one of his men at the entrance to the basement office and told she could not go there again. She had heard the man's name before. It was Faro. Well, he wasn't too smart. Since then, when she had seen him on the street, he always pretended he had not been watching her, but she knew that he had been.

To Annie, men were stupid even when they were smart. They could always be made to do as one wished—if one were not stupid one's self. She thought that she might give this Faro fellow a taste of his own medicine.

THIRTY SEVEN

They all sat in Cyrus's living room with several stacks of old newspapers in various places nearby. The old papers were what Cyrus had referred to earlier as his special source of information. The collection had been one of the advantages of making his home in Jerome. On the floor of the living room in his apartment were copies of several newspapers which had come and gone in the town over the years.

They had done as Cyrus had suggested: made their list and begun searching the most obvious sources. The list included the old church because of Mike's experience in it; the old car, even though they were all still skeptical about the idea of something spiritual being behind the strange combination of the wreck and the girl in antique clothing in the photograph Mike had taken; the highway itself coming down from the heights behind the town, because of Mike's dream of going over the side somewhere along its treacherous route; the section of street which had slipped downhill at one time in the town's history, again because of the dream; and finally, the copy of Spoon River Anthology Mike had found in the library on their first day in Jerome.

They had gone to the book first, with Mike reluctant to admit he had missed something as important as coded messages. Julia had a divided opinion about it. She was adamant about not admitting to anything supernatural being connected with the strange occurrences they had experienced while in the little town, but she could not help but gloat over the idea that she had found something before Mike had.

"I don't see it," he said to her as he thumbed quickly through the pages.

She reached for the old book. "Let me have it, Michael. Give it to me."

With irritation on his face, Mike handed her the book. Cyrus looked on with a glint in his eye that showed he was on Julia's side.

Confidently, she turned to the page she wanted and said, "Here. Here is where it begins."

Mike reached for the book but she pulled it away from him. "I'll show you, just look," she ordered, holding the page up so he could see the slight smudge beneath one of the letters in a word.

"That's just a bit of dirt," he said, a wry grin beginning to form on his lips.

But she remained silent and moved her finger across and down the page, pausing briefly at other similar marks until his preliminary expression of humor turned to the neutral blank that accompanied widened eyes and slightly opened mouth, signaling wonder and intense interest.

"See that?" she asked, her own smile shaping her mouth, her eyes bright in triumph. Her moving finger had touched on letters which when taken together spelled a word. The word was, "hello."

They went on to look at other pages which she unerringly turned to. In all, the little smudges, all beneath lowercase letters, spelled out the words: hello with us he got me child this is. This was followed by the names: madeleine, annie, harold, and bartholomew. The last words of what seemed like a connected message were: faro played and lost. Along with this was something Julia believed was a numerical code. But she had a difficult time convincing Michael that she was right.

"How can you call that a code?" he asked her, "It's simply

where someone was checking off numbered selections in the table of contents."

"Yes," she admitted, "it looks like that at first, but . . ."

"But, what, Julia? How can you differentiate between the same check mark over and over?"

Then Cyrus broke in. "Like this," he said, "I believe I know what she's thinkin'," and he looked at Julia with a smile. "Tell me if I'm wrong, Honey," he said. And he went on to explain what he thought was true. They both listened to him as he continued, "You think we can link the check-marked numbers in the table of contents against the order which the poems come in, I mean the poems with messages in them, don't you?" he asked.

She nodded her head in the affirmative.

"And so," he continued, "if we look at them check-marks in the table of contents, we see that there's a series of numbers marked which when read in order don't make no sense. But if we experiment with 'em, we might find a line of numbers which do add up and have some logic to 'em . . ."

Here, Julia could not help herself, and she interrupted, looking triumphantly up at Mike as she said, "And if you correctly apply that string of numbers to the titles of poems with the messages in them they will all work out!"

Mike had at last lost his skepticism, Quietly he took the book which Cyrus now held and began to examine it. "So, what do you think the numbers mean?" he asked.

"Well," said Julia, while looking at Cyrus and pausing.

The old man didn't need further encouragement. "I think it's like this," he began, "I think maybe it's a way to follow the words accordin' to the order they was made in so that the message makes sense."

Operating on that theory, they experimented with the numerical coding. The largest number checked was a three digit number. It didn't take long to find a combination that worked.

What they came up with was, "hello this is us madeleine annie bartholomew harold he got me with child played faro and lost."

Mike was suddenly enthralled. "I'll be damned," he breathed.

"You see what I mean?" said Julia excitedly.

"Yeah, Babe, I do. Holy moly! Whatta' y'think Cy?"

The old man had been as impressed as either of them, but he hadn't uttered a sound. In fact, he had been unknowingly holding his breath. He let it out now in a long gush of air and answered Mike, "Boy, we're on to somethin' here, for sure."

After the initial excitement of finding an actual message wore off a bit, they began to discuss the writings in the rest of the book. It took a while, for they had to read and re-read certain passages in order to find anything significant.

"I've looked at it all at least three times, now," said Mike, "and I've been unable to see anything there except comment on the poems themselves." He looked at Julia and Cyrus, shrugged his shoulders and held his hands palms up.

Julia spoke, then, "I agree. I can't see anything like a message or a code there, either. I think we'd better move on with what we've got so far."

"And what do we actually have?" asked Cyrus, then continuing, "'cause I think it's important that we establish that an' make it clear."

"Good point, Cy, "said Mike, "Let's focus on that. Obviously we have some names. A bunch of names isn't much to go on message-wise."

"That's true," said Julia, "but there is a message."

"Pregnancy, for sure," said Cyrus, "and probably a hint at infidelity of some kind, either that or rape." He looked at Mike, then at Julia.

"Yeah, I see that," agreed Mike.

"What's faro?" asked Julia.

"It's a card game," said Cyrus, "Nothin' unusual for this town."

"No, not in those days, anyway," said Mike. Then he became quiet for a moment.

"What are you thinking, Michael?" asked Julia.

He smiled at her and then grinned at Cyrus. The old man grinned back.

"He's thinkin' we're makin' fools of ourselves," chuckled Cyrus Dooley, rummaging in his shirt pocket for a cigarette.

While they waited patiently for him, Mike said, "No, I don't think we're making fools of ourselves. I just think I kinda' like this. It's right down my alley."

Julia almost snorted. She did not like any of it. Aside from meeting Cyrus Dooley, she would be just as happy if she and Mike had never arrived in Jerome, Arizona. At first, things had been alright, even fun. But the dreams Mike had been having, especially the last one with the smell and all in the little flat, well, she could do without it. And this message thing seemed to tie in with all the rest of the weird stuff, too.

"I'm glad you're having fun, Mike, but I'd just as soon forget it all and hit the road." She looked at Cyrus, then, "No offense to you, Cyrus. I'm glad we met you. But I don't believe in things like Mike does."

Cyrus reached out and took her by the hand. "Darlin'," he began, "if I was a few years younger, and Mike there wasn't already in the picture, I'd go with you myself. But, look here, Like I told Mike the other night, I ain't never seen a ghost. And in all the years I've lived in this so-called ghost town itself, I ain't never seen any evidence of anything 'cept people alive an' people dead. An' it's the live ones that can hurt you. But . . ." and his eyes glinted as he looked directly into hers before continuing, "somethin's goin' on here, don't you think? And whether it's live people or dead people that's behind it, we've sorta' got to keep on till we find out. Now, ain't that right?"

Looking at him through eyes that showed her anxiety, Julia said, "Alright, Cyrus, I suppose you're right. But I don't like it at all."

"Well, whatta' y'think, Cy?" asked Michael, obviously grateful to the old man for his help in convincing Julia not to give up, "What's our next step?"

With that, Cyrus said, "If all we have is them names an' these here papers, I think we should look for anything with one of the names on it, any story where one of these names is mentioned should tell us something, at least."

Mike and Julia both agreed. They spread some of the papers out before them on the floor and began to search. Sometimes the pages of the old papers were stuck together. At other times, the dried pages just crumbled into pieces and scraps. But they took their time and were as careful as the intensity of their interest would allow them to be. It wasn't long before their efforts were rewarded.

"Hey, here's something."

Both Julia and Cyrus put down the pages they had been looking through to attend to Mike's next words.

"What have you got?" asked Cyrus, looking closely at Michael who had gone on to read to himself after making the declaration that there was something of interest in the paper he held before him.

"It's about one of the names we're looking for. Listen to this," and Mike began to read aloud.

THIRTY EIGHT

Annie soon took steps to make good on her intentions. It should not be difficult to turn the oaf called Faro to her own needs. She was determined that he would become a line to Gilmour, who thought he had severed relations with Annie. And She was not going to allow the little man off so easily. It was his very resistance to her attempts to get closer to him, to find out what made him the way he was that drew her to him in the first place. She would not give up.

Annie took to meeting Gilmour's loose-jointed minion whenever she could. It was not a hard thing to do. She had only to be careful of Madeleine's watchfulness. Harry was no bother. He would not in any way interfere in her activities.

She made an appointment with Faro. Soon they met on a regular basis at various locations in town. One day they stood near a metal railing on the sidewalk running along Hull Avenue. Before them, and below the level on which they stood, lay a small playing field maintained by the town. Beyond that was Bittercreek Gulch. It contained the shacks of the Mexican and Eastern European communities as well as the United Verde Extension Mine. On the gulch's northern edge stood the Little Daisy Hotel which served as quarters for many of the men who worked the mines in Jerome. It was a grand edifice. The only other bright spot in this entire view was the adobe mansion on the east rim of the gulch which was owned by the Douglas Family who, in turn, owned and operated the United Verde Extension Mine.

Annie allowed herself only a brief look at the gray boards of the shacks and the tin roofs which sheltered the mine operations. Nor did she give much time to the hotel or the mansion. Beyond the descending slopes of the mountain, the valley lay in a slice of winter sun. She gazed on its lovely expanse.

Faro had his eyes on her. But to all who might see them there, they both appeared to be simply enjoying the view. Behind them, the jostle and the noise of people, mostly men, coming from and going to the shooting gallery nearby, as well as visiting the other businesses, told them that at least people who normally ran in the circles frequented by Madeleine Morgan or Harry Waldon would not likely be the ones to see them standing incongruously together.

Faro had just asked Annie if she knew what happened in the many whorehouses Jerome had, including one or two only a glance away from where they now stood. She had smiled inwardly at the question. She recognized it easily as an attempted foray into the realm of sex. He had made little feints before in that direction. Indeed, the subject was not ever far beneath the surface of any conversation the two of them had. She toyed with him. Sometimes she was quick to head him into another avenue of talk. At other times she teased him, allowing him more and more leeway until she could tell his mind had begun to cloud with its ever-present lust. Then she let him down hard, often ending the meeting with an unexpected comment that meant it was over.

At such times, he muttered to himself as he watched her walk away. If he could have seen her face during those moments, he would have seen her smiling to herself, gloating with pleasure at how she had pulled him along by his own emotions.

This time she did not intend to walk away. This time she meant for him to leave her. She turned to him with a twist to her lips that was almost a smirk as she answered his question with her own, "Do you?"

She held her gaze on his watery brown eyes which flicked away from hers and back again as he declared in a somewhat surprised tone, "Why, sure I do. I go in 'nere an' use 'em when I want to."

"Tell me about it," she urged. "I'd like to know just what does go on when a man enters a whorehouse and asks to do business there."

He began to snigger and turned from her to look out into the empty space before them. A silly grin spread across his long-jawed face and he shook his head once or twice as if getting rid of a fly which was bothering him. "Shoot," he said, "I guess I never told any of this to a girl before," and he laughed a little too loudly, glanced quickly at her and then looked away.

"I don't know where to start," he said.

But she was not going to allow him the luxury of avoiding his embarrassment. She continued to press him. "Do you just go in and pick them out?" she asked.

He looked back at her. "Yeah," he said, quietly this time, "sometimes it's like 'at. It depends on which place you go to."

"Can anyone go to any place he chooses?"

His expression darkened. His jaws clenched, closing his mouth. His lips, slightly puffed, sealed themselves while his brows furrowed and his eyes narrowed. Men like Faro could not go into any house of prostitution they chose. There were a few places which would not accept them, places reserved for only the elite of Jerome. Places for men like B.L. Buenig.

For a moment, the thought of Buenig brought back a flash of memory to Faro of that night on the street when he had thought the big man was going to break his face if he hit him again. But he and Pete had done for him, by-God! And his special whore, too. He'd seen to that one himself; walked in on her unexpectedly on an afternoon and caught her sleeping. hadn't even done anything to her, just killed her.

An' this one, this little bitch who should be at home in that big fancy house instead of down here on the street runnin' like some little whore herself; she had one of them high-falutin' sluts for a sister, the kind he could never have even if she was a whore. Dammit!

For a moment he almost said it all to Annie. But the admonition Gilmour had given him halted him. He let the anger that seethed in his mind subside before answering her. After a short pause he looked at her and said, "No, seems as if even in the world of whoredom some people thinks they's better'n others."

Before Annie could reply to this, Faro suddenly changed the direction of their conversation. "Say," he said, grinning this time, "I seen you 'an Mister Waldon in 'at big car of his the other day."

"Yes," she said, by way of answering the statement which was not only a statement but a question as well.

"What's it feel like to ride in 'at thing?"

And here youth betrayed her, took away the veneer she had used to keep him at bay, and with a prideful smile she declared, "It feels good. He's teaching me to drive it."

"Seems like 'at might be hard for a girl like you to do," he said, "I mean, 'at things mighty big 'an heavy lookin'."

"Yes, but I do it," she said.

He looked at her and said, "Dang it, I'd give somethin' to ride in it. Y'ever think of sneakin' it out sometime an' goin' for a spin by yourself?"

The heady thrill of the thought exploded in her mind. No, she had never considered such a thing. But if thinking about it made her feel as if she were on a merry-go-round, spinning so fast that she felt a sort of delicious emptiness filling her abdomen, exciting her with the danger of it all, then what might actually doing it make her feel?

She knew he was observing her, trying to fathom what might be in her mind as she pondered his question. She looked coolly at him and said with no hint of excitement or surprise, "I have thought of that. And I might do it, too," then she added, "one of these days. But, tell me, Faro, how is Regis? You know, I am fond of him. I can't understand why he won't let his friends come to see him."

It was now his turn to take care in answering. She was amused by the expression on his face. She could almost read his thoughts as easily as she could see the grime along the edge of his frayed shirt collar.

"I might be able to help you as far as Mister Gilmour goes," he said, "you come down to his office next Thursday at about ten in the mornin'. You knock. You hear me say come on in then you know it's alright. You hear anything else you know it's not."

"I will be in school next Thursday at ten O'clock. Can't I come after school?"

He looked at her with an expression he hoped resembled surprise, "You got somethin' against playin' hookey?"

"No, my sister does."

THIRTY NINE

They both looked expectantly at Mike. "Well," asked Julia, "whatcha' got?" She put down the paper she had been looking through and waited.

"Here it is," said Mike, "big headline, Valley Copper News, Thursday, May 18, 1926. Little Daisy Top Man Found Dead In Red-Light District. Mine executive found dead this morning at intersection of Hull and First Avenues. The body of Bartholomew Linnaeus Buenig, known to many in Jerome as B.L., was found by sheriff's deputies this morning. The body was lying with the head near the curb of the southeast corner of the intersection. Mr. Buenig's neck had been broken in addition to a wound to the head by a bludgeon of some sort. He had also been stabbed in the heart . . ." here, Mike stopped reading. "Shall I go on," he asked.

"You think that's the Bartholomew mentioned in the message?" asked Julia.

"Keep reading, Mike," urged Cyrus.

Mike continued, "The sheriff's department believes there were two assailants. Apparently the victim fought his killers. Cuts on Mr. Buenig's right hand indicate he struck something with a closed fist. The motive for this foul crime is thought to have been robbery.

The victim's wallet was missing along with a gold watch he always wore, according to those who knew him well. The deed was done sometime in the early morning or late evening according to the coroner. Speculation as to why Mr. Buenig was in that part of town during the time of the murder has been put forth. Mr. Buenig was known to enjoy walks during the evening. Funeral arrangements are being made by Miss Madeleine Morgan, a close friend. Services are to be held in the Holy St. Mary's Church. Burial will be in the Jerome cemetery this next Sunday, May 21."

"Well, there's your answer, Honey," Cyrus said to Julia.

"What do you mean," she asked.

"The name, Bartholomew," said Mike, by way of explanation, "in company with the name Madeleine, it has to be the one in the message. What do you think the paper meant by the term, 'close friend', Cyrus?"

"Just a nice way to say his mistress," said Cyrus, "Notice it said 'Miss', it wouldn't have been proper for any married woman to take over a man's funeral arrangements in them days, less'n it was her husband or relative, even in this town."

"So, how come we are finding just the articles we're looking for?" asked Julia, "It doesn't seem logical."

"Well, in the first place," said Cyrus," we ain't just findin' what we are lookin' for. Here's one about ol' man Clark dyin'. It's in the Jerome Chronicler, dated 1925. An' another article I run acrost a little bit ago was all about a gang of bootleggers caught doin' business out of the basement of the old theatre. I believe the paper was a Prescott paper." He searched through the papers nearby which he had already gone through and put aside, "Yeah, here it is, It's in the Sentinel. Says only the head of the gang was caught and identified but that the authorities are lookin' for others who might have been involved." He paused to read to himself momentarily, "Hah, this's different, it says they were tipped off by an anonymous out-of-state-informant."

"So, what's your point, Cy? asked Mike, for he, too, was beginning to wonder along the same lines as Julia.

"Just this," said Cyrus Dooley. Like I said, I got these old newspapers out of a house over on Leroux Street. Same place I found them old photos. I was rummagin' around in it one day and I found 'em all tied up neat with twine. So I gathered 'em all up an' brought 'em here. Whoever was collectin' these papers wasn't just doin' it at random. They was lookin' only for important stuff."

"Yeah, I guess I see that," said Michael, "if you look at the dates on them you can tell that was probably the case. You don't find days and weeks in consecutive order."

"That's right," said Cyrus, "what we got here is a collection, not just a bunch of old papers that somebody saved just to be savin'."

With that, they all three went back to searching. The sounds in the room soon settled to the rattling of the old papers as their pages were turned. Minutes went by, and then it was Juila who spoke.

"Hey, here's something."

Both men looked at her expectantly.

"Ah, I guess not, it's on the second page. It's about some old bum they found dead with no way to identify him. Rotted in some ravine for nearly a year." She continued to read then said, "All he had was a piece of paper in his back pocket, an I.O.U. with the name F. Potter on it."

"Poor bastard," Mike commented.

They continued to search through the collection of old papers. Suddenly Mike said, "Bingo!"

Julia and Cyrus waited quietly.

"It's an article about the work that was going on at the hospital; gives the names of the men on the board of development."

"And?" asked Julia.

"Says Harry Waldon is the president of the board," Mike answered.

"Any pictures?"

"No, just a list of names and titles."

"Alright," said Cyrus, "We got Bartholomew, Madeleine, and Harry together. Things look like they're comin' to a head."

At this point, Julia looked at Cyrus Dooley and said, "Cyrus, I don't think I can go back to that flat. I mean, I don't think I can ever sleep in that bed again."

The old man put aside the papers he had been thumbing through and leaned back against the front of the couch. "Well, hells bells, girl, you don't have to. You an' Mike can stay right here. I got room. We'll clean out one of them ol' rooms down the hall and you can put a bed up in there. It won't be fancy, but it won't stink neither. Why, I even have the spare bed and mattress stored around here somewheres."

Mike looked on quietly as Cyrus said this. "Babe," he began, in an effort to soothe Julia's fears, "Cy is right. To tell you the truth, I've been thinking the same thing."

"Well," and she shook her head from side to side, pursed her lips and looked apologetically at Cyrus, "I'm sorry about it, but I feel as if we have to, unless . . ." and she looked up at Mike who had moved from the floor to a chair.

"Unless what?" he asked, looking back at her.

"Unless we get in that little bug and leave this place," she declared.

Both men looked at each other then and Cyrus began to laugh. Mike simply smiled. Julia turned pleading eyes toward him, "Oh Michael," she said, drawing in a long sigh and stretching her arms above her head before settling back into position on the floor, "I guess I just want to leave all of this and remember it as some silly set of odd coincidences. I mean, here we are in a decayed little hole on some mountainside, being driven to scrabbling through newspapers because of some damned dreams and a jerk somewhere who wants to scare us with a crazy prank!" And she reached out and grabbed at some papers and threw them toward the wall. But her aim was bad and they hit Cyrus in the chest.

"Oh," she said, holding a hand to her face, "I'm sorry, Cyrus, I . . ." But she didn't finish. Like Mike, she was arrested by the old man's expression as he stared at one of the papers she had hit him with.

"What is it, Cy?" Mike asked quietly.

Cyrus Dooley looked up at him as if he were someone he had never seen before, then his eyes softened and he turned them toward Julia. "I think it's a little too late to start running away, Honey."

FORTY

Annie had not been fooled by Faro. She had seen behind his simple ruse as if he had been a child. Indeed, even though he was older than she was by at least ten years, he was not her equal intellectually. She had smiled to herself while watching him attempt to answer her questions about the procedures used in brothels. She had known that he was not able to simply use any one he pleased. But she wanted to pressure him, to see him squirm. Perhaps Regis would be in his office. She was not sure what she would do if he wasn't. She was convinced that Faro would ask her to come in. She knew what he wanted.

In another girl, certainly none of it would ever have gotten this far. Even in an adult woman of tarnished reputation, it would not have. But in Annie there was that mixture of intellect, guile, and sense of adventure which was paired with a precocious mind. Even her unique background, which was far more complete in the raw ways of the world than that of most decent women of the day in Jerome, was not enough to hold her back. In fact, it was the reality of her past, what she had learned from living with her mother and sister, that and suffering adversities few people had to endure that gave her a feeling of confidence which overshadowed that small bit of nagging fear in the back of her mind which said she should not go. If Regis was there it would be what she had hoped. And if not, maybe Faro wouldn't be such a beast after all.

When Thursday came, she went off to school as usual, but she never arrived. She went instead to the downtown area and kept as inconspicuous as she could until ten o'clock. Then she went into a side door of the theatre and thence to the basement below. She knocked on the door there and, as expected, heard Faro ask, "Who is it?"

He let her in with a grin on his face which he could not have erased had he been paid to. "You can come in but the boss ain't here."

A kind of controlled anger seized her as she walked slowly into the room while the leering oaf held the door open. So, she thought, Regis was not here. Probably on business somewhere, maybe it was a regular thing for him to be away on this day every week. Faro had known. Well, she wasn't any too surprised. Maybe she could turn things her way just the same.

Behind her, she heard the door close and the lock click. There was a chain lock above the regular one which Faro also put in place. She turned to face him.

"You think you're pretty smart, don't you?"

He ducked his head in embarrassment. "You didn't have to come," he mumbled through his wide-stretched lips.

She backed till she felt the edge of the big desk. "How about right here on top?" she offered.

He suddenly lost his grin. "Huh? Whatta' you mean?"

She turned and swept the surface of the desk clean with several movements of her arm. When she was finished, she faced Faro again and said through a smirk, "Right here, let's do it right here." And she began to take off her clothes. She threw her coat on the floor near the things from Gilmour's desk. Then she pulled her long skirt up and over her head. She stood before him, then, in an outer slip. Finally, she lifted that and was dressed only in her inner slip and underthings, looking odd with her feet still encased in the heavy winter shoes she wore against the cold and the wet.

"That's the boss's desk," Faro said with alarm, looking at her and then down at the floor where the scattered items from the desk lay.

"When you're having fun you gotta' take chances, Faro," she said. "You asked me to take a chance. I did. Now, how about it?"

He looked at her with a dumb expression. Suddenly, she knew that she was once more in charge. She could do this or not. There wasn't much in it for her, except a chance to score against Faro and the little Irishman as well. That might be enough to pay for the indignity of suffering this loose-jointed, leering bastard to mount her. Well, then getting on with it was the next step. Right on top of the desk where Regis worked. She couldn't help but laugh a little at the picture of him sitting there tomorrow. She was certain Faro would clean up the mess on the floor, and he wouldn't like telling Regis what he'd done today, not if he'd done it on top of the little man's prized desk.

"Whatta' you laughin' at," demanded Faro, "is somethin' funny? 'Cause this ain't no funny time, y'know."

"I know," she said, pulling her underslip up and over her head and throwing it on top of her dress and other things on the floor. She looked at him and closed her eyes halfway as she had often seen her mother do. Once, she had even listened, hidden beneath a bed, as Madeleine entertained a man in her room back in Texas.

It was not Annie's first time, though there had only been one other time for her. But a comparison of her reaction with Faro's would have indicated that it was his. He walked to the light switch on the wall and turned off the lights. Then she heard him sliding his feet along the floor as he made his way back to the desk. He talked as he approached, and his voice quavered as if he was shaking, either that or he was shivering.

"I ain't never done this before with no good . . . with nobody exceptin' a whore. I mean, I ain't callin' you nothin' bad an' all, but . . ." Then he bumped into the desk.

After that she could hear him struggling to get undressed so he might take the required position on top of her where she lay on the desk. Finally, he came to her, but he could not find his way. She reached down and guided him.

Suddenly, one of his feet slipped and he almost fell off her. It was an effort for her not to burst into laughter. But quietly she put an arm out and helped him keep his balance. It was when the end came that she enacted her planned mischief, both for him and his little boss who was not there. As Faro reached orgasm, she shifted beneath him so that he pulled out of her and, in a frenzy to find his way back, he ejaculated not only on her but on the surface of the fine finish that beautified the desk Regis Gilmour was so proud of.

"Unnhgh . . . Goddammit! Oh, hell! Shit fire, ooh!"

Beneath him, she turned away and grinned into the darkened room. "What's wrong?" she asked in her most tender voice.

"N . . . nothin'," he almost growled, rolling off her and standing.

"Turn on the light," she said, acting out her intended part. "Was that all? Was that it? Did you like it, Faro?" She could hear him shuffling toward the wall where the light switch was.

Suddenly, the lights came on. He stood with his hand still on the switch. He looked unhappy in his nakedness. He had removed all of his clothes except his underwear and his pants which lay around his ankles. Shaking his head, he said, "We gotta' clean all of this up." Then he looked toward the desk where she still lay, smiling at him. "Aw, hell" he declared, we got it all over the damned desk!"

She said innocently, "Got what on the desk?" What are you talking about?" Then she suddenly became all business, gathering her clothing and dressing herself as quickly as she could. "I'm sorry you are disappointed, Faro. I really am. After all, I did what you asked me to do. Now, I have to go. Do you know what people might think about me if they found out such a thing had taken place? Why, I hope that Regis Gilmour never finds it out," then, pretending to notice the condition of the desk's surface for the first time, she exclaimed, "Oh, did you put that on his desk, Faro?"

She finished dressing while he stood with mouth open and anguish on his face, then she walked to the door and unlocked it. She carried the picture with her of him standing dumbfounded as she passed through the doorway and closed the door behind her. With mischievous grin in place, she hurried from the building and onto the street.

She kept her head down as she walked up Jerome Avenue toward Main. The usual number of people, mostly men, was in evidence on the sidewalks. On the hill above the town's prime business section she could just see a corner of the roof on the big house. She'd tell Madeleine she had to leave school early because she did not feel well. That was her plan if she encountered her sister at home.

But Madeleine was not in the big house when Annie got there. She had said at breakfast that she might be away all afternoon at some women's group gathering. It was one reason Annie had finally decided to meet Faro. The odds had looked as if they were in her favor.

She quickly ran up the front stairs and down the big hall to her own bedroom. She took off her clothes and examined them for any signs of what she had just done. Her underpants were soiled. She laughed as she looked at them and thought of what was on them. How much more of that was on Regis's desk. And besides that, she had ruined it completely for Faro. All in all, she felt victorious.

Taking the soiled underpants in her hand and grabbing a clean pair along with a fresh linen under slip from her dresser drawer, she hurried down the hall to the bathroom. The big house had two bathrooms on the upper floors. She shared this one with her sister and Harry.

She turned the water on in the porcelain tub that stood on four legs along one side of the large room. The floor was covered in a most beautiful pattern of pea-green and purple linoleum. The tub and matching wash basin were of glistening white, while the toilet stool itself sat against another wall in gleaming gold and green. Its seat was of oak in a shiny finish. Along the other wall a great mirror ran for seven feet above a vanity counter. A soft throw rug lay in the middle of the room. She nudged it close to the bath tub as she stepped in and sank into the hot water. She poured in a favorite oil and submerged herself up to her nose. Closing her eyes, she relaxed, thinking of what had just taken place in the basement beneath the theatre. What fools men were to put so much importance into such a small thing.

*   *   *

It took time for Annie to learn that it hadn't been such a small thing at all. It was two months before she would allow herself to admit that, in fact, it had been a considerable thing indeed. She was pregnant. A heavy sadness enveloped her, then. She knew she had to tell someone, but she was not convinced that someone had to be Madeleine. It couldn't be Harry, either. She didn't know exactly why she felt unwilling to tell him about her meeting with Faro. But she knew she didn't want to. She reached a similar conclusion in regard to telling her sister. The obvious solution was to tell the priest, Father K. they called him.

She had concluded this one afternoon while wandering around the house alone. Madeleine was again out with some of her women friends. Annie felt bad about not confiding in Madeleine. Feelings of guilt were unusual for her, but even she felt the quandary she was in was impressive.

Passing along the hall, she came to the opened door to the big bedroom Madeleine and Harry shared. As she often did, she went inside.

Annie looked around admiringly at the changes her sister had brought to the room. The furniture was massive, and all in oak. But there were touches of Madeleine to be seen; the beautiful throw-rug on the polished hardwood floor was hers, so were the pictures on the walls, and the frilly, ruffled satin curtains. As well, the bedding had been selected by Madeleine. Along one wall she had placed a daybed of simple and tasteful design. Nearby was a chair with a small table and floor lamp at its side. Annie knew that her sister used that part of the room to give herself some privacy. The great bed was not hers, it was Harry's. The little daybed, done in two shades of brown metal and wicker, was a place where only she went.

Annie walked over to the daybed and lay down. She felt something hard beneath the pillow. She knew what it was. Reaching in her hand, she removed a book of poetry. She held it up to her face. She knew that Harry had given it to Madeleine soon after B.L. had been found murdered. Madeleine considered the poetry in it important in some way. She often wrote comments in it. Casually, Annie opened the book and began to read. Her sister's remarks about the poems were of interest to her. Suddenly, an idea was born.

It would take her a few days to devise the simple code, but she knew this was a way she could tell Madeleine of her dilemma. She would divulge the truth but, characteristically, she would do it in her own style. In the meantime, she'd like to see that Faro sweat a little.

FORTY ONE

Regis Gilmour was furious. "What? You did it to her on my own Goddammed desk! Goddamm it, Faro, you sonofabitch!"

"Boss, I mean, I didn't think about it, Boss. She didn't give me no choice, I . . . she . . ."

The little man, who had been walking back and forth in rage and frustration while listening to Faro, stopped in mid-stride. He turned to the lanky thug now and said in almost a whisper of disbelief, "She gave you no choice? Is that what you said, she gave you no choice?" Then with his voice increasing gradually in volume as he spoke, he said with extreme anger, "You had her in here, where by-God you knew damn well you shouldn't have had her in the first place, you had her in here with the Goddamned doors locked, her clothes on the floor, and you tell me she gave you no choice? When did you make this monumental mistake, because that's what you did you dumbassed bastard, you made a big mistake!"

"I guess it was a coupla' months ago," said Faro, his hands trembling with fear.

Gilmour turned away in disgust. His face was flaming red. He walked over to his desk and sat down in the big leather chair. His eyes seemed to be glued to the polished surface in front of him. He finally looked up and glared at Faro who stood miserable and at attention before the little man. His eyes strayed to that spot on the wooden surface of the desk in front of his boss.

"Do you know that I sometimes have coffee and a doughnut right here on my desk?" Gilmour asked quietly.

"I know, Boss."

"Gilmour looked away from Faro and then returned his eyes to that special area on the desk before him. With rising voice, he said, "I mean, sometimes I even have a sandwich for God's sake!"

"I'm sorry, Boss, you don't know how sorry I am 'at this here happened."

Gilmour shook his head in bewilderment, "How in hell did you get it all over the damned desk anyway? You're not supposed to get it on anything, maybe a little, but not a lot."

Faro didn't answer the question. Instead, he made another statement. This one caused Gilmour to leap to his feet and pound his fist into his palm. He made three quick trips back and forth in front of his hired henchman before stopping and demanding, "Whatta' you mean she's pregnant? You crazy sonofabitch, she's a damned kid in high school. All the damned whores in this horseshit town and you have to bring her to my office and fuck her right here on my desk and now you tell me she's pregnant. You lousy bastard!"

"It's alright, Boss," Faro said quietly, almost soothingly.

Filled with disbelief and disgust, Gilmour walked to his desk and sat in the big chair. This time he looked up at the face of his employee instead of down at the surface of the desk. "What the hell are you talkin' about?" he asked.

Faro shrugged. "Boss, you think I might could set down? I mean, I'm tired of standin', I mean."

"Sit," said Gilmour, nodding toward a nearby chair, and, as Faro took the offered seat, Gilmour continued, "Now, tell me, what do you mean it's gonna' be alright?"

Faro scooted back a bit in the chair so as to keep his long legs from being too close to the sides of his boss's desk before answering, "I'm gonna' kill her."

This time Gilmour simply sucked in his breath. Stunned, he sat still for several moments. Then he leaned toward Faro. "Now you listen to me," he said, "I don't want to hear any more of this crap. You hear me. We're running a business here, a good business!" He slammed his fist down on the desk top. Then, turning his hand over so he could examine it, he looked at it for a long time before directing his attention once more to Faro. "You bastard, I told you no bullshit. Now, you look here, I'm not the one who is in trouble, you are. I told that girl to stay away from me. I got witnesses."

"That would be me," said Faro. I heard you tell her."

Gilmour sighed heavily and sat back in his chair. He stuck his forefinger and thumb into his eyes and rubbed hard at them. "Alright," he said, "tell me the whole Goddamned thing. But don't be talking about killing anybody. We don't need the police lookin' for somebody wanted for murder who's also a part of our business."

FORTY TWO

Father K. waited for the traditional declaration of sinning, but it didn't come. Instead, the girl simply stated that she was pregnant.

"Who has done this thing to you, my child?" He, of course, had his own suspicions. A man who could involve himself in murder could certainly take a young girl who was nothing to him at all. He waited for her to confirm what he already thought. Again, he was surprised by what she said.

"It doesn't matter who did it, Father, I had a choice."

With a sigh which he was not successful in stifling, Father K. asked, "Have you told him?"

She laughed softly at the suggestion. It was funny to think of Faro in his doltish, lanky self as being the father of any child coming from her, but he was. "I've told him. We are going out in the car to have a long talk about it soon."

Father K. sat upright. Ah, he thought, the car. "So, you will use the car," he said, quietly, "Where will you go with him?"

Again she laughed. She knew what he was thinking. It was fun to play with men. All of them from the least to the so-called best had that one area of vulnerability. This one, now, he would be the hero if she allowed him to be. And why? Simply because he was aware of her as a female. She was a girl and he was a boy. How easy it was.

"It doesn't matter, Father, where we go, does it?"

"You are merely a child."

"I am more than that, now, Father. And I am the one who is acknowledging what I have done."

"And when will he admit to his . . . deeds?"

"He is not my concern, Father."

*   *   *

Next, Annie paid a visit to DeNelle. She found it to be a bit more difficult than the one made to Father K.

"I tol' you to stay 'way from that man an' anybody connected with him. I tol' you, child."

"You can get it done for me, DeNelle. I would have Madeleine do it but I don't want her to know."

DeNelle sighed and looked sadly at Annie. "Yes, we can get it done," she said, "it's somewhat late at two months. You sure it ain't any longer than that?"

"I know all about it, DeNelle. I've seen my mother and my sister go through the same thing. I know when it is and when it isn't. I know the signs."

DeNelle rose from the chair she had been sitting in and walked from her small front room into her even smaller kitchen. But her voice came to Annie easily from there. "Your motha' an' sistuh' wadn't no two months along when they did such things as you're askin' me to see to for you, now."

"I'll go someplace else," said Annie.

DeNelle came back into the room with the tea service. She set it down on a table between her chair and the loveseat Annie sat on. "That's what I'm worried about, you goin' to some quack." She was obvious in her distress over the matter. "I'll help you, child, but it ain't 'cause of your sistuh', an' it sho' ain't because I'm afraid of them that's responsible for this mess." She looked at Annie and shook her head with frustration, "You ain't nothin' but a baby yourself! Runnin' 'round here like you was meant to. I had a friend once talked to me 'bout you . . ."

"Who?" Annie interrupted.

"Never you mind. I said I would look out for you, an' I've tried," she shifted in the chair and took a sip of tea, put the cup down in its saucer and looked hard at Annie, "Lord, child! I was hopin' it might not come to this. An' I'll tell you one thing more, too," she leaned forward and shook her finger in Annie's face. "you come to me with anything like this again an' I'm goin' straight to your sistuh', Miss Madeleine, before I even let you in this front room. Now, you find a way to get ovuh' here in a day or two an' we'll see about this." Then she stood to open the door so Annie could leave.

"You won't tell Madeleine? You promise you won't?" Annie pleaded.

"Go on, get on out of here, now. I tol' you what I would do. Go on."

*   *   *

It was two days later and just at the end of the afternoon, in that pause between the dying of the day and the beginning of evening, when Annie took the car from the garage and picked Faro up on the south side of town on the road going over the mountain to Prescott.

"How'd you manage to get the car 'thout nobody knowin' it?" he asked, jumping into the front seat and looking around behind them to see if anyone had seen him get in.

She strained to put the car into a lower gear and keep the engine from stalling on the slight upgrade they were on. "Well," she grinned, after shifting the transmission and sending the big Cadillac growling ahead, "they went downtown to eat at a restaurant."

"Maybe they saw you drivin' along?" offered Faro.

"No," she said, shifting again and pulling the gear lever down so that the car was now in a higher gear, "they went to the Fashion. Madeleine said she wanted a good steak dinner. They wanted me to go with them but I begged off. How do you like my driving?"

"Let's go to the top and then turn around," he said, ignoring her question, "I'd like to drive her on the way down."

She didn't answer, but she drove toward the heights as he had requested. In the cold sky above them, the clouds began to darken. A storm was likely on its way, and she was glad the top was up on the car. She did not know how to work its mechanism. If Harry had left it down, they would be in trouble, now. She hoped that the weather wouldn't hinder her driving. It was getting darker by the minute. For it to be raining now would not be a good thing.

The thought of the weather bringing her trouble amused her. She had made arrangements to get rid of the real trouble. She had thought that she would tell him about it, reassure him that everything was going to be alright. But as they drove along, the idea that once she did, she would have less control of him, an idea which was not new to her, solidified in her mind. She would not tell him. Instead, she would keep the facts to herself and maintain the pressure she was sure, now, that he felt. There was one thing she wanted to know, and that was whether he had told Regis.

But he was not forthcoming with much as they drove up the roadway. She would have been concerned if not for his manner. He seemed calm and unworried. In fact, he seemed more interested in the prospect of driving the car than in the dilemma they had gotten themselves into.

It was almost dark when she turned the big machine off the road into a meadow near the top of the mountain and steered it in an arc that pointed it back down the way they had come. Rain spotted the flat face of the windshield.

"Why don't you stop it right here an' we'll switch places," he said.

She pushed in the clutch with effort and pulled the gear lever into neutral. The engine idled under the hood. She waited till he opened her door and then she scooted across to the passenger's side, allowing him to get in.

When he got in and shut the door, she said, "Let's just sit here a few minutes."

He turned to her and demanded, "What for?"

"Well, we have to deal with this . . . issue between us, Faro."

"Hell, it's cold up here, you know it? Specially with no damned windas' nor nothin' on this damned old thing to keep the wind an' rain out. We can talk about all this here stuff that's botherin' you back in town. Come on, whatcha' say?"

She turned away from him then in resignation. It was cold. And he was right about the absence of anything to keep the weather from blowing in beneath the fabric stretched across the frame of the car's roof.

"Well," she said, "maybe you're right. I hope you were telling me the truth about being able to drive the car."

"Don't you worry none, I can," he said, closing and opening the door one or two times before settling in the seat.

"Are you trying to wear it out?" she joked.

"Naw, just want to make sure the durn thing's shut. I don't want to fall out."

She laughed at him, then. "Really, Faro, have you ever driven a car before?"

For answer, he turned on the big headlamps, pushed in the clutch, dropped the shifter into low gear, and drove smoothly out of the meadow and onto the road. He looked at her with a grin as he shifted into the next gear without the slightest bit of shudder from the motor. She grinned back at him.

They went down the road, then. Above them, thunder exploded and rain fell heavily.

FORTY THREE

C yrus Dooley handed the paper he had been looking at to Michael without saying anything further. Julia watched Mike's face as it went white. She snatched at the paper which he was no longer looking at. Instead, he gazed into the darkness beyond the windows of Cyrus's apartment.

As she unfolded the paper and began to read it herself, she felt a sinking in her chest and a wave of heat seemed to envelop her head. Then she felt suddenly cold. The paper headlined the accident on 89A that had taken the life of a certain Annabelle Morgan. A car had gone over the side. The story went on to name Madeleine Morgan as the unfortunate victim's nearest relative. It named Harry Waldon as Madeleine Morgan's "very close friend." More details followed, such as the weather and the estimated time of the accident, also the absence of anyone else who may have been involved or might have witnessed the accident. There was a single photograph of the accident scene accompanying the article. Julia noted the date on the masthead; November 14, 1927.

It was shortly before midnight when they finally gave up on further searching through the old papers, as if what they had already found was much more than they had expected. After they sat and talked for another hour, Cyrus helped them make a bed in one of his vacant rooms. They cleaned out what little trash was in the room and brought in a mattress and some blankets.

"It ain't much, but it'll do," said Cyrus. "Tomorrow, we'll get a real bed and some furnishings in here for you." Then he looked toward the front of the room which held a window and a door that led onto the balcony running along the side of the old rooming house perched above the street that was 89A. "Just don't fall off that thing in the night," he finished with a chuckle.

Mike looked at him and said, "It's the same balcony you and I sat on the other night, isn't it?"

"It sure is, boy."

"I might sit out there for a while, but I won't fall off," Mike assured him."

"Well, you don't have to worry about me," said Julia, "I'm going to get into this bed and go right to sleep."

After Cyrus left them, and they both were in bed and the lights were out, Julia turned to Mike and asked, "You asleep?"

He wasn't. "No, my mind is going a million miles an hour, just turning all of this over and over, trying to figure it out."

They talked for more than an hour. Finally, she said, "Well, I've got to get some sleep. C'mere."

He rolled toward her, "Aw, Babe, I'm sorry I got us into this mess with my silly superstitious mind."

She kissed him, "I am too, but let's not talk any more about it. I'm all talked out. I've still got to pull a morning shift for old Rooster tomorrow."

He held her until she went to sleep. Then he lay on his back with eyes staring blindly into the darkness, glad she hadn't wanted to make love. After what had happened in the apartment they'd rented, he wondered if he could ever make love again.

In time, gentle rumbling signaled rain, then it was there. It fell hard at first, but finally settled into a steady patterning on the roof of the old building. He thought it might wake Julia, but she slept on. He eased himself out of bed and put on his clothes. It would be cold on the narrow balcony.

He went hunting for one of the chairs he and Cyrus had used the night before. Finding it, he carried it along the balcony until he was once more opposite the room where Julia lay on the makeshift bed. Then he put the chair down and sat in it. It was indeed cold. But the balcony was roofed. He wasn't going to get wet unless the rain increased and the wind blew.

Sitting there in the damp and the dark, he could feel the old town around him. It was like old papers stacked in a drafty corner of some old shed, like an old basement in winter; like rich, black loam turned over by a spade in an overgrown garden.

He smiled and shook his head at the tricks his own mind was trying to play on itself. And if I went on, he mused, I might compare it to that old graveyard in Georgia that time Luke tried to scare me. His friend, Luke, had told him all about an old graveyard that was abandoned, then dared him to meet him there after dark.

Mike had walked along the graveled country road in pitch darkness and finally reached the white cement entrance pillars leaning into the night. Inside the burial ground he stumbled along. Most of the time he could either see or sense the bulk of a tombstone he was about to blunder into in time to avoid it. But he eventually tripped and fell into the hollow that graves often become as the casket they contain rots and gives in to the weight of dirt above it.

God! It was as if the body, only a few feet below him, was about to reach out and embrace him with its rotten, bony arms and clutch him with its cold fingers. He leaped from the shrunken grave and almost screamed. It was then that he thought he saw something tall and white lurching out of the dark toward him. Of course it was his friend. He decided to turn the tables on him. Opening his shirt to expose his white undershirt, he howled as eerily as he could and lunged in his friend's direction. They both had a good laugh about it afterward.

But sitting on the balcony above the old highway as it came up the hill and into Jerome, he shuddered at the thought of lying in that old grave. This entire town was a grave. Life and death had begun to entwine themselves here long ago. And they had continued to exist side by side in the making of walls and streets and in the enacting of schemes and in the committing of deeds that were either good or bad or perhaps a bit of both. Life; it was flesh and blood and bones; it was love and hate; it was pain and pleasure, but it was always truth. Even when it lived in the form of a lie it was real. And its opposite, its eternal partner in existence, was death; the final truth.

They had discussed truth this night. A girl had been killed in a car that went over the side of the road going up the mountain from Jerome. He knew her name. Likely, according to what Cyrus said the address indicated, she had lived in that big house he had walked up to on his first day in Jerome. Was she the girl in his photograph? If there had only been a picture of her in the old news article; but there hadn't been, at least not one he could use to identify her with. The article had been accompanied by a rather bad photograph of the crowd at the site of the accident. But it had been in the early evening, and not much could be discerned from the picture. He had only words to help him, just words. And they were not enough. Even with his tendency to believe, his "going back" and all that it said about him, a part of him still held onto rationality and would not let go.

The girl had been alone in the car according to the paper. It had belonged to someone named H. Waldon. Harry Waldon. The girl had been the younger sister of a Miss Madeleine Morgan. Was the car the same one he had taken a photo of? The same one he had dreamed of? He couldn't make his mind conform to that idea. Yet the thought that the answer to these questions was yes kept nagging at him. Obviously someone in town knew what he was interested in. And they just as obviously did not like it; enough to befoul the very bed he slept in. How else to explain the smell in the apartment? Who was keeping tabs on him? Was it the person Julia thought she saw slipping away from the motorcycle pile-up?

This was the question they had all gone to bed with. It had numbed Julia's tired mind into submission. It had also affected Cyrus. He suddenly became very serious, serious and quite protective. It was he who had suggested they go to bed and talk it over in the morning. And it was he who had put an arm around Julia and assured her that everything was going to be alright, that surely there was some kind of explanation to be had. He had left them with more assurance, declaring that nothing would harm them in his house, and urging them not to worry, to get some sleep.

But Mike could not sleep. All around him lay things wishing to communicate with his soul. And he wanted to communicate with them as well. He wanted to, yet he shrunk from the thought. And that was not like him. Usually he wished to become one with the past. He could walk into an old building and see beyond all that was there in the present, see beyond it and into the years that had come before.

He loved those years coming before. They carried something more than mere existence, something greater than reality. They always made him yearn to reach out to them and become a part of them. And sometimes he almost could. To him, an old wall did not look old so much as it looked new. He could imagine it being built, could hear the scrape of the trowel as the mason loaded the bricks with mortar before placing one on top of the other. And he wondered about that mason; had he eaten a good breakfast that day? Did his boss approve of his work? Was he married? What would he tell his wife and children when he went home that evening? And, God! If he could only talk to him, talk to him and tell him about the changes that had taken place in the years which stood between them; see his eyes light up at the development of automobiles, airplanes, telephones; tell him that they were on the verge of curing cancer, that they had wiped out cholera, smallpox, pneumonia and diphtheria; that a second world war had come and gone and that America was the greatest and mightiest nation on earth! That they had recently dug a wooly mammoth out of the perma-frost and hauled it away on something called a helicopter;

that they intended to clone it, then explain cloning; that Darwin had been right, but a belief in God was more necessary than ever. And that quantum mechanics—explain that too—appeared to show that something like him was real, and photography and electronics were used to suggest that ghosts were, too!

He would reach out and touch the bricklayer's strong, work-worn hands and halt them in mid-motion, saying that his skill with mud and bricks, so highly touted in his time, was to one day give way completely, even as it was already beginning to in Jerome, to the crudity of poured reinforced concrete walls, then to concrete blocks, and then to a variety of other building materials and methods because, in the fabulous century ahead, bricks would be too expensive for ordinary building. He would tell the man to become an automobile mechanic. He would say that to him and then ask him what sports teams he favored, and if he ever had met a girl in town named Annabelle Morgan.

"Mike, you awake?"

Cyrus's voice coming so abruptly out of the darkness into the quiet pool that made up Mike's thoughts startled him, and he whipped around toward the sound of it with his hands before him as if to ward off a blow.

"Dammit, Cy, don't slip up on a man like that!"

Cyrus chuckled. "Sorry," he said, "I come to set with you." And he put the chair he had been carrying down next to Mike's.

"Well, you damned near caused me to fall off this balcony," Mike declared. But he was pleased to have the old man with him.

Cyrus sat down with a grunt and then a groan, "More rain, I see."

*   *   *

Below the buildings sitting along 89A on the slopes leading toward the valley, the storm drug its wet fingers across the thin topsoil of the old burial ground.

She rose in supernal form above the grave. The rain was nothing to her, except a thing to hide within. She could still be seen. Always that was true. It was one of the rules she existed by. As shadow or as substantial matter she was real. If only it were not so. If only she could have gone so long ago as the others who lay around her had gone; if only.

Before her the old town lay on the hillside. She could see it as it was and as it had been. She could not see it as it would be some day. That too, the inability to know what was to come, was one of the rules. She had pushed against these rules. Especially had she done so since the young man had come. And as punishment, perhaps as a warning, she had been unable to control the past, and it had relentlessly occurred and re-occurred within her memory at whatever speed and with whatever intensity it chose. She could no longer slow it or speed it or postpone it. Like fire out of control it came, and like fire it burned. She suffered. Time after time she had been at the cliff's edge and had seen the old car hauled over the side, dripping with the rain, dripping too with the heartache she had felt that night. Again and again she had driven alone over the same road in another rain storm and in another car; except, she had not been alone. Repeatedly, she had left the priest on the floor, awash in her hate, yet still thinking of her welfare. "Don't do this to yourself," he had said. If only she hadn't.

To her, the lives on the hillside before her were like stars; they could be seen to twinkle there in the dark. She was aware of them. She knew where the old man and the younger man were. The younger man had been a disappointment. He had dreamed, yes, but not the dreams she wanted.

Earlier, as she slid down from the old mansion at dusk, she had been tempted to intrude her senses; but only tempted. She had already given in too much to the temptation to tamper with the people, and it was not her right to tamper with the people. Oh, she could be a terrible force! But she was not there to torment others. To be tormented herself, this was the purpose behind her existence. And the only surcease from that torment was to come here and rise above his grave. It was like balm to her. Here, she could think of B.L. It was allowed. But nothing had ever indicated that he was more than the lump of rotting flesh and bones in the mouldering wood and cloth of the casket she had seen shiny and new as it was lowered into the hard, rock-filled earth all those years ago.

Only she was real, she and the old town and the people in it, and the bits and pieces of the past she must experience over and over. Like a dark column of smoke she swayed above the old grave. Once, she had sent fingerlings of herself into the earth to see. In terror she had jerked away from the thing there. She had never done that again.

At least his body was at peace and hidden from eyes that did not wish to see it as it was, eyes that obeyed a mind which wished to remember it as it had been. He had asked her once if she felt anything for him. She had only come to realize a short time earlier that she in fact did. She was sure it was love she felt growing within herself. But in answer to his question, she had said only that she respected and liked him, keeping her awareness of fledgling love a secret. If only she hadn't.

In the brief hours before dawn she collected herself and, with what for her was a low moan, began her ascent toward the old house. Within its walls, though there were places weak with dry rot and with areas of wet due to seepage of water from the slopes higher up and leakage from the roof, she could walk the creaking, sagging floors with the heavy and clumsy limbs of the thing that she had to endure as herself. But she could do so in peace from prying eyes. The old house was her own special darkness, her own mask for the world to see, her own place of misery.

FORTY FOUR

The next morning the town lay in the grip of rain. The sun provided only a gray light. It struggled to penetrate the front glass of Rooster's and reach the counter where Cyrus and Mike sat in their own kind of darkness.

Julia's face held a somber expression as she poured coffee for the two men. Looking at Mike, she said, "Let's just get our things together and put them in that little yellow bug and go. I tell you, Mike, it's what I want to do."

Cyrus looked at her and then at Mike and then back at her again. He smiled, too. "Y'know, maybe you ought'a do that. Just go and say to hell with it."

"Then what would you do?" Mike asked, looking directly at him and not smiling, waiting for an answer.

Cyrus returned the gaze for a moment before looking away and then back at his young friend. Taking a sip from his coffee, he stared at the surface of the counter, unable to answer.

"That's what I thought," said Mike. Then, looking at Julia, he said, "We are going to finish this thing. When we've done that, then we'll talk about leaving."

Julia moved away without a word to take care of other customers. Mike and Cyrus bent their heads and ate the breakfasts she had placed before them earlier. When they were done, Mike caught Julia's eye. She took their money at the cash register. Mike gave her a peck on the cheek, and as she watched, he and Cyrus walked out. Cyrus carried his usual pack. Mike had his camera on a sling. Julia noticed that he also had a small flashlight sticking out of the back pocket of his jeans. Just before the door closed behind them, Julia said, "Wait!"

She hurried from behind the counter and went outside with them. They stood together on the sidewalk. "What should I do if you don't come back right away? I mean, Mike, what if you don't come back?"

"You stay away from that old place up there, y'hear?" he ordered, "We'll be back in a few hours." She didn't say anything as he turned and spoke to Cyrus. "Come on, Cy," he said. The old man winked at her and smiled before following after Mike.

Julia knew that Cyrus was trying to reassure her, but it didn't help much. With her hands twisting and turning together, and shaking her head, she showed her anxiety as she turned and went back into the restaurant. The next hour was a write-off for her; she was there, taking orders and smiling and delivering food to customers, but her mind was on something else.

*   *   *

Cyrus and Mike paused at the corner of the lot where the old house stood. There was an odor coming from the weeds and vegetation in the yard which was a result of the rain, the same kind of odor one might smell in wet wood and decaying garbage.

Mike showed Cyrus how he had climbed from the street level to the yard above them. "I put my feet here and then was able to get high enough to grip the edge of the wall. Let me go first, I'll reach down and help pull you up."

After they both had climbed the wall, they stood in the untended yard among the growth of weeds and saplings. In the meager light allowed by the overcast sky, they examined their surroundings. Cyrus looked around with the sharp interest which comes from seeing something unique for the first time. Mike looked with renewed fervor. He had known when he stood here earlier in the week that he would be back, but he hadn't known it would be with such a mixture of eagerness and foreboding as he felt now. The old building almost spoke its disapproval.

"Lookit all the damned signs," said Cyrus.

"Yeah, somebody here wanted to be left alone at one time," said Mike. He pointed with his chin in the direction of the old hulk, "The car's over there."

Avoiding the saplings, they walked through the weeds and long grass toward the rusted carcass of the machine that had once been the talk of the little town of Jerome.

It sat on broken wheels of rotted rubber and decayed wooden spokes, with its big radiator facing the streets below. One bulbous light had been ripped away on that night it had soared out over the canyon, the other remained. Boys had long ago broken its glass with rocks thrown from the safety of temporary bravado. Weeds and saplings grew in the cavity containing the motor, their green vibrancy and pliant life in contrast with the clotted rust which froze the once powerful machine that had been built for movement into the still silence of immobility. It had lost one of its hood panels in its final flight. Its doors were still intact, though heavily dented. Along the top edge of one, a vicious scoring showed where it had landed upside down against the side of the mountain. What remnants of cloth and material remained held a faint scent of mildew. The thing lay exposed, yet keeping secrets still, like any fossil.

Running his hands along the top edge of the driver's door, Cyrus said, "She's been drug along on her top; windhield's gone, steerin' wheel's all bent. Looks like it might have rolled over some, too." Then he shook his head in wonder, "Humpf, big ol' Caddy. Shore took a spill. Probably been here all that time since then, too."

"Does it look like to you that it went over a cliff or something, Cyrus?" asked Mike.

The old man held his chin in one hand and looked at the wreck. "You can't tell," he said, "I suppose there's some in the business of tellin' such a thing who could answer that question. But if she went over somewhere, she never hit bottom 'cause her frame's still pretty straight. An' it was probably someplace where there was no guard rail or nothin'." He walked along the side of the wreck, peering at the length of it before speaking further. Then he said, "Doors'n fenders been banged up. Frame's twisted just a tiny bit, but there's no damage to the front or the back. See here?" and he went to the radiator in front, "Radiator's almost undamaged. She didn't land on her nose, that's for sure. An' even if she did hit a guard rail, they wasn't much in them days. Leastways, not like they are today. B'sides, sheda' hit it with her front wheels; this thing never had any kind of bumpers."

While Cyrus pulled out a cigarette and lit it, Mike considered what his friend had just said. Looking at the rusted wreck, he could understand the logic of Cyrus's comments. The car might have rolled over, but it had not impacted on its front end or its rear. How could it have sailed over a cliff and not shown evidence of the fall? It was a question which came natural to him, now, for he was certain this wreck had been the car he had dreamed of being in as it veered off the road into some kind of canyon or deep hole.

*   *   *

They stayed at the wreck for a while, taking pictures and talking. She was aware of them there. She needed no window to peer from, but she stood near a window in the upper level of the old house anyway. There, in the thing that she must take on as one wears clothing else one is naked, she stood behind the dry, rotten curtain to hide from them in case they should look upward.

There was no need to wonder at their intent. She knew what it was. They would come inside. And there, her wrath would await them. Others had come to the old place over the years. She had frightened all away with noises she made. Once, she had even spoken, but that had been in the beginning, when the thing she wore could still utter human speech. It had changed over the years to what it was now, a hideous and pitiful caricature of what she had been. Now, she thought of herself as separate from it. Lately, she had found it difficult to bear its horrid weight. But into it she must go at least some part of each day. It was decreed as one of the rules. And today it might be useful to have such rules. If they came in, she would allow them to look fully upon the filthy, rotted thing.

*   *   *

But they did not enter the house. "Let's look in the garage, Cyrus," said Mike, "maybe we can find something out about it in there. It was probably kept in there at one time anyway."

"Alright," agreed Cyrus, kneeling on the wet ground to rummage in his pack. "God, the knees!" he complained, "You get old, boy, it'll start in the knees." He took a small pry-bar from the pack. "We might need to help the door along some," he said, grinning up at his young friend.

"Wait a minute," said Mike, with an edge of protest in his voice, "I meant through the window, or a crack in the door or something. We can't just break in."

The old man smiled at this. "Son, I tol' you before, we might have to do a little breakin' an' enterin', but listen, I ain't never seen anybody usin' this place."

"How do you know there isn't anybody living here, Cyrus?"

"I just do, now come on."

Almost glad that Cyrus had overridden him, yet still feeling some trepidation, Mike followed the old man to the door at the side of the garage, the one which had been used to communicate from the garage to the house.

Cyrus had been right about the door. It was nailed shut. It also had a padlock dangling from a hasp. But both the lock and the hasp were hardly more than rust themselves. With a quick flip of the wrist, Cyrus stuck the bar beneath the hasp and pulled it away from the wood of the door-facing. Then he stuck the bar's chiseled edge beneath the rusted nails and pulled them free.

With a single creak from the hinges, the door opened inward into the gloom of the garage. A huff of stale air billowed past them as they stepped inside. Though it was dark, they could still see a little by the dim light that filtered through the cracks beneath the entrance doors, and along the edges of the tops of the walls where the trusses held up the roof. A single window, plastered over with old newspapers, showed lines of light around its four sides. Mike ran his hand along the wall and found the light switch. But either the bulb was no good or there was no electricity to the wires.

Beneath his feet, Mike felt what he assumed to be concrete. But there was a soft resistance there that he surmised was a layer of dust, thick enough to be felt through the soles of his shoes. This was confirmed when both he and Cyrus began to sneeze.

Somewhere in the middle of the space enclosed by the thin wooden walls, Mike could sense something large and solid. Reaching into his back pocket, he pulled out the little flashlight he had put there earlier. He clicked it on and its beam played over the wall in front of him. Hanging on nails driven into the studs were a few old tools, and a length of garden hose. He turned to his right and let the beam shine. Something large was there, shrouded in a dark, dull material.

Directing his light around in the gloom, Mike found a wooden box against one wall. Walking to it, he picked it up and shook it to make sure there was nothing lurking inside. A cloud of dust rose into the confined space of the garage.

Coughing and laughing at the same time, Cyrus asked him, "You afraid of spiders?"

Backing away from the dust cloud, Mike said, "I am, Cy, especially black widows."

"I doubt if there's been anything living in here in a long time for a spider to eat," said Cyrus.

"You never know," said Mike, going to the door and propping it open with the box.

At that moment, from somewhere in the old house a heavy sound rolled against the walls of the flimsy garage.

"What in hell was that!" exclaimed Cyrus, as a bit of wind tugged at the box holding the door open.

Mike didn't comment. Instead, he stood silhouetted against the dim light filtering into the building. He had heard the sound, but what he saw in the middle of the garage took thought of anything else completely out of his mind. "Cyrus," he said as if in a daze, "you got anything in that pack of yours we can use to get this dust off with?"

Cyrus Dooley turned around. Even shrouded in years of accumulated dust, the La Salle was arresting. "Damn," breathed Cyrus, and he walked forward to brush a hand against the machine. Instantly, a bright gleam of paint showed up in the ray of light from the flashlight Mike held. And they both began sneezing again.

"It's the damned dust," said Cyrus, "Tear some of that paper off'n that window!"

Mike handed him a few pieces of the old newspaper and they both began to work to remove the dust from the car. Finally, Mike took off his shirt and used it. When they finished, sitting before them was the machine Mike had seen in one of his dreams. Cyrus went to his pack again and got out a flashlight of his own.

"This ain't the one you went over the edge in is it?" he asked as he played his light on the car along with Mike's.

"No, Cy," said Mike, shaking his shirt to get the dust out of it before putting it back on, "It's the one I saw on the street with the woman in it and the man with the white suit."

"You sure, Mike?"

"Yes, I'm sure. She was so beautiful, and she seemed to be looking straight at me. But there was something about her . . . sadness, she seemed real sad."

The two men stopped talking as the presence of the La Salle totally captured their attention.

It sat there, where it had been since the night she had driven it back over the mountain from the direction of Prescott. Although it was soiled from dust, and stains from the rain it had once had on its gleaming body and light tan canvass top, it was still a thing of visual delight. The long hood with the bright vertical grille and porthole ventilators, five on a side, bespoke hidden power enclosed in elegance. Even as a two-seater, a coupe, it was a big car. It imbued the simple garage with the grandeur of its being in quiet grace.

Mike opened the driver's door. Inside, the dust accumulation was much less. "Look at it, Cyrus," he said in awe, "It's beautiful."

They examined the car as if it were a great treasure, stopping to exclaim to each other from time to time at how wonderful it was.

"Here's what made her move," declared Cyrus, lifting one of the wing panels of the hood to show the motor there. The big in-line eight was also covered in dust.

"I wonder if it'd still run," mused Mike.

"Sure," said Cyrus, "But you'd have to do some work on her first: check the wiring, drain the crankcase and fill it with new oil." Then, turning to walk along the side so as to examine the tires, he continued, "You'd have to make sure of the rubber, too. Ah, just as I thought."

"What?" asked Mike.

"Tires are no good, see?" And Cyrus kicked at the left rear tire. "Have to get some new tires, too. Boy, I wonder if we'd have to get 'em made special?"

"Cyrus," said Mike, turning to his friend, "This isn't our car, you know."

As they stood facing each other, with the idea of seeing the grand machine in working order on their minds, they heard the same sound they had heard earlier. It caused them to look toward the open door of the garage, then the sound came again. They were certain it originated from somewhere inside the old house.

Suddenly, a deep rumble rolled from the sky and lightning cracked against the earth close outside. Then the garage began to darken. Within seconds the dull drilling of rain on the tin roof filled the garage, and through the sound of it they could hear quick steps coming from somewhere out front. And they seemed to be getting nearer. Before either man could utter what thoughts he might have had, a female form suddenly filled the open doorway.

*   *   *

In the main bedroom of the old house, high above the level of the garage's concrete floor, she seethed with fury. Turning as quickly as she could, she moved through the double-doors of the room toward the hallway that ran past other rooms, long-since unused. But if her intent had been swiftness, the thing that she must occupy was not able to comply. It drug its right foot. Not even the powers of the universe themselves could compel rotted tendons to hold bones and muscles together in order to achieve movement. Still, movement there was, for with hatred and the other leg she drew herself along.

The flooring creaked with her weight, though it was not much. Dried and withered, she was uglier than anything life in her old age would have made her, but that which had kept her whole all through the years was not life, though it had attained a semblance of that state.

Could life hate? Then so could she. Could life feel jealousy and a need for revenge? Ah, so could she. Could life know remorse for what it had done and for what it had not done? Ah, well, so had she known such things. And still she had re-lived her transgressions; still she had been held in time like a thing in a pocket which fingers played with, rolled around, touched, fondled, and kept always in the darkness of that pocket. She wished to be lifted out and thrown away; wished to find herself cast into the emptiness of oblivion so that she could at last forget.

The priest had said for her not to do this to herself and she had done it! Harry had said it would take them into forever, but it had only taken him. She had been made to stay behind. B.L. had loved her and she had loved him. But she had not told him of her love. And then he was stolen from her. She had been wrong in all of it. But today, today it was for her to act. And she would do what she could!

The feeble light from outside threw shadows across shadows as she moved along the hallway. How easy it would be if she were allowed to exert her powers and flee from the earthbound thing with its dragging foot. Oh, if only she could do that; but she knew she couldn't. Still, she tried! With effort she attempted to escape in the form of a shadow herself, to fly from it, high above it, and then to seep down through the inner recesses of the walls of the old house and into that damned garage where they were and where they had no right to be! In rage she let out a bellow of hatred for them. Come to me, was her thought, oh, come to me.

*   *   *

Mike felt as if a jolt of electricity had shot through him when the strange sound emanated from the house rising above the garage. And seeing Julia suddenly in the doorway nearly froze him with fear. "Damn, Julia," he said, "You just scared the holy shit out of both of us!"

"Yeah, by-God, I'll have to go along with that," added Cyrus.

Startled by the sound they had all just heard, which had resounded from the old house just as she had entered the garage, Julia didn't respond to Mike's declaration. Instead, she stepped quickly over to him and huddled against him. "Oh, Michael," she asked, looking up at him with widened eyes, "What was that noise?"

"We don't know," answered Mike, holding her to him in an effort to calm her.

"Probably a loose shingle or somethin' in this here rain 'n all," offered Cyrus.

Julia looked at him thankfully and then, seeing that she had gotten Mike wet from the rain that had soaked her own sweater, she pulled away from him and said with a laugh that belied the fear still occupying her thoughts, "I'm glad to see you, both of you. I told Rooster I was sick so I could get off." Then she turned back to Mike and, after a moment more of holding him for reassurance, moved away from him and began to examine the interior of the garage.

"Ooh, this place is grim," she said, then she saw the car. Like the two men had done before her, she opened her mouth in silent amazement. Mike led her toward the beautiful machine, talking softly to her as they walked down its length. The old man stood and watched them only for a moment before he turned his attention elsewhere.

"Well, whatta' y'know?" he said, looking up at the roof of the old garage.

"What?" asked Mike, turning and following Cyrus's gaze.

"She don't leak. The roof don't leak," said Cyrus.

"That's because it's made of tin, Cy. I already thought about that. It probably wasn't built at the same time as the house. The roof on the house looked like some kind of shingles to me, and not wood either. Did they use asphalt shingles back then?"

"Hard to say, considerin' when that old bitch was built," Cyrus declared, nodding his head toward the house on the other side of the garage wall. "Scuze me, Julie," he apologized, "I didn't mean no disrespect."

The girl just smiled. It pleased her that the old man was so solicitous of her.

"Didn't they have slate roofs, then?" Mike held to the point. "Seems to me that I read about them, supposed to last forever."

"Yes," said Cyrus, "And some people got so tired of them that after a few years they painted over 'em. This," he jerked his head up at the tin above them, "would have been kinda' new in them days. It would have been light, not much weight could be carried by this building anyway. It's a two-by-four style of structure."

"Sounds like a drum," Julia noted, referring to the rain falling heavily on the tin. But as Cyrus had pointed out, the old roof, though rusted and sagging from time and age, did not leak.

"Now, that old house probably leaks like a sieve, no matter what kind of roof it has," said Mike.

"Yes," agreed Cyrus, "even if she has slate, she'll still be leakin' some after all these years. The slate itself has moved over time, what with freezin' and thawin' an' dryin'. The underlayment is what's really the first to go, y'know."

Julia was incredulous. "You aren't planning on going in there, are you?" Then sweeping an arm toward the La Salle, she continued, "Obviously, somebody lives here."

The two men looked at each other.

"Mike . . ." Julia started to protest but he cut her off.

"We have to go in there, Julia, At least I have to. This old car was in one of my dreams, and that wreck out there," he pointed beyond the walls of the garage, "is the one I took the pictures of, the one I dreamed about going over the side in."

"Oh, Michael!" She was frustrated and angry with him, but she knew when he had made up his mind it was no use to try to persuade him otherwise.

As they talked, Cyrus's attention once again wandered and he began to examine the La Salle further. He found that the canvas top had become quite brittle, rotted actually, in the years it had sat in the garage. He opened the other door and looked inside. Finally, he slipped in and sat in the passenger's seat. The leather held. He ran his hand across the dash, leaving streaks in the dust. He noted that the instruments were white on black and trimmed in silver. The silver gleamed in the beam of his flashlight. What a beautiful thing, he thought. Then, getting out, he examined the lines of the car, running his eye backward to the crisp shape of the rear end.

As casually as if he were going on an outing with friends and needed to open the rumble seat for an inspection before letting them sit in it, he placed a foot on the first step built into the side of the car for this purpose. There were three of them, all on the right rear: the first was a square, molded into the gleaming bumper, directly behind and a bit lower than the right tail light mounted on the down-curve of the fender. The light was small, cylindrical, and did not get in his way. Above this step, on the fender this time, was another square of chromed metal with rubber set in it for safe footing. The rubber was cracked, but it was still in good condition. One final step was placed on the highest point of the fender. With his feet on these last two steps, he leaned over and grasped the silver handle of the rumble seat. By this time, Mike and Julia had stopped discussing whether or not they should enter the old house, and had come closer to see what Cyrus was doing.

"Look here, Julie," said the old man, his voice touched with pride in things of his time, "Let me show you how it was in them days." And he lifted the hinged section of the car which formed the slope of the rear deck when it was closed and the back of the rumble seat when opened. He shined his light inside.

Immediately a rush of fetid air enveloped them. But none of them noticed the bad smell, not at first. It seemed to each of them that they peered forever into the leather interior of the space Cyrus had revealed. But in reality, it took only seconds for them to react.

Julia emitted a long scream. Her mouth opened and her eyes could not seem to grow large enough for her to take in what she saw. The men were equally stunned. They each drew in a quick breath.

"Goddamn!" said Cyrus.

Mike was silent. He began to feel as if he were having one of his going-back periods. But it didn't last long. Only for a brief moment did he catch a hint of other times, and a strong sense of some other person.

"The poor bastard," said Mike finally. Beside him, Cyrus breathed heavily. He was so disturbed that he reached for a cigarette but held it instead of lighting it.

"What kind of a suit did you say the man in your dream had?" he asked, almost in a whisper.

"White."

Cyrus expelled pent-up breath, then said, "You know we have to look through this here, uh, thing don't you?"

"I know, Cy. Do you think we ought to tell somebody about this now?"

"The police ain't gonna' think any of us did this deed, son. I am the only one of us old enough to have killed this man. And I was in Californy when it happened anyway."

"Why do you think somebody killed him, Cyrus?" asked Julia.

"I don't know Julie, I just do. For one thing, he's been stuffed here in this old car for a long time. Somebody had to have done that. He couldn't have done it himself."

"Maybe he committed suicide by pulling the door shut and then suffocating," Julia offered.

Mike went around to the other side of the car, the side closest to the head of the dead man. He shined his light on the corpse. "There isn't much left of him besides some skin and bones, and some hair. I don't see any sign of injury to the skull."

"Mike, don't touch it!" wailed Julia.

"Honey, it ain't alive no more," said Cyrus, trying to console her.

"I know, but it's yukky."

"No," said Mike, "all that yukky stuff dried up a long time ago," and he shined his light on dark brown and yellow stains that seemed to come from beneath the body and run down the white leather seat and then over the side of the plush cushions onto the floor of the little two-person compartment where they had puddled into a mess that had dried and hardened. "See? While he rotted in here he also dried up," and Mike touched a part of the stain. "It's dry, now. Why, you don't even smell anything."

"Yes, I do," asserted Julia. Then she turned to the old man. "Don't you smell it, Cyrus?"

"I'd call it right musty," said Cyrus, "but it ain't the worst I've run acrost."

"Uh, oh," said Mike.

"What?" demanded Julia.

Cyrus looked closely at Mike who was being careful to examine the corpse without touching it any more than he had to, an act which showed that he, too, felt a measure of revulsion.

Mike had found what at first he'd thought was a button. But as he grasped it he realized it was something else. He pulled against it. Gradually, as if removing a nail from a board, he pulled out a long, thin metal pin. The blood that had once covered it had turned black. It appeared to have gone into the chest of the once living being that now lay dried and still in the La Salle's rumble seat.

"This is what killed him," said Mike, holding up the thin length of metal and twirling it by the white bone knob that served as a handle, "Looks like it went between the ribs and into the chest."

"It's a hatpin," said Julia.

"I'll be damned," said Cyrus, "Killed by a woman."

The three of them stood around the rear of the La Salle in silence, looking at the evidence of a murder committed long ago, wondering at identities and motives. Before them, in the leather upholstered seat that had been its coffin, the body lay as it had been left in death all those years before.

"Look inside his coat," said Cyrus to Mike, "see if you can find his wallet, or somethin' with some identification."

Doing as he had been asked, with both Cyrus and Julia looking closely over his shoulder, Mike pulled forth a black leather billfold from one pocket. The other pocket held a piece of paper, folded and partially stained with what he was sure was blood. He put the folded paper down on the seat and examined the contents of the billfold. A California driver's license bore the name Harry Waldon. There was also money, and a picture of a beautiful, raven haired woman. Mike felt strangely familiar with the image. Taking the picture out and turning it over, he read the words, "My Madeleine."

Both Julia and Cyrus sucked in their breaths at what the wallet revealed. Putting the wallet on the seat beside the folded paper, Mike reached for his camera hanging from his shoulder and across his chest on a leather strap. He stood up over the opened rumble seat, using the steps built into the car for that purpose.

"Mike, what are you doing?" exclaimed Julia.

"Relax, Babe," he said, "I'm going to get this old car and what it has inside it on film."

"Then what? Can't we just get out of here?" she almost wailed.

"I told you, Julia, I have to go into that house."

*   *   *

Outside, the storm had lost its initial energy. The lightning no longer flashed as often against the darkened sky, and though an occasional rumble rolled morosely down the mountainside, the rain fell slowly, now. All the passion which the storm had begun with had been expended, and gloom alone pervaded the day.

On the upper landing, where she had been about to descend, anger welled in her being and she halted there. They had opened the back of the car. Oh, hateful hell! Oh, never would she have had that happen. Feelings roiled within her as hot as the molten material which had created part of the mountain on which the old house had sat during all the years of his death, sat in silence on the outside and rotted into hate and grief within.

Moaning, she turned back. She must retreat! Someway she must escape the rotted flesh and torn ligaments and bones that clicked and scraped together as she worked them. Her hideous body would do for scaring the living. Just the sight of its rotted flesh and leathern skin stretched over bone would send terror through most mortals, but there was another to contend with now. And facing it would require more than the disgusting transformation of the thing that was once alive, once beautiful, yea, even once desired!

With effort she moved along the upper hallway toward the main bedroom. The rain added a rhythmic backdrop of sound to the dragging of the one foot across the dust-covered and leak-spattered floor. And then she heard them at the back door. She heard the door protesting their fumbling fingers, their prying hands. If only she were free of the thing with its dragging foot; damn them to hell for their impudence!

She held her head so that the right side was turned to listen. It was a reflex action only, a habit left over from life. She had senses that needed no ears, no eyes. The entire left side of her face had long ago ceased to know even the imitation of life she had been caused to assume. Sealed off from the rest of her, it had become like some monstrous growth, come great, calloused glob, a weighty thing that was hideous to her. She projected her senses.

Ahh. A low rasping came from her fetid throat, it was what passed for a chuckle with her. They were afraid. One, especially, was frightened. She was amused at this fear. Let them come! They would walk through her house uninvited; they would look into all the rooms. Eventually they would mount the stairway. They would examine the rooms on the upper floor and . . . Ah, there it was, the other!

Her senses told her it had seeped into the musty, dust-plagued interior of the house. She had known that, once released from the seal of the forces which had kept it contained all these years, even as they had inflicted upon her the misery of her half-life, it would come. She must not meet it encased in this cursed left-over shell of living death that pulled its foot along the floor. The flesh at the knee and the ankle no longer functioned. Bone lay visible there, yellowed bone that time had touched; touched it even against the edict of the power which had kept her in the old house on the ancient mountain flanks in the town that, like the thing she had become, was neither dead nor living.

She could not be made to suffer this meeting she had never thought would be. Like a creature about to be cornered, she moved down the hallway, but slowly, too slowly. It was there, below, rolling as an unseen fog across the old wooden floors. It entered rooms there, seeking in silence. It knew! It knew even as she knew. It was not hampered by walls or locked doors. It needed no eyes.

She had to hurry! The bed, the daybed with its plain wood and wicker was hers. It had never been his. She had placed it there, had selected it for herself. Such heavy oaken things he had wanted; heavy and insufferable as he himself had been while lying upon her, taking her, even while he knew what he had done. Oh, damn him to hell and beyond! Had she not suffered enough?

The foot, it caught at things. It tugged against the floor. She could see the fog at the bottom of the stairs. It pooled there as if laughing, as if gloating; a dog from the Devil come for her, scenting her. Oh, God, what have I done to deserve such as this!

. . . *do not do this to yourself, I am a priest* . . . Arrgh unhgh! From the thing with the bad foot came the earthly sound of protest at the unwanted memory. Behind her the long hallway stretched past the rooms where life had walked once, where Annie had walked once. She struggled with the foot. The half-rotted lungs of the thing that held her made hoarse sounds, even though the need for air had long ago ceased. With bone protruding from deadened skin and the ivory tips of fingers stretching outward, she moved toward the large double doors of the great bedroom, where once he had stood and watched her against the light from the fading sun.

Aggh-aghh! He'd had no right to her. Only B.L. had had that right. If she had only known! The little daybed, she must reach it. It had been so pretty on that far-gone day when she had seen it in the store on Main Street and asked that it be delivered to the big house on the hill. It was stained now. Body fluids had soaked into it that would not go away, could only rot and stink and turn dark. She had lain there, the thing that drug its foot had lain there, it would lie there again. Oh, God, how long? She yearned for it all to end. Had the life of a priest been so pure against her own? Had the death of a man who had taken a young girl's virginity and caused death himself been such a sin? Not new, these questions for her, nor had they ever been answered.

Along the floor she moved in a shuffle that created a new track in the dust on the hardwood. The dust rose as she moved through it. Had they been in the entry hall and chanced to look upward, they could have seen her there. But they were in the big kitchen— as she well knew. They were no longer important to her.

At the bottom of the stairs, the thing that she feared began to flow upward. It had found her, now.

*   *   *

In the large kitchen, the three stood with the open door behind them letting in what light there was along with the rain and the dampness in the air. The retreating thunder had covered most of the sounds from the upstairs, but not all. Yet, they each chose not to mention what they had heard for the moment.

"God, look at the dust!"

"You could cook for a hundred people in a kitchen like this," said Cyrus, ignoring Mike's comment.

Julia was quiet. She stood and looked around the large room with fear gathering in her mind. Along one side ran sinks, counters, and a commercial-style range. Cabinets covered another wall. They went from the floor to the ceiling. Above the sinks was a line of metal storage bins and shelving. A portion of another wall contained several small windows along its top. Dirty and covered with cobwebs, these windows still managed to let in some light.

In the room's center stood a large table and a cutting block. Above it hung a metal ring festooned with knives and cleavers and long forks with spear-like tines. The ring also supported heavy metal pots and pans on hooks.

Mike took several pictures. The flash from the camera gave only enough light to suggest unknown objects in unseen spaces. But soon their eyes adjusted to the dim light inside the big room.

The floor was of red tile, its color showed where the dust had been washed away by water from the leaking roof. Around the drain in the middle of the floor, water had pooled into gray-green scum.

They stood and took it in. Julia lifted her head to examine the rack holding the knives and the other kitchenware. It had all discolored and become dull over time. The things had been cleaned and hung there by someone long years before. She wondered at who that person might have been.

After a minute or two more, Mike said, "Let's go into the rest of the house."

"Mike," protested Julia, "I don't like any of this."

Standing aside so that she might go ahead of him, Cyrus said with a pat on her shoulder, "Come on, honey, it's alright."

Mike sent him a look of thanks and was about to verbalize his appreciation as well when they heard a moaning sound.

"Dammit, Cy," he said, "you think somebody's here?"

"Naw, now, even if they was somebody here, Mike, they didn't have nothin' to do with what we found in the rumble seat of that old car out there. I told you, that deed was done many years ago. I figger that car in the garage is about a '34 model"

Mike and Julia looked at each other and then they both looked at Cyrus.

"Besides," the old man continued, "what I heard didn't sound like nothin' human anyways."

Julia turned a fearful face upward at him when he said that.

"I'm sorry, sugar," he said with a chuckle, "I didn't mean it to sound like that. What I meant was, it could have been an old board or somethin' causin' the wind to move over it and make that kind of sound."

Mike clenched his teeth. He could sense a heaviness around him. It lay beyond in the dark cavernous rooms that had once held the lives of people who in all likelihood had been involved in some way with that car and its dried-up corpse. The whole place had something to do with the dreams he had experienced in the few days since entering Jerome. He was convinced of that. God, he didn't want to have one of his going-back-in-time trances now.

He knew Julia was frightened, even as he was himself. Her presence was not something he had planned on. Yet, he couldn't make her leave. For one thing, she would have to walk back in the storm which, though weakened, still flashed a flicker of lightning and sent a latent rumble of thunder down the mountain once in a while.

"Look, Babe," he said, pulling her to him and embracing her, "why don't you wait for us right here?"

She pulled instantly away from him and, looking earnestly into his eyes, said, "Mike, I'm not staying here while you and Cyrus go off into the rest of this old hulk. No. You are not leaving me alone."

"But, what could hurt you here? he asked, waving his hand at the empty space in the big room, "You could always go back outside, the open door's right there."

"Mike, I'm not staying here alone."

He smiled at her, "I thought you didn't believe in the supernatural."

"I don't. And that dead man out there isn't supernatural. He's very real."

"Alright, then, but stay close to me and Cy."

"Don't you worry," she said.

With the light from both flashlights probing ahead, they moved through a small adjoining room to the dining room. It held a massive oak table and chairs for twelve. It had been set for a meal, long ago; a meal for two. The remnants of it were still there.

The draperies were shaded by the dust so that the dim light from outside limned them, giving an eerie quality to the scene. By the light from the windows as well as their flashlights, they could make out a trail on the floor.

"Them's funny lookin' footprints," said Cyrus.

"Yeah, Cy, you're right," Mike agreed, "and you know it's hard to tell exactly when they were made, but this place was already a mess whenever they were."

"You mean the dust was already heavy when whoever it was walked here?" asked Julia.

"That's right, honey," said Cyrus.

"God, look at it!" exclaimed Mike, playing the beam of his flashlight around the room. The wall was paneled in oak, cut and inlaid in a diamond design. The dust lay like chocolate along the etched and raised surfaces of the wood. Both Julia and Cyrus looked where his light directed them to. Then he played it around the rest of the room. Cyrus followed Mike's light with his own. The remaining walls had once been white. Now, muted by the dust and time, the color was a much different shade. Suddenly, the two beams passed something on the wall that stood out from it. Quickly, both men flicked their beams backward.

"It's a big picture frame," said Julia.

They stood in awe of the portrait shrouded in dust which still was unable to completely cloak the beauty that had been caught by the artist's brush. It was the painting Harry Waldon had commissioned those long years ago as he did everything in his power to salve the pain in Madeleine's heart at the passing of Buenig. Mike moved the weakening beam of his light over it.

"It's her," he said quietly.

"Who?" breathed Julia.

"The woman in the car out there in the garage, it's a copy of the photo in his wallet."

"What? Mike, you're not making any sense."

"The dream, Julia, the dream of the woman and man on the street. They were in that car."

"Well, we know who he was," said Cyrus.

"And this must be Madeleine Morgan," added Mike. And for a moment he felt he could almost hear her speak. Looking at the beautiful face, he felt a vague sense of having known her.

They all three stood enthralled. Then, after more than a few moments had passed, noting that his light was not as bright as he would like it to be, Cyrus said, "We'd better move on a little faster. Don't want to let it get dark an' run out of juice in these flashlights."

"You're right, Cy," agreed Mike, "Tell you what, you turn yours off, we'll use mine for now. When it gets too weak, we'll use yours."

"Let's just get on with it," urged Julia, "I don't want to be here when the sun goes down, even if we do have flashlights."

"We're going, Babe, but first I have to get a shot of that painting," said Mike.

As they moved from the dining room and into the great room that fronted the main entrance to the house and provided a setting for the central staircase, a low rumble from the storm shook itself through the old building.

In a little knot of three, now, the single beam of the flashlight slicing ahead of them into the darkened chambers, they moved through the once beautiful mansion and coughed at the dust rising from their feet, while exclaiming in wonder as the ever-weakening light touched on the many extraordinary pieces of art and furnishings.

Harry Waldon hadn't been conservative in decorating and furnishing the place. There was leather and beautiful woods and the gleaming of silver and gold, often on porcelain or mother-of-pearl, reflecting the art-deco style of the twenties that became a rage in the thirties and forties.

They explored all of the first floor and found only a very richly furnished house that had been abandoned to the years of empty quiet and unending falling of dust.

Just as Mike decided to lead them back to the bottom of the grand staircase, there was a series of odd sounds from above, as if cats were fighting. Spitting and snapping noises could be heard, and a brilliant flash of light seemed to burst throughout the darkened rooms.

*   *   *

Once the thing in the trunk of the car had been released to enter her house, she became oblivious to the three intruders searching the lower levels. In the great master bedroom high above them, she moved in her body-bound fashion toward the far wall and the daybed there. Behind her, in the double-doorway, the thing which pursued her collected itself into a funnel of gray mist and rose to the high ceiling. It remained there as her rotted and decayed form moved as quickly as it could toward the corner of the room.

There, she would be safe. The daybed was not his, it was her island in the sea of hate and punishment she had endured all the years since . . . since it had all happened. Let him come! Had she not paid? And why had she done it in the first place—had he paid for that?

She reached the daybed with its filth, and with a final gurgle, the old body collapsed upon it. She would be allowed to rise from that body now, she knew that she would be. Yet she only eased out of it a little. There would be the meeting, now.

. . . *You cannot avoid this.*

It was not sound. It was more like thought ringing silently in the mind. She replied in kind . . . *I do not wish to. I have lived and died here all these years while that wretched wreck has lain there rusting. I have come and gone and still remained here. I brought you back that night and I thought I could leave my conscience in the car with you. But I couldn't. I took a poison . . .*

. . . *You sought forever.*

. . . *Damn you to hell again! If not for you* . . . Enraged, she rose in a column of dark mist that reached from the floor to the ceiling.

She moved toward him, then. And like a pair of mighty serpents entwined in fierce battle, the dual plumes curled one upon the other. Twisting and turning, they flowed out of the big room and down the hallway. She uttered horrible sounds in her fury, he was quiet.

    . . . *I come not in hate.*

    . . . *It doesn't matter; I have hate enough for both of us. You made it to grow within me long ago and I became a creature of hatred . . .*

    . . . *I promised you forever.*

    . . . *You sent those I loved away forever.*

    . . . *They are waiting, Madeleine, they are waiting.*

She lashed him with all the fury she could produce. Silently he held against her.

    . . . *Madeleine, you can have it now . . . forever.*

With a crackle of white hot energy she pulled away from him . . . *Oh, if only you spoke true . . . I have endured so long, you do not know.*

    . . . *Yes, I know, Madeleine, I have been here too.*

    . . . *You deserved all of your misery, Harry, you caused it all!*

    . . . *Not all of it, Madeleine, not all.*

    . . . *Lies, all lies!* And again they wound against each other. Energized by her terrible hatred, they writhed over the flooring high in the old house, sometimes above its dusty surface, sometimes beneath it; often they flowed through the walls and into the high ceilings. They held against each other in this way until from out of the darkness of the long hallway there appeared a light brighter than any she had ever known. It seemed to her that, beyond the thing which was him, even past the brilliant luminescence which flashed suddenly throughout the upper part of the house, others could be seen there in the dark shadows. They seemed to beckon to her. Slowly, the old hallway began to stretch and increase in length; it became a hollow tube running out into the heavens over a tremendous distance. Oh, could it be? Toward her, now, like a star from far away that had descended to Earth and assumed human form, someone approached.

    "Annie," she said, "Is that you?" And it was in her real voice that she spoke, her voice which she had not heard for all the many years since she had begun her journey of penance. Oh, it was wonderful to hear the sweet modulations of it!

Then she felt a force upon her, not of the thing she had been struggling against, for it had pulled away, but a gentle urging as the new power made itself known.

"Oh, Annie," she sobbed as with a flooding of forgiveness and love she allowed herself to be drawn by it toward a place and an existence all in one; something she might have at one time in her life called eternity, only another word for forever.

Behind, in the old bedroom, complete death finally came to the half-decayed corpse. And the mist, all that remained of the man whose body lay in the back of the beautiful 1934 roadster, flowed down the hallway past its own place of sin to its own forever.

*   *   *

Downstairs, they took note of the light and the sounds.

"There's no electricity still in this ol' place, is there, Cy?"

"It damn shore acted like somethin' sparkin', though, didn't it?" answered Cyrus in a puzzled tone, "almost like a couple of crossed wires."

They all stood quiet for a moment or two. Then Mike said, "Come on, we have to go upstairs."

"Do we have to, Mike?" Julia whispered, "I mean, I don't see why." She clutched his arm. He could feel her quivering.

"Now listen, Babe, it's probably something relating to the storm, probably an open window or doorway somewhere up there that's making the noises we heard, and it just happened to do it when some lightning flashed."

But there was a strange feeling in his mind and he held her close for a moment before pulling her with him to the front of the house and the bottom of the big staircase. Cyrus followed, but he switched on his own light and flashed it around behind them as they moved along.

Once they'd arrived at the staircase, Mike sent the beam of his flashlight upward. Cyrus did the same with his. With the aid of both lights and the diluted light from outside, they could see the landings above them. Dark hallways branched off from them to run into the interior of the house's upper levels. Everything there was still.

"O.K., look," Mike began, "let's not let a little noise get us off track. What we want to find is anything that can tell us about the people who lived here—something besides the fact that they had a lot of money to spend."

"It's obvious it was that pore guy down there in the rumble seat of that old car. Harry Waldon. And that Madeleine, she lived here with him."

"We don't know that, Cy." said Mike.

"Well, why else would he have a painting of her on his wall?" protested Julia.

"Listen," said Mike, "you both know that we have to make sure, at least we have to do better than just come in here and look around on the first floor."

"Mike," breathed Julia, her eyes widening and her head swiveling as she tried to look everywhere at once, "this is a big house. And somebody is here, I know it."

"Julia, now calm down," said Mike, "How do you know it?"

"There," she said, pointing at the floor where his light beam showed the same kind of tracks in the dust they had found earlier in the dining room.

He played the light up the stairs, almost one step at a time. There they were, those same odd footprints they had seen before. It seemed that the stairway was well used. He put his foot on the first step and slowly began to move upward.

FORTY FIVE

As they reached the top of the stairs, the stench they had been aware of since the second story landing began to tug even more at their senses. It seemed to be coming from somewhere very close by. If it had been a visible thing, it would have resembled a web that ran in threads of decreasing circumference, from the grand old room at one end of the hallway, out along the balcony looking over the floors below, and down the stairway itself. It was everywhere, it seemed, where the strange footprints had left their sign in the dust. Despite the fact that it settled around them, they moved slowly onto the landing, cognizant of their original purpose in climbing the stairs to this point, for they had by-passed the second story since the footprints in the dust had too.

Of course, Michael and Julia recognized the smell as the same one they had experienced in their rented flat a couple of days earlier. They said so to Cyrus as they followed the trail in the dust along the long hallway toward the large double-doors at its end. They could barely see that they were open in the weak beam of Mike's flashlight.

When they finally reached the entrance to the room, they looked into the gloom there and probed it with their flashlights.

They hesitated to enter because of the odor, which was very strong, now. "It ain't hard to see why you didn't like it before," said Cyrus.

The inside of the chamber was covered in the same dust as everything else in the old house. The flashlight beams, working in concert, showed various pieces of furniture. A huge bed stood out from the south wall. It appeared to be neatly made-up. On the opposite wall, between two broken down French doors, was what appeared to be a fireplace. There was a large dresser and mirror, a table and chair with a lamp on it and what seemed to be some kind of papers. Occasionally, a picture on one of the walls came forward in the yellow beams of the flashlights as if it were some live thing, flushed from its hiding place in the dark. They looked at these with interest, but none contained images they found useful in their quest. Overall, the room seemed to have been left in a neat and well-kept condition that had only been touched by the weather and the years of settling dust.

"Here," said Mike to Cyrus, "put your light with mine into that corner over there."

Both dim fingers of light whisked as one to the corner. They revealed a small metal cot. There seemed to be someone lying on it. The men played their lights over the bed and its burden in silence, while Julia watched anxiously. It seemed to all of them that their own breathing was the loudest thing they had ever heard. Even the smell began to fade as fear enveloped them.

"M-Mike, Oh, Mike, let's go," moaned Julia.

It was then that Michael had one of his special experiences. He knew who or what was lying on the little cot, and he was not afraid. "Hush, Julia," he said gently. "Stay here with Cyrus," and he walked slowly over to stand close to the little daybed. He directed his light downward.

She had fallen with her left side up, the side which had dried and decayed in death even as the other side had lived in a kind of half-death. The bones of her face protruded through the dried skin of her cheek. Her hair hung in long, thin strands of brittle gray and black, large patches of her scalp showed where clumps of hair had been pulled out over the years. The hollow socket of her left eye looked blindly into the flashlight beam.

The flesh of her body had shrunk around her bones and dried into a mummified condition. Mike noticed that the left leg was turned and twisted as if it had been broken. She wore a sleeping gown that was rotted and torn, and grimy with age.

Moving the beam of his light over the bed, he saw something shiny just under her right shoulder.

"Cy, come here."

The old man let his breath go audibly and walked carefully over to Mike, where he spoke softly into his ear, "I'm here, boy," then, as he looked fully upon the corpse, he exclaimed, "My-God!"

Beside them both, Julia emitted a scream that sliced through the heavy atmosphere of the old room. She had followed Cyrus rather than be left alone, and when she saw the horrid thing on the little daybed, she could not control her reaction.

Mike quickly drew her to him as she shook and sobbed with fear. She continued to cry and tremble as he pulled her with him across the room toward one of the large windows. He grabbed at the curtain there, tearing part of it away. The feeble light of the late afternoon filtered into the old room as he stood with Julia and tried to calm her.

In the corner near the daybed and the corpse it held, Cyrus had seen the glint of something shiny as had Mike before him. He tried to see it better by leaning. This brought him closer to the corpse than he wanted to be, and in his efforts to remain as far from the body as possible and still see, he lost his balance. He tried immediately to regain it, but he slipped in the heavy dust on the hardwood floor and fell headlong on top of the rotten flesh and yellowed bones.

Everything turned then, the bed and all it contained. And as he fell on his back, the corpse fell on top of him. He lost his flashlight, it skittered toward a far wall, its cone of light turning alternately toward him and then away from him as it spun on the floor. Then it was his turn to scream.

"Arrghhh! Dammit to hell!"

Mike left Julia and hurried to retrieve Cyrus's flashlight. Then he turned his attention to the pile-up on the floor. Grabbing one of Cyrus's feet, he pulled him free of the tangle of corpse, bedding, and bed. The old man lashed out in every direction with his fists as Mike pulled him away. And as Mike released him, he glared back at the corner where the body lay now on the floor in a tangle of rotted bed clothing.

Mike handed him his flashlight and Cyrus got to his feet. They both shined their lights on the corpse, illuminating the face which seemed to look straight at them. One side was decayed flesh and protruding yellowed bone, while the other side was in a lesser state of decay. One eye remained. It was open, and it sent a shudder through them, for it seemed to light up as the two beams fell upon it.

"Holy shit!" said Cyrus.

"It's alright, it's alright," said Mike, putting a hand on his friend's arm in reassurance, "She's gone. She won't hurt us."

"How in hell do you know that?"

"I just do, Cy. She's gone."

Behind them, Julia still shook with fear. She walked hesitantly across the few feet of dusty floor and put an arm around Michael's waist. "Please, Mike," she implored in a quavering voice, "Can we leave this place?"

Hurriedly, Mike grabbed the papers they had seen earlier. He stuck them into his waistband. With one last flick of his light around the dreary old room he was about to turn and go when he saw again the glint of something near the overturned bed. Not relishing being near the corpse again, but wanting to see what it was that shined there, he crept across the floor and bent down to pick up what turned out to be a small glass bottle. He put it in his pocket and with a final look into the horrid death face of what he was sure was all that remained of the once beautiful Madeleine Morgan, he took one last picture. Then he turned and moved quickly from the room to join Julia and Cyrus Dooley in the hallway.

The three of them hurried down the old staircase and through the dining room to the large kitchen. They did not stop until they stood once more in the clean air of the outside. Below them, the lights of Jerome were already burning.

The storm had ended, but they knew the yard would be soaked. "Come on," said Mike, leading the way with Julia in tow, "Let's use the street this time."

"Wait a minute," said Cyrus, turning back, "might's well leave things as we found 'em. I need to nail that garage door shut, good an' tight." Then he froze and a look of dread and despair draped his face.

"I'll do it," said Mike, suddenly realizing what the old man was thinking.

"Do what, Mike? Why can't we just go?" Julia shuddered.

"We left the rumble seat open," Mike answered her while looking grimly at Cyrus.

The old man straightened and took a deep breath. "No, by-God; you two have been through enough. I'll do it. Just wait for me; I might want to have a conversation with you from inside that old garage while I'm doing what needs to be done."

"You sure, Cy?"

"Damn right, boy. Whatever might be in there might's well be as afraid of me as I am of it!" And the old man went inside the darkened garage where the beautiful La Salle sat with its one lone passenger lying in death in its leather upholstered rumble seat.

*   *   *

They spent the remainder of the evening drinking coffee, talking and looking through the papers they had taken from the old house. They turned out to be newspaper clippings. It wasn't difficult to find the unifying theme of each article. One clipped article headlined the death of B.L. Buenig. Another edition of the same paper dated more than a year later featured the tragedy of the accident involving Annabelle Morgan. Another clipping contained the story of Harry Waldon's separation from Madeleine Morgan and his subsequent departure from Jerome.

They had already seen some of the same articles in the collection of papers held by Cyrus. But this time they had the key. It was Madeleine Morgan, her name featured some way in almost every article. Still, it would take two other articles to provide the final answer. One had been overlooked by them because the publication was not a complete daily newspaper. Called the Copper District Shopping News, it was hardly more than a flyer. But one story and a picture in the edition they had taken from the old house told of the return to Jerome, "Perhaps for a visit with an old friend?" went the lead off phrase, of one Mister Harry Waldon.

The accompanying picture was of the 1934 La Salle parked with its big whitewalled tires turned into the curb on the left side of Main Street in front of a grocery store. A man in a white suit stood opening the door for a beautiful dark haired woman in a tight fitting hat of the nineteen twenties vintage. The woman was looking in the direction of what apparently was the camera. It was an exact duplication of the dream Michael had had about the same scene on that part of the street which had since slid downhill. The date was February 16, 1935.

Finally, there was a later issue of the Prescott Sentinel which reported the death of Father Jovan Kilryc Katichovic of an apparent heart attack in the confessional. It seemed there was suspicion of someone having been with him when he died, perhaps the person whose confession he might have been hearing. It was suggested by the writer of the article that that person should identify himself.

They speculated about the information provided by the old newspaper clippings.

"Looks like she had a relationship with B.L. Buenig," said Mike.

"I think she must have loved him," added Julia softly.

Cyrus was reflective. "I wonder," he began, "Let's look at this thing from the angle of who was likely murdered and who probably did it, or at least had some motive for doing it."

"Alright," said Mike, "We have Buenig . . ."

"Murdered," said Julia.

"There was the priest . . ." he paused to wait for her comment, but she seemed lost in a daze about B.L. Buenig and the possible romance between him and Madeleine Morgan.

"We can't tell about the priest 'cause the paper said he died of a heart attack," asserted Cyrus.

"Yes, but it also suggested somebody was there and could have gone for help—except they didn't," Michael declared.

"Maybe all of this explains your dreams, Mike," said Julia, seemingly recovered from her daydreaming.

"Whatta'y' mean?" Mike asked.

"Well, that one article with the picture of the car, do you think you might have seen it in the library or the Preservation Society's collection?"

He looked at her steadily for a long moment before replying, "I don't think so, but anything is possible."

"I think you did," she said with confidence, "I think you saw all of this somewhere in those old pictures and your subconscious mind did all the rest."

Cyrus rose stiffly. "Let's go out on the balcony if we're gonna' stay up all night again an' talk," he said. "You two go on out an' I'll just make us a fresh pot of coffee."

It was hours later that Cyrus left Mike and Julia still sitting in the cool early morning. The old town had finally become quiet as the tourists left to find their various places of lodging, either in Jerome or down the hill in the valley or up the mountainside in one of the camping areas there. There was no overnight camping allowed in the city limits, so those tourists who had driven motorhomes up the winding two-lane road into the tangle of Jerome's streets had to fire them up and brave the same streets in the dark of night. It was not a thing they would likely do again.

Mike had thought that with all the coffee and the excitement of finally getting somewhere in solving the mystery of the dreams and the two bodies they had found in the big house, not to mention the La Salle, that sleep would be too elusive for any of them. But he awoke in the clean sunshine of the late morning refreshed and with a wonderful feeling of peace and resolve.

"What's on your mind, Babe?" asked Julia, reaching across his chest to pull herself closer to him.

"It's time to go."

She sat up in bed and looked intently at him. "You mean it, Mike? You're not teasing?"

He laughed and drew her to him. They kissed, not the best thing to do first thing after waking. "Yuk!" he said with a big grin as he pulled away and sat up on the edge of the bed. "No, I'm not kidding."

He grabbed clean underwear from a suitcase and headed toward the hallway leading to the bathroom. "I hope there's plenty of hot water 'cause I'm gonna' use it all!"

She hurried after him. "I can get out of my gig at Rooster's. I'll call that girl and tell her she can have her old job back. She's probably ready to work now. It won't take long to pack the bug. We can be out of here in a couple of hours. Mike?"

He had continued walking down the hallway. Now he stopped and looked back at her.

"Yeah, well, there's just one thing I wanta' do in this old town before we leave. Ever since I had that horrible stinky dream, I've needed to."

"Go to the graveyard? I was wondering when you'd bring that up, seeing as how we haven't been there yet," she said, unwilling to follow further in her undressed state.

"Y'know what, Babe," he said, "I don't need to go to the graveyard. I don't think we should disturb those people any more. No, I meant something else."

"What?"

"You come on an' take a little ol' shower with me an' I'll tell you all about it."

She giggled, and followed him into the bathroom.

FORTY SIX

(the last)

They sat in the dim coolness of Mac's and listened to the Ruby Duo perform. A grin split Cyrus's craggy face as the two women played the song about Yarnell. It had become a hit—at least at Mac's.

. . . Yarnell, Yarnell, tell Phoenix go to hell . . . Yarnell . . .

Three couples were on the small dance floor. The men, all large, wearing tight jeans and leather wrist gauntlets as well as bandages in various places, danced heavily to the tune like great bandanna-bound whales. Their chrome and leather laden motorcycles, showing recent damage, were parked in a row just outside the opened double-doors of the bar. So was the little yellow Volkswagen. Its small trunk was full, as well as its back seat.

The streets also were filled, with tourists: older couples and younger couples, and families. Occasionally someone looked inside the darkened interior of the bar, but the presence of the motorcycles at curbside kept most people away, except for the young and the single.

"So, I guess the two of you are just gonna' drive off into the sunset?" Cyrus directed a smile at his young friends. He had to raise his voice to be heard over the music.

Julia returned his smile. "You won't believe it, Cyrus, but this one here," and she looked at Michael who looked away from both of them to hide his own smile, "this one here wants to go to Las Vegas where he can," she winked at Cyrus, "get away from so-called old things. Of which he says he has had enough for a while."

Cyrus shook his head in mock disbelief at Mike. "I'm surprised at you, boy, why old things is all you can find in Las Vegas. They go there to gamble, don't you know; haul 'em in on big buses."

They all had a laugh at this. Then Mike said, "It's true, Cy, we thought about it and decided that we want someplace where all the buildings are new. We don't want any more old Victorian houses for a while."

Mention of the house sobered them all for a moment. It caused each of them to remember the events of the last twenty-four hours.

"I've been wondering, Cy," Mike began.

The old man looked at his friend with a steady gaze. Yeah?" he said.

"Should we just leave it up there in that old garage?"

Cyrus dropped his head and looked down at the surface of the table before lifting his bottle of beer and taking a swig. "I know it's a purty thing," he said, "but if I've learned anything from all of this it's that there are some things we don't know nothin' about. That beautiful piece of road runnin' equipment was put there years ago by somebody who meant it to stay there. I don't intend otherwise. What about you?"

"I agree with you on that," Mike said, engaged in his own act of looking down and reflecting.

"And the story, you gonna' leave it alone, too?"

"I couldn't touch it, Cy," Mike said, shaking his head, still looking down at the table top, "I'd be afraid of having more dreams."

"Cyrus and Julia both laughed.

"No, I'm serious," Mike continued, raising his head and speaking in a somber tone, thinking of the things they had experienced in the old house. "He obviously got her sister pregnant, then he just as obviously killed her in that old Cadillac. He left, then came back in '35 and Madeleine killed him in revenge. And I dreamed some of it. That's all I need to know to make me mind my own business—the fact that I actually dreamed of it."

"And he probably allowed the priest to die, too. At least that's how I read it," added Julia.

"Well, the dates on them news clippin's don't support that," said Cyrus, "But whoever did let the priest die had some reason to be there confessin' when it happened."

"Anyway, Cy," said Mike, "It was a good thing we went into that old upstairs bedroom."

"You mean because we found them papers?" suggested Cyrus.

Mike nodded, and Cyrus continued, "What you gonna' do about them pictures you took up at that old place?"

"I don't know, yet," said Mike, "I guess when I get an urge to see it all again, if ever I do," his voice trailed off and nobody spoke for several moments.

When the song about Yarnell ended, and a space of relative quiet became available, the waitress arrived at their table with a tray and a towel. She took the empty bottles and wiped the top of the table, then stood expectantly. Mike placed a ten dollar bill on the table and said, "Give us another round, please."

After the waitress left, Cyrus leaned across the table and said in a very quiet voice, "I want you all to know that I ain't never been as damned skeered in my whole life as I was rollin' around on the floor with that thing." He leaned back and added, "I suppose you'll wanta' take them old clippin's with you?"

"No," said Mike, "you can have 'em. We read them all again last night, or was it this morning? Anyway, after you left to go to bed we stayed up a bit more, talking about that bottle we found."

"Why, it had to be poison'," declared Cyrus. "I thought we'd decided on that before I left."

"Oh, it was, Cyrus," agreed Julia. "Arsenic. The little bit of label still stuck on the bottle showed that.

"We weren't disputing that, Cy," said Mike. "We were just discussing how different things were back then and the different ways men and women found to do away with themselves."

"And how it was common practice to use arsenic then for rats," broke in Julia. "Why, you couldn't buy it today without a permit or something."

"There's just one thing," said Cyrus.

"What?" asked Mike.

"Well," began his friend, "that little book you found in the library; I still think she'd 'a kept somethin' like that."

"Kept it or thrown it away," said Julia. "Remember, Cyrus, it was from him. Probably broke her heart every time she looked at it."

"She wouldn't have donated it to the damned library, not with that code in it," said Cyrus. "If she did throw it away an' somebody found it . . ."

"I say whatever happened to it, that this Preservation Society in Jerome eventually got hold of it someway," declared Mike. "Anyway, we'll never know."

"And the smelly dream?"

Mike looked directly at Cyrus. "Had to be a trick, Cy. That's all I can figure."

"You're convinced of that?"

"Cy, you saw that body. It was dead. Been dead for a long time.

Julia leaned forward and used an index finger to underscore what she had to say, shaking it in both their faces. "That is what those tracks in the dust are all about. I think whoever made them also pulled the prank on Mike."

"Well," began Cyrus, "they'd of had to know of him dreamin'. Whatta' y' think they did, come up and rub stinky meat all around?"

"We've been doing a lot of talking about this entire thing in public places, Cy," said Mike, "a lot of it in Rooster's. And remember, Julia thought she saw somebody sneaking away from the accident scene that day."

The old man nodded in agreement. "Well, and the picture of the girl is, I suppose, at least a double-negative in your mind, even with the green eyes?"

Mike sucked in his breath and shook his head, then said, "Cy, we went over all of this last night. Did you go back up there after leaving us? Is there something you know that we don't?"

At that moment, the Ruby Duo began to play a piece of fast music. The bikers took to the floor again. Cyrus leaned back and fumbled at his shirt pocket for a cigarette. The waitress returned with fresh bottles.

"I thought you'd quit them things!" she exclaimed over the music.

The old man looked up at her and his eyes seemed to gleam with delight for a moment. "Where'n hell's ol' Ralph?" he asked. "Don't he usually work this place all by hisself?"

"Said he was gittin' tired of doin' that," the waitress replied.

Instead of going on with the repartee as he usually did, Cyrus let the girl leave, and then he went into his usual coughing spasm. When he finished, he looked at his two friends reflectively for a moment before he said, leaning toward them and speaking loudly in order to compete with the microphones of the Ruby Duo, "Well, I didn't go right to sleep when I went to bed either. But I damn sure didn't go back to that old house, I'll tell you that! There was somethin' on my mind I couldn't quite put my finger on right away, if you know what I mean. I took some of them old papers I've been keepin' all these years and began to rummage through 'em. Hell, I don't know why, but I rummaged and finally it came to me. Then I began to look in earnest."

"For what, Cy?" It was Julia.

"Well, Julie, do you remember that one thing we run acrost about that body found with the I.O.U. in its pocket?"

A look of surprise came to her face, and she nodded.

"That I.O.U. had the name F Potter on it, if you'll remember. I found the article again just to make sure. An' it got me to thinkin'."

This time it was Mike who asked the question. "What were you thinking, Cy?"

With a hard glint in his eyes, Cyrus said, "You know how we figured the girl's message meant that she got into gamblin', in a game called faro?"

Just as Cyrus pronounced the name, the music stopped and it was replaced by the curtain of sound made by people all talking at the same time. Once more it was quiet enough for them to speak without yelling at each other.

"Yeah,' said Mike, picking up the line of conversation, "you told us that was probably what she meant."

"Well, in all them newspaper clippin's that was kept up there in that old house, there wasn't none of 'em said anything about gamblin'."

"You're right, Cy," said Julia, and she looked at Mike through an expression of surprise, her mouth slightly open, her eyes wide and with just the touch of a smile on her parted lips.

Mike looked directly at Cyrus. "Cy, you don't think . . . ?"

"I do," said Cyrus Dooley, beaming with pride.

Julia wasn't buying into the theory. "Wait a minute, you two. Just because the I.O.U. said F Potter you think it meant Faro Potter? Come on, it could have been Frank or Fred or Floyd."

"Wonder why she didn't collect that article, too?" Mike said to Cyrus.

"Who knows," said the old man. "Maybe she just missed it. Maybe by that time she was such a recluse in that ol' house . . ."

"Aw, you guys!" Julie was still not in agreement.

Mike continued to ignore her protests. "Or," he said, "maybe we made a mistake in reading the message, or whoever created the message made a mistake.

"How do you mean?" asked Cyrus.

"Look, the message said, 'hello this is us madeleine annie bartholomew harold he got me with child played faro and lost,' all in lower case letters, right?"

"Right."

"But suppose it were, 'hello this is us madeleine annie bartholomew harold played faro and lost he got me with child,'?"

"Son, I'm beginnin' to see what you mean," said Cyrus. "An' if we made such a mistake, then so could anybody else."

"And so you two think that body with the I.O.U. was the one the message meant as faro? Well, I don't think so." Julia was adamant.

Cyrus looked at her and smiled. Mike frowned at her. But it was the old man who made an attempt to compromise with her. "Honey," he said, "it's just a theory I have. I could be wrong about it. Then he grinned mischievously, while reaching into his shirt pocket. "But there is one thing I know for a fact," he said, and he pulled out a folded piece of paper. It was the paper which had come from the inside pocket of the white pin-striped suit worn by the man they'd found dead in the La Salle's rumble seat. Mike had put it aside while examining the contents of the man's wallet.

"I picked it up when I went back into the garage to close the rumble seat and fasten the door," Cyrus said, "I was so blamed skeered when I picked it up, I forgot I had it till this mornin' when I changed shirts."

They both looked at him with the same question on their face.

"It's a poem," said Cyrus, "but it's also a testament to what a liar he was."

"What do you mean?" asked Julia. And Mike nodded agreement with her question. The old man was grinning, delighted that he had something to reveal to them.

"I told you my wife was a person who liked poetry. I kept some of her books. I used to look through one of 'em in particular, you know, kind of a way to remember her. Anyway, I recognized this right away. The original of it was written by a man named Wilford Pennington Clarke. The bird up there in that rumble seat . . ."

"Harry Waldon," said Julia.

"Yeah," continued Cyrus, "good ol' Harry. He copied it down

in longhand, substituted the name Madeleine for Caroline an' put his own name on it. Here it is." And he handed it over to Mike who took it and carefully spread the old paper out on the table so Julia could read it along with him.

Madeleine
"ME"

In the garden, in the afternoon, while the dying sun sends final plea
In scarlet streaks across the turquoise sky,
I hear the west wind tell your name;
And as the shadows fall in heavy blues and purple grays,
Within the chambers of my mind I listen to each syllable that
In orchestral chords is played, Dear Madeleine.

I sense you there as you descend the flagstones by the green,
A mist of passion drifts before my half-closed eyes,
Perfume of blossom rare, or only scent of you upon the air—unseen?
Oh, Madeleine, how deep our love, how sweet the need it cries!

I hear the very beating of your heart and, then, as you draw nigh,
There comes a rustle as if angels' wings had brushed aside eternal gates,
It's but the fabric wherein your beauty lies caressed, yet one
Soft touch from it and I can see, beyond the space the garden occupies,
The wondrous vale of paradise.
Oh, ecstasy in having thus to wait, and how divine, good Madeleine,
To be so sweetly with such blissful wonder blessed.

A smile rests on my face, my eyes are closed,
I have no need to see with you so near.
What we may say to each, each of us knows,
How tender—passing words we do not have to hear.
Ah, my lovely, so closely held within love's gentle folds are we that
Paired forever we shall be, and we shall transcend all of time, my own,
My dearest Madeleine.

"Oh," exclaimed Julia, "how beautiful!"

"I see he used the same moniker as he did in the little book," Mike commented, dryly.

"You mean, ME," said Cyrus.

"Yeah."

"He shore was a liar," said Cyrus.

"But he was right, don't you see," exclaimed Julia. "They are together for eternity. Up there, in that old house, he's in the garage and she's in the upstairs bedroom. Oh, it is so romantic."

The two men looked at each other and shook their heads in mock disdain for what they considered silly and overly emotional. The truth was that, in their own way, they were as foolish in this manner as Julia. Finally, Mike said, "Well, Babe, at least their bodies are up there together; and she killed him and in a way . . ."

"He killed her," interjected Cyrus. "And," he continued, "let's leave it at that, how about it? Ain't you two packed for a trip anyways?"

*   *   *

As they stood together on the sidewalk outside of Mac's, they all gazed upward at the old house on the slope above the town. For once, the monsoon seemed to have run out of moisture to drop on Jerome. The sun bathed it in light. The tourists walking by looked with curiosity at the little, yellow car parked next to the line of skinned-up motorcycles.

"You sure you're gonna' be able to live here, Cy, and see that every day and know what's there and not do anything about it?" asked Mike.

"What could I do? Tell about it and see that beautiful old car hauled out an' put on display for somebody else to make money from? B'sides, what about the body in the back seat?"

"And the other one in the upstairs room," breathed Julia.

"Not to mention," went on Cyrus, "that there may be somebody else here who knows all about this. Listen," and he held his palms up and said with a straight face, devoid of even the semblance of humor or guile, "I think you're right about somebody smearin' that stuff all over you. An' that same person knows about me and that we've been messin' around in that old house. Probably knows more'n we'll ever know about Madeleine Morgan an' that dead body in that rumble seat. You kids don't have to worry about me. Go on an' do your thing. An' then if someday you wanta' come back by here, hey, give me a knock on the door! If I'm still alive I'll answer. But there's one thing you can count on, the story of that old house an' the people who lived and died there is safe with me. All you gotta' do is peep in that ol' garage. If the La Salle's still there, you'll know I tol' you the truth—unless it's discovered in the meantime by somebody else.

"Cy?"

"Yeah, honey?"

She hugged the old man and kissed him on the cheek.

"Aw, hell, now . . ." Cyrus Dooley was embarrassed. He watched as Mike put the top down, and they got into the car. He tried not to show the sadness that he felt.

The Volkswagen rolled effortlessly down the long side of the triangle that made up the one way section of Main Street in Jerome, Arizona. They tried not to look up at the window of the apartment where they had stayed, but they couldn't resist.

Mike brought the bug to a halt at the juncture of Main and Hull Avenue. He remembered the rainy night he had stood at the front of the little flat and looked out into the dark. For a moment he almost went back to that time, but with a shake of his head he remained in the present. He looked down the street for traffic and pulled out onto 89A.

They coasted, now, down past the buildings on the hillside to their right, around the curve with the steep drop-off and out onto the hogback, past the high school, then right and down again. Finally, after one more curve, they reached the flatter and straighter sections of the road and he shifted into a higher gear. The bug's engine began to whistle.

Julia reached over and ran a hand along the curvature of Mike's forearm. He looked at her and they both smiled happily at each other. Then she turned to gaze over her shoulder. Past the retracted canvas top of the Volkswagen, the remnants of the old town lay spread out on Cleopatra Hill. It seemed so peaceful and innocent in the bright light of the afternoon sun. A part of her had changed because of it. She moved her fingers to touch the folded piece of paper tucked into a pocket on the sweater she wore. Cyrus had slipped it to her just as she had turned from him to get into the car. How long, she thought, will this place remain here on this mountainside, its old bones buried in long-gone years, while a part of it basks in the sunshine of the present, besieged by modern-day vehicles and their tourist owners moving unknowingly through the dark shadows of its past?

The End